...ow, among...

...Book Award, the

...he National Book Critics

Circle Award.

In 2005 *The Plot Against America* received the Society of American Historians' prize for 'the outstanding historical novel on an American theme for 2003–2004' and was named a Best Book of the Year by the *New York Times Book Review*, the *San Francisco Chronicle*, the *Boston Globe*, the *Chicago-Sun Times*, the *Los Angeles Times Book Review*, the *Washington Post Book World*, *Time*, *Newsweek*, and numerous other periodicals. In the United Kingdom, *The Plot Against America* won the W. H. Smith Award for the Best Book of the Year, making Roth the first writer in the forty-six-year history of the prize to win it twice.

In 2005 Philip Roth became the third living American writer to have his work published in a comprehensive, definitive edition by the Library of America. The last of the eight volumes is scheduled for publication in 2013.

ALSO BY PHILIP ROTH

Zuckerman Books

The Ghost Writer
Zuckerman Unbound
The Anatomy Lesson
The Prague Orgy
Exit Ghost
The Counterlife

American Pastoral
I Married a Communist
The Human Stain
Exit Ghost

Roth Books

The Facts
Deception
Patrimony
Operation Shylock
The Plot Against America

Kepesh Books

The Breast
The Dying Animal

Miscellany

Reading Myself and Others
Shop Talk

Other Books

Goodbye, Columbus
Letting Go
When She Was Good
Portnoy's Complaint
Our Gang
The Great American Novel
My Life as a Man
Sabbath's Theater
Everyman
Indignation

PHILIP ROTH

The Professor
of Desire

VINTAGE BOOKS
London

Published by Vintage 2000

8 10 9

Copyright © Philip Roth 1977

Philip Roth has asserted his right under the Copyright, Designs
and Patents Act, 1988 to be identified as the author of this work

First published in Great Britain in 1978
by Penguin Books

Vintage
Random House, 20 Vauxhall Bridge Road,
London SW1V 2SA

www.vintage-books.co.uk

Addresses for companies within The Random House Group Limited can be
found at: www.randomhouse.co.uk/offices.htm

The Random House Group Limited Reg. No. 954009

A CIP catalogue record for this book
is available from the British Library

ISBN 9780099389019

The Random House Group Limited supports The Forest
Stewardship Council (FSC), the leading international forest
certification organisation. All our titles that are printed on
Greenpeace approved FSC certified paper carry the FSC
logo. Our paper procurement policy can be found at
www.rbooks.co.uk/environment.

Printed and bound in Great Britain by
CPI Bookmarque, Croydon, CR0 4TD

For Claire Bloom

THE PROFESSOR OF DESIRE

T

emptation comes to me first in the conspicuous personage of Herbie Bratasky, social director, bandleader, crooner, comic, and m.c. of my family's mountainside resort hotel. When he is not trussed up in the elasticized muscleman's swim trunks which he dons to conduct rumba lessons by the side of the pool, he is dressed to kill, generally in his two-tone crimson and cream-colored "loafer" jacket and the wide canary-yellow trousers that taper down to enchain him just above his white, perforated, sharpie's shoes. A fresh slice of Black Jack gum is at the ready in his pocket while another is being savored, with slow-motion sassiness, in what my mother derisively describes as Herbie's "yap." Below the stylishly narrow alligator belt and the gold droop of key chain, one knee works away inside his trousers, Herbie keeping time to hides he alone hears being beaten in that Congo called his brain. Our brochure (from fourth grade on composed by me, in collaboration with the owner) headlines Herbie as "our Jewish Cugat, our Jewish Krupa—all rolled into one!"; further on he is described as "a second Danny

Kaye," and, in conclusion, just so that everyone understands that this 140-pound twenty-year-old is not nobody and Kepesh's Hungarian Royale is not *exactly* nowhere, as "another Tony Martin."

Our guests appear to be nearly as mesmerized by Herbie's shameless exhibitionism as I am. A newcomer will have barely settled into a varnished wicker rocker on the veranda before one of the old-timers arrived from the hot city the previous week starts giving him the lowdown on this wonder of our tribe. "And wait till you see the tan on this kid. He's just got that kind of skin—never burns, only tans. And from the first day in the sun. This kid has got skin on him right out of Bible times."

Because of a damaged eardrum, our drawing card—as it pleases Herbie to call himself, particularly into the teeth of my mother's disapproval—is with us throughout the Second World War. Ongoing discussion from the rocking chairs and the card tables as to whether the disability is congenital or self-inflicted. The suggestion that something other than Mother Nature might have rendered Herbie unfit to fight Tojo, Mussolini, and Hitler—well, I am outraged, personally mortified by the very idea. Yet, how tantalizing to imagine Herbie taking a hatpin or a toothpick in his own hands—taking an ice pick!—and deliberately mutilating himself in order to outfox his draft board.

"I wouldn't put it past him," says guest A-owitz; "I wouldn't put anything past that operator. What a pistol he is!" "Come on, he did no such thing. That kid is a patriotic kid like anybody else. I'll tell you how he went half deaf like that, and ask the doctor here if I'm not right: from banging on those drums," says guest B-owitz. "Oh, can that kid play drums," says C-owitz; "you could put him on the stage of the Roxy right now—and I think the only reason he ain't is that, like you say, he doesn't hear right from the drums themselves." "Still," says D-owitz, "he don't say definitely yes or no whether he did it with some instrument or something." "But that's the showman in him, keeping you hanging by suspense. His whole stock-in-trade is that he's crazy enough for anything— that's his whole *act*." "Still, even to kid around about it don't strike me right. The Jewish people have got their hands full as it is." "Please, a kid who dresses like that right down to the key chain, and with a build like that that he works on day and night, plus those drums, you think he is gonna do himself serious physical damage just out of spite to the war effort?" "I agree, one hundred percent. Gin, by the way." "Oh, you caught me with my pants down, you s.o.b. What the hell am I holding these jacks for, will somebody tell me? Look, you know what you don't find? You don't find a kid who is good-looking like this one, who is funny like he is too. To take that kind of looks, and to be funny, and to go crazy like that with the drums, that to me is something special in the annals of show business." "And what about at the pool? How about on the diving board? If Billy Rose laid eyes on him, clowning around in the water like that, he'd be in the Aquacade tomorrow." "And what about that voice on him?" "If only he wouldn't kid *around* with it—if only he would sing *serious*." "If that kid sang serious he could be in the Metropolitan Opera." "If he sang serious, he could be a cantor, for Christ sakes, with no problem. He could break your heart. Just imagine for yourself what he would look like in a white tallis with that tan!" And here at last I am spotted, working on a model R.A.F. Spitfire down at the end of the veranda rail. "Hey, little Kepesh, come here, you little eavesdropper. Who do you want to be like when you grow up? Listen to this—stop shuffling the cards a minute. Who's your hero, Kepaleh?"

I don't have to think twice, or at all. "Herbie," I reply, much to the amusement of the men in the congregation. Only the mothers look a little dismayed.

Yet, ladies, who else could it be? Who else is so richly endowed as to be able to mimic Cugie's accent, the shofar blowing, and, at my request, a fighter plane nose-diving over Berchtesgaden—*and* the Fuehrer going crazy underneath? Herbie's enthusiasm and virtuosity are such that my father must sometimes caution him to keep certain of his imitations to himself, unique though they may be. "But," protests Herbie, "my fart is perfect." "Could be, for all I know," replies the boss, "but not in front of a mixed crowd." "But I've been working on it for months. Listen!" "Oh, spare me, Bratasky, please. It just ain't exactly what a nice tired guest wants to hear in a casino after his dinner. You can appreciate that, can't you? Or can't you? I don't get you sometimes, where your brain is. Don't you realize that these are people who keep kosher? Don't you get it about women and children? My friend, it's simple—the shofar is for the High Holidays and the other stuff is for the toilet. Period, Herbie. Finished."

So he comes to imitate for me, his awestruck acolyte, the toots and the tattoos that are forbidden him in public by my Mosaic dad. It turns out that not only can he simulate the panoply of sounds—ranging from the faintest springtime sough to the twenty-one-gun salute—with which mankind emits its gases, but he can also "do diarrhea." Not, he is quick to inform me, some poor shlimazel in its throes—that he had already mastered back in high school—but the full Wagnerian strains of fecal *Sturm und Drang.* "I could be in Ripley's," he tells me. "You read Ripley's, don't you—then judge for yourself!" I hear the rasp of a zipper being undone. Then a most enviable stream belting an enamel bowl. Next the whoosh of the flush, followed by the gargle and hiccup of a reluctant tap commencing to percolate. And all of it emanating from Herbie's mouth.

I could fall down and worship at his feet.

"And catch *this!*" This is two hands soaping one another—but seemingly in Herbie's mouth. "All winter long I would go into the toilet at the Automat and just sit there and listen." "You would?" "Sure. I listen even to my own self every single time I go to the can." "You do?" "But your old man, he's the expert, and to him it's only one thing—dirty! 'Period!' " adds Herbie, and in a voice exactly like my old man's!

And he means every word he says. How come, I wonder. How can Herbie know so much and care so passionately about the tintinnabulations of the can? And why do tone-deaf philistines like my father care so little?

So it seems in summer, while I am under the demon drummer's spell. Then Yom Kippur comes and Bratasky goes, and what good does it do me to have learned what someone like that has to teach a growing boy? Our -witzes, -bergs, and -steins are dispersed overnight to regions as remote to me as Babylon—Hanging Gardens called Pelham and Queens and Hackensack—and the local terrain is reclaimed by the natives who till the fields, milk the cows, keep the stores, and work year round for the county and the state. I am one of two Jewish children in a class of twenty-five, and a feel for the rules and preferences of society (as ingrained in me, it seems, as susceptibility to the feverish, the flamboyant, the bizarre) dictates that, regardless of how tempted I may be to light my fuse and show these hicks a few of Herbie's fireworks, I do not distinguish myself from my schoolmates by anything other than grades. To do otherwise, I realize—and without my father even having to remind me—will get me nowhere. And nowhere is not where I am expected to go.

So, like a boy on a calendar illustration, I trudge nearly two miles through billowing snowdrifts down our mountain road to the school where I spend my winters excelling, while far to the south, in that biggest of cities, where anything goes, Herbie (who sells linoleum for an uncle during the day and plays with a Latin American combo on weekends) strives to perfect the last of his lavatory impressions. He writes of his progress in a letter that I carry hidden away in the button-down back pocket of my knickers and reread every chance I get; aside from birthday cards and stamp "approvals," it is the only piece of mail I have ever received. Of course I am terrified that if I should drown while ice skating or break my neck while sledding, the envelope postmarked BROOKLYN, NY will be found by one of my schoolmates, and they will all stand around my corpse holding their noses. My mother and father will be shamed forever. The Hungarian Royale will lose its good name and go bankrupt. Probably I will not be allowed to be buried within the cemetery walls with the other Jews. And all because of what Herbie dares to write down on a piece of paper and then mail through a government post office to a nine-year-old child, who is imagined by his world (and thus by himself) to be pure. Does Bratasky really fail to understand how decent people feel about such things? Doesn't he know that even sending a letter like this he is probably breaking a law, and making of me an accomplice? But if so, why do I persist in carrying the incriminating document around with me all day long? It is in my pocket even while I am on my feet battling for first place in the weekly spelling bee against the other finalist, my curly-haired co-religionist and the concert-pianist-to-be, brilliant Madeline Levine; it is in my pajama pocket at night, to be read by flashlight beneath the covers, and then to sleep with, next to my heart. "I am really getting down to a science how it sounds when you pull the paper off the roller. Which about gives me the whole shmeer, kid. Herbert L. Bratasky *and nobody else in the world* can now do taking a leak, taking a crap, diarrhea—*and* unrolling the paper itself. That leaves me just one mountain to climb—wiping!"

By the time I am eighteen and a freshman at Syracuse, my penchant for mimicry very nearly equals my mentor's, only instead of imitations à la Bratasky, I do Bratasky, the guests, and the characters on the staff. I impersonate our tuxedoed Rumanian headwaiter putting on the dog in the dining room—"This way, please, Monsieur Kornfeld . . . Madame, more derma?"—then, back in the kitchen, threatening in the coarsest Yiddish to strangle the drunken chef. I impersonate our Gentiles, the gawky handyman George, shyly observing the ladies' poolside rumba class, and Big Bud, the aging muscular lifeguard (and grounds attendant) who smoothly hustles the vacationing housewife, and then, if he can, her nubile offspring sunning her new nose job. I even do a long dialogue (tragical-comical-historical-pastoral) of my exhausted parents undressing for bed the night after the close of the season. To find that the most ordinary events out of my former life are considered by others to be so *entertaining* somewhat astonishes me—also I am startled at first to discover that not everybody seems to have enjoyed formative years so densely populated with vivid types. Nor had I begun to imagine that I was quite so vivid myself.

In my first few semesters at college I am awarded leading roles in university productions of plays by Giraudoux, Sophocles, and Congreve. I appear in a musical comedy, singing, and even dancing, in my fashion. There seems to be nothing I cannot do on a stage—there would seem to be nothing that can keep me *off* the stage. At the beginning of my sophomore year, my parents visit school to see me play Tiresias—older, as I interpret the role, than the two of them together—and afterward, at the opening-night party, they watch uneasily as I respond to a request from the cast to entertain with an imitation of the princely rabbi with the perfect diction who annually comes "all the way" from Poughkeepsie to conduct High Holiday services in the casino of the hotel. The following morning I show them around the campus. On the path to the library several students compliment me on my staggering rendition of old age the night before. Impressed—but reminding me also, with a touch of her irony, that not so long ago the stage star's diapers were hers to change and wash—my mother says, "Everybody knows you already, you're famous," while my father, struggling with disappointment, asks yet again, "And medical school is out?" Whereupon I tell him for the tenth time—*telling* him it's the tenth time—"I want to act," and believe as much myself, until that day when all at once performing, in my fashion, seems to me the most pointless, ephemeral, and pathetically self-aggrandizing of pursuits. Savagely I turn upon myself for allowing everyone, indeed, to know me already, to glimpse the depths of mindless vanity that the confines of the nest and the strictures of the sticks had previously prevented me from exposing, even to myself. I am so humiliated by the nakedness of what I have been up to that I consider transferring to another school, where I can start out afresh, untainted in the eyes of others by egomaniacal cravings for spotlight and applause.

Months follow in which I adopt a penitential new goal for myself every other week. I *will* go to medical school— and train to be a surgeon. Though perhaps as a psychiatrist I can do even more good for mankind. I will become a lawyer . . . a diplomat . . . why *not* a rabbi, one who is studious, contemplative, *deep* . . . I read *I and Thou* and the Hasidic tales, and home on vacation question my parents about the family's history in the old country. But as it is over fifty years since my grandparents emigrated to America, and as they are dead and their children by and large without any but the most sentimental interest in our origins in mid-Europe, in time I give up the inquiry, and the rabbinical fantasy with it. Though not the effort to ground myself in what is substantial. It is still with the utmost self-disgust that I remember my decrepitude in *Oedipus Rex*, my impish charm in *Finian's Rainbow*—all that cloying *acting!* Enough frivolity and manic showing off! At twenty I must stop impersonating others and Become Myself, or at least begin to impersonate the self I believe I ought now to be.

He—the next me—turns out to be a sober, solitary, rather refined young man devoted to European literature and languages. My fellow actors are amused by the way in which I abandon the stage and retreat into a rooming house, taking with me as companions those great writers whom I choose to call, as an undergraduate, "the architects of my mind." "Yes, David has left the world," my drama society rival is reported to be saying, "to become a man of the cloth." Well, I have my airs, and the power, apparently, to dramatize myself and my choices, but above all it is that I am an absolutist—a *young* absolutist —and know no way to shed a skin other than by inserting the scalpel and lacerating myself from end to end. I am one thing or I am the other. Thus, at twenty, do I set out to undo the contradictions and overleap the uncertainties.

During my remaining years at college I live somewhat as I had during my boyhood winters, when the hotel was shut down and I read hundreds of library books through hundreds of snowstorms. The work of repairing and refurbishing goes on daily throughout the Arctic months—I hear the sound of the tire chains nicking at the plowed roadways, I hear planks dropping off the pickup truck into the snow, and the simple inspiring noises of the hammer and the saw. Beyond the snow-caked sill I see George driving down with Big Bud to fix the cabanas by the covered pool. I wave my arm, George blows the horn . . . and to me it is as though the Kepeshes are now three animals in cozy, fortified hibernation, Mamma, Papa, and Baby safely tucked away in Family Paradise.

Instead of the vivid guests themselves, we have with us in winter their letters, read aloud and with no deficiency of vividness or volume by my father at the dinner table. *Selling himself* is the man's specialty, as he sees it; likewise, *showing people a good time*, and, no matter how ill-mannered they themselves may be, *treating them like human beings*. In the off-season, however, the balance of power shifts a little, and it is the clientele, nostalgic for the stuffed cabbage and the sunshine and the laughs, who divest themselves of their exacting imperiousness—"They sign the register," says my mother, "and every *ballagula* and his *shtunk* of a wife is suddenly the Duke and the Duchess of Windsor"—and begin to treat my father as though he too were a paid-up member of the species, rather than the target for their discontent, and straight man for their ridiculous royal routines. When the snow is deepest, there are sometimes as many as four and five newsy letters a week—an engagement in Jackson Heights, moving to Miami because of health, opening a second store in White Plains . . . Oh, how he loves getting news of the best and the worst that is happening to them. That proves something to him about what the Hungarian Royale means to people—that proves everything, in fact, and not only about the meaning of his hotel.

After reading the letters, he clears a place at the end of the table, and beside a plate full of my mother's *rugalech*, and in his sprawling longhand, composes his replies. I correct the spelling and insert punctuation where he has drawn the dashes that separate his single run-on paragraph into irregular chunks of philosophizing, reminiscence, prophecy, sagacity, political analysis, condolence, and congratulation. Then my mother types each letter on Hungarian Royale stationery—below the inscription that reads, "*Old Country Hospitality In A Beautiful Mountain Setting. Dietary Laws Strictly Observed. Your Proprietors, Abe and Belle Kepesh*"—and adds the P.S. confirming reservations for the summer ahead and requesting a small deposit.

Before she met my father on a vacation in these very hills—he was then twenty-one, and without a calling, spending the summer as a short-order cook—she worked for her first three years out of high school as a legal secretary. As legend has it, she had been a meticulous, conscientious young woman of astounding competence, who all but lived to serve the patrician Wall Street lawyers who employed her, men whose stature—moral *and* physical—she will in fact speak of reverentially until she dies. Her Mr. Clark, a grandson of the firm's founder, continues sending her birthday greetings by telegram even after he retires to Arizona, and every year, with the telegram in her hand, she says dreamily to my balding father and to little me, "Oh, he was such a tall and handsome man. And so dignified. I can still remember how he stood up at his desk when I came into his office to be interviewed for the job. I don't think I'll ever forget that posture of his." But, as it happened, it was a burly, hirsute man, with a strong prominent cask of a chest, Popeye's biceps, and no class credentials, who saw her leaning on a piano singing "Amapola" with a group of vacationers up from the city, and promptly said to himself, "I'm going to marry that girl." Her hair and her eyes were so dark, and her legs and bosom so round and "well developed" that he thought at first she might actually be Spanish. And the besetting passion for impeccability that had endeared her so to the junior Mr. Clark only caused her to be all the more alluring to the energetic young go-getter with not a little of the slave driver in his own driven, slavish soul.

Unfortunately, once she marries, the qualities that had made her the austere Gentile boss's treasure bring her very nearly to the brink of nervous collapse by the end of each summer—for even in a small family-run hotel like ours there is always a complaint to be investigated, an employee to be watched, linens to be counted, food to be tasted, accounts to be tallied . . . on and on and on it goes, and, alas, she can never leave a job to the person supposed to be doing it, not when she discovers that it is not being Done Right. Only in the winter, when my father and I assume the unlikely roles of Clark *père* and *fils*, and she sits in perfect typing posture at the big black Remington Noiseless precisely indenting his garrulous replies, do I get a glimpse of the demure and happy little *señorita* with whom he had fallen in love at first sight.

Sometimes after dinner she even invites me, a grade-school child, to pretend that I am an executive and to dictate a letter to her so that she can show me the magic of her shorthand. "You own a shipping company," she tells me, though in fact I have only just been allowed to buy my first penknife, "go ahead." Regularly enough she reminds me of the distinction between an ordinary office secretary and what she had been, which was a *legal* secretary. My father proudly confirms that she had indeed been the most flawless legal secretary ever to work for the firm—Mr. Clark had written as much to him in a letter of congratulation on the occasion of their engagement. Then one winter, when apparently I am of age, she teaches me to type. No one, before or since, has ever taught me anything with so much innocence and conviction.

But that is winter, the secret season. In summer, surrounded, her dark eyes dart frantically, and she yelps and yipes like a sheep dog whose survival depends upon driving his master's unruly flock to market. A single little lamb drifting a few feet away sends her full-speed down the rugged slope—a baa from elsewhere, and she is off in the opposite direction. And it does not stop until the High Holidays are over, and even then it doesn't stop. For when the last guest has departed, inventory-taking must begin —must! that minute! What has been broken, torn, stained, chipped, smashed, bent, cracked, pilfered, what is to be repaired, replaced, repainted, thrown out entirely, "a total loss." To this simple and tidy little woman who loves nothing in the world so much as the sight of a perfect, unsmudged carbon copy falls the job of going from room to room to record in her ledger the extent of the violence that has been wreaked upon our mountain stronghold by the vandal hordes my father persists in maintaining—over her vehement opposition—are only other human beings.

Just as the raging Catskill winters transform each of us back into a sweeter, saner, innocent, more sentimental sort of Kepesh, so in my room in Syracuse solitude goes to work on me and gradually I feel the lightweight and the show-off blessedly taking his leave. Not that, for all my reading, underlining, and note-taking, I become *entirely* selfless. A dictum attributed to no less notable an egotist than Lord Byron impresses me with its mellifluous wisdom and resolves in only six words what was beginning to seem a dilemma of insuperable moral proportions. With a certain strategic daring, I begin quoting it aloud to the coeds who resist me by arguing that I'm too smart for such things. "Studious by day," I inform them, "dissolute by night." For "dissolute" I soon find it best to substitute "desirous"—I am not in a palazzo in Venice, after all, but in upstate New York, on a college campus, and I can't afford to unsettle these girls any more than I apparently do already with my "vocabulary" and my growing reputation as a "loner." Reading Macaulay for English 203, I come upon his description of Addison's collaborator Steele, and, "Eureka!" I cry, for here is yet *another* bit of prestigious justification for my high grades and my base desires. "A rake among scholars, a scholar among rakes." Perfect! I tack it to my bulletin board, along with the line from Byron, and directly above the names of the girls whom I have set my mind to *seduce,* a word whose deepest resonances come to me, neither from pornography nor pulp magazines, but from my agonized reading in Kierkegaard's *Either/Or.*

I have only one male friend I see regularly, a nervous, awkward, and homely philosophy major named Louis Jelinek, who in fact is my Kierkegaard mentor. Like me, Louis rents a room in a private house in town rather than live in the college dormitory with boys whose rituals of camaraderie he too considers contemptible. He is working his way through school at a hamburger joint (rather than accept money from the Scarsdale parents he despises) and carries its perfume wherever he goes. When I happen to touch him, either accidentally or simply out of high spirits or fellow feeling, he leaps away as though in fear of having his stinking rags contaminated. "Hands off," he snarls. "What are you, Kepesh, still running for some fucking office?" Am I? It hadn't occurred to me. Which one?

Oddly, whatever Louis says of me, even in pique or in a tirade, seems significant for the solemn undertaking I call "understanding myself." Because he is not interested, as far as I can see, in pleasing anyone—family, faculty, landlady, shopkeepers, and certainly least of all, those "bourgeois barbarians," our fellow students—I imagine him to be more profoundly in touch with "reality" than I am. I am one of those tall, wavy-haired boys with a cleft in his chin who has developed winning ways in high school, and now I cannot seem to shake them, hard as I try. Especially alongside Louis do I feel pitifully banal: so neat, so clean, so *charming* when the need arises, and despite all my disclaimers to the contrary, not quite unconcerned as yet with appearances and reputation. Why can't I be more of a Jelinek, reeking of fried onions and looking down on the entire world? Behold the refuse bin wherein he dwells! Crusts and cores and peelings and wrappings—the perfect mess! Just look upon the clotted Kleenex beside his ravaged bed, Kleenex *clinging* to his tattered carpet slippers. Only seconds after orgasm, and even in the privacy of my locked room, I automatically toss into a wastebasket the telltale evidence of self-abuse, whereas Jelinek —eccentric, contemptuous, unaffiliated, and unassailable Jelinek—seems not to care at all what the world knows or thinks of his copious ejaculations.

I am stunned, can't grasp it, for weeks afterward won't believe it when a student in the philosophy program says in passing one day that "of course" my friend is a "practicing" homosexual. *My* friend? It cannot be. "Sissies," of course, I am familiar with. Each summer we would have a few famous ones at the hotel, little Jewish pashas on holiday, first brought to my attention by Herbie B. With fascination I used to watch them being carried out of the sunlight and into the shade, even as they dizzily imbibed sweet chocolate drinks through a pair of straws, and their brows and cheeks were cleansed and dried by the handkerchiefs of galley slaves called Grandma, Mamma, and Auntie. And then there were the few unfortunates at school, boys born with their arms screwed on like girls, who couldn't throw a ball right no matter how many private hours of patient instruction you gave them. But as for a practicing homosexual? Never, never, in all my nineteen years. Except, of course, that time right after my bar mitzvah, when I took a bus by myself to a stamp collectors' fair in Albany, and in the Greyhound terminal there was approached at the urinal by a middle-aged man in a business suit who whispered to me over my shoulder, "Hey, kid, want me to blow you?" "No, no, thank you," I replied, and quickly as I could (though without giving offense, I hoped) moved out of the men's room, out of the terminal, and made for a nearby department store, where I could be gathered up in the crowd of heterosexual shoppers. In the intervening years, however, no homosexual had ever spoken to me again, at least none that I knew of.

Till Louis.

Oh, God, does this explain why I am told to keep my hands to myself when our shirtsleeves so much as brush against each other? Is it because for him being touched by a boy carries with it the most serious implications? But, if so, wouldn't a person as forthright and unconventional as Jelinek come right out and say so? Or could it be that while my shameful secret with Louis is that under it all I am altogether ordinary and respectable, a closet Joe College, his with me is that he's queer? As though to prove how very ordinary and respectable I really am, I never ask. Instead, I wait in fear for the day when something Jelinek says or does will reveal the truth about him. Or has his truth been with me all along? Of course! Those globs of Kleenex tossed about his room like so many little posies . . . are they not intended to divulge? to *invite*? . . . is it so unlikely that some night soon this brainy hawk-nosed creature, who disdains, on principle, the use of underarm deodorant and is already losing his hair, will jump forth in his ungainly way from behind the desk where he is lecturing on Dostoevsky and try to catch me in an embrace? Will he tell me he loves me and stick his tongue in my mouth? And what will I say in response, exactly what the innocent, tempting girls say to me? "No, no, please don't! Oh, Louis, you're too smart for this! Why can't we just talk about books?"

But precisely because the idea frightens me so—because I am afraid that I may well be the "hillbilly" and "hayseed" that he delights in calling me when we disagree about the deep meaning of some masterpiece—I continue to visit him in his odoriferous room and sit across the litter from him there talking loudly for hours about the most maddening and vexatious ideas, and praying that he will not make a pass.

Before he can, Louis is dismissed from the university, first for failing to show up at a single class during an entire semester, and then for not even deigning to acknowledge the notes from his adviser asking him to come talk over the problem. Snaps Louis indignantly, sardonically, disgustedly, "*What* problem?" and darts and cranes his head as though the "problem," for all he knows, might be somewhere in the air above us. Though all agree that Louis's is an extraordinary mind, he is refused enrollment for the second semester of his junior year. Overnight he disappears from Syracuse (no goodbyes, needless to say) and almost immediately is drafted. So I learn when an F.B.I. agent with an undeflectable gaze comes around to question me after Louis deserts basic training and (as I picture it) goes to hide out from the Korean War in a slum somewhere with his Kierkegaard and his Kleenex.

Agent McCormack asks, "What about his homosexual record, Dave?" Flushing, I reply, "I don't know about that." McCormack says, "But they tell me you were his closest buddy." "They? I don't know who you mean." "The kids over on the campus." "That's a vicious rumor about him—it's totally untrue." "That you were his buddy?" "No, sir," I say, heat again rising unbidden to my forehead, "that he had a 'homosexual record.' They say those things because he was difficult to get along with. He was an unusual person, particularly for around here." "But you got along with him, didn't you?" "Yes. Why shouldn't I?" "No one said you shouldn't. Listen, they tell me you're quite the Casanova." "Oh, yes?" "Yeah. That you really go after the girls. Is that so?" "I suppose," turning from his gaze, and from the implication I sense in his remark that the girls are only a front. "That wasn't the case with Louis, though," says the agent ambiguously. "What do you mean?" "Dave, tell me something. Level with me. Where do you think he is?" "I don't know." "But you'd let me in on it, if you did, I'm sure." "Yes, sir." "Good. Here's my card, if you should happen to find out." "Yes, sir; thank you, sir." And after he leaves I am appalled by the way I have conducted myself: my terror of prison, my Lord Fauntleroy manners, my collaborationist instincts—and my shame over just about everything.

The girls that I go after.

Usually I pick them up (or at least *out*) in the reading room of the library, a place comparable to the runway of a burlesque house in its power to stimulate and focus my desire. Whatever is imperfectly suppressed in these neatly dressed, properly bred middle-class American girls is immediately apparent (or more often than not, immediately imagined) in this all-pervasive atmosphere of academic propriety. I watch transfixed the girl who plays with the ends of her hair while ostensibly she is studying her History—while I am ostensibly studying mine. Another girl, wholly bland tucked in her classroom chair just the day before, will begin to swing her leg beneath the library table where she idly leafs through a *Look* magazine, and my craving knows no bounds. A third girl leans forward over her notebook, and with a muffled groan, as though I am being impaled, I observe the breasts beneath her blouse push softly into her folded arms. How I wish I were those arms! Yes, almost nothing is necessary to set me in pursuit of a perfect stranger, nothing, say, but the knowledge that while taking notes from the encyclopedia with her right hand, she cannot keep the index finger of her left hand from tracing circles on her lips. I refuse— out of an incapacity that I elevate to a principle—to resist whatever I find irresistible, regardless of how unsubstantial and quirky, or childish and perverse, the source of the appeal might strike anyone else. Of course this leads me to seek out girls I might otherwise find commonplace or silly or dull, but I for one am convinced that dullness isn't their whole story, and that because my desire *is desire*, it is not to be belittled or despised.

"Please," they plead, "why don't you just talk and be nice? You can be so nice, if you want to be." "Yes, so they tell me." "But don't you see, this is only my body. I don't want to relate to you on that level." "You're out of luck. Nothing can be done about it. Your body is sensational." "Oh, don't start saying that again." "Your ass is sensational." "Please don't be crude. You don't talk that way in class. I love listening to you, but not when you insult me like this." "Insult? It's high praise. Your ass is marvelous. It's perfect. You should be thrilled to have it." "It's only what I sit on, David." "The hell it is. Ask a girl who doesn't own one quite that shape if she'd like to swap. That should bring you to your senses." "Please stop making fun of me and being sarcastic. *Please.*" "I'm not making fun of you. I'm taking you as seriously as anybody has ever taken you in your life. Your ass is a masterpiece."

No wonder that by my senior year I have acquired a "terrible" reputation among the sorority girls whose sisters I have attempted to seduce with my brand of aggressive candor. Given the reputation, you would think that I had already reduced a hundred coeds to whoredom, when in fact in four years' time I actually succeed in achieving full penetration on but two occasions, and something vaguely resembling penetration on two more. More often than not, where physical rapture should be, there logical (and illogical) discourse is instead: I argue, if I must, that I have never tried to mislead anyone about my desire or her desirability, that far from being "exploitive," I am just one of the few honest people around. In a burst of calculated sincerity—miscalculated sincerity, it turns out —I tell one of the girls how the sight of her breasts pressing against her arms had led me to wish I were those arms. And is this so different, I ask, pushing on with the charm, from Romeo, beneath Juliet's balcony, whispering, "See! how she leans her cheek upon her hand: / O! that I were a glove upon that hand, / That I might touch that cheek." Apparently it is quite different. During my last year at college there are times when the phone actually goes dead at the other end after I announce who is calling, and the few nice girls who are still willing to take their chances and go out alone with me are, I am told (by the nice girls themselves), considered nearly suicidal.

I also continue to earn the amused disdain of my high-minded friends in the drama society. Now the satirists among them have it that I have given up holy orders to take on our cheerleading squad; and a far cry, that, from enacting the sexual angst of Strindberg and O'Neill. Well, so they think.

In fact, there is only one cheerleader in my life to bring to me the unadulterated agonies of a supreme frustration and render ridiculous my rakish dreams, a certain Marcella "Silky" Walsh, from Plattsburg, New York. Doomed longing begins when I attend a basketball game one night to watch her perform, having met her in the university cafeteria line that afternoon and gotten a glimpse up close of that bounteous cushion, that most irresistible of bonbons, her lower lip. There is a cheer wherein each of the girls on the squad places one fist on her hip and with the other rhythmically pumps away at the air, all the while arching farther and farther back from the waist. To the seven other girls in brief, white, pleated skirts and bulky white sweaters the sequence of movements seems only so much peppy gymnastic display, to be executed with unsparing energy and at the edge of hilarity. Only in the slowly upturning belly of Marcella Walsh is there the smoldering suggestion (inescapable to me) of an offering, of an invitation, of a lust that is eager and unconscious and so clearly (to my eyes) begging to be satisfied. Yes, she alone seems (to me, to me) to sense that the tame and harnessed vehemence of this insipid cheer is but the thinnest disguise for the raw chant to be uttered while a penis propels into ecstasy that rising pelvis of hers. Oh, God, how can my coveting that pelvis thrust so provocatively toward the mouth of the howling mob, how can coveting those hard and tiny fists which speak to me of the pleasantest of all struggles, how can coveting those long and strong tomboyish legs that quiver ever so slightly as the arc is made and her silky hair (from which derives her pet name) sweeps back against the gymnasium floor —how can coveting the minutest pulsations of her being be "meaningless" or "trivial," "beneath" either me *or* her, while passionately rooting for Syracuse to win the NCAA basketball championship makes sense?

This is the line of reasoning that I take with Silky herself, and with which in time (oh, the time! the hours of debate that might have been spent cheering one another on to oceanic orgasms!) I hope to clear the way for those piercing erotic pleasures I have yet to know. Instead, I have to put aside logic, wit, candor, yes, and literary scholarship too, to put aside every reasonable attempt at persuasion—and at last all dignity as well—I have finally to turn as pitiful and craven as a waif in a famine before Silky, who has probably never seen anyone quite so miserable before, will allow me to shower kisses on her bare midriff. Since she really is the sweetest and most well-meaning of girls, hardly cruel enough or cold enough to reduce even a dirty-minded Romeo, a dean's list Bluebeard, a budding Don Giovanni and Johannes the Seducer to abject suppliance, I may kiss the belly about which I have spoken so "obsessively," but no more. "No higher and no lower," she whispers, from where I have her bent backward over a sink in the pitch-black laundry room of her dormitory basement. "David, no lower, I said. How can you even want to *do* a thing like that?"

So, between the yearnings and the myriad objects of desire, my world interposes its arguments and obstructions. My father doesn't understand me, the F.B.I. doesn't understand me, Silky Walsh doesn't understand me, neither the sorority girls nor the bohemians understand me—not even Louis Jelinek ever really understood me, and, unlikely as it sounds, this alleged homosexual (wanted by the police) has been my closest friend. No, nobody understands me, not even I myself.

I arrive in London to begin my fellowship year in literature after six days on a ship, a train ride up from Southampton, and a long ride on the Underground out to a district called Tooting Bec. Here, on an endless street of mock Tudor houses, and not in Bloomsbury, as I had requested, the King's College accommodations office has arranged lodgings for me in a private home. After I am shown to my grim little attic room by the retired army captain and his wife whose tidy, airless house this is—

and with whom, I learn, I will be taking my evening meals—I look at the iron bedstead on which I am to spend the next three hundred nights or so, and in an instant am bereft of the high spirits with which I had crossed the Atlantic, the pure joy with which I had fled from all the constraining rituals of undergraduate life, and from the wearisome concern of the mother and father whom I believe have ceased to nourish me. But Tooting Bec? This tiny room? My meals across from the captain's hairline mustache? And for what, to study Arthurian legends and Icelandic sagas? Why all this punishment just for being smart!

My misery is raw and colossal. In my wallet is the phone number of a teacher of paleography at King's given me by his friend, one of my Syracuse professors. But how can I phone this distinguished scholar and tell him within an hour of my arrival that I want to hand in my Fulbright and go home? "They chose the wrong applicant—I'm not serious enough to suffer like this!" With the captain's stout and kindly wife assisting—convinced by my coloring that I am Armenian, she mumbles to me all the while something about new carpets for the parlor—I find the phone in the hallway and dial. I am only inches from tears (I am really only inches from phoning collect to the Catskills), but scared and miserable as I am, it turns out that I am even more scared of confessing to being scared and miserable, for when the professor answers, I hang up.

Four or five hours later—night having fallen over Western Europe, and my first English meal of tinned spaghetti on toast having been more or less digested—I make for a London courtyard that I had learned about during the crossing. It is called Shepherd Market, and it provides me with an experience that alters considerably my attitude toward being a Fulbright fellow. Yes, even before I attend my first lectures on the epic and the romance, I begin to understand that for an unknown lad to have traveled to an unknown land may not have been a mistake after all. Terrified I am of course of dying like Maupassant; nonetheless, only minutes after peering timidly into the notorious alleyway, I have had a prostitute—the first whore of my life, and what is more, the first of my three sexual partners to date to have been born outside the continental United States (outside the state of New York, to be exact) and in a year prior to my own birth. Indeed, when she is astride me and is suddenly gravity's to do with as it wishes, I realize with an odd, repulsive sort of thrill that this woman whose breasts collide above my head like caldrons—whom I chose from among her competitors on the basis of these behemoth breasts and a no less capacious behind—was probably born prior to the outbreak of World War I. Imagine that, before the publication of *Ulysses*, before . . . but even as I am trying to place her in the century, I find that rather more quickly than I had planned—as though, in fact, one or the other of us is racing to make a train—I am being urged on to my big finale with the unbidden assistance of a sure, swift, unsentimental hand.

I discover Soho on my own the next night. I also discover in the *Columbia Encyclopedia* that I have lugged across the sea, along with Baugh's *Literary History of England* and the three paperback volumes of Trevelyan, that the final stages of *his* venereal disease finished Maupassant off at forty-three. Nonetheless, I still cannot think of anywhere I would rather be, following my dinner with the captain and the captain's wife, than in a room with a whore who will do whatever I wish—no, not after dreaming about paying for this privilege ever since I was twelve and had my allowance of a dollar a week to save up for anything I wanted. Of course if I chose whores less whorish-looking my chances of dying of VD rather than of old age might appreciably diminish. But what sense is there in having a whore who doesn't look and talk and behave like one? I am not in search of a girl friend, after all, not quite yet. And when I am ready for her it isn't to Soho that I take myself, but to lunch on a herring at a restaurant near Harrods called the Midnight Sun.

The mythology of the Swedish girl and her sexual freedom is, during these years, in its first effulgence, and despite the natural skepticism aroused in me by the stories of insatiable appetite and odd proclivities that I hear around the college, I happily play hooky from my ancient Norse studies in order to find out for myself just how much truth there may be in all this titillating school-boy speculation. Off then to the Midnight Sun, where the waitresses are said to be sex-crazed young Scandinavian goddesses who serve you their native dishes while dressed in colorful folk costumes, painted wooden clogs that display their golden legs to great advantage, and peasant bodices that cross-lace up the front and press into view the enticing swell of their breasts.

It is here that I meet Elisabeth Elverskog—and poor Elisabeth meets me. Elisabeth has taken a year off from the University of Lund in order to improve her English, and is living with another Swede, the daughter of friends of her family, who had left the University of Uppsala two years earlier to improve *her* English, and has not gotten around yet to going back. Birgitta, who entered England as a student and supposedly is taking courses at London University, works in Green Park collecting the penny rental for a deck chair, and, unbeknownst to Elisabeth's family, collecting such adventures as come her way. The basement flat Elisabeth shares with Birgitta is in a rooming house off Earl's Court Road inhabited mostly by students several tones darker than the girls. Elisabeth confesses to me that she is not too crazy about the place—the Indians, against whom she has no racial prejudice, distress her by cooking curried dishes in their rooms all hours of the night, and the Africans, against whom she has no racial prejudice either, sometimes reach out and touch her hair when they pass in the corridor, and though she understands why, and realizes they mean her no harm, it still makes her tremble a little each time it happens. However, in her compliant and good-natured way, Elisabeth has decided to accept the minor indignities of the hallway—and the general squalor of the neighborhood—as part of the adventure of living abroad until June, when she will return to spend the summer with her family at their vacation house in the Stockholm archipelago.

I describe for Elisabeth my own monkish accommodations and do an imitation that amuses her enormously of the captain and his wife telling me that they do not permit cohabitation on the premises, not even between themselves. And when I do an imitation of her own singsong English, she laughs still more.

For the first few weeks, small, dark-haired, and (to my mind) fetchingly buck-toothed Birgitta pretends to be asleep when Elisabeth and I arrive in their basement room and pretend not to be making love. I don't think the excitement I experience when we three suddenly give up the pretense is any greater than it was while we all held our breath and pretended that nothing out of the ordinary was going on. I am so dizzily elated over the change that has taken place in my life since I thought to have lunch at the Midnight Sun—indeed, since I subdued my fears and stepped into Shepherd Market to seek out the whoriest of whores—I am in such an egoistical frenzy over this improbable thing that is happening to me, not just with one but with two Swedish (or, if you will, *European*) girls, that I do not see Elisabeth slowly going to pieces from the effort of being a fully participating sinner in our intercontinental ménage, a half of what can only be called my harem.

Maybe I don't see it because she is in something of a frenzy of her own—a drowning frenzy, a wild thrashing about in order to stay afloat—and as a result seems often to be *enjoying* herself so much; that is, I take the excitement for pleasurable excitement, certainly so when we three go off with a picnic lunch and a tennis ball to spend a Sunday on Hampstead Heath. I teach the girls "running bases"—and could Elisabeth be more delighted by anything than to be caught in a screaming, hilarious rundown between Birgitta and myself?—and they teach me *brännboll*, bits and pieces of fly-catcher-up and stickball, which combine into a game they played in Stockholm as schoolchildren. When it rains we play cards together, gin or canasta. The old king, Gustav V, was a passionate gin-rummy player, I am told, as are Birgitta's mother and father and brother and sister. Elisabeth, whose circle of

Gymnasium friends had apparently idled away hundreds of afternoons at canasta, picks up gin rummy after just half an hour of watching a few games between Birgitta and me. She is captivated by the patter I deliver during the game, and takes immediately to using it herself —as did I at eight or so, back when I learned it all at the feet of Klotzer the Soda Water King (said by my mother to be the heaviest guest in Hungarian Royale history— when Mr. Klotzer lowered his behind onto our wicker, she had sometimes to cover her eyes—and a marathon monologuist and sufferer at the card table). Says Elisabeth, sadly arranging and rearranging the cards that Birgitta has dealt her, "I got a hand like a foot," and when she lays down her melds in triumph, it pleases her no end—it pleases *me* no end—to hear her ask of her opponent, "What's the name of the game, Sport?" Oh, and when she calls the wild card in canasta the "yoker"—well, that just slays me. How on earth can she be going to pieces? *I'm* not! And what about our serious and maddening discussions of World War II, during which I try to explain—and not always in a soft voice either—to explain to these two self-righteous neutralists just what was going on in Europe when we were all growing up? Isn't it Elisabeth who is in fact more vehement (and innocently simple-minded) than Birgitta, who insists, even when I practically threaten to *slap* some sense into her, that the war was "everybody's fault"? How then can I tell that she is not only going to pieces but also thinking from morning to night about how to do herself in?

After the "accident"—so we describe in the telegram to her parents the broken arm and the mild concussion Elisabeth sustains by walking in front of a truck sixteen days after I move from Tooting Bec into the girls' basement—I continue to hang my tweed jacket in her closet and to sleep, or to try to, in her bed. And I actually believe that I am staying on there because in my state of shock I am simply *unable* to move out as yet. Night after night, under Birgitta's nose, I write letters to Stockholm in which I set out to explain myself to Elisabeth; rather, I sit down at my typewriter to begin the paper I must soon deliver in my Icelandic Saga tutorial on the decline of skaldic poetry through the overuse of the kenning, and wind up telling Elisabeth that I had not realized she was trying only to please me, but altogether innocently— "altogether unforgivably"—had believed that, like Birgitta and like myself, she had been pleasing herself first of all. Again and again—on the Underground, in the pub, during a lecture—I take her very first letter, written from her bedroom the day she had arrived back home, and uncrumple it to reread those primary-school sentences that have the Sacco and Vanzetti effect every time—what an idiot I have been, how callous, how blind! *"Älskade David!"* she begins, and then, in her English, goes on to explain that she had fallen in love with me, not with Gittan, and had gone to bed with the two of us only because I wanted her to and she would have done anything I wanted her to do . . . and, she adds in the tiniest script, she is afraid she would again if she were to return to London—

I am not a strong girl as Gittan. I am just a weak one Bettan, and I can't do anything about it. It was like being in hell. I was in love with someone and what I did had nothing to do with love. It was like I no more was human being. I am so stupid and my english is strange when I write, I am sorry for that. But I know I must never again do what we three did as long as I live. So the silly girl have learned something.

Din Bettan

And, below this, Bettan's forgiving afterthought: *"Tusen pussar och kramar"*—a thousand kisses and hugs.

In my own letters I confess again and again that I had been blind to the nature of her real feeling for me—blind to the depth of my feelings for *her!* I call that unforgivable too, and "sad," and "strange," and when the contemplation of this ignorance of mine brings me nearly to tears, I call it "terrifying"—and mean it. And this in turn leads me to try to give both of us some hope by telling her that I have found a room for myself (in only a matter of days I do intend to inquire about one) in a university residence hall, and that henceforth she should write to me there—if she should ever want to write to me again—rather than at the old address, in care of Birgitta . . . And in the midst of composing these earnest apologias and petitions for pardon, I am overcome with the most unruly and contradictory emotions—a sense of unworthiness, of loathsomeness, of genuine shame and remorse, and simultaneously as strong a sense that I am not guilty of anything, that it is as much the fault of those Indians cooking curried rice at 2 a.m. as it is mine that innocent, undefended Elisabeth stepped in the path of that truck. And what *about* Birgitta, who was supposed to have been Elisabeth's protector, and who now merely lies on the bed across the room from me, studying her English grammar, unmoved utterly—or so she pretends—by my drama of self-disgust? As though, since it was Elisabeth's arm, rather than neck, that was broken by the truck, *she* is entirely in the clear! As though Elisabeth's behavior with us is for Elisabeth's conscience alone to reckon with . . . and not hers . . . and not mine. But surely, *surely*, Birgitta is no less guilty than I am of misusing Elisabeth's pliable nature. Or is she? Wasn't it Birgitta rather than me to whom Elisabeth would instinctively turn for affection whenever she needed it most? When, depleted, we lay together on the threadbare rug—for it was the floor, not the bed, we used mostly as our sacrificial altar— when we would be lying there, dead limbs amid the little undergarments, groggy, sated, and confused, it was invariably Birgitta who held Elisabeth's head and gently stroked her face and whispered lullaby words like the kindest of mothers. My arms, my hands, my words didn't seem to be of any use to anyone at that point. The way it worked, my arms, hands, and words meant everything —until I came, and then the two girls huddled up together like playmates off in a tree house, or in a tent where there is just no room for another . . .

Leaving my letter half-written, I go barging out into the street and walk halfway across London (in the direction of Soho generally) to bring myself under control. I try, on these Raskolnikovian sojourns (Raskolnikov, admittedly, as played by Pudd'nhead Wilson), to "think things through." That is, I should like, if I can, to be able to deal with this unexpected turn of events the way Birgitta does. And since I don't seem able to arrive at that kind of equanimity spontaneously—or marshal that kind of strength, if strength it is—how about if I try to *reason* my way into her shoes? Yes, use my Fulbright fellow's brain—it's got to be good for something over here! Think it through, damn it! It's not that difficult. You didn't roll around on these two girls so as to set yourself up in business as a saint! Far from it! You didn't think up the things you all did so as to please the old folks at home! Far from it! Either go back and play patty-cake with Silky Walsh, or stay where you are and want what you want! Birgitta is human too, you know! Strong and clearheaded is human too (if strong and clearheaded it is), and blubbering is not becoming, over the age of four! Nor is the naughty-boy bit! Elisabeth is perfectly right: Gittan is Gittan, Bettan is Bettan, and now it is about time you were you!

Well, "thinking things through" in this manner, it is never too long before I wind up recollecting that night when Birgitta and I kept asking and asking Elisabeth—hounding and hounding Elisabeth—about what we had already cross-examined one another: what was it she secretly wanted most, what was it that she only dared to think about herself and never in her life had had the courage to do or to have done to her? "What is it you've never been able to admit to anyone, Elisabeth, not even to yourself?" Clinging with ten fingers to the blanket dragged from the bed to cover us all on the floor, Elisabeth began softly to weep, and in that charming, musical English admitted she wanted to be had from behind while bending over a chair.

I found no satisfaction in her reply. Only after I had pressed her further, only after I had demanded, "But what else—what more? That's nothing!"—only then did she at last break down and "confess" that she wanted me to do it to her like that while her hands and feet were tied down. And maybe she did and maybe she didn't . . .

Passing through Piccadilly, I compose yet another paragraph of moral speculation for the latest letter intended to educate my innocent victim—and me. In truth, I am trying with what wisdom—and what prose resources and literary models—is mine to understand if in fact I have been what the Christians call wicked and what I would call inhuman. "And even if you had *actually* wanted what you told us you wanted, what law says that whatever secret longing one is asked to satisfy must be satisfied forthwith? . . ." We had used the belt from my trousers and a strap from Birgitta's knapsack to bind Elisabeth to a straight-backed chair. Once again the tears came rolling down her face, causing Birgitta to touch her cheek and to ask her, "Bettan, you want to stop now?" But Elisabeth's long trailing locks, that child's length of amber hair, whipped across her bare back, so vehemently did she shake her head in defiance. Defiance of whom, I wonder. Of what? Why, I don't begin to know a thing about her! "No," Elisabeth whispered. The only word she spoke from start to finish. "No stop?" I asked. "Or no go on? Elisabeth, do you understand me—? Ask her in Swedish, ask her—" But "no" is all she will answer; "no," and "no," and "no" again. And so it was that I proceeded as I sort of believed I was being directed to. Elisabeth weeps, Birgitta watches, and suddenly I am so excited by it all—by the panting, dog-like sounds the three of us are making, by what the three of us are *doing* —that all traces of reluctance drop away, and I know that I could do *anything*, and that I want to, and that I will! Why not four girls, why not five— ". . . who but the wicked would hold that whatever longing one is asked to satisfy must be satisfied forthwith? Yet, dearest, sweetest, precious girl, that appeared to be the very law under which we three had decided—had *agreed*—to live!" And by now I am in a hallway on Greek Street, where at last I stop thinking about what next to write to Elisabeth on the unfathomable subject of my iniquity, and thinking too about this unfathomable Birgitta—*has* she no remorse? no shame? no loyalty? no limits?—who must by now have read the half-written letter left by me in my Olivetti (and which surely will impress her with just how *deep* a sultan I am).

In a little room above a Chinese laundry, I try my luck with a thirty-shilling whore, a fading Cockney milkmaid called Terry the Tart who thinks me "a sexy bah-stard" and whose plucky lewdness had, once upon a time, a most startling effect upon the detonation of my seed. Now Terry's skills go for nought. She gives me her extraordinary collection of dirty pictures to look at; she describes, with no less imagination than Mrs. Browning, the ways in which she will love me; indeed, she praises to the skies the breadth and height of my member and its depth of penetration when last seen erect; but the fifteen minutes of hard labor she then puts in over the recumbent lump is without significant result. Taking such comfort as I can from the tender way Terry puts it—"Sorry, Yank, 'e seems a bit sleepy tonight"—I head back across London to our basement, finishing up as I go with that day's inquiry into the evil I may or may not have done.

As it turns out, I would have been better off applying all this concentration to the excessive use of the kenning in the latter half of the twelfth century in Iceland. That, in time, is something I could have made some sense of. Instead, I seem to get nowhere near the truth, or even the feel of the truth, in the prolix letters I regularly address to Stockholm, while the scholarly essay I finally read before my tutorial group prompts the tutor to invite me back to his office after class, to sit me down in a chair, and to ask, with only the faintest trace of sarcasm, "Tell me, Mr. Kepesh, are you sure you are serious about Icelandic poetry?"

A teacher taking me to task! As unimaginable, this, as my sixteen days in one room with two girls! As Elisabeth Elverskog's attempt at suicide! I am so stunned and humiliated by this chastisement (especially coming in the wake of the accusations that I have been leveling at myself in my capacity as Elisabeth's family's attorney) that I cannot find the courage to return to the tutorial ever again; like Louis Jelinek I do not even respond to the notes asking me to come talk to my tutor about my disappearance. Can it be? I am on my way to failing a course. *In God's name, what next?*

This.

One night Birgitta tells me that while I have been lying gloomily on Elisabeth's bed playing the "fallen priest" she has been doing something "a little perverse." Actually it goes back sometime, to when she had first arrived in London two years ago and had gone to see a doctor about a digestive problem. The doctor had told her that to make a diagnosis he would need a vaginal smear. He asked her to disrobe and arrange herself on the examination table, and then with either his hand or an instrument—she had been so startled at the time she still wasn't sure—had begun to massage between her legs. "Please, what is it that you are doing?" she had asked him. According to Birgitta, he'd had the nerve to say in response, "Look, do you think I like this? I've a bad back, my dear, and this posture doesn't help it any. But I must have a specimen and this is the only way I can get it." "Did you let him?" "I didn't know what else to do. How do I tell him to stop? I had just arrived three days here. I was frightened a little, you know, and I wasn't sure I understood his English. And he looked like a doctor. Tall and nice-looking and kind. And very nice clothes. And I thought maybe this is the way they do it here. He kept saying, 'Are you getting cramps yet, my dear?' At first I didn't know what that means—then I got my clothes on and I left. There were people in the waiting room, there was a nurse . . . He sent a bill for two guineas." "He did? And you paid it?" I ask. "No." "And?" I ask, wavering between incredulity and excitement. "Last month," says Birgitta, her English emerging even more deliberately than usual, "I go to him again. I started to think all the time of it. That's what I think of when you are writing all your letters to Bettan." Is that true, I wonder—is any of it true? "And?" I say. "Now once a week I go to his office. For my lunch hour." "And he masturbates you? You let him masturbate you?" "Yes." "Is this the truth, Gittan?" "I close my eyes and he does it to me with his hand." "And—then?" "I get dressed. I go back to the park." I am craving for more— and more lurid even than this—but there is none. He masturbates her, and he lets her go. Can this be true? Do such things happen? "What's his name? Where is his office?" To my surprise, without any reluctance, Birgitta tells me.

Some hours later, having failed to comprehend a single paragraph of *Arthurian Tradition and Chrétien de Troyes* (an invaluable source, I have been told, for the paper now due in my other tutorial), I rush out to a telephone kiosk at the end of our street and search the directory for the doctor's name—and find it, and at the Brompton Road address! Tomorrow morning first thing I will call him up —I will say (perhaps even in my Swedish accent), "Dr. Leigh, you had better watch out, you had better leave your hands off foreign young girls or you are going to get yourself in a lot of trouble." But it seems that I do not really want to reform the lascivious doctor so much as to find out (inasmuch as I can) whether Birgitta's story is true. Not that I know for sure even yet whether I want it to be true or not. Wouldn't I be better off if it weren't?

When I get back to the flat I undress her. And she submits. With what self-possession does she submit—she and submission are thick as thieves! We are both panting and greatly worked up. I am clothed and she is naked. I call her a little whore. She begs me to pull her hair. How hard she wants it pulled I am not sure—no one has ever asked such a thing of me before. God, how far I have come from kissing Silky's navel in the dormitory laundry room just last spring! "I want to know you're here," she cries—"do it more!" "Like this?" "Yes!" "Like this, my whore? my filthy little Birgitta whore!" "Ah, yes! Ah, yes, yes!"

An hour earlier I had been fearful that it might be decades before I was potent again, that my punishment, if such it was, might even last *forever*. Now I spend a night overcome by a passion whose harsh energies I have never allowed myself to begin to know before; or maybe it is that I have never before known a girl of roughly my own age to whom such forcefulness would have been anything other than an outrage. I have been so steeped in cajoling and wheedling and begging my way toward pleasure that I had not known I was actually capable of such a *besiegement* of another, or that I wished to be besieged and assaulted in turn. Straddling her head with my legs, I force my member into her mouth as though it were at once the lifeline that will prevent her suffocation and the instrument upon which she will strangle. And, as though I am her saddle, she plants herself upon my face and rides and rides and rides. "Tell me things!" cries Birgitta, "I like to be told things! Tell me all kind of things!" And in the morning there is no remorse for anything said or done—far from it. "We appear to be two of a kind," I say. She laughs and says, "I know that a long time." "That's why I stayed, you know." "Yes," she replies, "I know that."

Yet I continue writing to Elisabeth (though no longer in Birgitta's presence). In care of a university residence hall—an American friend has arranged to receive my mail in his box there, and forward it to me—Elisabeth sends a photograph showing that her arm is no longer in a cast. On the back of the photograph she has printed, "Me." I write immediately to thank her for the picture of herself healed and healthy again. I tell her that I am making progress in my Swedish grammar book, that I pick up a *Svenska Dagbladet* on Charing Cross Road each week and try at least to read the front-page stories with the aid of the English-Swedish pocket dictionary she gave me. And though in fact it is Birgitta's newspaper that I take a stab at translating—during the time previously reserved for sweating over my Eddas—while I am writing to Elisabeth

I believe I am doing it for her, for our future, so that I can marry her and settle down in her homeland, eventually to teach American literature there. Yes, I believe I could yet fall in love with this girl who wears around her neck a locket with her father's picture in it . . . indeed, that I should have already. Her face *alone* is so lovable! Look at it, I tell myself—look, you idiot! Teeth that couldn't be whiter, the ripe curve of her cheeks, enormous blue eyes, and the reddish-amber hair that I once told her—it was the night I received the little dictionary inscribed "From me to you"—was best described in English by "tresses," a poetical word out of fairy stories. "Common" is the English word which she tells me (after looking in the dictionary) best describes her nose. "It is a farm girl's nose," she says, "it is like the thing you plant in the garden to grow tulips." "Not quite." "How do you say that?" "Tulip bulb." "Yes. When I am forty I will look horrible because of this tulip bulb." But the nose is just the nose of millions and millions, and, on Elisabeth, actually touching in its utter lack of pride or pretension. Oh, what a sweet face, so full of the happiness of her childhood! the frothiness of her laugh! her innocent heart! This is the girl who knocked me out just by saying "I got a hand like a foot!" Oh, how incredibly moving a thing it is, a person's innocence! How it catches me off guard each time, that unguarded trusting look!

Yet, work myself up as I will over her photograph, it is with slender little Birgitta, a girl a good deal less innocent and vulnerable—a girl who confronts the world with a narrow foxy face, a nose delicately pointed and an upper lip ever so slightly protruding, a mouth ready, if need be, to answer a charge or utter a challenge—that I continue to live out my year as a visiting fellow in erotic daredevilry.

Of course, strolling around Green Park renting out deck chairs to passers-by, Birgitta is tendered invitations almost daily by men visiting London as tourists, or men out prowling on their lunch hour, or men on their way home to wives and children at the end of the day. Because of the opportunities for pleasure and excitement afforded by these meetings, she had decided against returning to Uppsala after her year's leave of absence and had given up her courses in London, too. "I think I get a better English education this way," says Birgitta.

One March afternoon when suddenly the sun appears, out of the blue, over dreary London, I take the Underground to the park and, sitting under a tree, I watch her, some hundred yards away, engaged in conversation with a gentleman nearly three times my age who is reclining in one of the deck chairs. It is almost an hour before the conversation ends, the gentleman rises, makes a formal bow in her direction, and departs. Could it be somebody she knows? Somebody from home? Could it be Dr. Leigh from the Brompton Road? Without telling her, I travel to the park every afternoon for almost a week and, keeping back in the shadows of the trees, spy upon her at work. I am surprised at first to find myself so enormously excited each time I see Birgitta standing over a deck chair in which a man is seated. Of course, all they ever do is talk. That is all I ever see. Never once do I see either a man touching Birgitta or Birgitta touching a man. And I am almost certain she does not make assignations and go off with any of them after work. But what excites me is that she might, that she could . . . that if I proposed such a thing to her, she probably would

44

do it. "What a day," she says at dinner one evening. "The whole Portuguese navy is here. Feee! What men!" But if I were to say . . .

Only a few weeks later she startles me one evening by saying, "Do you know who came to see me today? Mr. Elverskog." "Who?" "Bettan's father." I think: They have found my letters! Oh, why did I put in writing that stuff about tying her hands to the chair! It's me they're after, the *two* families! "He came to see you here?" "He knows where I work," say Birgitta, "so he came there." Is Birgitta lying to me, is she doing something "a little perverse" again? But how can she possibly know that all along I have been terrified of Elisabeth breaking down and turning us in, and of her father coming after me, with a Scotland Yard detective, or with his whip . . . "What's he doing in London, Gittan?" "Oh, his business—I don't know. He just came to the park to say hello." *And did you go off to his hotel room with him, Gittan? Would you like to make love with Elisabeth's father? Wasn't he the tall, distinguished-looking gentleman who bowed farewell to you that sunny day in March? Isn't he the old man I saw you listening to so avidly several months ago? Or was that the doctor who likes to play doctor with you in his office? What was he saying to you, that man, just what was he proposing that held your attention so?*

I don't know what to think, and so I think everything.

In bed later, when she wants to be excited by hearing "all kinds of things," I come to the very brink of saying to her, "Would you do it with Mr. Elverskog? Would you do it with a sailor, if I told you to? Would you do it with him for money?" I don't, not simply for fear that she will say yes (as she might, if only for the thrill of saying it), but because I might reply, "Then go ahead, my little whore."

At the end of the term Birgitta and I take a hitchhiking trip on the Continent, looking at museums and cathedrals during the day, and then after dark, in cafés and *caves* and tavernas, training our sights on girls. About leading Birgitta back into this, I have no such scruples as I had in London about tempting her to visit Mr. Elverskog in his hotel. "Another girl" is one of those "things" with which we have aroused one another continually during the months since Elisabeth's departure. To find other girls is, in fact, one of the reasons we are on this holiday. And we are not bad at it, not at all. To be sure, alone neither Birgitta nor I is ever quite so cunning or brave, but together it seems that we strongly reenforce one another's waywardness and, as the nights go by, become more and more adroit at charming perfect strangers. Yet, no matter how skillfully, how *professionally*, we come to maneuver as a team, I still go a little weak and dizzy when it appears that we have actually succeeded in finding a willing third and all of us get up as one to go find a quieter place to talk. Birgitta reports similar symptoms in herself —though out on the street wins my admiration by daring to reach out and push away from her face the hair of the game young student who is daring to see what develops. Yes, seeing my partner so plucky and confident, I recover my faculties—and my balance—and give each of the girls an arm, and, now, without so much as a quiver in my voice, with my worldly mix of irony and bonhomie, say, "Let's go, friends—come along!" And all the while I am thinking what I have been thinking now for months: *Is this happening? This, too?* For in my wallet along with Elisabeth's picture is a photo of her family's seaside house, sent to me just before I received my lamentable grades and boarded the boat-train with Birgitta. I have been invited to visit her on tiny Trångholmen and to stay on the island as long as I wish. And why don't I? And marry her there! Her father knows nothing, and he never will. The whip, the detective, the scenes of vengeful murderous rage, the secret plot to make me pay for what I have done to his daughter—that is all my imagination running wild. Why not let my imagination run another way? Why not imagine Elisabeth and myself rowing past the rocky shore and the tall pine trees, all the way down the length of the island to where the Waxholms ferry docks each day? Why not imagine her family beaming and waving at us when we return in the boat with the milk and the mail? Why not imagine this sweet Elisabeth on the porch of the Elverskogs' pretty barn-red house, pregnant with the first of our Swedish-Jewish children? Yes, there is Elisabeth's unfathomable and wonderful love and there is Birgitta's unfathomable and wonderful daring, *and whichever I want I can have*. Now isn't *that* unfathomable! Either the furnace or the hearth! Ah, this must be what is meant by the possibilities of youth.

More youthful possibilities. In Paris, in a bar not far from the Bastille, where the infamous marquis had himself been punished for his vile and audacious crimes, a prostitute sits in a corner with us and, while she jokes with me in French about my crew cut, is busy stroking Birgitta beneath the table. In the midst of our excitement—for I also have a hand moving under the table—a man looms up, berating me for the indignities that I am making my young wife submit to. I rise with a throbbing heart to explain that we happen not to be husband and wife,

47

that we are students, that what we do is our business—but, despite my excellent pronunciation and perfect grammatical constructions, he pulls a hammer out of his overalls, and raises it into the air. "*Salaud!*" he cries. "*Espèce de con!*" Hand in hand with Birgitta, and for the first time ever, I run for my life.

We do not discuss what will happen when the month is over. Rather, each thinks: Given what has been, what else can be? That is, I assume that I will return to America alone in order to resume my education, this time *seriously,* and Birgitta assumes that when I leave she will pack her knapsack and come with me. Birgitta's parents have already been told that she is thinking of going to study next in America for a year, and apparently that is all right with them. Even if it weren't, Birgitta would probably still do as she pleased.

When I rehearse the difficult conversation that must take place sooner or later, I hear myself sounding very limp and whiny indeed. Nothing I can say comes out right, nothing she can say sounds wrong—and yet it is I, of course, who invent the dialogue. "I am going to Stanford. I am going back to get my degree." "So?" "I have terrible dreams about school, Gittan. Nothing like this has ever happened to me before. I fucked up my Fulbright but good." "Yes?" "And, as for the two of us—" "Yes?" "Well, I don't see that we have any future. Do *you*? I mean we would never be able to go back to ordinary sex. That can never work for us—we've upped the ante much too high. We've gone too far to go back." "We have?" "I think so, yes." "But it wasn't my idea alone, you know." "I didn't say that it was." "So then we stop going too far." "But *we* can't. Oh, come on, you know that." "But I do whatever you want." "That's not possible any longer. Or are you saying that I've had you in my power all along, that you're another Elisabeth I've corrupted?" She smiles her fetching buck-toothed smile. "Who then is the other Elisabeth?" she asks. "*You*? Oh, but that is not so. You say so yourself. You are a whoremaster by nature, you are a polygamist by nature, there is even the rapist in you—" "Well, maybe I've changed my mind about all that; maybe I was foolish to say such things." "But how can you change your mind about what is your nature?" she asks.

In reality, going home to resume my serious education hardly requires that I fight my way, a little helplessly, a little foolishly, through this thicket of flattering objections. No, no challenging debate about my "nature" is necessary for me to be free of her and our fantastical life of thrilling pleasures—at least not right then and there. We are undressing for bed in a room we have rented for the night in a town in the Seine Valley, some thirty kilometers from Rouen, where I intend the next day to visit Flaubert's birthplace, when Birgitta begins to reminisce about the silly dreams that used to be awakened in her as a teenager by the name California: convertible cars, millionaires, James Dean— I interrupt: "I'm going to California by myself. I'm going by myself—on my own."

Minutes later she is dressed again and her knapsack is ready for the road. My God, she is bolder even than I imagined! How many such girls can there be in the world? She dares to do everything, and yet she is as sane as I am. Sane, clever, courageous, self-possessed—and wildly lascivious! Just what I've always wanted. Why am

I running away, then? In the name of what? More
Arthurian legends and Icelandic sagas? Look, if I were
to empty my pockets of Elisabeth's letters and Elisabeth's
photographs—and empty my imagination of Elisabeth's
father—if I were to give myself completely over to what
I have, to whom I am with, to what may actually *be* my
nature—"Don't be ridiculous," I say, "where can you find
a room at this hour? Oh, damn it, Gittan, I *have* to go to
California alone! I've got to go back to school!"

In response, no tears, no anger, and no real scorn to
speak of. Though not too much admiration for me as a
shameless carnal force. She says from the door, "Why
did I like you so much? You are such a boy," and that is
all there is to the discussion of my character, all, apparently, that her dignity requires or permits. Not the
masterful young master of mistresses and whores, not
the precocious dramatist of the satyric and the lewd, and
something of a fledgling rapist too—no, merely "a
boy." And then gently, so very gently (for despite being
a girl who moans when her hair is pulled and cries for
more when her flesh is made to smart with a little pain,
despite her Amazonian confidence in the darkest dives
and the nerves of iron that she can display in the chancy
hitchhiking world, aside from the stunning sense of in-
alienable right with which she does whatever she likes,
that total immunity from remorse or self-doubt that
mesmerizes me as much as anything, she is also
courteous, respectful, and friendly, the perfectly brought-
up child of a Stockholm physician and his wife), she
closes the door after her so as not to awaken the family
from whom we have rented our room.

Yes, easily as that do young Birgitta Svanström and

young David Kepesh rid themselves of each other. Ridding himself of what he is *by nature* may be a more difficult task, however, since young Kepesh does not appear to be that clear, quite yet, as to what his nature is, exactly. He is awake all night wondering what he will do if Birgitta should steal back into the room before dawn; he wonders if he oughtn't to get up and lock the door. Then when dawn arrives, when noon arrives, and she is nowhere to be found, neither in the town of Les Andelys nor in Rouen—not at the Grosse Horloge; not at the Cathedral; not at the birthplace of Flaubert or the spot where Joan of Arc went up in flames—he wonders if he will ever see the likes of her and their adventure again.

Helen Baird appears some years later, when I am in the final stretch of graduate studies in comparative literature and feeling triumphant about the determination I have mustered to complete the job. Out of boredom, restlessness, impatience, and a growing embarrassment that naggingly informs me I am too old to be sitting at a desk still being tested on what I know, I have come near to quitting the program just about every semester along the way. But now, with the end in sight, I utter my praises aloud while showering at the end of the day, thrilling myself with simple statements like "I did it" and "I stuck it out," as though it is the Matterhorn I have had to climb in order to qualify for my orals. Following the year with Birgitta, I have come to realize that in order to achieve anything lasting, I am going to have to restrain a side of myself strongly susceptible to the most bewildering and debilitating sort of temptations, temptations that as long ago as that night outside Rouen I already recognized as inimical to my overall interests. For, far as I had gone with Birgitta, I knew how very easy it would have been for me to have gone further still—more than once, I remember the thrill it had given me imagining her with men other than myself, imagining her taking money to bring home in her pocket . . . But *could* I have gone on to that so easily? Actually have become Birgitta's pimp? Well, whatever my talent may have been for that profession, graduate school has not exactly encouraged its development . . . Yes, when the battle appears to have been won, I am truly relieved by my ability to harness my good sense in behalf of a serious vocation—and not a little touched by my virtue. Then Helen appears to tell me, by example and in so many words, that I am sadly deluded and mistaken. Is it so as never to forget the charge that I marry her?

Hers is a different brand of heroism from what, at that time, I take mine to be—indeed, it strikes me as its antithesis. A year of U.S.C. at eighteen, and then she had run off with a journalist twice her age to Hong Kong, where he was already living with a wife and three children. Armed with startling good looks, a brave front, and a strongly romantic temperament, she had walked away from her homework and her boy friend and her weekly allowance and, without a word of apology or explanation to her stunned and mortified family (who thought for a week she had been kidnapped or killed), taken off after a destiny more exhilarating than sophomore year in the sorority house. A destiny that she had found—and only recently abandoned.

Just six months earlier, I learn, she had given up everyone and everything that she had gone in search of eight years before—all the pleasure and excitement of roaming among the antiquities and imbibing the exotica of gorgeous places alluringly unknown—to come back to California and begin life anew. "I hope I never again have to live through a year like this last one" is nearly the first thing she says to me the night we meet at a party given by the wealthy young sponsors of a new San Francisco magazine "of the arts." I find Helen ready to tell her story without a trace of shyness; but then I had not been shy myself, once we'd been introduced, about meandering away from the girl I'd arrived with, and hunting her down through the hundreds of people milling around in the town house. "Why?" I ask her—the first of the whys and whens and hows she will be obliged to answer for me—"What's the year been like for you? What went wrong?" "Well, for one thing, I haven't been anywhere for six months at a stretch since I did my time as a coed." "Why did you come back, then?" "Men. Love. It all got out of hand." Instantly I am ready to attribute her "candor" to a popular-magazine mentality—and a predilection for promiscuity, pure and simple. Oh, God, I think, so beautiful, and so corny. It seems from the stories she goes on to tell me that she has been in fifty passionate affairs already—aboard fifty schooners already, sailing the China Sea with men who ply her with antique jewelry and are married to somebody else. "Look," she says, having sized up how I seem to have sized up such an existence, "what do you have against passion anyway? Why the studied detachment, Mr. Kepesh? You want to know who I am—well, I'm telling you." "It's quite a saga," I say. She asks, with a smile, "Why shouldn't it be? Better a 'saga' than a lot of other things I can think of. Come now, what do you have against passion anyway? What harm has it ever done you? Or should I ask, what good?" "The question right now is what it has or hasn't done for you." "Fine things. Wonderful things. God knows, nothing I'm ashamed of." "Then why are you here and not there, being impassioned?" "Because," Helen answers, and without any irony at all for protection—which may be what makes me begin to surrender some of my own, and to see that she is not only stunning-looking, she is also real, and here with me, and maybe even mine if I should want her—"Because," she tells me, "I'm getting on."

At twenty-six, getting on. Whereas the twenty-four-year-old Ph.D. candidate who is my date for the evening —and who eventually leaves the party in a huff, without me—had been saying on the way over that, sorting her index cards in the library just that afternoon, she had been wondering if and when her life would ever get underway.

I ask Helen what it was like to come back. We have left the party by now and are across from one another in a nearby bar. Less passively than I, she has given the slip to the companion with whom she started the evening. If I want her . . . but do I? *Should* I? Let me hear first what it had been like coming back from running away. For me, of course, there had been far more relief than letdown, and I had been adrift for only a year. "Oh, I signed an armistice with my poor mother, and my kid sisters followed me around like a movie star. The rest of the family gaped. Nice Republican girls didn't do what I did. Except that seems to be all I ever met everywhere I went, from Nepal to Singapore. There's a small army of us out there, you know. I'd say half the girls who fly out of Rangoon on that crate that goes to Mandalay are generally from Shaker Heights." "And now what do you do?" "Well, first I have to figure out some way to stop crying. I cried every day I was back for the first few months. Now that seems to be over, but, frankly, from the way I feel when I wake up in the morning I might as *well* be in tears. It's that it was all so beautiful. Living in all that loveliness—it was overwhelming. I never stopped being thrilled. I got to Angkor every single spring, and in Thailand we would fly from Bangkok up to Chiengmai with a prince who owned elephants. You should have seen him with all his elephants. A nut-colored little old man moving like a spider in a herd of the most enormous animals. You could have wrapped him twice around in one of their ears. They were all screaming at one another, but he just walked along, unfazed. You probably think seeing that is, well, seeing only that. Well, that isn't what I thought. I thought, 'This is what it is.' I used to go down in the sailboat—this is in Hong Kong—to get my friend from work at the end of the day. He sailed with the boat boy to work in the morning and then at night we sailed home together, right down between the junks and the U.S. destroyers." "The good colonial life. It isn't for nothing they hate giving up those empires. But I still don't understand precisely why you gave up yours."

And in the weeks that follow I continue to find it hard to believe—despite the tiny ivory Buddhas, the jade carvings, and the row of rooster-shaped opium weights that are arranged by her bedside table—that this way of life ever really was hers. Chiengmai, Rangoon, Singapore, Mandalay . . . why not Jupiter, why not Mars? To be sure, I know these places exist beyond the Rand McNally map on which I trace the course of her adventures (as once I traced down an adventure of Birgitta's in the London phone directory), and the novels of Conrad where I first encountered them—and so, of course, do I know that "characters" live and breathe who choose to make their destiny in the stranger cities of the world . . . What then fails to persuade me completely that living, breathing Helen is one of them? My being with her? Is the unbelievable character Helen in her diamond-stud earrings or is it the dutiful graduate teaching assistant in his wash-and-dry seersucker suit?

I even become somewhat suspicious and critical of her serene, womanly beauty, or rather, of the regard in which she seems to hold her eyes, her nose, her throat, her breasts, her hips, her legs—why, even her feet would seem to her to have charming little glories to be extolled. How does she come by this regal bearing anyway, this aristocratic sense of herself that seems to derive almost entirely from the smoothness of skin, the length of limb, the breadth of mouth and span of eyes, and the fluting at the very tip of what she describes, without batting an eyelid (shadowed in the subtlest green), as her "Flemish" nose? I am not at all accustomed to someone who bears her beauty with such a sense of attainment and self-worth. My experience—running from the Syracuse undergraduates who did not want to "relate" to me "on that level," to Birgitta Svanström, for whom flesh was very much there to be investigated for every last thrill—has been of young women who make no great fuss about their looks, or believe at least that it is not seemly to show that they do. True, Birgitta knew well enough that her hair cut short and carelessly nicely enhanced her charming fur-

tiveness, but otherwise how she framed her unpainted
face was not a subject to which she appeared to give
much thought from one morning to the next. And Elisabeth, with an abundance of hair no less praiseworthy
than Helen's, simply brushed it straight down her back,
letting it hang there as it had since she was six. To Helen,
however, all that marvelous hair—closest in shading to
the Irish setter—seems to be in the nature of a crown, or
a spire, or a halo, there not simply to adorn or embellish
but to express, to symbolize. Perhaps it is only a measure
of how narrow and cloistered my life has become—or perhaps it is in fact the true measure of a courtesanlike
power that emanates from Helen's sense of herself as an
idolized object that might just as well have been carved of
one hundred pounds of jade—but when she twists her
hair up into a soft knot at the back of her head, and draws
a black line above her lashes—above eyes in themselves
no larger and no bluer than Elisabeth's—when she dons
a dozen bracelets and ties a fringed silk scarf around her
hips like Carmen to go out to buy some oranges for
breakfast, the effect is not lost upon me. Far from it. I
have from the start been overcome by physical beauty in
women, but by Helen I am not just intrigued and aroused,
I am also alarmed, and made deeply, deeply uncertain—
utterly subjugated by the authority with which she claims
and confirms and makes singular her loveliness, yet as
suspicious as I can be of the prerogatives, of the *place*,
thereby bestowed upon her in her own imagination. Hers
seems to me sometimes such a banalized conception of
self and experience, and yet, all the same, enthralling and
full of fascination. *For all I know, maybe she is right.*

"How come," I ask—still asking, still apparently very

much hoping to expose what is fiction in this fabulous character she calls herself and in the Asiatic romance she claims for a past—"how come *you* gave up the good colonial life, Helen?" "I had to." "Because the inheritance money had made you independent?" "It's six thousand lousy dollars a year, David. Why, I believe even ascetic college teachers make that much." "I only meant that you might have decided youth and beauty weren't going to get you through indefinitely." "Look, I was a kid, and school meant nothing to me, and my family was just like everyone else's—sweet and boring and proper, and living lo these many years under a sheet of ice at 18 Fern Hill Manor Road. The only excitement came at mealtime. Every night when we got to dessert my father said, 'Is that it?' and my mother burst into tears. And so at the age of eighteen I met a grown man, and he was marvelous-looking, and he knew how to talk, and he could teach me plenty, and he knew what I was all about, which nobody else seemed to know at all, and he had wonderful elegant ways, and wasn't really a brutal tyrant, as tyrants go; and I fell in love with him—yes, in two weeks; it happens and not just to schoolgirls, either—and he said, 'Why don't you come back with me?' and I said yes—and I went." "In a 'crate'?" "Not that time. Paté over the Pacific and fellatio in the first-class john. Let me tell you, the first six months weren't a picnic. I'm not in mourning over that. You see, I was just a nicely brought-up kid from Pasadena, that's all, really, in her tartan skirt and her loafers —my friend's *children* were nearly as old as I was. Oh, splendidly neurotic, but practically my age. I couldn't even learn to eat with chopsticks, I was so scared. I remember one night, my first big opium party, I somehow

wound up in a limousine with four of the wildest pansies
—four Englishmen, dressed in gowns and gold slippers.
I couldn't stop laughing. 'It's surreal,' I kept saying, 'it's
surreal,' until the plumpest of them looked down his
lorgnette at me and said, 'Of course it's surreal, dear,
you're nineteen.' " "But you came back. Why?" "I can't go
into that." "Who was the man?" "Oh, you are becoming
a *cum laude* student of real life, David." "Wrong. Learned
it all at Tolstoy's feet."

I give her *Anna Karenina* to read. She says, "Not bad—
only it wasn't a Vronsky, thank God. Vronskys are a dime
a dozen, friend, and bore you to tears. It was a man—very
much a Karenin, in fact. Though not at all pathetic, I
hasten to add." *That* stops me for a moment: what an
original way to see the famous triangle! "Another husband," I say. "Only the half of it." "Sounds mysterious; sounds like high drama. Maybe you ought to write it
all down." "And perhaps you ought to lay off reading what
all has been written down." "And do what instead with
my spare time?" "Dip a foot back into the stuff itself."
"And there's a book about that, you know. Called *The
Ambassadors*." I think: And there's also a book about you.
It's called *The Sun Also Rises* and her name is Brett and
she's about as shallow. So is her whole crew—so, it seems,
was yours. "I'll bet there's a book about it," says Helen,
gladly rising, with her confident smile, to the bait. "I'll
bet there are thousands of books about it. I used to see
them all lined up in alphabetical order in the library.
Look, so there is no confusion, let me only mildly over-
state the case: I hate libraries, I hate books, and I hate
schools. As I remember, they tend to turn everything
about life into something slightly other than it is—

'slightly' at best. It's those poor innocent theoretical book-worms who do the teaching who turn it all into something worse. Something ghastly, when you think about it." "What do you see in me, then?" "Oh, you really hate them a little too. For what they've done to you." "Which is?" "Turned you into something—" "Ghastly?" I say, laughing (for we are having this little duel beneath a sheet in the bed beside the little bronze opium weights). "No, not quite. Into something slightly other, slightly . . . wrong. Everything about you is just a little bit of a lie— except your eyes. They're still you. I can't even look into them very long. It's like trying to put your hand into a bowl of hot water to pull out the plug." "You put things vividly. You're a vivid creature. I've noticed your eyes too." "You're misusing yourself, David. You're hopelessly intent on being what you're not. I get the sense that you may be riding for a very bad fall. Your first mistake was to give up that spunky Swede with the knapsack. She sounds a little like a guttersnipe, and—I have to say it— from the snapshot looks to me a little squirrely around the mouth, but at least she was fun to be with. But of course that's a word you just despise, correct? Like 'crate' for beat-up airplane. Every time I say 'fun' I see you positively wincing with pain. God, they've really done a job on you. You're so damn smug, and yet I think secretly you know you lost your nerve." "Oh, don't simplify me *too* much. And don't romanticize my 'nerve' either—okay? I like to have a good time now and then. I have a good time sleeping with you by the way." "By the way, you have more than a good time sleeping with me. You have the best time you've ever had with anybody. And, dear friend," she adds, "don't simplify me either."

"Oh, God," says Helen, stretching languorously when morning comes, "fucking is such a lovely thing to do."

True, true, true, true, true. The passion is frenzied, inexhaustible, and in my experience, singularly replenishing. Looking back to Birgitta, it seems to me, from my new vantage point, that we were, among other things, helping each other at age twenty-two to turn into something faintly corrupt, each the other's slave and slaveholder, each the arsonist and the inflamed. Exercising such strong sexual power over each other, *and* over total strangers, we had created a richly hypnotic atmosphere, but one which permeated the inexperienced *mind* first of all: I was intrigued and exhilarated at least as much by the idea of what we were engaged in as by the sensations, what I felt and what I saw. Not so with Helen. To be sure, I must first accustom myself to what strikes me at the height of my skepticism as so much theatrical display; but soon, as understanding grows, as familiarity grows, and feeling with it, I begin at last to relinquish some of my suspiciousness, to lay off a little with my interrogations, and to see these passionate performances as arising out of the very fearlessness that so draws me to her, out of that determined abandon with which she will give herself to whatever strongly beckons, and regardless of how likely it is to bring in the end as much pain as pleasure. I have been dead wrong, I tell myself, trying to dismiss hers as a corny and banalized mentality deriving from *Screen Romance*—rather, she is *without* fantasy, there is no *room* for fantasy, so total is her concentration, and the ingenuity with which she sounds her desire. Now, in the aftermath of orgasm, I find myself weak with gratitude and the profoundest feelings of self-surrender. I am the least guarded, if not the simplest, organism on earth. I don't even know what to say at such moments. Helen does, however. Yes, there are the things that this girl knows and knows and knows. "I love you," she tells me. Well, if something has to be said, what makes more sense? So we begin to tell each other that we are lovers who are in love, even while my conviction that we are on widely divergent paths is revived from one conversation to the next. Convinced as I would like to be that a kinship, rare and valuable, underlies and nourishes our passionate rapport, I still cannot wish away the grand uneasiness Helen continues to arouse. Why else can't we stop—can't I stop—the fencing and the parrying?

Finally she agrees to tell me why she gave up all she'd had in the Far East: tells me either to address my suspiciousness directly or to enrich the mystique I cannot seem to resist.

Her lover, the last of her Karenins, had begun to talk about arranging for his wife to be killed in an "accident." "Who was he?" "A very well-known and important man" is all she is willing to say. I swallow that as best I can and ask: "Where is he now?" "Still there." "Hasn't he tried to see you?" "He came here for a week." "And did you sleep with him?" "Of course I slept with him. How could I resist sleeping with him? But in the end I sent him back. It nearly did me in. It was hideous, seeing him go for good." "Well, maybe he'll go ahead and have his wife killed anyway, as an enticement—" "Why must you make fun of him? Is it so impossible for you to understand that he's as human as you?" "Helen, there are ways of dealing with a mate you want to be rid of, short of homicide. You can just walk out the door, for one thing." "Can you, 'just'? Is that the way they do it in the Comparative Literature Department? I wonder what it will be like," she says, "when you can't have something you want." "Will I blow somebody's brains out to get it? Will I push somebody down the elevator shaft? What do you think?" "Look, *I'm* the one who gave up everything and nearly died of it— because I couldn't bear to hear the idea even *spoken*. It terrified me to know that he could even *have* such a thought. Or maybe it was so excrutiatingly tempting that *that's* why I went running. Because all I had to say was yes; that's all he was waiting for. He was desperate, David, and he was serious. And do you know how easy it would have been to say what he wanted to hear? It's only a word, it takes just a split second: yes." "Only maybe he asked because he was so sure you'd say no." "He couldn't be sure. *I* wasn't sure." "But such a well-known and important man could certainly have gone ahead then and had the thing done on his own, could he not—and without your knowing he was behind it? Surely such a well-known and important man has all kinds of means at his disposal to get a measly wife out of the way: limousines that crash, boats that sink, airplanes that explode in mid-air. Had he done it on his own to begin with, what *you* thought about it all would never even have come up. If he asked your opinion, maybe it was to *hear* no." "Oh, this is interesting. Go on. I say no, and what does he gain?" "What he has: the wife *and* you. He gets to keep it all, and to cut a very grand figure into the bargain. That you ran, that the whole idea took on reality for you, had moral consequences for you— well, he probably hadn't figured on getting that kind of rise out of a beautiful, adventurous, American runaway."

"Very clever, indeed. A plus, especially the part about 'moral consequences.' All that's wrong is that you haven't the faintest understanding of what there was between us. Just because he's someone with power, you think he has no feelings. But there are men, you know, who have both. We met two times a week for two years. Sometimes more—but never less. And it never changed. It was never anything but perfect. You don't believe such things happen, do you? Or even if they do, you don't want to believe they matter. But this happened, and to me and to him it mattered more than anything." "But so has coming back happened. So did sending him away happen. So did your terror happen and your revulsion. This guy's machinations are beside the point. It mattered to you, Helen, that your limit had been reached." "Maybe I was mistaken and that was only so much sentimentality about myself. Or some childish kind of hope. Maybe I should have stayed, gone beyond my limit—and learned that it wasn't beyond me at all." "You couldn't," I say, "and you didn't."

And who, oh, who is being the sentimentalist now?

It appears then that the capacity for pain-filled renunciation joined to the gift for sensual abandon is what makes her appeal inescapable. That we never entirely get along, that I am never entirely *sure*, that she somehow lacks depth, that her vanity is so enormous, well, all that is nothing—isn't it?—beside the esteem that I come to have for this beautiful and dramatic young heroine, who has risked and won and lost so much already, squarely facing up to appetite. And then there is the beauty itself. Is she not the single most desirable creature I have ever known? With a woman so physically captivating, a woman whom I cannot take my eyes from even if she is only drinking her coffee or dialing the phone, surely with someone whose smallest bodily movement has such a powerful sensuous hold upon me, I need hardly worry ever again about imagination tempting me to renewed adventures in the base and the bewildering. Is not Helen the enchantress whom I had already begun searching for in college, when Silky Walsh's lower lip stirred me to pursue her from the university cafeteria to the university gymnasium and on to the dormitory laundry room—that creature to me *so* beautiful that upon her, and her alone, I can focus all my yearning, all my adoration, all my curiosity, all my lust? If not Helen, who then? Who ever will intrigue me more? And, alas, I still so need to be intrigued.

Only if we marry . . . well, the contentious side of the affair will simply dwindle away of itself, will it not, an ever-deepening intimacy, the assurance of permanence, dissolving whatever impulse remains, on either side, for smugness and self-defense? Of course it would not be quite such a gamble if Helen were just a little more like this and a little less like that; but, as I am quick to remind myself—imagining that I am taking the *mature* position —that is not how we are bestowed upon each other in the world this side of dreams. Besides, what I call her "vanity" and her "lack of depth" is just what makes her so interesting! So then, I can only hope that mere differences of "opinion" (which, I readily admit—if that will help—I am often the first to point up and to dramatize) will come to be altogether beside the point of the passionate attachment that has, so far, remained undiminished in spite of our abrasive, rather evangelical dialogues. I can only hope that just as I have been mistaken about her motives before, I am wrong again when I suspect that what she secretly hopes to gain by marriage is an end to her love affair with that unpathetic Karenin in Hong Kong. I can only hope that it is in fact I whom she will marry and not the barrier I may seem to be against the past whose loss had very nearly killed her. I can only hope (for I can never know) that it is I with whom she goes to bed, and not with memories of the mouth and the hands and the member of that most perfect of all lovers, he who would murder his wife in order to make his mistress his own.

Doubting and hoping then, wanting and fearing (anticipating the pleasantest sort of lively future one moment, the worst in the next), I marry Helen Baird—after, that is, nearly three full years devoted to doubting-hoping-wanting-and-fearing. There are some, like my own father, who have only to see a woman standing over a piano singing "Amapola" to decide in a flash, "There—there is my wife," and there are others who sigh, "Yes, it is she," only after an interminable drama of vacillation that has led them to the ineluctable conclusion that they ought never to see the woman again. I marry Helen when the weight of experience required to reach the monumental decision to give her up for good turns out to be so enormous and so moving that I cannot possibly imagine life without her. Only when I finally know *for sure* that *this must end now*, do I discover how deeply wed I already am by my thousand days of indecision, by all the scrutinizing appraisal of possibilities that has somehow made an affair of three years' duration seem as dense with human event as a marriage half a century long. I marry Helen then—and she marries me—at the moment of impasse and exhaustion that must finally come to all those who spend years and years and years in these clearly demarcated and maze-like arrangements that involve separate apartments and joint vacations, assumptions of devotion and designated nights apart, affairs terminated with relief every five or six months, and happily forgotten for seventy-two hours, and then resumed, oftentimes with a delicious, if effervescent, sexual frenzy, following a half-fortuitous meeting at the local supermarket; or begun anew after an evening phone call intended solely to apprise the relinquished companion of a noteworthy documentary to be rerun on television at ten; or following attendance at a dinner party to which the couple had committed themselves so long ago it would have been unseemly not to go ahead and, together, meet this last mutual social obligation. To be sure, one or the other might have answered the obligation by going off to the party alone, but alone there would have been no accomplice across the table with whom to exchange signs of boredom and amusement, nor afterward, driving home, would there have been anyone of like mind with whom to review the charms and deficiencies of the other guests; nor, undressing for bed, would there have been an eager, smiling friend lying unclothed atop the bed sheet to whom one allows that the only truly engaging person present at the table happened to have been one's own previously underrated mate manqué.

We marry, and, as I should have known and couldn't have known and probably always knew, mutual criticism and disapproval continue to poison our lives, evidence not only of the deep temperamental divide that has been there from the start, but also of the sense I continue to have that another man still holds the claim upon her deepest feelings, and that, however she may attempt to hide this sad fact and to attend to me and our life, she knows as well as I do that she is my wife only because there was no way short of homicide (or so they say) for her to be the wife of that very important and well-known lover of hers. At our best, at our bravest and most sensible and most devoted, we do try very hard to hate what divides us rather than each other. If only that past of hers weren't so vivid, so grandiose, so operatic—if somehow one or the other of us could forget it! If I could close this absurd gap of trust that exists between us still! Or ignore it! Live *beyond* it! At our best we make resolutions, we make apologies, we make amends, we make love. But at our worst . . . well, our worst is just about as bad as anybody's, I would think.

What do we struggle over mostly? In the beginning— as anyone will have guessed who, after three years of procrastination, has thrown himself headlong and half convinced into the matrimonial flames—in the beginning we struggle over the toast. Why, I wonder, can't the toast go in while the eggs are cooking, rather than before? This way we can get to eat our bread warm rather than cold. "I don't believe I am having this discussion," she says. "Life isn't toast!" she finally screams. "It is!" I hear myself maintaining. "When you sit down to eat toast, life is toast. And when you take out the garbage, life is garbage. You can't leave the garbage halfway down the stairs, Helen. It belongs in the can in the yard. Covered." "I forgot it." "How can you forget it when it's already in your hand?" "Perhaps, dear, because it's garbage—and what difference does it make anyway!" She forgets to affix her signature to the checks she writes and to stamp the letters she mails, while the letters I give her to mail for me and the household turn up with a certain regularity in the pockets of raincoats and slacks months after she has gone off to deposit them in the mailbox. "What do you think about between Here and There? What makes you so forgetful, Helen? Yearnings for old Mandalay? Memories of the 'crate' and the lagoons and the elephants, of the dawn coming up like thunder—" "I can't think about your letters, damn it, every inch of the way." "But why is it you think you've gone outside with the letter in your hand to *begin* with?" "For some air, that's why! To see some sky! To breathe!"

Soon enough, instead of pointing out her errors and oversights, or retracing her steps, or picking up the pieces, or restraining myself (and then going off to curse her out behind the bathroom door), I make the toast, I make the eggs, I take out the garbage, I pay the bills, and I mail the letters. Even when she says, graciously (trying, at *her* end, to bridge the awful gap), "I'm going out shopping, want me to drop these—" experience, if not wisdom, directs me to say, "No—no, thanks." The day she loses her wallet after making a withdrawal from the savings account, I take over the transactions at the bank. The day she leaves the fish to rot under the car's front seat after going out in the morning to get the salmon steaks for dinner, I take over the marketing. The day she has the wool shirt that was to have been dry-cleaned laundered by mistake, I take over going to the cleaners. With the result that before a year is out I am occupied—and glad of it—some sixteen hours a day with teaching my classes and rewriting into a book my thesis on romantic disillusionment in the stories of Anton Chekhov (a subject I'd chosen before even meeting my wife), and Helen has taken increasingly to drink and to dope.

Her days begin in jasmine-scented waters. With olive oil in her hair to make it glossy after washing, and her face anointed with vitamin creams, she reclines in the tub for twenty minutes each morning, eyes closed and the precious skull at rest against a small inflated pillow; the woman moves only to rub gently with her pumice stone the rough skin on her feet. Three times a week the bath is followed by her facial sauna: in her midnight-blue silk kimono, embroidered with pink and red poppies and yellow birds never seen on land or sea, she sits at the counter of our tiny kitchenette, her turbaned head tilted over a bowl of steaming water sprinkled with rosemary and camomile and elder flower. Then, steamed and painted and coiffed, she is ready to dress for her exercise class—and wherever else it is she goes while I am at school: a close-fitting Chinese dress of navy-blue silk, high at the collar and slit to the thigh; the diamond-stud earrings; bracelets of jade and of gold; her jade ring; her sandals; her straw bag.

When she returns later in the day—after Yoga, she decided to go into San Francisco "to look around": she talks (has talked for years) of plans to open a Far East antique shop there—she is already a little high, and by dinnertime she is all smiles: mellow, blotto, wry. "Life is toast," she observes, sipping four fingers of rum while I season the lamb chops. "Life is leftovers. Life is leather soles and rubber heels. Life is carrying forward the balance into the new checkbook. Life is writing the correct amount to be paid out onto each of the stubs. *And* the correct day, month, and year." "That is all true," I say. "Ah," she says, watching me as I go about setting the table, "if only his wife didn't forget what she puts in to broil and leave everything to burn; if only his wife could remember that when David had dinner in Arcadia, his mother always set the fork on the left and the spoon on the right and never never both on the same side. Oh, if only his wife could bake and butter his potato the way Mamma did in the wintertime."

By the time we are into our thirties we have so exacerbated our antipathies that each of us has been reduced to precisely what the other had been so leery of at the outset, the professorial "smugness" and "prissiness" for which Helen detests me with all her heart—"You've actually done it, David—you are a full-fledged young fogy"—no less in evidence than her "utter mindlessness," "idiotic wastefulness," "adolescent dreaminess," etc. Yet I can never leave her, nor she me, not, that is, until outright disaster makes it simply ludicrous to go on waiting for the miraculous conversion of the other. As much to our wonderment as to everyone else's, we remain married nearly as long as we had been together as lovers, perhaps because of the opportunity this marriage now provides for each of us to assault head-on what each takes to be his demon (and had seemed at first to be the other's salvation!). The months go by and we remain together, wondering if a child would somehow resolve this crazy deadlock . . . or an antique shop of her own for Helen . . . or a jewelry shop . . . or psychotherapy for us both. Again and again we hear ourselves described as a strikingly "attractive" couple: well dressed, traveled, intelligent, worldly (especially as young academic couples go), a combined income of twelve thousand dollars a year . . . and life is simply awful.

What little spirit smolders on in me during the last months of the marriage is visible only in class; otherwise, I am so affectless and withdrawn that a rumor among the junior faculty members has me "under sedation." Ever since the approval of my dissertation I have been teaching, along with the freshman course "Introduction to Fiction," two sections of the sophomore survey in "general" literature. During the weeks near the end of the term when we study Chekhov's stories, I find, while reading aloud to my students passages which I particularly want them to take note of, that each and every sentence seems to me to allude to my own plight above all, as though by now every single syllable I think or utter must first trickle down through my troubles. And then there are my classroom daydreams, as plentiful suddenly as they are irrepressible, and so obviously inspired by longings for miraculous salvation—reentry into lives I lost long ago, reincarnation as a being wholly unlike myself—that I am even somewhat grateful to be depressed and without anything like the will power to set even the mildest fantasy in motion.

"I realized that when you love you must either, in your reasoning about that love, start from what is higher, more important than happiness or unhappiness, sin or virtue in their usual meaning, or you must not reason at all." I ask my students what's meant by these lines, and while they tell me, notice that in a far corner of the room the poised, soft-spoken girl who is my most intelligent, my prettiest—and my most bored and arrogant—student is finishing off a candy bar and a Coke for lunch. "Oh, don't eat junk," I say to her, silently, and see the two of us on the terrace of the Gritti, squinting through the shimmer over the Grand Canal across to the ocher façade of the perfect little palazzo where we have taken a shuttered room . . . we are having our midday meal, creamy pasta followed by tender bits of lemoned veal . . . and at the very table where Birgitta and I, arrogant, nervy youngsters not much older than these boys and girls, sat down to eat on the afternoon we pooled much of our wealth to celebrate our arrival in Byron's Italy . . .

Meanwhile, my other bright student is explaining what the landowner Alyohin means at the conclusion of "About Love" when he speaks of "what is higher . . . than happiness or unhappiness, sin or virtue in their usual meaning." The boy says, "He regrets that he didn't yield to his feeling and run off with the woman he fell in love with. Now that she's going away, he's miserable for having allowed conscience and scruples, and his own timidity, to forbid him confessing his love to her just because she is already married and a mother." I nod, but clearly without comprehension, and the clever boy looks dismayed. "Am I wrong?" he asks, turning scarlet. "No, *no*," I say, but all the while I am thinking, "What are you doing, Miss Rodgers, dining on Peanut Chews? We should be sipping white wine . . ." And then it occurs to me that, as an undergraduate at U.S.C., Helen probably looked rather like my bored Miss Rodgers in the months before that older man—a man of about my age!—plucked her out of the classroom and into a life of romantic adventure . . .

Later in the hour, I look up from reading aloud out of "Lady with a Lapdog" directly into the innocent and uncorrupted gaze of the plump, earnest, tenderhearted Jewish girl from Beverly Hills who has sat in the front row all year long writing down everything I say. I read to the class the story's final paragraph, in which the adulterous couple, shaken to find how deeply they love one another, try vainly "to understand why he should have a wife and she a husband." "And it seemed to them that in only a few more minutes a solution would be found and a new, beautiful life would begin; but both of them knew very well that the end was still a long, long way away and that the most complicated and difficult part was only just beginning." I hear myself speaking of the moving transparency of the ending—no false mysteries, only the harsh facts directly stated. I speak of the amount of human history that Chekhov can incorporate in fifteen pages, of how ridicule and irony gradually give way, even within so short a space, to sorrow and pathos, of his feel for the disillusioning moment and for those processes wherein actuality seemingly pounces upon even our most harmless illusions, not to mention the grand dreams of fulfillment and adventure. I speak of his pessimism about what he calls "this business of personal happiness," and all the while I want to ask the chubby girl in the front row, who is rapidly recording my words in her notebook, to become my daughter. I want to look after her and see that she is safe and happy. I want to pay for her clothes and her doctor bills and for her to come and put her arms around me when she is feeling lonely or sad. If only it were Helen and I who had raised her to be so sweet! But how could we two raise anything?

And later that day, when I happen to run into her walking toward me on the campus, I feel impelled yet again to say to someone who is probably no more than ten or twelve years my junior that I want to adopt her, want her to forget her own parents, about whom I know nothing, and let me father and protect her. "Hi, Mr. Kepesh," she says, with a little wave of the hand, and that affectionate gesture does it, apparently. I feel as though I am growing lighter and lighter, I sense an emotion coming my way that will pick me up and turn me over and deposit me I know not where. Am I going to have my nervous collapse right here on the walk in front of the library? I take one of her hands in mine—I am saying, through a throat clogged with feeling, "You're a good girl, Kathie." She ducks her head, her forehead colors. "Well," she says, "I'm glad somebody around here likes me." "You're a good girl," I repeat, and release the soft hand I am holding and go home to see if childless Helen is sober enough to prepare dinner for two.

About this time we are visited by an English investment banker named Donald Garland, the first of Helen's Hong Kong friends ever to be invited to dine with us in our apartment. To be sure, she has on occasion made herself spectacularly beautiful so as to go into San Francisco to have lunch with somebody or other out of paradise lost, but never before have I seen her approach such a meeting in this mood of happy, almost childlike anticipation. Indeed, in the past there have been times when, having spent hours getting made up for the luncheon engagement, she would emerge from the bathroom in her drabbest robe, announcing herself unable to leave the house to see anyone. "I look hideous." "You don't at all." "I do," and with that she returns to bed for the day.

Donald Garland, she tells me now, is "the kindest man" she has ever known. "I was taken to lunch at his house my first week in Hong Kong, and we were the best of friends from then on. We just adored each other. The center of the table was strewn with orchids he'd picked from his garden—in my honor, he said—and the patio where we ate looked out over the crescent of Repulse Bay. I was eighteen years old. He must have been about fifty-five. My God. Donald is probably seventy! I could never believe he was over forty; he was always so happy, so youthful, so thrilled with everything. He lived with the most easygoing and good-natured American boy. Chips must have been about twenty-six or -seven then. On the phone this afternoon Donald told the most terrible news—one morning two months ago Chips died of an aneurysm at breakfast; just keeled over dead. Donald took the body back to Wilmington, Delaware, and buried it, and then he couldn't leave. He kept booking plane tickets and canceling. Now, finally, he's on his way home."

Chips, Donald, Edgar, Brian, Colin . . . I have no response to make, no interrogations or cross-examination, nothing faintly resembling sympathy, curiosity, or interest. Or patience. I had long ago heard all I could stand about the doings of the wealthy Hong Kong circle of English homosexuals who had "adored" her. I exhibit only a churlish sort of surprise to find that I am to be a party to this very special reunion. She shuts her eyes tightly, as though she must obliterate me momentarily from sight just in order to survive. "Don't talk to me like that. Don't take that terrible tone. He was my dearest friend. He saved my life a hundred times." *And why did you risk it a hundred times?* But the interrogatory accusation, and the terrible tone that goes with it, I manage to squelch, for by now even I know that I am being diminished far more by my anger at everything she does and did than by those ways of hers I ought to have learned to disregard, or to have accepted with a certain grace, long, long ago . . . Only as the evening wears on, and Garland becomes increasingly spirited in his reminiscences, do I wonder if she has invited him to the apartment so that I might learn at first hand just how very far from the apex she has fallen by insanely joining her fate to this fogy's. Whether or not that is her intention, it is something like the result. In their company I am no easygoing, good-natured Chips, but entirely the Victorian schoolmaster whose heart stirs only to the crack of the whip and the swish of the cane. In a vain attempt to force this pious, sour, censorious little prig out of my skin, I try hard to believe that Helen is simply showing this man who has meant so much to her and been so kind to her, and who has himself just suffered a terrible blow, that all is well in her life, that she and her husband live comfortably and amicably, and that her protector hasn't to worry about her any longer. Yes, Helen is only acting as would any devoted daughter who wished to spare a doting father some harsh truth . . . In short: simple as the explanation for Garland's presence might have seemed to someone else, it is wholly beyond my grasp, as though now that living with Helen has ceased to make the least bit of sense, I cannot discover the truth about anything.

At seventy, delicate, small-boned Garland still does have a youthful sort of charm, and a way about him at once worldly and boyish. His forehead is so fragile-looking it seems it could be cracked with the tap of a spoon, and his cheeks are the small, round, glazed cheeks of an alabaster Cupid. Above the open shirt a pale silk scarf is tied around his neck, almost completely hiding from view the throat whose creases are the only sign of his age. In that strangely youthful face all there is to speak of sorrow are the eyes, soft, brown, and awash with feeling even while his crisp accent refuses to betray the faintest hint of grief.

"Poor Derek was killed, you know." Helen did not know. She puts her hand to her mouth. "But *how*? Derek," she says, turning to me, "was an associate in Donald's firm. A very silly man sometimes, very muddled and so on, but such a good heart, really—" My dead expression sends her quickly back to Garland. "Yes," he says, "he was a very kind person, and I was devoted to him. Oh, he could talk and go on, but then you just had to tell him, 'Derek, that's enough now,' and he'd shut up. Well, two Chinese boys thought that he hadn't given them enough money, so they kicked him down a flight of stairs. Broke Derek's neck." "How terrible. How awful. Poor, poor man. And what," asks Helen, "has happened to all his animals?" "The birds are gone. Some sort of virus wiped them out the week after he was killed. The rest Madge adopted. Madge adopted them and Patricia looks after them. Otherwise, those two won't have anything to do with each other." "Again?" "Oh yes. She can be a good bitch, that Madge, when she wants to be. Chips did her house over for her a year ago. She nearly drove the poor boy crazy with her upstairs bath." Helen tries yet again to bring me into the company of the living: she explains that Madge and Patricia, who own houses down along the bay from Donald, were stars of the British cinema in the forties. Donald rattles off the names of the movies they made. I nod and nod, just like an agreeable person, but the smile I make a stab at presenting him does not begin to come off. The look Helen has for me does, however, quite effectively. "And how does Madge look?" Helen asks him. "Well, when she makes up, she still looks wonderful. She ought never to wear a bikini, of course." I say, "Why?" but no one seems to hear me. The evening ends with Garland, by now a little drunk, holding Helen's hand and telling me about a famous masquerade party held in a jungle clearing on a small island in the Gulf of Siam owned by a Thai friend of his, half a mile out to sea from the southern finger of Thailand. Chips, who designed Helen's costume, had put her all in white, like Prince Ivan in *The Firebird*. "She was ravishing. A silk Cossack shirt and full silk trousers gathered into soft silver kid boots, and a silver turban with a diamond clasp. And around her waist a jeweled belt of emeralds." Emeralds? Bought by whom? Obviously by Karenin. Where's the belt now, I wonder? What do you have to return and what do you get to keep? You certainly get to keep the memories, that's for sure. "A little Thai princess burst into tears at the very sight of her. Poor little thing. She'd come wearing everything but the kitchen stove and expected people to swoon. But the one who looked like royalty that night was this dear girl. Oh, it was quite a to-do. Hasn't Helen ever shown you the photographs? Don't you have photographs, dear?" "No," she says, "not any more." "Oh, I wish I'd brought mine. But I never thought I'd see you—I didn't even know who I was when I left home. And remember the little boys?" he says, after a long sip from his brandy glass. "Chips, of course, got all the little native boys stripped down, with just a little coconut shell around their how-dee-dos, and Christmas tinsel streaming down around their necks. What a sight they were when the wind blew! Well, the boat landed, and there were these little chaps to greet the guests and to lead us up a torch-lined path to the clearing where we had the banquet. Oh, my goodness, yes—Madge came in the dress that Derek wore for his fortieth birthday party. Never would spend money, if she could help it. Always angry about something, but mostly it's the money everyone's stealing from her. She said, 'You can't just go to one of these things, you have to have something wonderful to wear.' So I said to her, only as a joke, mind you, 'Why don't you come in Derek's dress? It's white chiffon covered with Diamonte and with a long train. And cut very low in the back. You'll look lovely in it, darling.' And Madge said, 'How could it be cut low in the back, Donald? How in the world could Derek have worn it? What about the hair on his back, and all that disgusting rubbish?' And I said, 'Oh, darling, he only shaves once every three years.' You see," Garland says to me, "Derek was rather the old Guards officer type—slim, elegant, very pink-complexioned, altogether the most extraordinarily hairless person. Oh, there's a photograph of Helen you must see, David. I must send it to you. It's Helen being led from the boat by these enchanting little native boys streaming Christmas tinsel. With her long legs and all that silk clinging to her, oh, she was absolute perfection. And her face—her face in that photograph is classic. I must send it to you; you must have it. She was the most ravishing thing. Patricia said about Helen, the first moment she laid eyes on her— that was at lunch at my house, and the darling girl still had the most ordinary little clothes—but Patricia said then she had star quality, that without a doubt she could be a film star. And she could have been. She still has it.

She always will." "I know," replies the schoolmaster, silently swishing his cane.

After he leaves, Helen says, "Well, there's no need to ask what you thought of him, is there?" "It's as you said: he adores you." "Really, just what has empowered you to sit in judgment of other people's passions? Haven't you heard? It's a wide, wide world; room for everybody to do whatever he likes. Even you once did what you liked, David. Or so the legend goes." "I sit in judgment of nothing. What I sit in judgment of, you wouldn't believe." "Ah, yourself. Hardest on yourself. Momentarily I forgot." "I sat, Helen, and I listened and I don't remember saying anything about the passions or preferences or private parts of anybody from here to Nepal." "Donald Garland is probably the kindest man alive." "Fine with me." "He was always there when I needed someone. There were weeks when I went to live in his house. He protected me from some terrible people." *Why didn't you just protect yourself by staying away from them?* "Good," I say; "you were lucky and that was great." "He likes to gossip and to tell tales, and of course he got a little maudlin tonight—look what he's just been through. But he happens to know what people are, just how much and just how little—and he is devoted to his friends, even the fools. The loyalty of those kind of men is quite wonderful, and not to be disparaged by anyone. And don't you be misled. When he is feeling himself he can be like iron. He can be unmovable, and marvelous." "I am sure he was a wonderful friend to you." "He still is!" "Look, what are you trying to tell me? I don't always get the gist of things these days. Rumor has it my students are going to give *me* the final exam, to see if they've been able to get anything through my skull. What are we talking about now?" "About the fact that I am still a person of consequence to quite a few people, even if to you and the learned professors and their peppy, dowdy little wives I am beneath contempt. It's true I'm not clever enough to bake banana bread and carrot bread and raise my own bean sprouts and 'audit' seminars and 'head up' committees to outlaw war for all time, but people still look at me, David, wherever I go. I could have married the kind of men who *run* the world! I wouldn't have had to look far, either. I hate to have to say such a vulgar, trashy thing about myself, but it's what you're reduced to saying to someone who finds you repulsive." "I don't find you repulsive. I'm still awestruck that you chose me over the president of ITT. How can someone unable even to finish a little pamphlet on Anton Chekhov feel anything but gratitude to be living with the runner-up for Queen of Tibet? I'm honored to have been chosen to be your hair shirt." "It's debatable who is the hair shirt around here. I am repugnant to you, Donald is repugnant to you—" "Helen, I neither liked the man nor disliked the man. I did my level fucking best. Look, my best friend as long ago as college was practically the only queer *there*. I had a queer for a friend in 1950—before they even existed! I didn't know what one was, but I had one. I don't care *who* wears *whose* dress—oh, fuck it, forget it, I quit."

Then on a Saturday morning late in the spring, just as I have sat down at my desk to begin marking exams, I hear the front door of our apartment open and shut— and finally the dissolution of this hopeless misalliance has begun. Helen is gone. Several days pass—hideous days, involving two visits to the San Francisco morgue, one with Helen's demure, bewildered mother, who insists on flying up from Pasadena and bravely coming along with me to look at the broken body of a drowned "Caucasian" woman, age thirty to thirty-five—before I learn her whereabouts.

The first telephone call—informing me that my mate is in a Hong Kong jail—is from the State Department. The second call is from Garland, who adds certain lurid and clarifying details: she had gone from the Hong Kong airport directly by taxi to the well-known ex-lover's mansion in Kowloon. He is the English Onassis, I am told, son and heir of the founder of the MacDonald-Metcalf Line, and king of the cargo routes from the Cape of Good Hope to Manila Bay. At Jimmy Metcalf's home, she had not even been allowed past the servant posted at the door, not after her name had been announced to Metcalf's wife. And when, some hours later, she left her hotel to tell the police of the plan made some years earlier by the president of MacDonald-Metcalf to have this wife run down by a car, the officer on duty at the police station made a telephone call and subsequently a packet of cocaine was found in her purse.

"What happens now?" I ask him. "My God, Donald, now what?"

"I get her out," says Garland.

"Can that be done?"

"It can."

"How?"

"How would you think?"

Money? Blackmail? Girls? Boys? I don't know, I don't care, I won't ask again. *Whatever works, do it.*

"The question is," says Garland, "what happens when

Helen is free? I can, of course, make her quite comfortable right here. I can provide her with all she needs to pull herself together again, and to go on. I want to know what you think is for the best. She cannot afford to be caught in between again."

"In between what? Donald, this is all a little confusing. I have no idea what's best, frankly. Tell me, please, why didn't she go to you when she got there?"

"Because she got it in her head to see Jimmy. She knew that if she'd come first to me I would never have let her go anywhere near him. I know the man, better than she does."

"And you knew she was coming?"

"Yes, of course."

"The night you were here for dinner."

"No, no, my dear boy. Only a week ago. But she was to have cabled. I would have been at the airport to meet her. But she did it Helen's way."

"She shouldn't have," I say dumbly.

"The question is, does she come back to you or stay with me? I'd like you to tell me which you think is best."

"You're sure she's getting out of jail, you're sure the charges will be dropped—"

"I wouldn't have phoned to say what I'm saying otherwise."

"What happens then . . . well, it's up to Helen, isn't it? That is, I'd have to talk to her."

"But you can't. I'm lucky I could. We're lucky she isn't in irons already and halfway to Malaysia. Our police chief is not the most charitable of men, except on his own behalf. And your rival is not Albert Schweitzer."

"That is apparent."

"She used to tell me, 'It's so difficult to go shopping with Jimmy. If I see something I like, he buys me twelve.' She used to say to him, 'But, Jimmy, I can only wear one at a time.' But Jimmy never understood, Mr. Kepesh. He does everything by twelves."

"Okay, I believe that."

"I don't want anything further to go wrong for Helen—ever," says Garland. "I want to know exactly where Helen stands, and I want to know now. She has been through years of hell. She was a marvelous, dazzling creature, and life has treated her hideously. I won't allow either one of you to torture her again."

But I can't tell him where she stands—I don't know where *I* stand. First, I say, I must reach Helen's family and calm their fears. He will hear from me.

Will he? Why?

As though I have just reported that her daughter has been detained by a club meeting after school, Helen's mother says, politely, "And when will she be home?"

"I don't know."

But this does not appear to faze the adventuress's mother. "I do hope you'll keep me informed," she says, brightly.

"I will."

"Well, thank you for calling, David."

What else can the mother of an adventuress do but thank people for calling and keeping her informed?

And what does the husband of an adventuress do while his wife is in jail in the Far East? Well, at dinnertime I prepare an omelette, make it very carefully, at just the right heat, and serve it to myself with a little chopped parsley, a glass of wine, and a slice of buttered toast. Then

I take a long hot shower. He doesn't want me to torture her; all right, I won't torture her—but best of all, I won't torture myself. After the shower I decide to get into my pajamas and to do my night's reading in bed, all by myself. No girls, not yet. That will come in its own sweet time. Everything will. Can it be? I am back where I was six years ago, the night before I ditched my sensible date and took Hong Kong Helen home from that party. Except that now I have my job, I have my book to complete, and I seem to have this comfortable apartment, so charmingly and tastefully decorated, all to myself. What is Mauriac's phrase? "To revel in the pleasures of the unshared bed."

For some hours my happiness is complete. Have I ever heard or read of something like this happening, of a person being catapulted out of his misery *directly* into bliss? The common wisdom has it that it works the other way around. Well, I am here to say that on rare occasions it seems to work this way too. My God, I do feel good. I will not torture her, or myself, ever again. Fine with me.

Two hundred and forty minutes of this, more or less.

With a loan from Arthur Schonbrunn, a colleague who had been my thesis adviser, I buy a round-trip ticket and fly off to Asia the next day. (At the bank I discover that the entire balance in our savings account had been withdrawn by Helen the week before, for her one-way air ticket, and to start her new life.) On the plane there is time to think—and to think and to think and to think. It must be that I want her back, that I can't give her up, that I am in love with her whether I've known it or not, that she is my destiny—

Not one word of this stuff convinces me. Most are words

I despise: Helen's kind of words, Helen's kind of thinking. I can't live without this, he can't live without that, my woman, my man, my destiny . . . Kid stuff! Movie stuff! *Screen Romance!*

Yet if this woman is not *my woman*, what am I doing here? If she is not *my destiny*, why was I on the phone from 2 to 5 a.m.? Is it just that pride won't permit me to abdicate in favor of her homosexual protector? No, that's not what's done it. Nor am I Acting Responsibly, or out of shame, or masochism, or vindictive glee . . .

Then that leaves love. Love! At this late date! Love! After all that's been done to destroy it! More love, suddenly, than there was anywhere along the way!

I spend the rest of my waking hours on that flight remembering every single charming, sweet, beguiling word she has ever spoken.

Accompanied by Garland—grim, courteous, impeccably now the banker and businessman—a Hong Kong police detective, and the clean-cut young man from the American consulate who is also there to meet my airplane, I am taken to a jail to see my wife. As we leave the terminal for the car, I say to Garland, "I thought she was to be out by now." "The negotiations," he says, "seem to involve more interests than we had imagined." "Hong Kong," the young consulate officer informs me wryly, "is the birthplace of collective bargaining." Everybody in the car seems to know the score, except me.

I am searched and then allowed to sit with her in a tiny room whose door is dramatically locked behind us. The sound of the lock catching makes her reach wildly for my hand. Her face is blotchy, her lips are blistered, her eyes . . . her eyes I cannot look into without my innards crumbling. And Helen smells. And as for all that I felt for her up in the air, well, I simply cannot bring myself to love her like that down here on the ground. I have never loved her quite like that down on the ground before, and I'm not going to start in a jail. I am not that kind of an idiot. Which maybe makes me some other kind of idiot . . . but that I will have to determine later.

"They planted cocaine on me." "I know." "He can't get away with that," she says. "He won't. Donald is going to get you out of here." "*He has to!*" "He is, he's doing it. So you don't have to worry. You'll be out very soon now." "I have to tell you something terrible. All our cash is gone. The police stole it. He told them what to do to me —and they did it. They laughed at me. They touched me." "Helen, tell me the truth now. I have to know. We all have to know. When you get out of here, do you want to stay on with Donald in his house? He says he will look after you, he—" "But I can't! No! Oh, don't leave me here, please! Jimmy will kill me!"

On the return flight Helen drinks until the stewardess says she cannot serve her another. "I'll bet you were even faithful to me," she says, oddly "chatty" suddenly. "Yes, I'll bet you were," she says, serene in a dopey sort of way now that the whiskey has somewhat dimmed the horrors of incarceration and she is beyond the nightmare of Jimmy Metcalf's revenge. I don't bother to answer one way or the other. Of the two meaningless copulations of the last year there is nothing to say; she would only laugh if I were to tell her who her rivals had been. Nor could I expect much sympathy were I to try to explain to her how unsatisfying it had been to deceive her with women who hadn't a hundredth of her appeal to me—who hadn't a hundredth of her character, let alone her loveliness—and whose faces I could have spit into when I realized how much of *their* satisfaction derived from putting Helen Kepesh in her place. Quickly enough—*almost* quickly enough—I had seen that deceiving a wife as disliked as Helen was by other women just wasn't going to be possible without humiliating myself in the process. I hadn't a Jimmy Metcalf's gift for coldly rearing back and delivering the grand and fatal blow to my opponent; no, vengeance was his style and contentious melancholia was mine . . . Helen's speech is badly slurred by liquor and fatigue, but now that she has had a bath, and a meal, and a change of clothes, and a chance to make up her face, she intends to have a conversation, her first in days and days. She intends now to resume her place in the world, and not as the vanquished, but as herself. "Well," she says, "you didn't have to be *such* a good boy, you know. You could have had your affairs, if that would have made you any happier. I could have taken it." "Good to know that," I say. "It's you, David, who wouldn't have survived in one piece. You see, I've been faithful to you, whether you believe it or not. The only man I've been faithful to in my life." Do I believe that? Can I? And if I should? Where does *that* leave me? I say nothing. "You don't know yet where I used to go sometimes after my exercise class." "No, I don't." "You don't know why I went out in the morning wearing my favorite dress." "I had my ideas." "Well, they were wrong. I had no lover. Never, never with you. Because it would have been too hideous. You couldn't have taken it—and so I didn't do it. You would have been crushed, you would have forgiven me, and you would never have been yourself again. You would have gone around bleeding forever." "I went around bleeding anyway. We both went around bleeding. Where did you go all dressed up?" "I went out to the airport." "And?" "And I sat in the Pan Am waiting room. I had my passport in my handbag. And my jewelry. I sat there reading the paper until somebody asked if I wanted to have a drink in the first-class lounge." "And I'll bet somebody always did." "Always—that's right. And I'd go there and have a drink. We would talk . . . and then they would ask me to go away with them. To South America, to Africa, everywhere. A man even asked me to come with him on a business trip to Hong Kong. But I never did it. Never. Instead, I came back home and you started in on me about the checkbook stubs." "You did this how often?" "Often enough," she replies. "Enough for what—to see if you still had the power?" "No, you idiot, to see if *you* still had the power." She begins to sob. "Will it startle you," she asks, "to hear that I think we should have had that baby?" "I wouldn't have risked it, not with you." My words knock the wind out of her, what wind is left. "Oh, you shit, that was unnecessary, there are less cruel ways . . ." she says. "Oh, why didn't I let Jimmy kill her when he wanted to!" she cries. "Quiet down, Helen." "You should see her now—she stood there, ten feet inside the hallway, glaring out at me. You should see her —she looks like a whale! That beautiful man goes to bed with a whale." "I said quiet down." "He told them to plant cocaine on me—on me, the person he loves! He let them take my purse and steal my money! And how I loved that man! I only left him to save him from committing a murder! And now he hates me for being too decent, and you despise me for being indecent, and the truth of it is that

I'm better and stronger and braver than both of you. At least I was—and I was when I was only twenty years old! *You* wouldn't risk a baby with *me*? What about someone like *you*? Did it ever occur to you that about a baby it may have been the other way around? No? Yes? Answer me! Oh, I can't wait to see the little sparrow you do take the risk with. If only you had taken it into your hands long ago, years ago—at the beginning! I should have had nothing to say about it!" "Helen, you're exhausted and you're loaded and you don't know what you're saying. A lot you cared about having a baby." "A lot I did, you fool, you dope! Oh, why did I come on this airplane with you! I could have stayed with Donald! He needs someone as much as I do. I should have stayed with him in his house, and told *you* to go on home. Oh, why did I lose my nerve in that jail!" "You lost it because of your Jimmy. You thought when you got out he'd kill you." "But he wouldn't —that was crazy! He only did what he did because he loves me so, and I loved him! Oh, I waited and I waited and I waited—I've waited for you for six years! Why didn't you take me into your world like a man!" "Maybe you mean why didn't I take you out of yours. I couldn't. The only kind to take *you* out is the kind who took you in. Sure, I know about my terrible tone, and the scornful looks I can give, but I never went and got a hit-man in about the toast, you know. Next time you want to be saved from a tyrant, find another tyrant to do the job. I admit defeat." "Oh, God, oh, Jesus God, why must they be either brutes or choirboys? Stewardess," she says, grabbing the girl's arm as she passes in the aisle, "I don't want a drink, I've had enough. I only want to ask a question of you. Don't be frightened. Why are they either brutes or choirboys, do you know?" "Who, madam?" "Don't you find that in your travels from one continent to the other? They're even afraid, you know, of a sweet little thing like you. That's why you have to go around grinning like that. Just look the bastards right in the eye and they're either at your knees or at your throat."

When at last Helen has fallen asleep—her face rolling familiarly on my shoulder—I take the final exams out of my briefcase and begin where I had had to leave off a hundred or so hours ago. Yes, I have taken my schoolwork with me—and a good thing too. I cannot imagine how I could get through the million remaining hours of the flight without these examination papers to hang on to. "Without this . . ." and see myself strangling Helen with the coil of her waist-long hair. Who strangles his lover with her hair? Isn't it somebody somewhere in Browning? Oh, who cares!

"The search for intimacy, not because it necessarily makes for happiness, but because it is necessary, is one of Chekhov's recurrent themes."

The paper I have chosen to begin with—to begin again with—is by Kathie Steiner, the girl I had dreamed of adopting. "Good," I write in the margin alongside her opening sentence; then I reread it and after "necessary" make an insertion mark and write, "for survival(?)." And all the while I am thinking, "And miles below are the beaches of Polynesia. Well, dear, dazzling creature, a lot of good that does us! Hong Kong! The whole damn thing could have taken place in Cincinnati! A hotel room, a police station, an airport. A vengeful megalomaniac and some crooked cops! And a would-be Cleopatra! Our savings gone on this trashy Grade-B thriller! Oh, this voyage is the marriage itself—traversing four thousand miles of the exotic globe twice over, and for no good reason at all!"

Struggling to fix my attention once again on the task at hand—and not on whether Helen and I should have had a child, or who is to blame because we didn't; refusing to charge myself yet again with all I could have done that I didn't do, and all I did that I shouldn't have—I return to Kathie Steiner's final exam. Jimmy Metcalf instructs the police: "Kick her ass a little, gentlemen, it'll do the whore some good," while I subdue my emotions by reading carefully through each of Kathie's pages, correcting every last comma fault, reminding her about her dangling-modifier problem, and dutifully filling the margin with my commentary and questions. Me and my "finals"; my marking pen and my paper clips. How the Emperor Metcalf would enjoy the spectacle—likewise Donald Garland and his uncharitable chief of police. I suppose I ought to laugh a little myself; but as I am a literature professor and not a policeman, as I am someone who long ago squeezed out what little of the tyrant was ever in him—from the look of things, maybe squeezed out just a bit too much—instead of laughing it all off, I come to Kathie's concluding sentence, and am undone. The hold I have had on myself since Helen's disappearance dissolves like that, and I must turn my face and press it into the darkened window of the humming airship that is carrying us back home to complete, in orderly and legal fashion, the disentanglement of our two wrecked lives. I cry for myself, I cry for Helen, and finally I seem to cry hardest of all with the realization that somehow not every last thing *has* been destroyed, that despite my consuming obsession with my marital unhappiness and my dreamy desire to call out to my young students for their help, I have somehow gotten a sweet, chubby, unharmed and as yet unhorrified daughter of Beverly Hills to end her sophomore year of college by composing this grim and beautiful lament summarizing what she calls "Anton Chekhov's overall philosophy of life." But can Professor Kepesh have taught her this? How? *How*? I am only just beginning to learn it on this flight! "We are born innocent," the girl has written, "we suffer terrible disillusionment before we can gain knowledge, and then we fear death—and we are granted only fragmentary happiness to offset the pain."

I am finally extracted from the rubble of my divorce by a job offer from Arthur Schonbrunn, who has left Stanford to become chairman of the comparative literature program at the State University of New York on Long Island. I have already begun seeing a psychoanalyst in San Francisco—only shortly after I began seeing the lawyer—and it is he who recommends that when I return East to teach I continue therapy with a Dr. Frederick Klinger, whom he knows and can recommend as someone who is not afraid to speak up with his patients, "a solid, reasonable man," as he is described to me, "a specialist," I am told, "in common sense." But are reason and common sense what I need? Some would say that I have ruined things by far too narrow a devotion to exactly these attributes.

Frederick Klinger is solid, all right: a hearty, round-faced fellow, full of life, who, with my permission, smokes cigars throughout the sessions. I don't much like the aroma myself, but allow it because smoking seems even further to concentrate the keenness with which Klinger attends to my despair. Not many years older than me, and sporting fewer gray hairs than I have lately begun to show, he exudes the contentment and confidence of a successful man in his middle years. I gather from the phone calls which, to my distress, he takes during my hour, that he is already a key figure in psychoanalytic circles, a member of the governing bodies of schools, publications, and research institutes, not to mention the last source of hope for any number of souls in disrepair. At first I find myself somewhat put off by the sheer relish with which the doctor seems to devour his responsibilities —put off, to be truthful, by nearly everything about him: the double-breasted chalk-stripe suit and the floppy bow tie, the frayed Chesterfield coat growing tight over the plumpening middle, the *two* bursting briefcases at the coat rack, the photos of the smiling healthy children on the book-laden desk, the tennis racket in the umbrella stand—put off even by the gym bag pushed behind the big worn Eames chair from which, cigar in hand, he addresses himself to my confusion. Can this snazzy, energetic conquistador possibly understand that there are mornings when on the way from the bed to the toothbrush I have to struggle to prevent myself from dropping down and curling up on the living-room floor? I don't entirely understand the depth of this plunge myself. Having failed at being a husband to Helen—having failed at figuring out how to make Helen a wife—it seems I would rather sleep through my life now than live it.

How, for instance, have I come to be on such terrible terms with sensuality? "You," he replies, "who married a *femme fatale*?" "But only to de-fatalize her, to de-fang her, along the way. All that nagging at her, at Helen, about the garbage and the laundry and the toast. My mother couldn't have done a better job. About every last detail!" "Too divine for details, was she? Look, she isn't the Helen born of Leda and Zeus, you know. She's of the earth, Mr. Kepesh—a middle-class Gentile girl from Pasadena, California, pretty enough to get herself a free trip to Angkor Wat every year, but that's about it, in the way of supernatural achievement. And cold toast is cold toast, no matter how much jewelry the cook may have accumulated over the years from rich married men with a taste for young girls." "I was frightened of her." "Sure you were." His phone rings. No, he cannot possibly be at the hospital before noon. Yes, he has seen the husband. No, the gentleman does not seem willing to cooperate. Yes, that is most unfortunate. Now back to this uncooperative gentleman. "Sure you were frightened," he says, "you couldn't trust her." "I *wouldn't* trust her. And she *was* faithful to me. I believe that." "Neither here nor there. Some game she was playing with herself, that's all. What value did it have when the fact is that the two of you had no real business together ever? From the sound of it the only thing each of you did *totally* out of character was to marry the other." "I was frightened of Birgitta, too." "My God," he exclaims, "who wouldn't have been?" "Look, either I'm not making myself clear or you don't even want to begin to understand me. I'm saying that these were special creatures, full of daring and curiosity —and freedom. They were not ordinary young women." "Oh, I understand that." "Do you? I think sometimes that you'd prefer to assign them both to some very tawdry category of humankind. But what made them special is that they weren't tawdry, not to me, neither one of them.

97

They were exceptional." "Granted." The phone rings. Yes, what is it? I am in session, yes. No, no, go ahead. Yes. Yes. Of course he understands. No, no, he's pretending, pay no attention. All right, increase the dosage to four a day. But no more. And call me if he continues crying. Call me anyway. Goodbye. "Granted," he says, "but what were you supposed to do, having *married* one of these 'special creatures'? Spend days as well as nights fondling her perfect breasts? Join her opium den? The other day you said the only thing you learned from six years with Helen was how to roll a joint." "I think saying that is what is known as courting the analyst's favor. I learned plenty." "The fact remains—you had your work to do." "The work is just a habit," I say, without disguising my irritation with his dogged "demythologizing." "Perhaps," I wearily suggest, "reading books is the opiate of the educated classes." "Is it? Are you thinking of becoming a flower child?" he says, lighting up a new cigar. "Once Helen and I were sunbathing in the nude on a beach in Oregon. We were on a vacation, driving north. After a while we spotted a guy watching us from off in some brush. We started to cover up, but he came toward us anyway and asked if we were nudists. When I said no he gave us a copy of his nudist newspaper in case we wanted to subscribe." Klinger laughs loudly. "Helen said to me that God Himself must have sent him because it had been, by that time, fully ninety minutes since I'd read anything." Again Klinger laughs with genuine amusement. "Look," I tell him, "you just don't know what it was like when I first met her. It's not to be so easily disparaged. You don't know what I was like, nor can you—nor can I, any more—seeing me in this shape.

But I was a fearless sort of boy back in my early twenties. More daring than most, especially for that woebegone era in the history of pleasure. I actually did what the jerk-off artists dreamed about. Back when I started out on my own in the world, I was, if I may say so, something of a sexual prodigy." "And you want to be one again, in your thirties?" I don't even bother to answer, so narrow and wrongheaded does the common sense he's mastered strike me. "Why allow Helen," Klinger continues, "who has disfigured herself so in the frantic effort to be the high priestess of Eros—who very nearly destroyed you with her pronouncements and insinuations —why allow her judgment power over you still? How long do you intend to let her go on rebuking you where you feel weakest? How long do you intend to go on *feeling* weak over such utter foolishness? What was this 'daring' search of hers—?" The telephone. "Excuse me," he says. Yes, this is he. Yes, go ahead. Hello—yes, I can hear you very well. How is Madrid? What? Well, of course he's suspicious, what did you expect? But you just tell him that he is behaving stupidly and then forget it. No, of course you don't want to get into a fight. I understand. Just say it, and then try to have some courage. You can stand up to him. Go back up to the room and tell him. Come on now, you know very well you can. All right. Good luck. Have a good time. I said, then go out and have a good time. Goodbye. "What was this search of hers," he says, "but so much evasion, a childish flight from the real attainable projects of a life?" "Then, on the other hand," I say, "maybe the 'projects' are so much evasion of the search." "Please, you like to read and write about books. That, by your own testimony, gives you enormous satisfaction—did, at any rate, and will again, I assure you. Right now you're fed up with everything. But you like being a teacher, correct? And from what I gather you are not uninspired at it. I still don't know what alternative you have in mind. You want to move to the South Seas and teach great books to the girls in sarongs at the University of Tahiti? You want to have a go at a harem again? To be a fearless prodigy again, playing at Jack and Jill with your little Swedish daredevil in the working-class bars of Paris? You want a hammer over your head again—though maybe this time one that finds the mark?" "Burlesquing what I'm talking about doesn't do me any good, you know. It's obviously not going back to Birgitta that's on my mind. It's going ahead. I can't go *ahead*." "Perhaps going ahead, on that road anyway, is a delusion." "Dr. Klinger, I assure you that I am sufficiently imbued by now with the Chekhovian bias to suspect as much myself. I know what there is to know from 'The Duel' and other stories about those committed to the libidinous fallacy. I too have read and studied the great Western wisdom on the subject. I have even taught it. I have even practiced it. But, if I may, as Chekhov also had the ordinary good sense to write: in psychological matters, 'God preserve us from generalizations.'" "Thank you for the literature lesson. Tell me this, Mr. Kepesh: can you really be in the doldrums about what has befallen her—over what you seem to think you have 'done' to her—or are you just trying to prove to us that you are a man of feeling and conscience? If so, don't overdo it. Because *this* Helen was bound to spend a night in jail, sooner or later. Destined for it long before she met you. From the sound of it, it's how she landed on you—in the hope of being saved from the hoosegow, and the other inevitable humiliations. And that you know, as well as I do."

But whatever he may say, however he may bully, burlesque, or even try a smidgen of charm in order to get me to put the marriage and divorce behind me, I am, whether he believes it or not, never altogether immune from self-recrimination when stories reach me of the ailments that are said to be transforming the one-time Occidental princess of the Orient into a bitter hag. I learn of a debilitating case of rhinitis that cannot seem to be checked by drugs and necessitates that she live with a tissue continuously rubbing away at her nose—at the fluted nostrils that flare as though catching the wind when she achieves her pleasure. I hear tell of extensive skin eruptions, on the cunning fingers ("You like this? . . . this? . . . oh, you do like it, my darling!"), and on her wide, lovely lips ("What do you see first in a face? The eyes or the mouth? I like that you discovered my mouth first"). But then Helen's is not the only flesh slowly taking its revenge, or doing penance, or losing heart, or removing itself from the fray. Eating hardly anything, I have dropped since the divorce to scarecrow weight, and for the second time in my life I am bereft of my potency, even for an entertainment as unambitious as self-love. "I should never have come home from Europe," I tell Klinger, who has at my request put me on an anti-depressant drug, which pries me out of bed in the morning but then leaves me for the rest of the day with vague, otherworldly feelings of encapsulation, of vast unpassable reaches between myself and the flourishing hordes. "I should have gone all the way and become Birgitta's pimp.

I'd be a happier, healthier member of society. Somebody else could teach the great masterworks of disillusionment and renunciation." "Yes? You would rather be a pimp than an associate professor?" "That's one way of putting it." "Put it your own way." "This something in me that I turned against," I say in a fit of hopelessness, "before I even understood it, or let it have a life . . . I throttled it to death . . . killed it, practically overnight. And why? Why on earth was *murder* required?"

In the weeks that follow I attempt, between phone calls, to describe and chronicle the history of this something that, in my hopeless and de-energized state, I continue to think of as "murdered." I speak at length now not just of Helen but of Birgitta as well. I go back to Louis Jelinek, even to Herbie Bratasky, speak of all that each meant to me, what each excited and alarmed, and of how each was dealt with, in my way. "Your rogues' gallery," Klinger calls them one day in the twentieth or thirtieth week of our debate. "Moral delinquency," he observes, "has its fascination for you." "Also," I say, "for the authors of *Macbeth* and *Crime and Punishment*. Sorry to have mentioned the names of two works of art, Doctor." "Quite all right. I hear all sorts of things here. I'm used to it." "I do seem to get the feeling that it's somehow against house rules for me to call upon my literary reserves in these skirmishes of ours, but the only point I'm trying to make is that 'moral delinquency' has been on the minds of serious people for a long time now. And why 'delinquents,' anyway? Won't 'independent spirits' do? It's no *less* accurate." "I only mean to suggest that they aren't wholly harmless types." "Wholly harmless types probably lead rather constricted lives, don't you think?"

"On the other hand, one oughtn't to underestimate the pain, the isolation, the uncertainty, and everything else unpleasant that may accompany 'independence' of this kind. Look at Helen now." "Please, look at me now." "I am. I do. I suspect that she is worse off. You at least haven't put *all* your eggs in that basket." "I cannot maintain an erection, Dr. Klinger. I cannot maintain a smile, for that matter." Whereupon his phone rings.

Fastened to no one and to nothing, drifting, drifting, sometimes, frighteningly, sinking; and, with the relentlessly clever and commonsensical doctor, quarreling, bickering, and debating, arguing yet again the subject which had been the source of so much marital bitterness—only when I am supine it is generally I who wind up taking Helen's part, while he who sits up takes mine.

Each winter my parents come down to New York City to spend three or four days visiting family, friends, and favorite guests. In times gone by, we all used to stay on West End Avenue with my father's younger brother, Larry, a successful kosher caterer, and his wife, Sylvia, the Benvenuto Cellini of strudel, and, in childhood, my favorite aunt. Until I was fourteen, I would, to my astonished delight, be put to bed there in the same room with my cousin Lorraine. Sleeping beside a bed with a live girl in it—a "developing" girl, at that—going out to dine at Moskowitz and Lupowitz (on food described by my father as *nearly* as good as what is prepared in the kitchen of the Hungarian Royale), waiting in subfreezing temperatures to get in to see the Rockettes, sipping cocoa amid the thick draperies and the imposing furniture sets of haberdashery wholesalers and produce merchants whom I have known only in their voluminous half-sleeve shirts and their drooping swim trunks, and who are called by my father the Apple King and the Herring King and the Pajama King—everything about these New York visits hold a secret thrill for me, and invariably from "overexcitement" I develop a "strep throat" on the drive home, and back on our mountaintop have to spend at least two or three days in bed recovering. "We didn't visit Herbie," I say sullenly, only seconds before our departure—to which my mother invariably responds, "A summer isn't enough with him? We have to travel to Brooklyn to make a special trip?" "Belle, he's teasing you," my father says, but on the sly shakes a fist in my direction, as though for mentioning the Fart King to my mother I deserve no less than a blow to the head.

Now that I am back East and my uncle and aunt live in Cedarhurst, Long Island, I respond by phone to a letter from my father and invite my parents to stay in my apartment rather than at a hotel when they come down for their annual winter visit. The two rooms on West Seventy-fifth Street are not actually mine but, through an ad in the *Times,* have been sublet, furnished, from a young actor who has gone to try his luck in Hollywood. There is a crimson damask on the bedroom walls, perfumes lined up on a bathroom shelf, and, in boxes that I discover at the rear of the linen closet, a half-dozen wigs. The night I find them I indulge my curiosity and try a couple on. I look like my mother's sister.

Near the beginning of my occupancy, the phone rings one night and a man asks, "Where's Mark?" "He's in California. He'll be there for two years." "Yeah, sure. Look, you just tell him Wally's in town." "But he's not here. I have an address for him out there." I begin to recite it, but the voice, grown gruff and agitated now, interrupts: "Then who are you?" "His tenant." "Is that what they call it in the thee-yater? What do you look like, sweetpants? You got big blue eyes too?" When the calls persist, I have the telephone number changed, but then it is through the intercom that connects my apartment to the downstairs hallway of the brownstone that the repartee continues. "You just tell your little pal—" "Mark is in California, you can reach him out there." "Ha ha—that's a good one. What's your name, honey? Come to the doorway and we'll see whether I can reach you." "Come on, Wally, leave me alone. He's gone. Go away." "You like the rough stuff too?" "Oh, take off, will you?" "Take what off, sweetpants? What do you want me to take off?" So the flirtation goes.

Nights when I am at my loneliest, nights when I start talking to myself and to people who are not present, I sometimes have to suppress a powerful urge to call for help into the intercom. What holds me back isn't that it makes no sense but, rather, the fear that one of my neighbors or, what is worse, Patient Wally will be standing in the entryway just as my strident cry comes through; what I fear is the kind of help I might get—if not my homosexual suitor, the Bellevue emergency squad. So I go into the bathroom instead, close the door behind me, and leaning over the mirror to look at my own drawn face, I let it out. "I want somebody! I want somebody! I want somebody!" Sometimes I can go on like this for minutes at a time in an attempt to bring on a fit of weeping that will leave me limp and, for a while at least, empty of longing for another. I of course am not *so* far gone as to believe that screaming aloud in a closed-off room will make the somebody I want appear. Besides, who is it? If I knew I wouldn't have to holler into the mirror—I could write or phone. *I want somebody*, I cry —and it is my parents who arrive.

I carry their suitcases upstairs while my father lugs the Scotch cooler in which are packed some two-dozen round plastic containers of cabbage soup, matzoh-ball soup, kugel, and flanken, all frozen and neatly labeled. Inside the apartment my mother takes an envelope from her purse—"DAVID" is typed exactly at the center and underlined in red. The envelope contains instructions for me typewritten on hotel stationery: time required for the defrosting and heating of each dish, details as to seasoning. "Read it," she says, "and see if you have any questions." My father says, "How about if he reads it after you get out of your coat and sit down?" "I'm fine," she says. "You're tired," he tells her. "David, you have enough room in your freezer? I didn't know how big a freezer you had here." "Mamma, room to spare," I say lightly. But when I open the refrigerator she groans as though her throat has just been slit. "One this and one that, and that's it?" she cries. "Look at that lemon, it looks older than I do. How do you eat?" "Out, mostly." "And your father told me I was overdoing it." "You've been tired," he says to her, "and you *were* overdoing." "I knew he wasn't taking care of himself," she says. "You're the one who has to take care of herself," he says. "What is it?" I ask, "what's the matter with you, Ma?" "I had a little pleurisy, and your father is making it into a production. I get a little pain when I knit for too long. That's the whole outcome of all the money thrown away on doctors and tests."

She does not know—nor do I, until my father comes with me the next morning to buy a paper and some things for breakfast and then to walk me gravely up toward where Larry and Sylvia used to put us all up on West End Avenue—that she is dying of cancer that has spread from the pancreas. This then explains his letter saying, "Maybe if we could stay with you this one time . . ." Does it also explain her request to visit landmarks she has not been to in decades? I almost believe she knows just what is happening and this display of exuberance is to spare *him* from knowing she knows. Each protecting the other from the horrible truth—my parents like two brave and helpless children . . . And what can I do about it? "But dying—*when*?" I ask him as we turn back, the two of us in tears, to my apartment. For several moments he cannot answer. "That's the worst of it," he manages finally to say. "Five weeks, five months, five years—five *minutes*. Every doctor tells me something different!"

And back at the apartment she asks me again, "Will you take us to Greenwich Village? Will you take us to the Metropolitan Museum of Art? When I worked for Mr. Clark one of the girls used to eat the most delicious green noodles at an Italian restaurant in Greenwich Village. I wish I could remember the name. It couldn't be Tony's, could it, Abe?" "Honeybunch," my father says, his voice already tinged with grief, "it wouldn't even be there after all this time." "We could look—and what if it was!" she says, turning with excitement to me. "Oh, David, how

Mr. Clark loved the Museum of Art! Every Sunday when his sons were growing up he took them there to see the paintings."

I accompany them everywhere, to see the famous Rembrandts at the Metropolitan, to look for a Tony's that serves green noodles, to visit their oldest and dearest friends, some of whom I haven't seen in over fifteen years but who kiss and embrace me as though I were still a child, and then, because I am a professor, ask me serious questions about the world situation; we go, as of old, to the zoo and to the planetarium, and finally on a pilgrimage to the building where she was once a legal secretary. Following lunch in Chinatown, we stand at the corner of Broad and Wall Streets on a chilly Sunday afternoon, and, as always, with perfect innocence, she reminisces about her days with the firm. And how different for her it would have been, I think, had she stayed on to be one of Mr. Clark's girls for life, one of those virgin spinsters who adore the fatherly boss and play auntie on holidays to the boss's children. Without the interminable demands of a family-run resort hotel, she might actually have known some serenity, have lived in accordance with her simple gifts for tidiness and order rather than at their mercy. On the other hand, she would never have known my father and me—*we* would never have been. If only, if only . . . If only what? She has cancer.

They sleep in the double bed in the bedroom while I lie awake under a blanket on the living-room sofa. My mother is about to vanish—that's what it comes down to. And her last memory of her only child will be of his meager, rootless existence—her last memory will be of this lemon I live with! Oh, with what disgust and remorse do I recall the series of mistakes—no, the one habitual and recurrent mistake—that has made these two rooms my home. Instead of being enemies, of providing one another with the *ideal* enemy, why couldn't Helen and I have put that effort into satisfying each other, into steady, dedicated living? Would that have been so hard for two such strong-willed people? *Should* I have said at the very outset, "Look, we're having a child"? Lying there listening to my mother breathing her last, I try to infuse myself with new resolve: I must, I *will*, end this purposeless, pointless . . . and into my thoughts comes Elisabeth, of all people, with the locket around her neck and her broken arm healed. How sweet, how welcoming she would be to my widowed father! But without an Elisabeth, what can I do for him? How ever will he survive up there on his own? Oh, why must it be Helen and Birgitta at one extreme or life with a lemon at the other?

As the sleepless minutes pass—or, rather, do not seem to pass at all—all the thoughts that can possibly distress me seem to coalesce into an unidentifiable nonsense word that will not let me be. To free myself from its insipid thralldom, I begin to toss angrily from one side of the couch to the other. I feel half in, half out of deep anesthesia—immersed back in the claustrophobic agonies of the recovery room, which I last saw at the age of twelve, following my appendectomy—until the word resolves itself at last into nothing other than the line of keys, read from left to right, on which my mother taught me to rest the tips of my fingers when I learned typing from her on the hotel's Remington Noiseless. But now that I know the origin of this commonplace alphabetical scrambling, it is worse even than before. As though it *is* a word after all, and the one that holds within its unutterable syllables all the pain of her baffled energies and her frenetic life. And the pain of my own. I suddenly see myself struggling with my father over her epitaph, the two of us are hurling each other against enormous pieces of rock, while I insist to the stonecutter that ASDFGHJKL be carved beneath her name on the tombstone.

I cannot sleep. I wonder if it is possible that I will never be able to sleep again. All my thoughts are either simple or crazy, and after a while I cannot distinguish which is which. I want to go into the bedroom and get into their bed. I rehearse in my mind how I will do it. To ease them out of their initial timidity, I will just sit first at the edge of the bed and quietly talk to them about the best of the past. Looking down at their familiar faces side by side on the fresh pillowcases, at their two faces peering out at me from above the sheet drawn up to their chins, I will remind them of how very long it's been since last we all snuggled up together under a single blanket. Wasn't it in a tourist cabin just outside Lake Placid? Remember that little box of a room? Was it 1940 or '41? And, am I right, didn't it cost Dad just one dollar for the night? Mother thought that it would be good for me to see the Thousand Islands and Niagara Falls during my Easter vacation. That's where we were headed, in the Dodge. Remember, you told us how Mr. Clark took his little boys each summer to see the sights of Europe; remember all those things you told me that I had never heard before; God, remember me and the two of you and the little Dodge back before the war . . . and then, when they are smiling, I will take off my robe and crawl into the bed between them. And before she dies, we will all hold each other through one last night and morning. Who will ever know, aside from Klinger, and why should I care what he or anyone makes of it?

Near midnight the doorbell rings. At the intercom in the kitchenette I depress the lever and ask, "Who is it?"

"The plumber, sweetpants. Last time you were out. How's your leak, fixed yet?"

I don't respond. My father has come into the living room in his robe. "Somebody you know? At this hour?"

"Just some clown," I say, as the bell rings now to the rhythm of "Shave and a Haircut."

"What is it?" my mother calls from the bedroom.

"Nothing, Ma. Go to sleep."

I decide to speak into the intercom one more time. "Cut it out or I'm going to call the cops."

"Call 'em. Nothing I'm doing is actionable, kiddo. Why don't you just let me up? I'm not half bad, you know. I'm all bad."

My father, standing now at my elbow and listening, has gone a little white.

"Dad," I say, "go back to bed. It's just one of those things that happen in New York. It's nothing."

"He knows you?"

"No."

"Then how does he know to come here? Why does he talk like that?"

A pause, and the bell is ringing again.

Thoroughly irritated now, I say, "Because the fellow I sublet from is a homosexual—and, as best I can gather, this was a friend of his."

"A Jewish fellow?"

"Who I rented from? Yes."

"Jesus," snaps my father, "what the hell is the *matter* with a guy like that?"

"I think I'm going to have to go downstairs."

"By yourself?"

"I'll be all right."

"Don't be crazy—two is better than one. I'll come with you."

"Dad, that's not necessary."

From the bedroom my mother calls, "Now what?"

"Nothing," my father says. "The bell is stuck. We're going downstairs to fix it."

"At this hour?" she calls.

"We'll be right back," my father says to her. "Stay in bed." To me he whispers, "You got some kind of stick, a bat or something?"

"No, no—"

"What if he's armed? You got an umbrella, at least?"

In the meantime, the ringing has stopped. "Maybe he's gone," I say.

My father listens.

"He's gone," I say. "He left."

My father, however, has no intention of going back to bed now. Closing the door to the bedroom—"Shhhh," he whispers to my mother, "everything's fine, go to sleep"— he comes to sit across from the sofa. I can hear how heavily he is breathing as he prepares himself to speak. I am not all that relaxed myself. Propped stiffly up against the pillow, I wait for the bell to start ringing again.

"You're not involved"—he clears his throat—"with something you want to tell me about . . ."

"Don't be silly."

"Because you left us, Davey, when you were seventeen years old and since then there has been no interfering with the kind of influences you let yourself under."

"Dad, I'm not under any 'influences.'"

"I want to ask you a question. Outright."

"Go ahead."

"It's not about Helen. I never asked you about that, and I don't want to start now. I always treated her like a daughter-in-law. Didn't I, didn't your mother, always with respect—?"

"Yes, absolutely."

"I held my tongue. We didn't want her to turn against us. She can have nothing against us to this day. All things considered, I think we did excellent. I am a liberal person, son—and in my politics even more than liberal. Do you know that in 1924 I voted for Norman Thomas for the governor of New York with the first vote I ever cast? And in '48 I voted for Henry Wallace—which maybe was meaningless and a mistake, but the point is that I was probably the only hotel owner in the whole country who voted for somebody that everybody was calling a Communist. Which he wasn't—but the point is, I have never been a narrow man, never. You know—and if you don't, you should—it was never that the woman was a shiksa that bothered me. Shiksas are a fact of life, and they are not going to go away just because Jewish parents might like it better that way. And why should they? I am a believer in all the races and religions living together in harmony, and that you married a Gentile girl was never the point to your mother and me. I think we did excellent on that score. But that doesn't mean I could stomach the rest of her and her attitudes. The truth of the matter, if

113

you want to know, is that I didn't have a good night's sleep in the three years you were married."

"Well, neither did I."

"Is that true? Then why the hell didn't you get out right off the bat? Why did you get in that damn mess to begin with?"

"You want me to go over that territory, do you?"

"No, no—you're right—the hell with it. As far as I'm concerned, if I never hear her name again, that won't be too soon. You are all I care about."

"What do you want to ask?"

"David, what is Tofrinal, that I see it in the medicine chest, a big bottle full? What are you taking this drug for?"

"It's an anti-depressant. Tofranil."

He hisses. Disgust, frustration, disbelief, contempt. I must first have heard that sound out of him a hundred years ago, when he had to fire a waiter who wet his bed and stank up the attic where the help slept. "And *why* do you need that? Who told you to take a thing like that and put it in your bloodstream?"

"A psychiatrist."

"You go to a psychiatrist?"

"Yes."

"*Why?*" he cries.

"To keep me afloat. To figure things out. To have someone to talk to . . . confidentially."

"Why not a *wife* to talk to? That's what a wife is for! I mean this time a *real* wife, not somebody who it must have cost you your whole school salary just to pay the beauty parlors. All this is all *wrong*, son. It is no way to live! A psychiatrist, and being on strong drugs, and people

114

showing up at all hours—people who aren't even people—"

"There is nothing to get worked up about."

"There is *everything* to get worked up about."

"No, no," I say, lowering my voice. "Dad, there is only Mother . . ."

He puts a hand over his eyes and quietly begins to cry. With his other hand he makes a fist which he waves at me. "This is what I have had to be all my life! *Without* psychiatrists, *without* happy pills! I am a man who has never said die!"

And once again, the downstairs doorbell.

"Forget it. Let it ring. Dad, he'll go away."

"And then come back? I'll crack his head open, and, believe me, then he'll go away for good!"

Here the bedroom door opens and my mother appears in her nightgown. "Who are you cracking in the head?"

"Some lousy stinking fairy who won't leave him alone!"

The bell again: two shorts, a long; two shorts, a long. Wally is drunk.

Her eyes tearful now, my tiny mother says, "And how often does this go on?"

"Not often."

"But—why don't you report him?"

"Because by the time the police come he'd be gone. You don't want the police for something like this."

"And you swear to me," says my father, "this is nobody you know?"

"I swear to you."

My mother comes into the living room and sits beside me. She takes my hand and clutches it. The three of us listen to the bell—mother, father, and son.

"You know what would fix the son of a bitch once and for all?" my father says. "Boiling water."

"*Abe!*" cries my mother.

"But it would teach him where he don't belong!"

"Dad, you mustn't make too much of it."

"And don't you make so little! Why do you hang *around* with such people?"

"But I don't."

"Then why do you live in a place like this, where they show up and make trouble for you? Do you need more trouble still?"

"Calm down, please," says my mother. "It isn't *his* fault some maniac rings his doorbell. This is New York. He told you. This is what happens."

"That doesn't mean you leave yourself unprotected, Belle!" Jumping up from his chair, he rushes to the intercom. "Hey! You!" he shouts. "Cut it out! This is David's father—!"

Stroking her arm—already skeletal—I whisper, "It's okay, it's all right, he's not working the thing right anyway. Don't worry, Ma, please—the fellow can't even hear him."

"—you want third-degree burns, we'll give them to you! Do what you want to do in some gutter somewhere, but if you know what's good for you, don't come near my son!"

Two months later, in the hospital in Kingston, my mother dies. After the funeral guests have all left, my father urges me to take the food she has frozen for me only the month before, the last things cooked by her on this earth. I say, "And what are *you* going to eat?" "I was a short-order man before you were even born. Take it. Take what she made for you." "Dad, how are you going to live here by yourself? How are you possibly going to manage the season? Why did you shoo everybody away? Don't be so brave. You can't stay up here alone." "I can look after myself fine. Her going is not something we didn't expect. Please, take it. Take it all. She wanted you to. She said whenever she remembered the inside of your refrigerator, she saw red. She cooked for you," he says, his voice trembling, "and then she went away." He begins to sob. I put my arms around him. "Nobody understood her," he says, "the guests, never, *never*. She was a good person, Davey. When she was young, everything thrilled her, the littlest things even. She had a nervous nature only when the summer got hectic and out of control. So they made fun of her. But do you remember the winter? The peace and the quiet? The fun we had? Remember the letters at night?" Those words do it: for the first time since her death the morning before, I break down completely. "Of course I do, sure I do." "Oh, sonny, that's when she was herself. Only who knew it?" "We did," I tell him, but he repeats, with an angry sob, "And who knew it!"

He carries the frozen food in a shopping bag out to my car. "Here, please, in her memory." And so I return to New York with the half-dozen containers each bearing the same typewritten label: "Tongue with Grandma's famous raisin sauce—2 portions."

Within a week, I am driving back up to the country again, this time with my Uncle Larry, to take my father to Cedarhurst, where he will move in with his brother and sister-in-law. Though only temporarily, he says while we pack his suitcase in the car; just till he is over the shock. In a few days he is sure he will be himself. He has to be, that's all there is to it. "I've been working since I'm fourteen years old. You don't give in to a thing like this," he says. "You tighten your belt and you go on." Besides, it is winter, and there is always the risk up there of fire. Yes, the handyman and his wife will be living on the grounds, but that is no guarantee against the possibility of the hotel burning down in his absence.

It is true, of course, that dozens of mysterious fires have broken out in abandoned hotels and boardinghouses ever since the region began to pass out of fashion as a Jewish summer resort at about the time I was going off to college, but as he and my mother have been able, even in recent years, to hang on to a remnant of their aging clientele and to keep the main house open and the grounds respectable-looking, the arsonists had never before seemed to him a real threat. But now on the drive down the Thruway they are all he can think about. He names for my uncle and me the local hoodlums—"Men, thirty- and forty-year-old men!"—whom he has always suspected of setting the fires. "No, no," he says to my uncle, who has offered his standard analysis as to where the trouble begins, "not even anti-Semites. Too stupid even for that! Just plain de-mented no-good idiots, fit for the lunatic asylum. Just peo-ple who like to see flames! And when it is in ashes, you know who they will accuse? I've seen it a dozen times. Me! That I did it for the insurance money! Because my wife is gone and I want to get out! The blame will fall on my good name! And half the time you know who else I some-times think that does it? The volunteer fire fighters themselves! Yes—so they can rush out in the fire engines in the middle of the night and ride up and down the mountain in their helmets and boots!"

Even after he is comfortably installed in what used to

be Lorraine's bedroom, there is no calming his fears for the empire built of his sweat and his blood. Every night I call him on the phone and he tells me he cannot get to sleep for worrying about a fire. And he has other things to worry about now as well. "That fairy never came back, did he?" "No," I say, knowing it best to lie. "See—it paid to threaten him. Unfortunately that's all some people understand, is the fist," says my father, who has never struck another person in his life. "And how are Uncle Larry and Aunt Sylvia?" I ask. "Wonderful. They couldn't be kinder. Every other word is 'Stay.'" "Well, that sounds reassuring," I say. But no, another ten days, he tells me, and the worst of being without her will be over. Has to be. He has to get back up there while the damn place is still in one piece!

And then it is another five days, and then another, until at last, following an emotional Sunday car ride alone with me, he agrees to put the Hungarian Royale up for sale. His face in his hands, he says, "But I never said die in my life." "There's no shame in it, Dad. Things have just changed." "But I don't *give* up," he cries. "Nobody is going to see it that way," I say, and drive him back to his brother's.

And during this time hardly a night passes when I do not think about the girl I knew for barely two months back when I was a twenty-two-year-old sexual prodigy, the girl who wore a locket around her neck with her father's picture in it. I even think of writing to her, in care of her parents. I even get up out of bed and search through my papers, looking for the Stockholm address. But by now Elisabeth must certainly be married and a mother two or three times over, and assuredly she does not think of me. No woman alive thinks of me, certainly not with love.

Though my department chairman Arthur Schonbrunn is a handsome and exquisitely groomed middle-aged man of unflagging charm and punctiliousness—as adroit and gracious a social being as I have ever seen in action —his wife, Deborah, is someone for whom I have never been able to work up much enthusiasm, even when I was Arthur's favorite graduate student and she was frequently my affectionate and hospitable hostess. In those first years at Stanford, I used to spend a certain amount of my time, in fact, trying to figure out what bound a man so scrupulous about the amenities, so tirelessly concerned to oppose, from the highest principles, the burgeoning political assaults upon university curriculum—what bound such a man of conscience to a woman whose very favorite public performance was in the role of the dizzy dame whose beguiling charm is her reckless and impudent "candor"? The very first time I was invited by Arthur to have dinner with the two of them, I remember thinking at the end of the evening's conversation—conversation consisting largely of Deborah's coquettishly "outrageous" chatter—"This is surely the loneliest man alive." How pained and disenchanted I was at twenty-three by this first look into my fatherly professor's domestic life . . . only to be told by Arthur the following day about his wife's "wonderful powers of observation" and her "gift" for "getting right to the heart of the problem." And, along these lines, I remember another night, years later, when Arthur and I were working late in our offices—that is, Arthur was at work, while I was immobile at my desk, hopeless as usual about the loveless impasse Helen and I had reached and hadn't the strength or the courage to resolve. When Arthur saw me apparently looking even more benumbed than usual, he came in and, until 3 a.m., tried his best to protect me from the crazier sort of solutions that might enter the head of a dreadfully unhappy husband having trouble getting himself to go home. Time and again he reminded me of the fine piece of work my thesis had been. The important thing now was to get back to revising it for book publication. Indeed, much that Arthur said to me that night sounded very like what Dr. Klinger was eventually to say to me about me, my work, and Helen. And I, in turn, poured out my grievances, and at one point lowered my face to my desk and wept. "I figured it was that bad," said Arthur. "We both did. But much as we care for you, we never felt it was our business to say anything. We've had enough experience by now to know that always comes between friends, sooner or later. But still there were days when I wanted to shake you for being such a fool. You don't know how many times I talked to Debbie about what could be done to get you to save yourself from all this unhappiness. Nothing was more upsetting for us than remembering what you'd been like when you first got here, and then seeing what was happening to you with her. But I couldn't do a thing, David, unless you came to me—and that's not how you go about things. You're someone who goes so far with people, and no further, and the result is that you're rather more alone with yourself than many people are. I'm not so unlike that myself."

Near the end of his vigil—and for the first time ever—

Arthur spoke about his own personal life almost as though we were men of the same age and rank. In his twenties, when he was an instructor at Minnesota, he too had been involved with "a wildly neurotic and destructive woman." Scandalous public quarrels, two harrowing abortions, despair so enormous that he had actually come to think that suicide was the only way he might ever be able to extricate himself from his confusion and pain. He showed me a small scar on his hand, where this mad, pathetic little librarian, whom he could not stand and yet could not leave, had once stabbed him with a table fork at breakfast . . . And while Arthur tried to give me hope (and guidance) by associating his own early misfortune—and subsequent recovery—with what I was going through, I only wanted to say, "But how dare you? What do you call what you have now? Debbie is so *common;* her spontaneity so much guile-filled play-acting; her candor so much tactless showing-off; capricious for the company; devilish for Daddy—Arthur, none of it means a thing, audacious behavior with nothing at stake! While Helen—my God, Helen is a hundred times, Helen is a thousand times . . ." But of course I rose to no such heights of virtuous indignation, uttered no words so foolish as these about the falsity and shallowness of his wife as against the integrity, intelligence, charm, beauty, and bravery of mine—uxoriousness, after all, being his line, and certainly that night, dreams of uxoricide being somewhat more like mine.

Is this chivalry of Arthur's to be pitied or envied? Is my former mentor and current benefactor a little bit of a liar, a little bit of a masochist, or is he just in love? Or is it that

Debbie, with her slightly shrill kittenishness and vaguely slatternly good looks, is the touch of the disreputable that makes bearable an otherwise stiflingly decorous life?

"Vizzied" is the diagnosis rendered by our resident poet, Ralph Baumgarten: "vizzied" or "vizzified"—both adjectives deriving from "vizzy," an uncommon noun of Baumgarten's strewn throughout his verse, rhyming with "fizzy" and "tizzy," closely related to "fuzzy" and "buzz," and referring, of course, to the pudenda. The vizz-ridden—to this class of husbands is Arthur Schonbrunn consigned by the unmarried poet—are those who slavishly conform to standards of propriety and respectability which, as Baumgarten sees it, have been laid down by generations of women to disarm and domesticate men. Of which domestication the poet himself is clearly having none. I tend to agree with Baumgarten that it is in part because of his own decidedly undeferential attitude toward the other gender—and his sexual predilections generally—that the young literary roughneck is not to be reappointed when his contract here runs out. However, if he has, by his manner, earned the disdain of certain of our colleagues and their wives, it has not caused him to be any less flagrant about what he likes and how he likes it. For him flagrancy appears to be much of the fun. "Picked up a girl at the Modern Museum, and on our way out we ran into your pals, Kepesh. Debbie hustled the girl off to the ladies' room to get the latest lowdown on me, and Arthur, in the course of his pleasantries, asked how long Rita and I had been friends. I told him about an hour and a half. I said we were leaving because the museum seemed to afford no comfortable corner where we might go down on each other. But what, I wondered, did Arthur make of her plump little behind? Well, he wouldn't tell me. Gave me a lecture on compassion, instead."

No arguing that Baumgarten throws a rather large net out to catch his little minnows in. When the two of us are walking on the streets of Manhattan, hardly a woman under fifty or a girl over fifteen passes by from whom he does not attempt to extract information that he manages to intimate is absolutely vital to his survival. "Gee, what a nice coat!" he says, flashing his grin at a young woman in a ratty fur pushing a baby carriage. "Oh, thanks." "May I ask what it's made of? What kind of an animal was that? I never saw a coat quite like that before." "This? It's a fake." "*Really*?" Within minutes he is barely this side of stupefaction (not all of it feigned, either) at learning that this young woman in the fake fur is already divorced, the mother of three small children, and a dropout from the University of Two Thousand Miles Away. To me, standing self-consciously off to the side, he calls, "Did you hear that, Dave? This is Alice. Alice was born in Montana—yet here she is wheeling a baby carriage in New York." And no less than Baumgarten, the young mother herself now seems a little wonderstruck to have been transported such a distance in a mere twenty-four years.

Success with strangers, Baumgarten informs me, resides in never asking a question of them that can't be answered without thinking, and then being wholly attentive to the reply, no matter how pedestrian. "You remember your James, Kepesh—'Dramatize, dramatize.' Get these people to understand that who they are and where they're from and what they wear is *interesting*. In a manner of speaking, *momentous*. *That's* compassion. And, please, display no irony, will you? Your problem is you scare 'em off with your wonderful feel for the complexity of things. My experience is that the ordinary woman in the streets doesn't cotton to irony, really. It's irony, really, that pisses her off. She wants attention. She wants appreciation. She surely doesn't want to match wits with you, boy. Save all that subtlety for your critical articles. When you get out there on the street, *open up*. That's what streets are *for*."

During my first months at the university I discover that when Baumgarten's name comes up at faculty gatherings there is always someone around who cannot stand the sight of him, and is more than willing to say why. Debbie Schonbrunn holds that the "abomination-in-residence" would be comical were he not so—the word is a favorite of hers and Arthur's—"destructive." Of course in response I need say nothing: just drink my drink and start back to New York. "Oh, he's not so bad," I tell her. "In fact," I add, "I sort of like him." "And what is there to 'like' so?" Go home, Kepesh. That empty apartment is where you belong; between this predictable discussion and that faggy apartment, there is no doubt where you will be better off. "What is there to *dislike* so?" I reply. "Where do I begin?" asks Deborah; "his contempt for women, for one thing. He is a murderous, conscienceless womanizer. He hates women." "Looks to me as though he rather likes them." "David, you are being contrary and disingenuous, and just a little hostile, and I'm really not sure why. Ralph Baumgarten is an abomination and so is his poetry. I have never read anything so dehumanized in my life. Read that first book of his and see for yourself just how much he likes girls." "Well, I haven't read him yet"—a lie—"but we've had lunch a few times. He isn't so reprehensible, as far as I can see. Could be, Deborah, that the poetry isn't exactly the man." "Ah, but it *is*: mean and smug and overbearing and actually quite stupid. And what *about* 'the man'? That walk of his, that *glide*; those army clothes; that face—well, actually he hasn't got a face, has he? Just mean, flat eyes and that surly grin. The mystery is how any girl can even go near him." "Well, he must have something." "Or *they* lack something. Really, you have such innate elegance and he is a carrion vulture right down to his claws, and why you would want even to associate with him . . ." "I get along with him," I say, shrugging my shoulders, and *now* put down my drink and go on home.

Soon enough, news reaches me as to what Debbie's powers of observation have uncovered in our conversation. It is what I should have expected, certainly, and probably what I deserve. The only surprise, really, is my surprise—that, and the vulnerability.

It seems that at a dinner party at the Schonbrunns' the hostess had announced to all in attendance that Baumgarten has become David Kepesh's "alter ego," "acting out fantasies of aggression against women" David harbors as a consequence of his marriage and its "mortifying" ending. The mortifying ending in Hong Kong—the cocaine, the cops, the works—as well as mortifying tidbits from the beginning and the middle were then narrated for the edification of all. I am given these details by a nice enough man, a guest at the Schonbrunns', who is no part of this story, and who thought he was doing me a good turn.

A correspondence ensues. Initiated by me and, alas, perpetuated by me too.

Dear Debbie:

Word has reached me that at a dinner party last week you were talking a little freely about my private affairs—namely, my marriage, my "mortifications," and what you are said to have described as my "aggressive fantasies against women." How would you know about my fantasies, if I may ask? And why should Helen and I be the subject for dinner conversation among people most of whom I have never even met? For the sake of a friendship with Arthur which goes back some time now, and which we have only just had the chance to rekindle, I hope that you will refrain in the future from discussing with perfect strangers my aggressive fantasies and my mortifying history. Otherwise, it is going to be difficult for me to be myself with Arthur, and, of course, with you.

Sincerely,
David

Dear David:

I do apologize for blabbing to people who don't know you, and won't do it again. Although I would do anything if you'll tell me the name of the s.o.b. who spilled his and/or her guts. Just so they don't set their teeth in my rack of lamb again!

To salve your wounds, I want to add, first, that your name only came up in passing—alas, you weren't the subject of a whole night's conversation—and, second, I think you have every justification for resenting Helen as much as you do, and, third, it isn't really so strange or shameful that your anger with Helen should take the form for now of an association with a young man who punishes women the way that vulture

127

does. But, if you view your friendship with him one way, and I see it another, that's certainly all right with me—as I think it should be with you.

Lastly, if I spoke thoughtlessly about Helen to my dinner guests, it is probably because back at Stanford she was, as you well know, rather ostentatious about herself, and consequently a prime topic of conversation among any number of people, including your friends. And you yourself were not averse to talking about her with us, whenever you came home with Arthur.

But, dear David, enough of this is enough. Will you come to have dinner with us—how is this Friday night? Come, by yourself or with somebody (other than the Visigoth) if you like. If you bring a girl I promise I won't breathe a word about your misogyny all the time you're here.

Love,
Debbie

P.S. I'd give anything to know the name of the skunk who turned me in.

Dear Debbie:

I can't say that your reply strikes me as satisfactory. You seem not at all to grasp how indiscreet you were with what you know, and think you know, about me. Surely that I shared certain confidences with Arthur, and he in turn shared them with you, cannot be offered to me as a mitigating factor. Do you understand why? Nor do I see how you can fail to realize that my marriage is still painful to me, and the pain is not lessened when I learn that it is being discussed like so much soap opera by people to whom I once unburdened myself of some of my troubles.

The spirit in which your letter was written only seems to have worsened the situation for me, and I don't see any way to accept your invitation.

David

Dear David:

I'm sorry you found my note unsatisfactory. Actually it was purposely superficial in tone—I rather thought it suited what you considered my crime.

Do you really see me as some harridan hell-bent on sullying your spotless reputation or invading your privacy by vicious, hurtful innuendo? Obviously you do, and that's monstrous, of course, but simply because you believe it to be so, doesn't make it so.

I apologized for speaking carelessly about you to strangers, because I know I do that sometimes. I assumed that what came back to you was just that—foolish and careless. I know I never said anything so awful it would cause you any pain. Remembering back to your own judgments of yourself with the ladies—stories of your student days, remember?—I never dreamt you saw yourself as being beyond reproach. I will admit I never saw you as a perfect angel in relation to women, but neither did I think that summed you up as a person. I did enjoy you and care for you as a friend.

I must say I would be very sorry to hear that you had flailed out at any of those others who were your friends in California just because they were "indiscreet" enough to mention you in conversation. And to mention you not out of unkindness, or viciousness or malice, but only because they happen to know all you have been through.

I am afraid that your letter tells me more about you than I care to know.

Debbie

Dear David:

Debbie is replying to your last letter, but now I feel compelled to mix in too.

It seems to me that Debbie made an effort, stopping short of abject prostration before you, to apologize for what she considered a just complaint. At the same time she tried to indicate by her joking tone that what she did was not as serious as you seem to feel. I agree with her from what I know about the situation, and it strikes me that your last letter, with its aggressive, exasperated, self-righteous tone, is more seriously hurtful than anything Deborah may have been guilty of. I have no idea, by the way, what you think Deborah may have said about you (a little documentation would have helped here), but I can assure you that it was little more than dinner-table conversation that lasted a few minutes and maligned you in no way. I suspect that you may have said a lot worse about her in passing conversations (though presumably not before strangers). It seems to me that friends ought to be more willing to forgive each other their occasional frailties.

Sincerely,
Arthur

Dear Arthur:

You can't have it both ways: that Debbie took "a joking tone" or, as she put it, a "purposely superficial . . . tone" because that best expressed her attitude toward what was bothering me, and that simultaneously she "made an effort short of abject prostration" before me. Debbie's indiscretion was of course forgivable, and I indicated as much in my first letter. But that she should continue, not only to be so obtuse, but to be so casual about all this, leads me to view her lapse as something other than an example of "occasional frailty" displayed by a friend.

David

Dear David:

I have hesitated about replying to your last letter because it left me with very little to say. I find it incredible you could even imagine Deborah ever meant you any harm.

It is also somewhat incredible that you fail to see that in blowing up this situation as you have, you are arguing only too well for the truth of Deborah's observation about the aggressive nature of your attitude toward women these days. Rather than pressing on with the attack, why don't you stop and think for a moment why it was you refused to accept the apology she made for her tactlessness at the outset—why did you prefer instead to jeopardize our friendship in order to beat her over the head with her alleged misconduct?

Short of divorcing Debbie and sending her out in the street in rags, I don't know what I can do that would prove sufficient to restore friendly relations between you. I'd be grateful to hear any suggestions.

Sincerely,
Arthur

It is Klinger who mercifully utters the magic formula that puts an end to all this. I tell him what I intend to say in my next message to Arthur—already half typed in a second draft—about the Freudian noose that he would now like to tighten around my neck. And I am still a little wild about his request, two letters back (and tucked between parentheses), for "a little documentation." What does he think we are, student and teacher, still Ph.D. candidate and dissertation adviser? Those letters weren't sent him for a grade! I don't care how beholden I am supposed to be—I won't have them saying I am something I am not! I will not be maligned and belittled by her reckless neurotic slander! Nor will I let Helen be slandered either! "Aggressive fantasies"! All that means is I can't stand *her*! And why the hell *doesn't* he throw her out into the street in rags? It's a marvelous idea! I'd *respect* him for it! The whole community would!

When my day's tirade has run its course, Klinger says, "So she gossips about you—who the hell pays any attention?"

Eleven words, but all at once I am, yes, mortified, and see *myself* for the neurotic fool. So peevish! So purposeless still! Without focus, without meaning—without a single friend! And making only enemies! My angry letters to the Devoted Couple constitute the whole of my critical writing since my return to the East, all I have been able to marshal sufficient concentration, stamina, and wisdom to get down on paper. Why, I spend entire evenings rewriting them for brevity and tone . . . while my Chekhov book has all but been abandoned. Imagine—drafts and drafts, and of what? Nothing! Oh, something about the drift of things doesn't look right to me, Doctor. Fending off Wally, fighting with Debbie, hanging on for dear life to your apron strings—oh, where is the way of living that will make all this nothingness *truly* nothing, instead of being all I have and all I do?

Strangely, my run-in with the Schonbrunns serves to enliven a friendship with Baumgarten that hadn't really amounted to much before—or, not so strangely at all, given those old vested interests contending for a say in my new and barely lived-in life. Following what I take to be doctor's orders, I abandon the Schonbrunn correspondence—though indignant rejoinders, *clinching* rejoinders, continue to provide lively company as I drive along the Expressway to school each morning—and then late one afternoon, acting on what I assume at the time to be a harmless impulse, I stop at Baumgarten's office and ask him to join me for coffee. And the following Sunday evening, when I return from a visit to my father and find that back in my apartment I am, on the scale of loneliness, hovering near a hundred—right up there with my own dad—I turn down the flame under the soup I am warming in my little spinster's saucepan, and telephone Baumgarten to invite him to come share the very last container of food prepared and frozen by my mother.

Soon we are meeting once a week for dinner at a small Hungarian restaurant on upper Broadway, not far from where each of us lives. No more than Wally is Baumgarten the someone for whom I used to cry out before the bathroom mirror during my first months of mourning in New York (the mourning that preceded the mourning for the only one of us who actually died). But then that longed-for someone may very likely never turn up—because in fact she already did: was here, was mine, and has been lost, destroyed because of some terrible mechanism that causes me to challenge and challenge—finally to challenge to the death—what once I thought I wanted most. Yes, I miss Helen! Suddenly I *want* Helen! How meaningless and ridiculous all those arguments seem now! What a gorgeous, lively, passionate creature! Bright, funny, mysterious—and gone! Oh, why on earth did I do what I did? It all should have been so different! And when, if ever, will there be another?

So—little more than a decade of adult life behind me, and already I have the sense that all my chances have been used up; indeed, pondering my past over that pathetic little enameled saucepan, I invariably feel as though I have not simply been through a bad marriage but in fact through all the female sex, and that I am so constructed as to live harmoniously with no one.

Over cucumber salad and stuffed cabbage (not bad, but nothing to compare, I inform Baumgarten—and sounding not so unlike my father—to the Hungarian Royale in its heyday), I show him an old picture of Helen, as inviting and seductive a passport photo as may ever have passed through customs. I have unstapled it from her International Driver's License, which turned up only recently—to each his own discordances and incongruities—in a carton of Stanford papers, among my lecture notes on François Mauriac. I bring Helen's photograph to dinner with me, then wonder for half the meal whether to take it out of my wallet or, rather, wonder why I would. Some ten days earlier I had brought the picture to his office to show to Klinger, intending to prove to him that, blind as I may have been to certain dire consequences, I was by no means blind to everything.

"A real beauty," says Baumgarten when, with some of the anxiety of a student handing in a plagiarized paper, I pass the picture across the table. And then I am hanging on to his every word! "A queen bee, all right," he says. "Yes, sir, and followed aloft by the drones." He is a long time savoring it. Too long. "Makes me jealous," he informs me, and not to be polite either. He is reporting a genuine emotion.

Well, I think, at least *he* won't disparage her, or me . . . yet I am reluctant to go ahead now and try to puzzle out anything truly personal in Baumgarten's presence, as though any challenge he might offer to Klinger's perspective—and the willingness with which I now try to yield to it—might actually send me reeling, perhaps even all the way back to where I was when I would start off the day on my knees. It hardly pleases me, of course, to feel so susceptible still to this sort of confusion, or to feel so very thinly protected from the elements by my therapy, or to find that, at this moment, I seem to share Debbie Schonbrunn's sense of Baumgarten as a source of contamination. The fact is that I *do* look forward to our evening out together, that I *am* interested in listening to the stories he tells, stories, as with Helen, of someone on the friendliest of terms with the sources of his excitement, and confidently opposed to—in fact, rather amused by—all that stands in opposition. Yet it is also a fact that my attachment to Baumgarten is increasingly marked by uncertainty, by what amount at times almost to seizures of doubt, the stronger our friendship grows.

Baumgarten's family story is pretty much a story of pain and little else. The father, a baker, died only recently, destitute and alone on the ward of a V.A. hospital—he had deserted his family sometime during Baumgarten's adolescence ("later rather than sooner"), and only after years of horrific depressions that had all but turned family life into one long tearful wake. Baumgarten's mother had worked for thirty years stitching gloves in a loft near Penn Station, fearful of the boss, of the shop steward, of the subway platform and the third rail, then at home afraid of the cellar stairs, the gas oven, the fuse box, even of a hammer and a nail. She had suffered a disabling stroke when Ralph was at college, and since has been staring at the wall in a Jewish home for the aged and infirm in Woodside. Every Sunday morning when her youngest child pays his visit—wearing that cocky grin on his face, bearing the *Sunday News* under his arm, and in his hand carrying a little paper bag from the delicatessen with her bagel in it—the nurse precedes him into the room with a perky introduction intended to give a lift to the frail little woman sitting like a sack in her chair, safe at last from all the world's weaponry: "Guess who's here with the goodies, Mildred. Your professor!"

Aside from those expenses of the mother's care which are not covered by the government and which Baumgarten pays out of his university salary, there has also fallen to him a father's responsibilities to his older sister, who lives in New Jersey with three children and a husband who haplessly runs a dry-cleaning store there. The three kids Uncle Baumgarten describes as "dummies"; the sister he describes as "lost," raised from infancy on the mother's terrors and the father's gloom, and now, at about my age, alive to nothing but a welter of superstitions which, says Baumgarten, have come through untouched from the shtetl. Because of her looks, and her clothes, and the odd things she says to her children's schoolmates, she is known as the "gypsy lady" in the Paramus housing development where the family lives.

It surprises me, hearing tales of this mercilessly beaten-down clan from its inextinguishable survivor, that Baumgarten has never, to my knowledge, written a single line about the way in which his unhappy family is unlike any other, or about why he cannot turn his back on the wreckage, despite the disgust aroused in him by memories of his upbringing in this household of the dead. No, not a single word on that subject in his two books of verse, the first impudently titled, at twenty-four, *Baumgarten's Anatomy*, and the most recent, called after a line from an erotic poem of Donne's, *Behind, Before, Above, Between, Below*. I must admit to myself—if not to a Schonbrunn—that after a week of Baumgarten as bedtime reading, the interest I have long had in the fittings and fixtures of the other sex seems to me just about sated. Yet, narrow as his subject strikes me—or, rather, his means of exploration—I find in the blend of shameless erotomania, microscopic fetishism, and rather dazzling imperiousness a character at work whose unswerving sense of his own imperatives cannot but arouse my curiosity. But then at first even watching him eat his dinner arouses my curiosity— it is as hard at times for me to watch as it is to look away. Is it really the untamed animal in him that causes this carnivore to tear at the meat between his teeth with such stupendous muscle power, or does he not masticate his food genteelly simply because the rest of us agree to do it that way? Where *did* he first eat flesh, in Queens or in a cave? One night the sight of Baumgarten's incisors severing the meat from the bone of his breaded veal chop sends me home later to my bookshelves to take down the collection of Kafka's stories and to reread the final paragraph of "A Hunger Artist," the description of the young panther who is put into the sideshow cage to replace the professional abstinent after he expires of starvation. "The food he liked was brought without hesitation by the attendants, he seemed not even to miss his freedom; his noble body, furnished almost to the bursting point with all that it needed, seemed to carry freedom around with it too; somewhere in its jaws it seemed to lurk . . ."

Yes, and what "it" lurks in these strong jaws? Freedom also? Or something more like the rapacity of one once very nearly buried alive? Are his the jaws of the noble panther or of the starved rat?

I ask him, "How come you've never written about your family, Ralph?" "Them?" he says, giving me his indulgent look. "Them," I say, "and you." "Why? So I can read to a full house at the Y? Oh, Kepesh"—five years my junior, he nonetheless enjoys talking to me as though I am the kid and, too, something of an unredeemable square— "spare me the subject of the Jewish family and its travails. Can you actually get worked up over another son and another daughter and another mother and another father driving each other nuts? All that loving; all that hating; all those meals. And don't forget the *menschlichkeit*. And the baffled quest for dignity. Oh, and the *goodness*. You can't write that stuff and leave out the goodness. I understand somebody has just published a whole book on our Jewish literature of goodness. I expect any day to read that an Irish critic has come out with a work on conviviality in Joyce, Yeats, and Synge. Or an article by some good old boy from Vanderbilt on hospitality in the Southern novel: 'Make Yourself at Home: The Theme of Hospitality in Faulkner's "A Rose for Emily."'"

"I just wondered if it might not give you access to other feelings."

He smiles. "Let the other guys have the other feelings, okay? They're used to having them. They *like* having them. But virtue isn't my bag. Too bo-ring." A favorite word, sung by Baumgarten with the interval of a third between the two syllables. "Look," he says, "I can't even take that much of Chekhov, that holy of holies. Why isn't he ever implicated in the shit? You're an authority. Why is the brute never Anton but some other slob?"

"That's a strange way to go at Chekhov, you know, expecting Céline. Or Genet. Or you. But then maybe the brute isn't always Baumgarten, either. It doesn't sound that way when you tell me about those visits to Paramus, or to the old-age home. Sounds more like Chekhov, actually. The family serf."

"Don't be too sure. Besides, besides, why bother to write that kind of stuff down? Has it not been done—and done? Do they need me too to scratch my name on the Wailing Wall? For me the books count—my own included—where the writer incriminates *himself*. Otherwise, why bother? To incriminate the other guy? Best leave that to our betters, don't you think, and that cunning Yiddish theater they've evolved, called Literary Criticism. Ah, those noble middle-aged Jewish sons, with their rituals of rebellion and atonement! Ever read them on the front of the Sunday *Times*? All the closet cunt hunters coming on like old man Tolstoy. All that sympathy for the humble of the earth, all that guarding of the sacred flame, which, by the way, don't cost them a fucking dime. Look, all those deeply suffering Jewish culture-bearers *need* a fallen Jewish ass to atone for their sins on in public—so why not mine? Keeps their wives in the dark; gives their girl friends someone sensitive to suffering to suck off; and goes a very long way with the Brandeis Kollege of Musical Knowledge. Every year I read in the papers about the powers-that-be up there awarding them merit badges for their neckerchiefs. Virtue, virtue, who's got the virtue? Biggest Jewish racket since Meyer Lansky in his prime."

Yes, he is steamed up now, and with no regard for the loudness of his voice or the windmilling of his arms—and not without pleasure in his broadside biliousness—he goes on about the lasciviousness (well known to all Manhattan, Baumgarten claims) of the "esteemed professor" who demolished his second book of poems in an omnibus review in the *Times*. "No 'culture,' no 'heart,' and what is worse, no 'historical perspective.' As if the esteemed professor has historical perspective when he is sticking it into some graduate assistant! No, they don't like it too much when you get down in there and burrow away just for the sake of the fishy little vizzy in your face. No, no, if you're a real man of letters in the humanist tradition you have historical perspective while you're doing it."

Not till we down our tea and strudel does he finish (for the night) with his investigation into the hypocrisies, pieties, and bo-ring-ness generally of the literary world and the humanist tradition (largely as it is embodied in the reviewers of his books and the members of his department), and begin to speak, with a different sort of relish, of his other chosen arena of assertion. Like so many of his stories of the pleasant surprises that the hunt turns up, what he narrates over the dregs of dessert touches upon certain old but vivid recollections of my own. Indeed, there are times when, listening to him speak with such shamelessness of the wide range of his satisfactions, I feel that I am in the presence of a parodied projection of myself. A parody—a possibility. Maybe Baumgarten feels somewhat the same about me, and *this* explains the curiosity at either end. I am a Baumgarten locked in the Big House, caged in the kennels, a Baumgarten Klingered and Schonbrunned into submission—while he is a Kepesh, oh, what a Kepesh! with his mouth frothing and his long tongue lolling, leash slipped and running wild.

Why am I here with him? Passing time, sure, sure—and meanwhile, what is passing in and out of me? In the presence of the appetitious Baumgarten, am I looking to be exposed ever so mildly to the virulent strain, and thereby immunized for good? Or am I half hoping to be reinfected? Have I taken the healing of myself into my own hands at last, or is it rather that the convalescence is over, and I am just about ready to begin to conspire *against* the doctor and his bo-ring admonitions?

"One night last winter," he says, eyeing the round rear end of the largish Hungarian waitress who is trundling in carpet slippers back to the kitchen to make us some more tea, "I was browsing in Marboro's—" And I can see him browsing already; I *have* seen it, a dozen times at least. BAUMGARTEN: Hardy? GIRL: Why—yes. BAUMGARTEN: *Tess of the d'Urbervilles,* is that what you've got there? GIRL (*looking at the book jacket*): That's right, it is—"—and I started talking to this nice red-cheeked girl who told me she had just come down on the train from visiting her family in Westchester. Sitting a couple of seats in front of her there'd been a fellow in a suit and tie and an overcoat who kept looking back at her over his shoulder and jacking off under the coat. I asked her what she did about it. 'What do you think I did?' she said. 'I looked him right in the eye, and when we got into Grand Central, I went up to him, and I said, "Hey, I think we should meet, I'd like to meet you."' Well, he took off, started running out of the station, but the girl kept right on him, trying to explain to him that she was *serious*— she liked the way he looked, she admired his courage, she was terrifically flattered by what he had done, but the guy disappeared into a taxi before she could convince him that he was in for a good time. Anyway, we struck it off, you might say, and went back to her apartment. It was over on the East River, in one of those hi-rise villages. When we got there she showed me the view up the river, and the kitchen with all the cookbooks, and then she wanted me to take off her clothes and tie her to the bed. Well, I haven't played with a rope since Troop 35, but I managed. Did it with dental floss, Kepesh, twelve yards of it—got her spread-eagled, arms and legs, just the way she wanted. Took me forty-five minutes. And you should have heard the sounds coming out of that girl. You should have seen what she looked like, excited like that. Very stirring image. Makes you understand the creeps more. Anyway, she told me to go and get the poppers out of the medicine chest. Well, there weren't any, they were all gone. It seems one of her friends had stolen them. So I told her I had some coke at home, and I'd get it if she wanted me to. 'Go, get it, get it,' she said. So I went. But when I came downstairs from my place and got a taxi to start back to hers, I realized that I didn't know her name—and for the life of me I couldn't remember which of those fucking buildings she lived in. Kepesh, I was stymied," he says, and reaching across the table with a thumb and forefinger to get the strudel crumbs off my plate, manages to sweep my water glass into my lap with the cuff of his army coat. For some reason Baumgarten always eats in his coat. Maybe Jesse James did, too. "Oops," he cries, seeing the glass go down, but of course this isn't the first time; indeed, "oops" may be the four-letter word that most frequently falls from Baumgarten's lips, certainly while he is turning the table into his trough. "Sorry," he says; "you all right?" "It'll dry," I say, "it always does. Go on. What did you do?"

"What *could* I do? Nothing. I started wandering from one building to the next, looking at the names on the directories. Jane was her first name, or so she said, so whenever I saw a 'J,' like a schmuck I rang the buzzer. Couldn't find her, of course, though I had several promising conversations. Anyway, a guard came up and asked me what I was looking for. I told him I must be in the wrong building, but when I went out he followed me into the portico area there, and so I hung around for about a minute or two, looking up and admiring the moon. And then I went home. And after that I bought the *Daily News* on the way to school every day. I looked in there for weeks to see if the cops had found a skeleton tied to a bed with dental floss over on the decadent East Side. Finally I just gave up. Then this summer I was coming out of a movie down on Eighth Street, and there standing in line to get in for the next show is the same girl. Plain Jane. And you know what she says? She spots me, and a smile spreads across her face, and she says, 'Far out, man.' "

Skeptical, but laughing, I say, "That all happened, huh?"

"Dave, just walk the streets and say hello to the folks. *Everything* happens."

And then, after Baumgarten has asked the waitress—new to our restaurant, and whose aging, peasanty overflow he had decided he must get to know—whether she can recommend someone to give him Hungarian lessons; after he has taken her name and number—"Live alone there, do you, Eva?"— he excuses himself and goes to the back of the restaurant, where there is a pay phone.

In order to write down Eva's telephone number, he has emptied his coat pocket of a handful of papers and envelopes, on which, I see, he already has recorded the names and whereabouts of those others of her sex who have crossed his path during the day. The number of whomever he is calling now he has carried off with him to the phone, leaving the little mess of personal papers for me to contemplate at my leisure, the papers and the life that goes with them.

With a fingernail, I am able to flick into view the last paragraph of a letter neatly typewritten on heavy cream-colored stationery.

. . . I've gotten you your fifteen-year-old (eighteen, actually, but fleshwise I'll swear you'd never know the difference, and anyway, fifteen is *jail*)—a succulent sophomore, and not just young but a real beauty besides, a sweet girl and worldly both, and altogether I can't see how you could improve on her. I found her for you all by myself, her name is Rona and we are having lunch next week, so if you meant it (assuming you do remember mentioning this fancy), I will open negotiations at this time. I feel reasonably confident of success. Kindly semaphore your intentions next time you're in the office, one blink for yes, two for no, if I should go ahead. So there's my half of the bargain—I'm procuring for you, as desired and with my heart somewhere up near my mouth—now *please* put me in touch with the orgiasts. The only good reasons for no that I can think of are (a) you are involved there yourself—and in that case I would simply abstain from those soirees, if you prefer—or (b) you're afraid of being compromised by somebody at the heart of the Kremlin—then just give me the name and I'll say I heard about it elsewhere than you. Otherwise, why not give your (slightly atrophied) faculty of human sympathy a little workout (I've read somewhere it was once believed to be an essential quality for a poet) as long as it won't cost you anything, and bring a little ray of sunshine into the dim life of a (rapidly) fading spinster.

Your chum,
T.

And who is "T," I wonder, in the "Kremlin"? The assistant to the provost or the director of student health? And who—on another piece of paper—is "L"? Her words crossed out and rewritten on every line; her felt-tipped pen on the brink of anemia—what does *she* want of the poet with the slightly atrophied heart? Is "L"'s the pleading voice Baumgarten is so patiently listening to in the telephone booth? Or is that "M," or "N" or "O" or "P"—?

Ralph, I refuse to be sorry about last night unless you can point out in a *believable* way there was something twisted or mean about my wanting to see you. I had thought that if I could only sit in the same room with a man who wasn't trying to push me or convince me or confuse me, someone whom I liked and respected, that I might get closer to something in myself that matters and is real. I was under the impression that you didn't live in a dream world, and have sometimes wondered since the baby whether I do. I didn't want to make love. Sometimes you act like someone who is adept at removing a lady's drawers and that's all. I certainly won't make any more spontaneous visits after 10 p.m. It is just that wanting and needing to talk to someone with whom I am *not* involved, I chose you, when, I admit, in some way I want to be involved, some part wanting to be in your arms, when the other part insists that what I really need is your friendship, your

145

advice—*and* distance. I guess I don't quite want to admit that you move me. But that doesn't mean I don't think there is something crazy about you—

Inside the booth, Baumgarten hangs up the phone and so I stop reading his fan mail. We pay Eva, Baumgarten collects his property, and together—his "pal" on the phone is best left to herself this evening, he informs me —we head toward the nearest Bookmasters, where, as usual, one or the other of us will lay out five dollars for five remaindered books he most likely will never get around to reading. "Inebriate of cunt and print!" as my secret sharer exclaims somewhere in the song of himself behind, before, above, between, below.

It takes two full weeks, six whole sessions, before I am able to tell the psychoanalyst to whom I am supposed to tell everything that only a little later that evening we had met a high school girl shopping for a paperback for her English class. (BAUMGARTEN: Emily or Charlotte? GIRL: Charlotte. BAUMGARTEN: *Villette* or *Jane Eyre*? GIRL: I never heard of the first one. *Jane Eyre*.) Breezy, street-wise, and just a little terrified, she had accompanied us back to Baumgarten's one room, and there, on his Mexican rug, amid several piles of his own two erotic books of verse, she had auditioned for a modeling job for the new erotic picture magazine being started on the West Coast by our bosses, the Schonbrunns. Magazine to be called *Cunt*. "The Schonbrunns," he explains, "are sick and tired of pulling their punches."

A lanky strawberry blonde in fringed leather jacket

and jeans, the girl had told us straight out, while being interviewed in the bookstore, that she would not be at all shy about taking off her clothes for a photographer—so, at Baumgarten's, she is given one of his Danish magazines to look at, for the inspiration in it.

"Could you do this, Wendy?" he asks her earnestly as she sits on the sofa leafing through the magazines with one hand and, with the other, holding the Baskin-Robbins ice cream cone that Baumgarten (the impeccable scenarist) couldn't resist buying for her on the way home. ("What's your favorite flavor, Wendy? Go ahead, please, have a double dip, have sprinkles, have everything. How about you, Dave? Want some Chocolate Ribbon, too?") Clearing her throat, she closes the magazine in her lap, bites into what remains of the cone, and casually as she can manage, says, "That's a little far for me." "What isn't?" he asks her; "just tell me what isn't." "Maybe something more along the lines of *Playboy*," she says.

Working together then, something like teammates moving the ball across the midcourt line against a tight defense, something like two methodical day laborers driving a post into the ground with alternating blows of their mallets—something like Birgitta and myself back on the continent of Europe during the Age of Exploration—we manage, by bringing her through a series of provocative postures in progressive stages of undress, to get her flat on her back in her bikini underpants and her boots. And that, says the seventeen-year-old senior from Washington Irving High—trembling ever so slightly as she gazes up at our four eyes looking down—that is as far as she will go.

What next? That her limit is to be *the* limit is understood by Baumgarten and myself without any consultation. I make that clear to Klinger—also point out that no tears were shed, no force used, not so much as a fingertip touched her flesh.

"And this happened when?" Klinger asks me.

"Two weeks ago," I say, and rise from the couch to get my coat.

And leave. I have withheld my confession for two full weeks, and even now, until the end of the hour. Consequently, I am able just to walk out the door, and do not have to add—and never will—that it was not a recidivist's shame that deterred me from narrating the incident earlier, but rather the small color snapshot of Klinger's teenage daughter, in faded dungarees and school T-shirt, taken on a beach somewhere and displayed in a triptych frame on his desk between photographs of his two sons.

And then the summer after I return East I meet a young woman altogether unlike this small band of consolers, counselors, tempters, and provocateurs—the "influences," as my father would have it—off whom my benumbed and unsexed carcass has been careening since I've been a womanless, pleasureless, passionless man on his own.

I am invited for a weekend on Cape Cod by a faculty couple I have just gotten to know, and there I am introduced to Claire Ovington, their young neighbor, who is renting a tiny shingled bungalow in a wild-rose patch near the Orleans beach for herself and her golden Labrador. Some ten days after the morning we spend talking together on the beach—after I have sent her a painfully charming letter from New York, and consulted for several clammy hours with Klinger—I take the impulse by the horns and return to Orleans, where I move into the local inn. I am drawn at first by the same look of soft voluptuousness that had (against all seemingly reasonable reservations) done so much to draw me to Helen, and which has touched off, for the first time in over a year, a spontaneous surge of warm feeling. Back in New York after my brief weekend visit, I had thought only about her. Do I sense the renewal of desire, of confidence, of capacity? Not quite yet. During my week at the inn, I cannot stop behaving like an overzealous child at dancing class, unable to go through a door or to raise a fork without the starchiest display of good manners. And after the *self-display* of that letter, that bravura show of wit and self-assurance! Why did I listen to Klinger? "Of course, go—what can you lose?" But what does *he* have to lose if I fail? Where's his tragic view of life, damn it? Impotence is no joke—it's a plague! People kill themselves! And alone in my bed at the inn, after yet another evening of keeping my distance from Claire, I can understand why. In the morning, just before I am to leave for New York once again, I arrive at her bungalow for an early breakfast, and midway through the fresh blueberry pancakes try to redeem myself a little by admitting to my shame. I don't know how else to get out of this with at least some self-esteem intact, though why I will ever have to care about self-esteem again I cannot imagine. "I seem to have come all the way up here—after writing to you like that, and then arriving out of nowhere—well, after all that fanfare, I seem to have come upon the scene and . . . disappeared." And now moving over me—moving right up to the roots of my hair—I feel something very like the shame that I must have imagined I could avoid *by* disappearing. "I must seem odd to you. At this point I seem odd to myself. I've seemed odd to myself for some time now. I'm only trying to say that it's nothing you've done or said that's made me behave so coldly." "But," she says, before I can begin another round of apology about this "oddity" that I am, "it's been so pleasant. In a way it's been the sweetest thing." "It has?" I say, fearful that I am about to be humbled in some unforeseen way. "*What* has?" "Seeing somebody shy for a change. It's nice to know it still exists in the Age of Utter Abandon."

God, as tender within as without! The tact! The calm! The *wisdom!* As physically alluring to me as Helen—but there the resemblance ends. Poise and confidence and determination, but, in Claire, all of it marshaled in behalf of something more than high sybaritic adventure. At twenty-four, she has earned a degree from Cornell in experimental psychology, a master's from Columbia in education, and is on the faculty of a private school in Manhattan, where she teaches eleven- and twelve-year-olds, and, as of the coming semester, will be in charge of the curriculum-review committee. Yet, for someone who, as I come to learn, emanates in her professional role a strong aura of reserve, a placid, coolheaded, and seemingly unassailable presence, she is surprisingly innocent and guileless about the personal side of her life, and, as regards her friends, her plants, her herb garden, her dog, her cooking, her sister Olivia, who summers on Martha's Vineyard, and Olivia's three children, she has about as much reserve as a healthy ten-year-old girl. In all, this translucent mix of sober social aplomb and domestic enthusiasms and youthful susceptibility is simply irresistible. What I mean is *no resistance is necessary.* A tempter of a kind to whom I can at last succumb.

Now it is as if a gong has been struck in my stomach when I recall—and I do, daily—that I had written Claire my clever, flirtatious letter, and then had very nearly been content to leave it at that. Had even told Klinger that writing out of the blue to a voluptuous young woman I had spoken with casually on a beach for two hours was a measure of just how hopeless my prospects had become. I had almost decided against showing up for breakfast that last morning on the Cape, so fearful was I of what my convalescent desire might have in store for me were I, with a suitcase in one hand and my plane ticket in the other, to try to put it to a crazy last-minute test. How ever *did* I manage to make it past my shameful secret? Do I owe it to sheer luck, to ebullient, optimistic Klinger, or do I owe everything I now have to those breasts of hers in that bathing suit? Oh, if so, then bless each breast a thousand times! For now, now I am positively exultant, thrilled, astonished—grateful for everything about her, for the executive dispatch with which she orders her life as for the patience that she brings to our lovemaking, that canniness of hers that seems to sense exactly how much raw carnality and how much tender solicitude it is going to require to subdue my tenacious anxiety and renew my faith in coupling and all that may come in its wake. All the pedagogic expertise bestowed upon those sixth-graders is now bestowed upon *me* after school—such a gentle, tactful tutor comes to my apartment each day, and yet always the hungry woman with her! And those breasts, those breasts—large and soft and vulnerable, each as heavy as an udder upon my face, as warm and heavy in my hand as some fat little animal fast asleep. Oh, the look of this large girl above me when she is still half stripped! And, mind you, an assiduous keeper of records as well! Yes, the history of each passing day in calendar books going back through college, her life's history in the photographs she has been taking since childhood, first with a Brownie, now with the best equipment from Japan. And those lists! Those wonderful, orderly lists! I too write out on a yellow pad what I plan to accomplish each day, but by bedtime I seem never to find a soothing little check mark beside each item, confirming that the letter has been dispatched, the money withdrawn, the article xeroxed, the call made. Despite my own strong penchant for orderliness, passed along through the maternal chromosomes, there are still mornings when I can't even locate the list I drew up the night before, and, usually, what I don't feel like doing one day, I am able to put off to the next without too many qualms. Not so with Mistress Ovington—to every task that presents itself, regardless of how difficult or dreary, she gives her complete attention, taking each up in its turn and steadfastly following it through to its conclusion. And, to my great good luck, reconstituting my life is apparently just such a task. It is as though at the top of one of her yellow pads she has spelled out my name and then, beneath, in her open spherical hand, written instructions to herself, as follows: "Provide DK with— 1. Loving kindness. 2. Impassioned embraces. 3. Sane surroundings." For within a year the job is somehow done, a big check mark beside each life-saving item. I give up the anti-depressants, and no abyss opens beneath me. I sublet the sublet apartment, and, without being wracked too much by memories of the handsome rugs, tables, dishes, and chairs once jointly owned by Helen and me and now hers alone, I furnish a new place of my own. I even accept an invitation to a dinner party at the Schonbrunns', and at the end of the evening politely kiss Debbie's cheek while Arthur paternally kisses

Claire's. Easy as that. Meaningless as that. At the door, while Arthur and Claire conclude the conversation they'd been having at dinner—about the curriculum that Claire is now devising for the upper grades—Debbie and I have a moment to chat privately. For some reason—alcoholic intake on both sides, I think—we are holding hands! "Another of your tall blondes," says Debbie, "but this one seems a bit more sympathetic. We both find her very sweet. And very bright. Where did you meet?" "In a brothel in Marrakesh. Look, Debbie, isn't it about time you got off my ass? What does that mean, my 'tall blondes'?" "It's a fact." "No, it is not even a fact. Helen's hair was auburn. But suppose it was cut from the same bolt as Claire's— the fact is that 'blondes,' in that context, and that tone, is, as you may even know, a derogatory term used by intellectuals and other serious people to put down pretty women. I also believe it is dense with unsavory implication when addressed to men of my origin and complexion. I remember how fond you used to be at Stanford of pointing out to people the anomaly of a literate chap like myself coming from the 'Borscht Belt.' That too used to strike me as a bit reductive." "Oh, you take yourself too seriously. Why don't you just admit you have a penchant for these big blondes and leave it at that? It's nothing to be ashamed of. They do look lovely up on water skis with all that hair streaming. I bet they look lovely everywhere." "Debbie, I'll make a deal with you. I'll admit I know nothing about you, if you'll admit you know nothing about me. I'm sure you have a whole wondrous being and inner life that I know nothing about." "Nope," she says, "this is it. This is the whole thing. Take it or leave it." Both of us begin to laugh. I say, "Tell me, what does

Arthur see in you? It's really one of the mysteries of life. What do you have that I'm blind to?" "Everything," she replies. Out in the car, I give Claire an abridged version of the conversation. "The woman is warped," I say. "Oh, no," says Claire, "just silly, that's all." "She tricked you, Clarissa. Silly is the cover—assassination is the game." "Ah, sweetie," says Claire, "it's *you* she's tricked."

So much for my rehabilitation back into society. As for my father and his awesome loneliness, well, now he takes the train from Cedarhurst to have dinner in Manhattan once a month; he can't be coaxed in any more often, but in truth, before there was the new apartment, and Claire to help with the conversation and the cooking, I didn't work at coaxing him that hard, no, not so each of us could sit and peer sadly at the other picking at his spareribs, two orphans in Chinatown . . . not so I could wait to hear him ask over the lichee nuts, "And that guy, he hasn't come back to bother you, has he?"

And, to be sure, from the maw of that maelstrom called Baumgarten I withdraw my toes a little. We still have lunch together from time to time, but the grander feasts I leave him to partake of on his own. And I do not introduce him to Claire.

My, how easy life is when it's easy, and how hard when it's hard!

One night, after dinner at my apartment, while Claire is preparing her next day's lessons at the cleared dining table, I finally get up the nerve, or no longer seem to need "nerve," to reread what there is of my Chekhov book, shelved now for more than two years. In the midst of the laborious and deadly competence of those fragmentary chapters intended to focus upon the subject of romantic disillusionment, I find five pages that are somewhat read-able—reflections growing out of Chekhov's comic little story, "Man in a Shell," about the tyrannical rise and cele-brated fall—"I confess," says the goodhearted narrator after the tyrant's funeral, "it is a great pleasure to bury people like Belikov"—the rise and fall of a provincial high school official whose love of prohibitions and hatred of all deviations from the rules manages to hold a whole town of "thoughtful, decent people" under his thumb for fifteen years. I go back to reread the story, then to reread "Gooseberries" and "About Love," written in sequence with it and forming a series of anecdotal ruminations upon the varieties of pain engendered by spiritual imprisonment—by petty despotism, by ordinary human complacency, and finally, even by the inhibitions upon feeling necessary to support a scrupulous man's sense of decency. For the next month, with a notebook on my lap, and some tentative observations in mind, I return to Chekhov's fiction nightly, listening for the anguished cry of the trapped and misera-ble socialized being, the well-bred wives who during din-ner with the guests wonder "Why do I smile and lie?", and the husbands, seemingly settled and secure, who are "full of conventional truth and conventional deception." Simultaneously I am watching how Chekhov, simply and clearly, though not quite so pitilessly as Flaubert, reveals the humiliations and failures—worst of all, the destruc-tive power—of those who seek a way *out* of the shell of restrictions and convention, out of the pervasive boredom and the stifling despair, out of the painful marital situa-tions and the endemic social falsity, into what they take to be a vibrant and desirable life. There is the agitated young wife in "Misfortune" who looks for "a bit of excitement" against the grain of her own offended respectability; there is the lovesick landowner in "Ariadne," confessing with Herzogian helplessness to a romantic misadventure with a vulgar trampy tigress who gradually transforms him into a hopeless misogynist, but whom he nonetheless waits on hand and foot; there is the young actress in "A Boring Story," whose bright, hopeful enthusiasm for a life on the stage, and a life with men, turns bitter with her first experiences of the stage and of men, and of her own lack of talent—"I have no talent, you see, I have no talent and . . . and lots of vanity." And there is "The Duel." Every night for a week (with Claire only footsteps away) I reread Chekhov's masterpiece about the weaseling, slovenly, intelligent, literary-minded seducer Layevsky, immersed in his lies and his self-pity, and Layevsky's antagonist, the ruthless punitive conscience who all but murders him, the voluble scientist Von Koren. Or so it is that I come to view the story: with Von Koren as the ferociously rational and merciless prosecutor called forth to challenge the sense of shame and sinfulness that is nearly all that Layevsky has become, and from which, alas, he no longer can flee. It is this immersion in "The Duel" that finally gets me writing, and within four months the five pages extracted from the old unfinished rehash of my thesis on romantic disillusionment are transformed into some forty thousand words entitled *Man in a Shell*, an essay on license and restraint in Chekhov's world—longings fulfilled, pleasures denied, and the pain occasioned by both; a study, at bottom, of what makes for Chekhov's pervasive pessimism about the methods—scrupulous, odious, noble, dubious—by which the men and women of his time try in vain to achieve "that sense of personal freedom" to which Chekhov himself is so devoted. My first book! With a dedication page that reads "To C.O."

"She is to steadiness," I tell Klinger (and Kepesh, who must never, never, never forget), "what Helen was to impetuosity. She is to common sense what Birgitta was to indiscretion. I have never seen such devotion to the ordinary business of daily life. It's awesome, really, the way she deals with each day as it comes, the attention she pays minute by minute. There's no dreaming going on there—just steady, dedicated *living*. I trust her, that's the point I'm making. That's what's done it," I announce triumphantly, "trust."

To all of which Klinger eventually replies goodbye then and good luck. At the door of his office on the spring afternoon of our parting, I have to wonder if it can really be that I no longer need bucking up and holding down and hearing out, warning, encouragement, consent, consolation, applause, and opposition—in short, professional doses of mothering and fathering and simple friendship three times a week for an hour. *Can* it be that I've come through? Just like that? Just because of Claire? What if I awaken tomorrow morning once again a man with a crater instead of a heart, once again without a man's capacity and appetite and strength and judgment, without the least bit of mastery over my flesh or my intelligence or my feelings . . .

"Stay in touch," says Klinger, shaking my hand. Just as I could not look squarely at him the day I neglected to mention the impact on my conscience of his daughter's snapshot—as though suppressing that fact I might be spared his unuttered judgment, or my own—so I cannot let his eyes engage mine when we say farewell. But now it is because I would prefer not to give vent to my feelings of elation and indebtedness in an outburst of tears. Sniffing all sentiment back up my nose—and firmly, for the moment, suppressing all doubt—I say, "Let's hope I don't have to," but once out on the street by myself, I repeat the incredible words aloud, only now to the accompaniment of the appropriate emotions: "I've come through!"

The following June, when the teaching year is over for the two of us, Claire and I fly to the north of Italy, my first time back in Europe since I'd gone prowling there with Birgitta a decade earlier. In Venice we spend five days at a quiet pensione near the Accademia. Each morning we eat breakfast in the pensione's aromatic garden and then, in our walking shoes, weave back and forth across the bridges and alleyways that lead to the landmarks Claire has marked on the map for us to visit that day. Whenever she takes her pictures of these palazzos and piazzas and churches and fountains I wander off aways, but always looking back to get a picture of her and her unadorned beauty.

Each evening after dinner under the arbor in the garden, we treat ourselves to a little gondola ride. With Claire beside me in the armchair that Mann describes as "the softest, most luxurious, most relaxing seat in the world," I ask myself yet again if this serenity truly exists, if this contentment, this wonderful accord is real. *Is* the worst over? Have I no more terrible mistakes to make? And no more to pay on those behind me? Was all that only so much Getting Started, a longish and misguided youth out of which I have finally aged? "Are you sure we didn't die," I say, "and go to heaven?" "I wouldn't know," she replies; "you'll have to ask the gondolier."

Our last afternoon I blow us to lunch at the Gritti. On the terrace I tip the headwaiter and point to the very table where I had imagined myself sitting with the pretty student who used to lunch on Peanut Chews in my classroom; I order exactly what I ate that day back in Palo Alto when we were studying Chekhov's stories about love and I felt myself on the edge of a nervous collapse—only this time I am not imagining the delicious meal with the fresh, untainted mate, this time both are real and I am well. Settling back—I with a cold glass of wine; Claire, the teetotaling daughter of parents who overimbibed, with her *acqua minerale*—I look out across the gleaming waters of this indescribably beautiful toy town and I say to her, "Do you think Venice is really sinking? The place seems in vaguely the same position as last time I was here."

"Who were you with then? Your wife?"

"No. It was my Fulbright year. I was with a girl."

"Who was that?"

Now, how endangered or troubled would she feel, what, if anything, do I risk awakening if I go ahead and tell her all? Oh, how dramatically put! What did "all" consist of—any more, really, than a young sailor goes out to find in his first foreign port? A sailor's taste for a little of the lurid, but, as things turned out, neither a sailor's stomach nor strength . . . Still, to someone so measured and orderly, someone who has turned all her considerable energy to making normal and ordinary what had for her been heartbreakingly irregular in her childhood home, I think it best to answer, "Oh, nobody, really," and let the matter drop.

Whereupon the nobody who has been no part of my life for over ten years is all I can think of. In that Chekhov class the mismatched husband had recalled sunnier days on the terrace of the Gritti, an unbruised, audacious, young Kepesh still running around Europe scot-free; now on the terrace of the Gritti, where I have come to celebrate the triumphant foundation of a sweet and stable new life, to celebrate the astonishing renewal of health and happiness, I am recalling the earliest, headiest hours of my sheikdom, the night in our London basement when it is my turn to ask Birgitta what it is *she* most wants. What I most want the two girls have given me; what Elisabeth most wants we are leaving for last—she does not know . . . for in her heart, as we are to discover when the truck knocks her down, she wants none of it. But Birgitta has desires about which she is not afraid to speak, and which we proceed to satisfy. Yes, sitting across from Claire, who has said that my semen filling her mouth makes her feel that she is drowning, that this is something she just doesn't care to do, I am remembering the sight of Birgitta kneeling before me, her face upturned to receive the strands of flowing semen that fall upon her hair, her forehead, her nose. "*Här!*" she cries, "*här!*", while Elisabeth, wearing her pink woolen robe, and reclining on the bed, looks on in frozen fascination at the naked masturbator and his half-clothed suppliant.

As if such a thing matters! As if Claire is withholding anything that *matters!* But admonish myself as I will for amnesia, stupidity, ingratitude, callowness, for a lunatic and suicidal loss of all perspective, the rush of greedy lust I feel is not for this lovely young woman with whom I have only recently emerged into a life promising the most profound sort of fulfillment, but for the smallish buck-toothed comrade I last saw leaving my room at midnight some thirty kilometers outside Rouen over ten years ago, desire for my own lewd, lost soul mate, who, back before my sense of the permissible began its inward collapse, welcomed as feverishly and gamely as did I the uncommon act and the alien thought. Oh, Birgitta, go away! But this time we are in our room right here in Venice, a hotel on a narrow alleyway off the Zattere, not very far from the little bridge where Claire had taken my picture earlier in the day. I tie a kerchief around her eyes, careful to knot it tightly at the back, and then I am standing over the blindfolded girl and—ever so lightly to begin with—whipping her between her parted legs. I watch as she strains upward with her hips to catch the bite of each stroke of my belt on her genital crease. I watch this as I have never watched anything before in my life. "Say all the things," Birgitta whispers, and I do, in a low, subdued growl such as I have never used before to address anyone or anything.

For Birgitta then—for what I would now prefer to dismiss as a "longish and misguided youth"—a surging sense of lascivious kinship . . . and for Claire, for this truly passionate and loving rescuer of mine? Anger; disappointment; disgust—contempt for all she does so marvelously, resentment over that little thing she will not deign to do. I see how very easily I could have no use for her. The snapshots. The lists. The mouth that will not drink my come. The curriculum-review committee. Everything.

The impulse to fly up from the table and telephone Dr. Klinger I suppress. I will not be one of those hysterical patients at the other end of the overseas line. No, not that. I eat the meal when it is served, and sure enough, by the time the dessert is to be ordered, yearnings for Birgitta begging me and Birgitta beneath me and Birgitta below me, all such yearnings have begun to subside, as left to themselves those yearnings will. And the anger disappears too, to be replaced by shame-filled sadness. If Claire senses the rising and ebbing of all this distress—and how can she not? how else understand my silent, icy gloom?—she decides to pretend ignorance, to talk on about her plans for the curriculum-review committee until whatever has cast us apart has simply passed away.

From Venice we drive a rented car to Padua to look at the Giottos. Claire takes more pictures. She will have them developed when we get home and then, sitting cross-legged on the floor—the posture of tranquillity, of concentration, the posture of a very good girl indeed —paste them, in their proper sequence, into the album for this year. Now northern Italy will be in the bookcase at the foot of the bed where her volumes of photographs are stored, now northern Italy will be forever *hers*, along with Schenectady, where she was born and raised, Ithaca, where she went to college, and New York City, where she lives and works and lately has fallen in love. And I will be there at the foot of the bed, along with her places, her family, and her friends.

Though so many of her twenty-five years have been blighted by the squabbling of contentious parents—arguments abetted, as often as not, by too many tumblers of

Scotch—she regards the past as worth recording and remembering, if only because she has outlasted the pain and disorder to establish a decent life of her own. As she likes to say, it is the only past she has got to remember, hard as it may have been when the bombs were bursting around her and she was trying her best to grow up in one piece. And then, of course, that Mr. and Mrs. Ovington put more energy into being adversaries than into being the comforters of their children does not mean that their daughter must deny *herself* the ordinary pleasures that ordinary families (if such there be) take as a matter of course. To all the pleasant amenities of family life—the exchanging of photographs, the giving of gifts, the celebration of holidays, the regular phone calls—both Claire and her older sister are passionately devoted, as though in fact she and Olivia are the thoughtful parents and their parents the callow offspring.

From a hotel in a small mountain town where we find a room with a terrace and a bed and an Arcadian view, we make day trips to Verona and Vicenza. Pictures, pictures, pictures. What is the opposite of a nail being driven into a coffin? Well, that is what I hear as Claire's camera clicks away. Once again I feel I am being sealed up into something wonderful. One day we just walk with a picnic lunch up along the cowpaths and through the flowering fields, whole nations of minute bluets and lacquered little buttercups and unreal poppies. I can walk silently with Claire for hours on end. I am content just to lie on the ground propped up on one elbow and watch her pick wild flowers to take back to our room and arrange in a water glass to place beside my pillow. I feel no need for anything more. "More" has no meaning. Nor does Birgitta appear to have meaning any longer, as though "Birgitta" and "more" are just different ways of saying the same thing. Following the performance at the Gritti, she has failed to put in anything like such a sensational appearance again. For the next few nights she does come by to pay me a visit each time Claire and I make love—kneeling, always kneeling, and begging for what thrills her most—but then she is gone, and I am above the body I am above, and with that alone partake of all the "more" I now could want, or want to want. Yes, I just hold tight to Claire and the unbeckoned visitor eventually drifts away, leaving me to enjoy once again the awesome fact of my great good luck.

On our last afternoon, we carry our lunch to the crest of a field that looks across high green hills to the splendid white tips of the Dolomites. Claire lies stretched out beside where I am sitting, her ample figure gently swelling and subsiding with each breath she draws. Looking steadily down at this large, green-eyed girl in her thin summer clothes, at her pale, smallish, oval, unmarred face, her scrubbed, unworldly prettiness—the beauty, I realize, of a young Amish or Shaker woman—I say to myself, "Claire is enough. Yes, 'Claire' and 'enough'—they, too, are one word."

From Venice we fly by way of Vienna—and the house of Sigmund Freud—to Prague. During this last year I have been teaching the Kafka course at the university— the paper that I am to read a few days from now in Bruges has Kafka's preoccupations with spiritual starvation as its subject—but I have not as yet seen his city, other than in books of photographs. Just prior to our departure I had graded the final examinations written by my fifteen students in the seminar, who had read all of the fiction, Max Brod's biography, and Kafka's diaries and his letters to Milena and to his father. One of the questions I had asked on the examination was this—

In his "Letter to His Father" Kafka writes, "My writing is all about you; all I did there, after all, was to bemoan what I could not bemoan upon your breast. It was an intentionally long-drawn-out leave-taking from you, yet, although it was enforced by you, it did take its course in the direction determined by me . . ." What does Kafka mean when he says to his father, "My writing is all about you," and adds, "yet it did take its course in the direction determined by me"? If you like, imagine yourself to be Max Brod writing a letter of your own to Kafka's father, explaining what it is your friend has in mind . . .

I had been pleased by the number of students who had taken my suggestion and decided to pretend to be the writer's friend and biographer—and, in describing the inner workings of a most unusual son to a most conventional father, had demonstrated a mature sensitivity to Kafka's moral isolation, to his peculiarities of perspective and temperament, and to those imaginative processes by which a fantasist as entangled as Kafka was in daily existence transforms into fable his everyday struggles. Hardly a single benighted literature major straying into ingenious metaphysical exegesis! Oh, I am pleased, all right, with the Kafka seminar and with myself for what I've done there. But these first months with Claire, what hasn't been a source of pleasure?

Before leaving home I had been given the name and telephone number of an American spending the year teaching in Prague, and, happily, as it turns out (and what doesn't these days?), he and a Czech friend of his, another literature professor, have the afternoon free and are able to give us a tour of old Prague. From a bench in the Old Town Square we gaze across at the palatial building where Franz Kafka attended Gymnasium. To the right of the columned entryway is the ground-floor site of Hermann Kafka's business. "He couldn't even get away from him at school," I say. "All the worse for him," the Czech professor replies, "and all the better for the fiction." In the imposing Gothic church nearby, high on one wall of the nave, a small square window faces an apartment next door where, I am informed, Kafka's family had once lived. So Kafka, I say, could have sat there furtively looking down on the sinner confessing and the faithful at prayer . . . and the interior of this church, might it not have furnished, if not every last detail, at least the atmosphere for the Cathedral of *The Trial*? And those steep angular streets across the river leading circuitously to the sprawling Hapsburg castle, surely they must have served as inspiration for him too . . . Perhaps so, says the Czech professor, but a small castle village in northern Bohemia that Kafka knew from his visits to his grandfather is thought to have been the principal model for the topography of *The Castle*. Then there is the little country village where his sister had spent a year managing a farm and where Kafka had gone to stay with her during a spell of illness. Had we time, says the Czech professor, Claire and I might benefit from an overnight visit to the countryside. "Visit one of those xenophobic little towns, with its smoky taverna and its buxom barmaid, and you will see what a thoroughgoing realist this Kafka was."

For the first time I sense something other than geniality in this smallish, bespectacled, neatly attired academic—I sense all that the geniality is working to suppress.

Near the wall of the castle, on cobbled Alchemist Street—and looking like a dwelling out of a child's bedtime story, the fit habitation for a gnome or elf—is the tiny house that his youngest sister had rented one winter for Kafka to live in, another of her efforts to help separate the bachelor son from father and family. The little place is now a souvenir shop. Picture postcards and Prague mementos are being sold on the spot where Kafka had meticulously scribbled variants of the same paragraph ten times over in his diary, and where he had drawn his sardonic stick figures of himself, the "private ideograms" he hid, along with practically everything else, in a drawer. Claire takes a picture of the three literature professors in front of the perfectionist writer's torture chamber. Soon it will be in its place in one of the albums at the foot of her bed.

While Claire goes off with the American professor, and her camera, for a tour of the castle grounds, I sit over tea with Professor Soska, our Czech guide. When the Russians invaded Czechoslovakia and put an end to the Prague Spring reform movement, Soska was fired from his university post and at age thirty-nine placed in "retirement" on a minuscule pension. His wife, a research scientist, also was relieved of her position for political reasons and, in order to support the family of four, has been working for a year now as a typist in a meat-packing plant. How has the retired professor managed to keep up his morale, I wonder. His three-piece suit is impeccable, his gait quick, his speech snappy and precise—how does he do it? What gets him up in the morning and to sleep at night? What gets him through each day?

"Kafka, of course," he says, showing me that smile again. "Yes, this is true; many of us survive almost solely on Kafka. Including people in the street who have never read a word of his. They look at one another when something happens, and they say, 'It's Kafka.' Meaning, 'That's the way it goes here now.' Meaning, 'What else did you expect?'"

"And anger? Is it abated any when you shrug your shoulders and say, 'It's Kafka'?"

"For the first six months after the Russians came to stay with us I was myself in a continuous state of agitation. I went every night to secret meetings with my friends. Every other day at least I circulated another illegal petition. And in the time remaining I wrote, in my most precise and lucid prose, in my most elegant and thoughtful sentences, encyclopedic analyses of the situation which then circulated in *samizdat* among my colleagues. Then one day I keeled over and they sent me to the hospital with bleeding ulcers. I thought at first, all right, I will lie here on my back for a month, I will take my medicine and eat my slops, and then—well, then *what*? What will I do when I stop bleeding? Return to playing K. to their Castle and their Court? This can all go on interminably, as Kafka and his readers so well know. Those pathetic, hopeful, striving K.'s of his, running madly up and down all those stairwells looking for their solution, feverishly traversing the city contemplating the new development that will lead to, of all things, their success. Beginnings, middles, and, most fantastical of all, endings—that is how they believe they can force events to unfold."

"But, Kakfa and his readers aside, will things change if there is no opposition?"

The smile, disguising God only knows the kind of expression he would *like* to show to the world. "Sir, I have made my position known. The entire country has made its position known. This way we live now is not what we had in mind. For myself, I cannot burn away what remains of my digestive tract by continuing to make this clear to our authorities seven days a week."

"And so what do you do instead?"

"I translate *Moby Dick* into Czech. Of course, a translation happens already to exist, a very fine one indeed. There is absolutely no need for another. But it is something I have always thought about, and now that I have nothing else pressing to be accomplished, well, why not?"

"Why that book? Why Melville?" I ask him.

"In the fifties I spent a year on an exchange program, living in New York City. Walking the streets, it looked to me as if the place was aswarm with the crew of Ahab's ship. And at the helm of everything, big or small, I saw yet another roaring Ahab. The appetite to set things right, to emerge at the top, to be declared a 'champ.' And by dint, not just of energy and will, but of enormous rage. And *that*, the rage, that is what I should like to translate into Czech . . . if"—smiling—"that *can* be translated into Czech.

"Now, as you might imagine, this ambitious project, when completed, will be utterly useless for two reasons. First, there is no need for another translation, particularly one likely to be inferior to the distinguished translation we already have; and second, no translation of mine can be published in this country. In this way, you see, I am able to undertake what I would not otherwise have dared to do, without having to bother myself any longer worrying whether it is sensible or not. Indeed, some nights when I am working late, the futility of what I am doing would appear to be my deepest source of satisfaction. To you perhaps this may appear to be nothing but a pretentious form of capitulation, of self-mockery. It may even appear that way to me on occasion. Nonetheless, it remains the most serious thing I can think to do in my retirement. And you," he asks, so very genially, "what draws you so to Kafka?"

"It's a long story too."

"Dealing with?"

"Not with political hopelessness."

"I would think not."

"Rather," I say, "in large part, with sexual despair, with vows of chastity that seem somehow to have been taken by me behind my back, and which I lived with against my will. Either I turned against my flesh, or it turned against me—I still don't know quite how to put it."

"From the look of things, you don't seem to have suppressed its urgings entirely. That is a very attractive young woman you are traveling with."

"Well, the worst is over. *May* be over. At least is over for *now*. But while it lasted, while I couldn't be what I had always just assumed I was, well, it wasn't quite like anything I had ever known before. Of course you are the one on intimate terms with totalitarianism—but if you'll permit me, I can only compare the body's utter single-mindedness, its cold indifference and absolute contempt for the well-being of the spirit, to some unyielding, authoritarian regime. And you can petition it all you like, offer up the most heartfelt and dignified and logical sort of appeal—and get no response at all. If anything, a kind of laugh is what you get. I submitted my petitions through a psychoanalyst; went to his office every other day for an hour to make my case for the restoration of a robust libido. And, I tell you, with arguments and perorations no less involuted and tedious and cunning and abstruse than the kind of thing you find in *The Castle*. You think poor K. is clever—you should have heard me trying to outfox impotence."

"I can imagine. That's not a pleasant business."

"Of course, measured against what you—"

"Please, you needn't say things like that. It is *not* a pleasant business, and the right to vote provides, in this matter, little in the way of compensation."

"That is true. I did vote during this period, and found it made me no happier. What I started to say about Kafka, about reading Kafka, is that stories of obstructed, thwarted K.'s banging their heads against invisible walls, well, they suddenly had a disturbing new resonance for me. It was all a little less remote, suddenly, than the Kafka I'd read in college. In my own way, you see, I had come to know that sense of having been summoned— or of imagining yourself summoned—to a calling that turns out to be beyond you, yet in the face of every compromising or farcical consequence, being unable to wise up and relinquish the goal. You see, I once went about living as though sex were sacred ground."

"So to be 'chaste' . . ." he says, sympathetically. "Most unpleasant."

"I sometimes wonder if *The Castle* isn't in fact linked to Kafka's own erotic blockage—a book engaged at every level with not reaching a climax."

He laughs at my speculation, but as before, gently and with that unrelenting amiability. Yes, just so profoundly compromised is the retired professor, caught, as in a mangle, between conscience and the regime—between conscience and searing abdominal pain. "Well," he says, putting a hand on my arm in a kind and fatherly way, "to each obstructed citizen his own Kafka."

"And to each angry man his own Melville," I reply. "But then what are bookish people to do with all the great prose they read—"

"—but sink their teeth into it. Exactly. Into the books, instead of into the hand that throttles them."

Late that afternoon, we board the streetcar whose number Professor Soska had written in pencil on the back of a packet of postcards ceremoniously presented to Claire at the door of our hotel. The postcards are illustrated with photographs of Kafka, his family, and Prague landmarks associated with his life and his work. The handsome little set is no longer in circulation, Soska explained to us, now that the Russians occupy Czechoslovakia and Kafka is an outlawed writer, *the* outlawed writer. "But you do have another set, I hope," said Claire, "for yourself—?" "Miss Ovington," he said, with a courtly bow, "I have Prague. Please, permit me. I am sure that everyone who meets you wants to give you a gift." And here he suggested the visit to Kafka's grave, to which it would not, however, be advisable for him to accompany us . . . and motioning with his hand, he drew our attention to a man standing with his back to a parked taxicab some fifty feet up the boulevard from the door of the hotel: the plainclothesman, he informs us, who used to follow him and Mrs. Soska around in the months after the Russian invasion, back when the professor was helping to organize the clandestine opposition to the new puppet regime and his duodenum was still intact. "Are you sure that's him, here?" I had asked. "Sufficiently sure," said Soska, and stooping quickly to kiss Claire's hand, he moved with a rapid, comic stride, rather like a man in a walking race, into the crowd descending the wide stairs of the passageway to the underground. "My God," said Claire, "it's too awful. All that terrible smiling. And that getaway!"

We are both a little stunned, not least of all, in my case, for feeling myself so safe and inviolable, what with the passport in my jacket and the young woman at my side.

The streetcar carries us from the center of Prague to the outlying district where Kafka is buried. Enclosed within a high wall, the Jewish graveyard is bounded on one side by a more extensive Christian cemetery— through the fence we see visitors tending the graves there, kneeling and weeding like patient gardeners—and on the other by a wide bleak thoroughfare bearing truck traffic to and from the city. The gate to the Jewish cemetery is chained shut. I rattle the chain and call toward what seems a watchman's house. In time a woman with a little boy appears from somewhere inside. I say in German that we have flown all the way from New York to visit Franz Kafka's grave. She appears to understand, but says no, not today. Come back Tuesday, she says. But I am a professor of literature and a Jew, I explain, and pass a handful of crowns across to her between the bars. A key appears, the gate is opened, and inside the little boy is assigned to accompany us as we follow the sign that points the way. The sign is in five different tongues—so many peoples fascinated by the fearful inventions of this tormented ascetic, so many fearful millions: Khrobu/ К могиле/Zum Grabe/To the Grave of/à la tombe de/ FRANZE KAFKY.

Of all things, marking Kafka's remains—and unlike anything else in sight—a stout, elongated, whitish rock, tapering upward to its pointed glans, a tombstone phallus. That is the first surprise. The second is that the family-haunted son is buried forever—still!—between the mother and the father who outlived him. I take a pebble from the gravel walk and place it on one of the little mounds of pebbles piled there by the pilgrims who've preceded me. I have never done so much for my own grandparents, buried with ten thousand others alongside an expressway twenty minutes from my New York apartment, nor have I made such a visit to my mother's tree-shaded Catskill grave site since I accompanied my father to the unveiling of her stone. The dark rectangular slabs beyond Kafka's grave bear familiar Jewish names. I might be thumbing through my own address book, or at the front desk looking over my mother's shoulder at the roster of registered guests at the Hungarian Royale: Levy, Goldschmidt, Schneider, Hirsch . . . The graves go on and on, but only Kafka's appears to be properly looked after. The other dead are without survivors hereabouts to chop away the undergrowth and to cut back the ivy that twists through the limbs of the trees and forms a heavy canopy joining the plot of one extinct Jew to the next. Only the childless bachelor appears to have living progeny. Where better for irony to abound than à la tombe de Franze Kafky?

Set into the wall facing Kafka's grave is a stone inscribed with the name of his great friend Brod. Here too I place a small pebble. Then for the first time I notice the plaques affixed to the length of cemetery wall, inscribed to the memory of Jewish citizens of Prague exterminated in Terezin, Auschwitz, Belsen, and Dachau. There are not pebbles enough to go around.

With the silent child trailing behind, Claire and I head back to the gate. When we get there Claire snaps a picture of the shy little boy and, using sign language, instructs him to write down his name and address on a piece of paper. Pantomiming with broad gestures and stagy facial expressions that make me wonder suddenly just how childish a young woman she is—just how childlike and needy a man I have become—she is able to inform the little boy that when the photograph is ready she will send a copy to him. In two or three weeks Professor Soska is also to receive a photograph from Claire, this one taken earlier in the day outside the souvenir shop where Kafka had once spent a winter.

Now why do I want to call what joins me to her childish? Why do I want to call this happiness names? Let it happen! Let it be! Stop the challenging before it even starts! You need what you need! Make peace with it!

The woman has come from the house to open the gate. Again we exchange some remarks in German.

"There are many visitors to Kafka's grave?" I ask.

"Not so many. But always distinguished people, Professor, like yourself. Or serious young students. He was a very great man. We had many great Jewish writers in Prague. Franz Werfel. Max Brod. Oskar Baum. Franz Kafka. But now," she says, casting her first glance, and a sidelong, abbreviated one at that, toward my companion, "they are all gone."

"Maybe your little boy will grow up to be a great Jewish writer."

She repeats my words in Czech. Then she translates the reply the boy has given while looking down at his shoes. "He wants to be an aviator."

"Tell him people don't always come from all over the world to visit an aviator's grave."

Again words are exchanged with the boy, and, smiling pleasantly at me—yes, it is only to the Jewish professor that she will address herself with a gracious smile—she says, "He doesn't mind that so much. And, sir, what is the name of your university?"

I tell her.

"If you would like, I will take you to the grave of the man who was Dr. Kafka's barber. He is buried here too."

"Thank you, that is very kind."

"He was also the barber of Dr. Kafka's father."

I explain to Claire what the woman has offered. Claire says, "If you want, go ahead."

"Better not to," I say. "Start with Kafka's barber, and by midnight we may end up by the grave of his candlestick maker."

To the graveyard attendant I say, "I'm afraid that's not possible right now."

"Of course your wife may come too," she starchily informs me.

177

"Thank you. But we have to get back to our hotel."

Now she looks me over with undisguised suspiciousness, as though it well may be that I am not from a distinguished American university at all. She has gone out of her way to unlock the gate on a day other than the one prescribed for tourists, and I have turned out to be less than serious, probably nothing but a curiosity seeker, a Jew perhaps, but in the company of a woman quite clearly Aryan.

At the streetcar stop I say to Claire, "Do you know what Kafka said to the man he shared an office with at the insurance company? At lunchtime he saw the fellow eating his sausage and Kafka is supposed to have shuddered and said, 'The only fit food for a man is half a lemon.'"

She sighs, and says, sadly, "Poor dope," finding in the great writer's dietary injunction a disdain for harmless appetites that is just plain silly to a healthy girl from Schenectady, New York.

That is all—yet, when we board the streetcar and sit down beside each other, I take her hand and feel suddenly purged of yet another ghost, as de-Kafkafied by my pilgrimage to the cemetery as I would appear to have been de-Birgittized once and for all by that visitation on the terrace restaurant in Venice. My obstructed days are behind me—along with the *un*obstructed ones: no more "more," and no more nothing, either!

"Oh, Clarissa," I say, bringing her hand to my lips, "it's as though the past can't do me any more harm. I just don't have any more regrets. And my fears are gone, too. And it's all from finding you. I'd thought the god of women, who doles them out to you, had looked down on me and said, 'Impossible to please—the hell with him.' And then he sends me Claire."

That evening, after dinner in our hotel, we go up to the room to prepare for our early departure the next day. While I pack a suitcase with my clothes and with the books I have been reading on the airplanes and in bed at night, Claire falls asleep amid the clothing she has laid out on the comforter. Aside from the Kafka diaries and Brod's biography—my supplemental guidebooks to old Prague—I have with me paperbacks by Mishima, Gombrowicz, and Genet, novels for next year's comparative literature class. I have decided to organize the first semester's reading around the subject of erotic desire, beginning with these disquieting contemporary novels dealing with prurient and iniquitous sexuality (disquieting to students because they are the sort of books admired most by a reader like Baumgarten, novels in which the author is himself pointedly implicated in what is morally most alarming) and ending the term's work with three masterworks concerned with illicit and ungovernable passions, whose assault is made by other means: *Madame Bovary,* *Anna Karenina,* and "Death in Venice."

Without awakening her, I pick Claire's clothes off the bed and pack them in her suitcase. Handling her things, I feel overwhelmingly in love. Then I leave her a note saying that I have gone for a walk and will be back in an hour. Passing through the lobby I notice that there are now some fifteen or twenty pretty young prostitutes seated singly, and in pairs, beyond the glass doorway of the hotel's spacious café. Earlier in the day there had been just three of them, at a single table, gaily chatting together. When I asked Professor Soska how all this is organized under socialism, he had explained that most of Prague's whores are secretaries and shopgirls moonlighting with tacit government approval; a few are employed full-time by the Ministry of the Interior to get what information they can out of the various delegations from East and West that pass through the big hotels. The covey of miniskirted girls I see seated in the café are probably there to greet the members of the Bulgarian trade mission who occupy most of the floor beneath ours. One of them, who is stroking the belly of a brown dachshund puppy that lies cuddled in her arms, smiles my way. I smile back (costs nothing) and then am off to the Old Town Square, where Kafka and Brod used to take their evening stroll. When I get there it is after nine and the spacious melancholy plaza is empty of everything except the shadows of the aged façades enclosing it. Where the tourist buses had been parked earlier in the day there is now only the smooth, worn, cobblestone basin. The place is empty—of all, that is, except mystery and enigma. I sit alone on a bench beneath a street lamp and, through the thin film of mist, look past the looming figure of Jan Hus to the church whose most sequestered proceedings the Jewish author could observe by peering through his secret aperture.

It is here that I begin to compose in my head what at first strikes me as no more than a bit of whimsy, the first lines of an introductory lecture to my comparative literature class inspired by Kafka's "Report to an Academy," the story in which an ape addresses a scientific gathering. It is only a little story of a few thousand words, but one that I love, particularly its opening, which seems to me one of the most enchanting and startling in literature: "Honored Members of the Academy! You have done me the honor of inviting me to give your Academy an account of the life I formerly led as an ape."

"Honored Members of Literature 341," I begin . . . but by the time I am back at the hotel and have seated myself, with pen in hand, at an empty table in a corner of the café, I have penetrated the veneer of donnish satire with which I began, and on hotel stationery am writing out in longhand a formal introductory lecture (not un-influenced by the ape's impeccable, professorial prose) that I want with all my heart to deliver—and to deliver not in September but at this very moment!

Seated two tables away is the prostitute with the little dachshund; she has been joined by a friend, whose fa-vorite pet seems to be her own hair. She strokes away at it as though it is somebody else's. Looking up from my work, I tell the waiter to bring a cognac to each of these petite and pretty working girls, neither of them as old as Claire, and order a cognac for myself.

"Cheers," says the prostitute pleasing her puppy, and after the three of us smile at one another for a brief, en-ticing moment, I go back to writing what seem to me then and there somehow to be sentences of the most enormous consequence for my happy new life.

Rather than spend the first day of class talking about the reading list and the general idea behind this course, I would like to tell you some things about myself that I have never before divulged to any of my students. I have no business doing this, and until I came into the room and took my seat I wasn't sure I would go through with it. And I may change my mind yet. For how do I justify disclosing to you the most intimate facts of my personal life? True, we will be meeting to discuss books for three hours a week during the coming two semesters, and from experience I know, as you do, that under such conditions a strong bond of affection can develop. However, we also know that this does not give me license to indulge what may only be so much impertinence and bad taste.

As you may already have surmised—by my style of dress, as easily as from the style of my opening remarks—the conventions traditionally governing the relationship between student and teacher are more or less those by which I have always operated, even during the turbulence of recent years. I have been told that I am one of the few remaining professors who address students in the classroom as "Mr." and "Miss," rather than by their given names. And however you may choose to attire yourselves—in the getup of garage mechanic, panhandler, tearoom gypsy, or cattle rustler—I still prefer to appear before you to teach wearing a jacket and a tie . . . though, as the observant will record, generally it will be the same jacket and the same tie. And when women students come to my office to confer, they will see, if they should even bother to look, that throughout the meeting I will dutifully leave open to the outside corridor the door to the room where we sit side by side. Some of you may be further amused when I remove my watch from my wrist, as I did only a moment ago, and place it beside my notes at the beginning of each class session. By now I no longer remember which of my own professors used to keep careful track of the passing hour in this way, but it would seem to have made its impression on me, signaling a professionalism with which I like still to associate myself.

All of which is not to say that I shall try to keep hidden from you the fact that I am flesh and blood—or that I understand that you are. By the end of the year you may even have grown a little weary of my insistence upon the connections between the novels you read for this class, even the most eccentric and off-putting of novels, and what you know so far of life. You will discover (and not all will approve) that I do not hold with certain of my colleagues who tell us that literature, in its most valuable and intriguing moments, is "fundamentally non-referential." I may come before you in my jacket and my tie, I may address you as madam and sir, but I am going to request nonetheless that you restrain yourselves from talking about "structure," "form," and "symbols" in my presence. It seems to me that many of you have been intimidated sufficiently by your junior year of college and should be allowed to recover and restore to respectability those interests and enthusiasms that more than likely drew you to reading fiction to begin with and which you oughtn't to be ashamed of now. As an experiment you might even want during the course of this year to try living without any classroom terminology at all, to relinquish "plot" and "character" right along with those very exalted words with which not a few of you like to solemnize your observations, such as "epiphany," "persona," and, of course, "existential" as a modifier of everything existing under the sun. I suggest this in the hope that if you talk about *Madame Bovary* in more or less the same tongue you use with the grocer, or your lover, you may be placed in a more intimate, a more interesting, in what might even be called a more *referential* relationship with Flaubert and his heroine.

In fact, one reason the novels to be read during the first semester are all concerned, to a greater or lesser degree of obsessiveness, with erotic desire is that I thought that readings organized around a subject with which you all have some sort of familiarity might help you even better to locate these books in the world of experience, and further to discourage the temptation to consign them to that manageable netherworld of narrative devices, metaphorical motifs, and mythical archetypes. Above all, I hope that by reading these books you will come to learn something of value about life in one of its most puzzling and maddening aspects. I hope to learn something myself.

All right. This much said by way of stalling, the time has come to begin to disclose the undisclosable—the story of the *professor's* desire. Only I can't, not quite yet, not until I have explained to my own satisfaction, if not to your parents', why I would even think to cast you as my voyeurs and my jurors and my confidants, why I would expose my secrets to people half my age, almost all of whom I have never previously known even as students. Why for me an audience, when most men and women prefer either to keep such matters entirely to themselves or to reveal them only to their most trusted confessors, secular or devout? What makes it compellingly necessary, or at all appropriate, that I present myself to you young strangers in the guise not of your teacher but as the first of this semester's texts?

Permit me to reply with an appeal to the heart.

I love teaching literature. I am rarely ever so contented as when I am here with my pages of notes, and my marked-up texts, and with people like yourselves. To my mind there is nothing quite like the classroom in all of life. Sometimes when we are in the midst of talking—when one of you, say, has pierced with a single phrase right to the heart of the book at hand—I want to cry out, "Dear friends, cherish this!" Why? Because once you have left here people are rarely, if ever, going to talk to you or listen to you the way you talk and listen to one another and to me in this bright and barren little room. Nor is it likely that you will easily find opportunities elsewhere to speak without embarrassment about what has mattered most to men as attuned to life's struggles as were Tolstoy, Mann, and Flaubert. I doubt that you know how very affecting it is to hear you speak thoughtfully and in all earnestness about solitude, illness, longing, loss, suffering, delusion, hope, passion, love, terror, corruption, calamity, and death . . . moving because you are nineteen and twenty years old, from comfortable middle-class homes most of you, and without much debilitating experience in your dossiers yet—but also because, oddly and sadly, this may be the last occasion you will ever have to reflect in any sustained and serious way upon the unrelenting forces with which in time you will all contend, like it or not.

Have I made any clearer why I should find our classroom to be, in fact, the *most* suitable setting for me to make an accounting of my erotic history? Does what I have just said render any more legitimate the claim I should like to make upon your time and patience and tuition? To put it as straight as I can—what a church is to the true believer, a classroom is to me. Some kneel at Sunday prayer, others don phylacteries each dawn . . . and I appear three times each week, my tie around my neck and my watch on my desk, to teach the great stories to you.

Class, oh, students, I have been riding the swell of a very large emotion this year. I'll get to that too. In the meantime, if possible, bear with my mood of capaciousness. Really, I only wish to present you with my credentials for teaching Literature 341. Indiscreet, unprofessional, unsavory as portions of these disclosures will surely strike some of you, I nonetheless would like, with your permission, to go ahead now and give an open account to you of the life I formerly led as a human being. I am devoted to fiction, and I assure you that in time I will tell you whatever I may know about it, but in truth nothing lives in me like my life.

The two pretty young prostitutes are still unattended, still sitting across from me in their white angora sweaters, pastel miniskirts, dark net stockings, and elevating high-heel shoes—rather like children who have ransacked Mamma's closet to dress as usherettes for a pornographic movie house—when I rise with my sheaf of stationery to leave the café.

"A letter to your wife?" says the one who strokes the dog and speaks some English.

I cannot resist the slow curve she has thrown me. "To the children," I say.

She nods to the friend who is stroking her hair: yes, they know my type. At eighteen they know all the types.

Her friend says something in Czech and they have a good laugh.

"Goodbye, sir; nighty-night," says the knowing one, offering a harmless enough smirk for me to carry away from the encounter. I am thought to have gotten my kick by buying two whores a drink. Maybe I did. Fair enough.

In our room I find that Claire has changed into her nightdress and is sleeping now beneath the blankets. A note for me on the pillow: "Dear One—I loved you so much today. I *will* make you happy. C."

Oh, I *have* come through—on my pillow is the proof!

And the sentences in my hands? They hardly seem now to be so laden with implication for my future as they did when I was hurrying back to the hotel from the Old Town Square, dying to get my hands on a piece of paper so as to make *my* report to *my* academy. Folding the pages in two, I put them with the paperbacks at the bottom of my suitcase, there along with Claire's note that promises to make her dear one happy. I feel absolutely triumphant: capacious indeed.

When I am awakened in the early morning by a door slamming beneath our room—down where the Bulgarians are sleeping, one of them no doubt with a little Czech whore and a dachshund puppy—I find I cannot begin to reconstruct the meandering maze of dreams that had so challenged and agitated me throughout the night. I had expected I would sleep marvelously, yet I awaken perspiring and, for those first timeless seconds, with no sense at all of where I am in bed or with whom. Then, blessedly, I find Claire, a big warm animal of my own species, my very own mate of the other gender, and encircling her with my arms—drawing her sheer creatureliness up against the length of my body—I begin to recall the long, abusive episode that had unfolded more or less along these lines:

I am met at the train by a Czech guide. He is called X, "as in the alphabet," he explains. I am sure he is really Herbie Bratasky, our master of ceremonies, but I do nothing to tip my hand. "And what have you seen so far?" asks X as I disembark.

"Why, nothing. I am just arriving."

"Then I have just the thing to start you off. How would you like to meet the whore Kafka used to visit?"

"There is such a person? And she is still alive?"

"How would you like to be taken to talk with her?"

I speak only after I have looked to be sure that no one is eavesdropping. "It is everything I ever hoped for."

"And how was Venice without the Swede?" X asks as we step aboard the cemetery streetcar.

"Dead."

The apartment is four flights up, in a decrepit building by the river. The woman we have come to see is nearly eighty: arthritic hands, slack jowls, white hair, clear and sweet blue eyes. Lives in a rocking chair on the pension of her late husband, an anarchist. I ask myself, "An anarchist's widow receiving a government pension?"

"Was he an anarchist all his life?" I ask.

"From the time he was twelve," X replies. "That was

when his father died. He once explained to me how it happened. He saw his father's dead body, and he thought, 'This man who smiles at me and loves me is no more. Never again will any man smile at me and love me as he did. Wherever I go I will be a stranger and an enemy all my life.' That's how anarchists are made, apparently. I take it you are not an anarchist."

"No. My father and I love each other to this day. I believe in the rule of law."

From the window of the apartment I can see the gliding force of the famous Moldau. "Why, there, boys and girls, at the edge of the river"—I am addressing my class—"is the *piscine* where Kafka and Brod would go swimming together. See, it is as I told you: Franz Kafka was real, Brod was not making him up. And so am I real, nobody is making me up, other than myself."

X and the old woman converse in Czech. X says to me, "I told her that you are a distinguished American authority on the works of the great Kafka. You can ask her whatever you want."

"What did she make of him?" I ask. "How old was he when she knew him? How old was she? When exactly was all this taking place?"

X (interpreting): "She says, 'He came to me and I took a look at him and I thought, "What is this Jewish boy so depressed about?"' She thinks it was in 1916. She says she was twenty-five. Kafka was in his thirties."

"Thirty-three," I say. "Born, class, in 1883. And as we know from all our years of schooling, three from six is three, eight from one doesn't go, so we must borrow one from the preceding digit; eight from eleven is three, eight from eight is zero, and one from one is zero—and that is why thirty-three is the correct answer to the question: How old was Kafka when he paid his visits to this whore? Next question: What, if any, is the relationship between Kafka's whore and today's story, 'The Hunger Artist'?"

X says, "And what else would you like to know?"

"Was he regularly able to have an erection? Could he usually reach orgasm? I find the diaries inconclusive."

Her eyes are expressive when she answers, though the crippled hands lie inert in her lap. In the midst of the indecipherable Czech I catch a word that makes my flesh run: Franz!

X nods gravely. "She says that was no problem. She knew what to do with a boy like him."

Shall I ask? Why not? I have come not just from America, after all, but out of oblivion, to which I shall shortly return. "What was that?"

Matter-of-fact still, she tells X what she did to arouse the author of—"Name Kafka's major works in the order of their composition. Grades will be posted on the department bulletin board. All those who wish recommendations for advanced literary studies will please line up outside my office to be whipped to within an inch of their lives."

X says, "She wants money. American money, not crowns. Give her ten dollars."

I give over the money. What use will it be in oblivion? "No, that will not be on the final."

X waits until she is finished, then translates: "She blew him."

Probably for less than it cost me to find out. There is

such a thing as oblivion, and there is such a thing as fraud, which I am also against. Of course! This woman is nobody, and Bratasky gets half.

"And what did Kafka talk about?" I ask, and yawn to show just how seriously I now take these proceedings.

X translates the old woman's reply word for word: "I don't remember any more. I didn't remember the next day probably. Look, these Jewish boys would sometimes say nothing at all. Like little birds, not even a squeak. I'll tell you one thing, though—they never hit me. And they were clean boys. Clean underwear. Clean collars. They would never dream to come here with so much as a soiled handkerchief. Of course everybody I always would wash with a rag. I was always hygienic. But they didn't even need it. They were clean and they were gentlemen. As God is my witness, they never beat on my backside. Even in bed they had manners."

"But is there anything about Kafka in particular that she remembers? I didn't come here, to her, to Prague, to talk about nice Jewish boys."

She gives some thought to the question; or, more likely, no thought. Just sits there trying out being dead.

"You see, he wasn't so special," she finally says. "I don't mean he wasn't a gentleman. They were all gentlemen."

I say to Herbie (refusing to pretend any longer that he is some Czech named X), "Well, I don't really know what to ask next, Herb. I have the feeling she may have Kafka confused with somebody else."

"The woman's mind is razor-sharp," Herbie replies.

"Still, she's not exactly Brod on the subject."

The aged whore, sensing perhaps that I have had it, speaks again.

Herbie says, "She wants to know if you would like to inspect her pussy."

"To what possible end?" I reply.

"Shall I inquire?"

"Oh, please do."

Eva (for this, Herbie claims, is the lady's name) replies at length. "She submits that it might hold some literary interest for you. Others like yourself, who have come to her because of her relationship with Kafka, have been most anxious to see it, and, providing of course that their credentials established them as serious, she has been willing to show it to them. She says that because you are here on my recommendation she would be delighted to allow you to have a quick look."

"I thought she only blew him. Really, Herb, of what possible interest could her pussy be to me? You know I am not in Prague alone."

Translation: "Again, she frankly admits she doesn't know of what interest anything about her is to anyone. She says she is grateful for the little money she is able to make from her friendship with young Franz, and she is flattered that her callers are themselves distinguished and learned men. Of course, if the gentleman does not care to examine it—"

But why not? Why come to the battered heart of Europe if not to examine just this? Why come into the world at all? "Students of literature, you must conquer your squeamishness once and for all! You must face the unseemly thing itself! You must come off your high horse! There, *there* is your final exam."

It would cost me five more American dollars. "This is a flourishing business, this Kafka business," I say.

"First of all, given your field of interest, the money is tax-deductible. Second, for only a fiver, you are striking a decisive blow against the Bolsheviks. She is one of the last in Prague still in business for herself. Third, you are helping preserve a national literary monument—you are doing a service for our suffering writers. And last but not least, think of the money you have given to Klinger. What's five more to the cause?"

"I beg your pardon. What cause?"

"Your happiness. We only want to make you happy, to make you finally you, David dear. You have denied yourself too much as it is."

Despite her arthritic hands Eva is able on her own to tug her dress up until it is bunched in her lap. Herbie, however, has to hold her around with one arm, shift her on her buttocks, and draw down her underpants for her. I reluctantly help by steadying the rocking chair.

Accordioned kidskin belly, bare ruined shanks, and, astonishingly, a triangular black patch, pasted on like a mustache. I find myself rather doubting the authenticity of the pubic hair.

"She would like to know," says Herbie, "if the gentleman would care to touch it."

"And how much does that go for?"

Herbie repeats my question in Czech. Then to me, with a courtly bow, "Her treat."

"Thanks, no."

But again she assures the gentleman that it will cost him nothing. Again the gentleman courteously declines.

Now Eva smiles—between her parted lips, her tongue, still red. The pulp of the fruit, still red!

"Herb, what did she say just then?"

"Don't think I ought to repeat it, not to you."

"What was it, Herbie? I demand to know!"

"Something indecent," he says, chuckling, "about what Kafka liked the most. His big thrill."

"*What was it?*"

"Oh, I don't think your dad would want you to hear that, Dave. Or your dad's dad, and so on, all the way back to the Father of the Faithful and the Friend of God. Besides, it may just have been a malicious remark, gratuitously made, with no foundation in fact. She may only have said it because you insulted her. You see, by refusing to touch a finger to her famous vizz you have cast doubt—perhaps not entirely inadvertently either—on the very meaning of her life. Moreover, she is afraid you will go back to America now and tell your colleagues that she is a fraud. And then serious scholars will no longer come to pay their respects—which, of course, would mark the end for her, and if I may say so, the end too for private enterprise in our country. It would constitute nothing less than the final victory of the Bolsheviks over free men."

"Well, except for this new Czech routine of yours—which, I have to admit, could have fooled just about anybody but me—you haven't changed, Bratasky, not a bit."

"Too bad I can't say the same about you."

Here Herbie approaches the old woman, her face now sadly tear-streaked, and cupping his fingers as though to catch the trickle of a stream, he places his hands between her bare legs.

"Coo," she gurgles. "Coo. Coo." And closing her blue eyes, she rubs her cheek against Herbie's shoulder. The tip of her tongue I see protruding from her mouth. The pulp of the fruit, still red.

Upon returning from our travels through the beautiful cities—after I dreamed in Prague of visiting Kafka's whore, we flew the next morning to Paris, and three days later to Bruges, where at a conference on modern European literature I read the paper entitled "Hunger Art" —we decide to split the rent on a small house in the country for July and August. How better to spend the summer? But once the decision is made, all I can think about is the time I last lived in daily proximity to a woman, the tomb-like months just before the Hong Kong fiasco, when neither of us could so much as bear the sight of the other's shoes on the floor of the closet. Consequently, before I sign the lease for the perfect little house that we've found, I suggest that probably it would be best not to sublet either of our apartments in the city for the two months—a small financial sacrifice, true, but this way there will always be a place to retreat to if anything untoward should happen. I actually say "untoward." Claire—prudent, patient, tender Claire—understands well enough what I mean as I jabber on in this vein, the pen in my hand, and the agent who drew up the lease casting unamused glances from the other end of his office. Raised by heavyweight battlers from the day she was born until she was able to leave for school and a life of her own, an independent young woman now since the age of seventeen, she has no argument against having a nest to fly off to, as well as the nest that is to be shared, for so long as the sharing is good. No, we won't rent our apartments, she agrees. Whereupon, with the solemnity of the Japanese Commander-in-Chief sitting down aboard MacArthur's battleship to surrender an empire, I affix my signature to the lease.

A small, two-storied white clapboard farmhouse, then, set halfway up a hillside of dandelions and daisies from a silent, untraveled rural road, and twenty miles north of the Catskill village where I was raised. I have chosen Sullivan County over Cape Cod, and that too is fine with Claire—proximity to the Vineyard and to Olivia seems not to matter to her quite the way it did just the year before. And for me the gentle green hills and distant green mountains beyond the dormer windows take me back to the bedroom vista of my childhood—exactly my view from the room at the top of the "Annex"—and augment the sense I already have with her that I am living at last in accordance with my true spirit, that, indeed, I am "home."

And for the spirit what a summer it is! From the daily regimen of swimming in the morning and hiking in the afternoon we each grow more and more fit, while within, day by day, we grow fat as our farmer neighbor's hogs. How the spirit feasts on just getting up in the morning! on coming to in a whitewashed sunlit room with my arms encircling her large, substantial form. Oh, how I do love the size of her in bed! That *tangibility* of hers! And the weight of those breasts in my hands! Oh, very different, this, from all the months and months of waking up with nothing to hold on to but my pillow!

Later—is it not yet eleven? *really*? we have eaten our cinnamon toast, taken our dip, stopped in town to buy food for dinner, brooded over the newspaper's front page, and it is only ten-fifteen?—later, from the rocker on the porch where I do my morning writing, I watch her toil in the garden. Two spiral notebooks are arranged beside me. In one I work at planning the projected book on Kafka, to be called, after my Bruges lecture, *Hunger Art,* while in the other, whose pages I approach with far greater eagerness—and where I am having somewhat more success—I move on to the substance of the lecture whose prologue I had begun composing in the hotel café in Prague, the story of *my* life in its most puzzling and maddening aspects, *my* chronicle of the iniquitous, the ungovernable and the thrilling . . . or (by way of a working title), "How David Kepesh comes to be sitting in a wicker rocker on a screened-in porch in the Catskill Mountains, watching with contentment while a teetotaling twenty-five-year-old sixth-grade teacher from Schenectady, New York, creeps about her flower garden in what appear to be overalls handed down from Tom Sawyer himself, her hair tied back with a snip of green twister seal cut from the coil with which she stakes the swooning begonias, her delicate, innocent Mennonite face, small and intelligent as a raccoon's, and soil-smudged as though in preparation for Indian night at the Girl Scout jamboree—and his happiness in her hands."

"Why don't you come out and help with the weeds?" she calls—"Tolstoy would have." "He was a big-time novelist," I say; "they have to do that sort of thing, to gain Experience. Not me. For me it's enough to see you crawling on your knees." "Well, whatever pleases," she says.

Ah, Clarissa, let me tell you, all that *is* pleases. The pond where we swim. Our apple orchard. The thunderstorms. The barbecue. The music playing. Talking in bed. Your grandmother's iced tea. Deliberating on which walk to take in the morning and which at dusk. Watching you lower your head to peel peaches and shuck corn . . . Oh, nothing, really, is what pleases. But what nothing! Nations go to war for this kind of nothing, and in the absence of such nothing, people shrivel up and die.

Of course by now the passion between us is no longer quite what it was on those Sundays when we would cling together in my bed until three in the afternoon—"the primrose path to madness," as Claire once described those rapacious exertions which end finally with the two of us rising on the legs of weary travelers to change the bed linens, to stand embracing beneath the shower, and then to go out of doors to get some air before the winter sun goes down. That, once begun, our lovemaking should have continued with undiminished intensity for almost a year—that two industrious, responsible, idealistic schoolteachers should have adhered to one another like dumb sea creatures, and, at the moment of overbrimming, have come to the very brink of tearing flesh with cannibalized jaws—well, that is somewhat more than I ever would have dared predict for myself, having already served beyond the call of duty—having already staked so much and lost so much—under the tattered scarlet standard of His Royal Highness, my lust.

Leveling off. Overheated frenzy subsiding into quiet physical affection. That is how I choose to describe what is happening to our passion during this blissful summer. Can I think otherwise—can I possibly believe that, rather than coming to rest on some warm plateau of sweet coziness and intimacy, I am being eased down a precipitous incline and as yet am nowhere near the cold and lonely cavern where I finally will touch down? To be sure, the faintly brutal element has taken it on the lam; gone is the admixture of the merciless with the tender, those intimations of utter subjugation that one sees in the purplish bruise, the wantonness one thrills to in the coarse word breathed at the peak of pleasure. We no longer *succumb* to desire, nor do we touch each other everywhere, paw and knead and handle with that unquenchable lunacy so alien to what and who we otherwise are. True, I am no longer a little bit of a beast, she is no longer a little bit of a tramp, neither any longer is quite the greedy lunatic, the depraved child, the steely violator, the helplessly impaled. Teeth, once blades and pincers, the pain-inflicting teeth of little cats and dogs, are simply teeth again, and tongues are tongues, and limbs are limbs. Which is, as we all know, how it must be.

And I for one will not quarrel, or sulk, or yearn, or despair. I will not make a religion of what is fading away —of my craving for that bowl into which I dip my face as though to extract the last dram of a syrup I cannot guzzle down fast enough . . . of the harsh excitement of that pumping grip so strong, so rapid, so unyielding, that if I do not moan that there is nothing left of me, that I am stupefied and numb, she will, in that stirring state of fervor bordering on heartlessness, continue until she has milked the very life from my body. I will not make a religion of the marvelous sight of her half-stripped. No, I intend to nurse no illusions about the chance for a great revival of the drama we would seem very nearly to have played out, this clandestine, uncensored, underground theater of four furtive selves—the two who pant in performance, the two who pantingly watch—wherein regard for the hygienic, the temperate, and the time of day or night is all so much ridiculous intrusion. I tell you, I am a new man—that is, I am a *new* man no longer—and I know when my number is up: now just stroking the soft, long hair will do, just resting side by side in our bed each morning will do, awakening folded together, mated, in love. Yes, I am willing to settle on these terms. This will suffice. No more *more*.

And before whom am I on my knees trying to strike such a bargain? Who is to decide how far from Claire I am going to slide? Honored members of Literature 341, you would think, as I do, that it would, it should, it must, be me.

Late in the afternoon of one of the loveliest days of August, with nearly fifty such days already stored away in memory and the deep contentment of knowing that there are still a couple dozen more to come, on an afternoon when my feeling of well-being is boundless and I cannot imagine anyone happier or luckier than myself, I receive a visit from my former wife. I will think about it for days afterward, imagining each time the phone rings or I hear the sound of a car turning up the steep drive to the house that it is Helen returning. I will expect to find a letter from her every morning, or rather a letter about her, informing me that she has run off again to Hong Kong, or that she is dead. When I awaken in the middle of the night to remember how once I lived and how I live now—and this still happens to me, too regularly—I will cling to my sleeping partner as though it is she who is ten years my senior—twenty, thirty years my senior—rather than the other way around.

I am out by the orchard in a canvas lounge chair, my legs in the sun and my head in the shade, when I hear the phone ringing inside the house, where Claire is getting ready to go swimming. I have not yet decided—of such decisions are my days composed—whether I'll go along with her to the pond, or just stay on quietly doing my work until it is time to water the marigolds and open the wine. Since lunch I have been out here—just myself, the bumblebees, and the butterflies, and, from time to time, Claire's old Labrador, Dazzle—reading Colette and taking notes for the course known by now around the house as Desire 341. Leafing through a pile of her books, I have been wondering if there has ever been in America a novelist with a point of view toward the taking and giving of pleasure even vaguely resembling Colette's, an American writer, man or woman, stirred as deeply as she is by scent and warmth and color, someone as sympathetic to the range of the body's urgings, as attuned to the world's every sensuous offering, a connoisseur of the finest gradations of amorous feeling, who is nonetheless immune to fanaticism of any sort, except, as with Colette, a fanatical devotion to the self's honorable survival. Hers seems to have been a nature exquisitely susceptible to all that desire longs for and promises—"these pleasures which are lightly called physical"—yet wholly untainted by puritan conscience, or murderous impulse, or megalomania, or sinister ambitions, or the score-settling rage of class or social grievance. One thinks of her as egotistic, in the sharpest, crispest sense of the word, the most pragmatic of sensualists, her capacity for protective self-scrutiny in perfect balance with the capacity to be carried away—

The top sheet of my yellow pad is spattered and crisscrossed with the fragmentary beginnings of a lecture outline—running down one margin is a long list of modern novelists, European as well as American, among whom Colette's decent, robust, bourgeois paganism still seems to me unique—when Claire comes out of the kitchen's screen door, wearing her bathing suit and carrying her white terry-cloth robe over her arm.

The book in her hand is Musil's *Young Törless*, the copy I'd just finished marking up the night before. How delighted I am with her curiosity about these books I will be teaching! And to look up at the swell of her breasts above the bikini's halter, well, that is yet another of this wonderful day's satisfactions.

"Tell me," I say, taking hold of the calf of her nearest leg, "why is there no American Colette? Or could it be Updike who comes the closest? It's surely not Henry Miller. It's surely not Hawthorne."

"A phone call for you," she says. "Helen Kepesh.".

"My God." I look at my watch, for all the help that

will give. "What time would it be in California? What can she want? How did she find me?"

"It's a local call."

"*Is* it?"

"I think so, yes."

I haven't yet moved from the chair. "And that's what she said, Helen *Kepesh*?"

"Yes."

"But I thought she'd taken her own name back."

Claire shrugs.

"You told her I was here?"

"Do you want me to tell her you aren't?"

"What can she *want*?"

"You'll have to ask her," says Claire. "Or maybe you won't."

"Would it be so very wrong of me just to go in there and put the phone back on the hook?"

"Not wrong," says Claire. "Only unduly anxious."

"But I *feel* unduly anxious. I feel unduly *happy*. This is all so perfect." I spread ten fingers across the soft swell of flesh above her halter. "Oh, my dear, dear pal."

"I'll wait out here," she says.

"And I *will* go swimming with you."

"Okay. Good."

"So wait!"

It would be neither cruel nor cowardly, I tell myself, looking down at the phone on the kitchen table—it would just be the most sensible thing I could do. Except, of the half-dozen people closest to my life, Helen happens still to be one. "Hello," I say.

"Hello. Oh, hello. Look, I feel odd about phoning you,

David. I almost didn't. Except I seem to be in your town. We're at the Texaco station; across from a real-estate office."

"I see."

"I'm afraid it was just too hard driving off without even calling. How are you?"

"How did you know I was staying here?"

"I tried you in New York a few days ago. I called the college, and the department secretary said she wasn't authorized to give out your summer address. I said I was a former student and I was sure you wouldn't mind. But she was adamant about Professor Kepesh's privacy. Quite a moat, that lady."

"So how did you find me?"

"I called the Schonbrunns."

"My, my."

"But stopping off here for gas is really just accidental. Strange, I know, but true. And not as strange, after all, as the truly strange things that happen."

She is lying and I'm not charmed. Through the window I can see Claire holding the unopened book in her hand. We could already be in the car on the way down to the pond.

"What do you want, Helen?"

"You mean from you? Nothing; nothing at all. I'm married now."

"I didn't know."

"That's what I was doing in New York. We were visiting my husband's family. We're on our way to Vermont. They have a summer house there." She laughs; a very appealing laugh. It makes me remember her in bed. "Can you believe I've never been to New England?"

"Well," I say, "it's not exactly Rangoon."

"Neither is Rangoon any more."

"How is your health? I heard that you were pretty sick."

"I'm better now. I had a hard time for a while. But it's over. How are *you*?"

"My hard time is over too."

"I'd like to see you, if I could. Are we that far from your house? I'd like to talk to you, just for a little—"

"About what?"

"I owe you some explanations."

"You don't. No more than I owe you any. I think we'd both be better off at this late date without the explanations."

"I was mad, David, I was going crazy— David, these are difficult things to say surrounded by cans of motor oil."

"Then don't say them."

"I have to."

Out on my chair, Claire is now leafing through the *Times*.

"You better go swimming without me," I say. "Helen's coming here; with her husband."

"She's married?"

"So she says."

"Why *was* it Helen 'Kepesh' then?"

"Probably to identify herself to you. To me."

"Or to herself," says Claire. "Would you rather I weren't here?"

"Of course not. I meant I thought you'd *prefer* going swimming."

"Only if *you* prefer—"

"No, absolutely not."

"Where are they now?"

"Down in town."

"She came all this way—? I don't understand. What if we hadn't been at home?"

"She says they're on their way to his family's house in Vermont."

"They didn't take the Thruway?"

"Honey, what's happened to you? No, they didn't take the Thruway. Maybe they're taking the back roads for the scenery. What's the difference? They'll come and they'll go. You were the one who told *me* not to be unduly anxious."

"But I wouldn't want you to be hurt."

"Don't worry. If that's why you're staying—"

Here suddenly she stands, and at the edge of tears (where I have never before seen her!) she says, "Look, you so *obviously* want me out of the way—" Quickly she starts toward where our car is parked on the other side of the house, in the dust bowl by the old collapsing barn. And I run after her, just behind the dog, who thinks it is all a game.

Consequently we are beside the barn, waiting together, when the Lowerys arrive. As their car makes its way up the long dirt drive to the house, Claire slips her terry-cloth robe on over her bathing suit. I am wearing a pair of corduroy shorts, a faded old T-shirt, battered sneakers, an outfit I've probably had since Syracuse. Helen will have no trouble recognizing me. But will I recognize her? Can I explain to Claire—should I have?—that really, all I want is to *see* . . .

I had heard that, on top of all her debilitating ailments,

she had gained some twenty pounds. If so, she has by now lost all that weight, and a bit more. She emerges from the car looking exactly like herself. She is paler-complexioned than I remember—or rather, she is not pale in the cleansed, Quakerish way to which I am now accustomed. Helen's pallor is luminous, transparent. Only in the thinness of her arms and neck is there any indication that she has been through a bad time with her health, and, what is more, is now a woman in her mid-thirties. Otherwise, she is the Stunning Creature once again.

Her husband shakes my hand. I had been expecting someone taller and older—I suppose one usually does. Lowery has a close-cropped black beard, round tortoiseshell glasses, and a compact, powerful, athletic build. Both are dressed in jeans and sandals and colored polo shirts and have their hair cut in the Prince Valiant style. The only jewelry either wears is a wedding ring. All of which tells me practically nothing. Maybe the emeralds are home in the vault.

We walk around as though they are prospective buyers who have been sent up by the real-estate agent to look at the house; as though they are the new couple from down the road who have stopped by to introduce themselves; as though they are what they are—ex-wife with new husband, someone now meaning nothing, artifact of relatively little remaining historical interest uncovered during an ordinary day's archaeological excavation. Yes, giving her the directions to our so perfect lair turns out to have been neither a foolish nor, God knows, a *dangerous* mistake. Otherwise, how would I have known that I have been wholly de-Helenized too, that the woman can neither harm me nor charm me, that I am unbewitchable by all but the most loving and benign of feminine spirits. How right Claire was to caution me against being unduly anxious; before, of course, she went ahead and—doubtless because of my own confusion upon hanging up the phone—became unduly anxious herself.

Claire is up ahead now with Les Lowery. They are headed toward the blackened, ruined oak tree at the edge of the woods. Early in the summer, during a dramatic daylong storm, the tree was struck by lightning and severed in two. While we all walked together around the house and through the garden, Claire had been talking, just a little feverishly, about the wild thunderstorms of early July; a little feverishly, and a little childishly. I had not imagined beforehand just how ominous Helen would seem to her, given the tales of her troublemaking that I have told; I suppose I had not realized how often I must have told them to her in the first months we were together. No wonder she has latched on to the quiet husband, who does in fact seem closer to her in age and spirit, and who, it turns out, is also a subscriber to *Natural History* and the *Audubon Magazine*. Some minutes earlier, on the porch, she had identified for the Lowerys the unusual Cape Cod seashells arranged in a wicker tray in the center of the dining table, between the antique pewter candlesticks that were her grandmother's gift upon her graduation from college.

While my mate and her mate are examining the burned-out trunk of the oak tree, Helen and I drift back to the porch. She is telling me all about him, still. He is a lawyer, a mountain climber, a skier, he is divorced, has two adolescent daughters; in partnership with an architect he has already made a small fortune as a housing developer; lately he has been in the news for the work he has been doing as investigating counsel for a California State Legislature committee unraveling connections between organized crime and the Marin County Police . . . Outside I see that Lowery has moved past the oak tree and onto the path that cuts up through the woods to the steep rock formations that Claire has been photographing all summer. Claire and Dazzle appear to be headed back down to the house.

I say to Helen, "He looks a bit young to be *such* a Karenin."

"I'm sure I'd be sardonic too," she replies, "if I were you and thought I was still me. I was surprised you even came to the phone. But that's because you are a nice man. You always were, actually."

"Oh, Helen, what's going on here? Save the 'nice man' stuff for my tombstone. You may have a new life, but this lingo . . ."

"I had a lot of time to think when I was sick. I thought about—"

But I don't want to know. "Tell me," I say, interrupting her, "how was your conversation with the Schonbrunns?"

"I spoke to Arthur. She wasn't home."

"And how did he take hearing from you after all this time?"

"Oh, he took it quite well."

"Frankly I'm surprised he offered assistance. I'm surprised you asked him for it. As I remember, he was never a great fan of yours—nor you of theirs."

"Arthur and I have changed our minds about each other."

"Since when? You used to be very funny about him."

"I'm not any more. I don't ridicule people who admit what they want. Or at least admit to what they don't have."

"And what does Arthur want? Are you telling me that all along Arthur wanted *you*?"

"I don't know about all along."

"Oh, Helen, I find this hard to believe."

"I never heard anything easier to believe."

"And what exactly is it I'm supposed to be believing, again?"

"When we two got back from Hong Kong, when you moved out and I was alone, he telephoned one night and asked if he could come over to talk. He was very concerned about you. So he came from his office—it was about nine—and he talked about your unhappiness for nearly an hour. I said finally that I didn't know what any of it had to do with me any more, and then he asked if he and I might meet in San Francisco for lunch one day. I said I didn't know, I was feeling pretty miserable myself, and he kissed me. And then he made me sit down and he sat down and he explained to me in detail that he hadn't expected to do that, and that it didn't mean what I thought it meant. He was happily married still, and after all these years he still had a strong physical relationship with Debbie, and in fact he owed her his whole life. And then he told me a harrowing story about some crazy girl, some librarian he had almost married in Minnesota, and how she had once gone after him with a fork at breakfast and stabbed his hand. He'd never gotten over what might have happened to him if he had caved in and married her

—he thinks it actually might have ended in a murder. He showed me the scar from the fork. He said his salvation was meeting Debbie, and that he owes everything he's accomplished to her devotion and love. Then he tried to kiss me again, and when I said I didn't think it was a good idea, he told me I was perfectly right and that he had misjudged me completely and he still wanted to have lunch with me. I really couldn't take any more confusion, so I said yes. He arranged for us to eat at a place in Chinatown where, I assure you, nobody he knew or I knew or *anybody* knew could possibly see us together. And that was it. But then that summer, when they moved East, he began writing letters. I still get them, every few months or so."

"Go on. What do they say?"

"Oh, they're awfully well-written," she says, smiling. "He must write some of those sentences ten times over before he's completely satisfied. I think they may be the kind of letters the poetry editor of the college magazine writes late at night to his girl friend at Smith. 'The weather, as clear and as sharp as a fish spine,' and so on. And sometimes he includes lines from great poems about Venus, Cleopatra, and Helen of Troy."

" 'Lo, this is she that was the world's desire.' "

"That's right—that's one of them. I thought it was a bit insulting, actually. Except I suppose it can't be because it's so 'great.' Anyway, he always somehow or other lets me know that I don't have to answer; so I don't. Why are you smiling? It's really rather sweet. Well, it's *something*. Who'da thunk it?"

"I smile," I say, "because I've had my own Schonbrunn letters—from her."

"Now, *that's* hard to believe."

"No, not if you saw them. No great lines of poetry for me."

Claire is still some fifty or so feet away, yet both of us stop speaking as she makes her way back to the house. Why? Who knows why!

And if only we hadn't! Why didn't I just talk nonsense, tell a joke, *recite* a poem, *anything* so that Claire hadn't to come through the screen door into this conspiratorial silence. Hadn't to come in to see me sitting across from Helen, charmed in spite of myself.

Immediately she becomes stony—and reaches a deci-. sion. "I'm going swimming."

"What's happened to Les?" asks Helen.

"Took a walk."

"You sure you don't want some iced tea?" I ask Claire. "Why don't we all have some iced tea?"

"No. Bye." That single adolescent syllable of farewell for the guest, then she's gone.

From where I am sitting I am able to watch our car pass down the hill to the road. What does Claire think we are plotting? What *are* we plotting?

Says Helen, when the car is out of sight, "She's terribly sweet."

"And I'm a 'nice man,' " I say.

"I'm sorry if I upset your friend by coming here. I didn't mean to."

"She'll be all right. She's a strong girl."

"And I mean you no harm. That isn't why I wanted to see you."

I am silent.

"I did mean you harm once, that's true," she says.

"You weren't solely responsible for the misery."

"What you did to me you did without wanting to; you did because you were provoked. But I think now that I actually set out to torture you."

"You're rewriting history, Helen. It's not necessary. We tormented each other, all right, but it wasn't out of malice. It was confusion, and it was ignorance, and it was other things too, but had it been malice, we wouldn't have been together for very long."

"I used to burn that fucking toast on purpose."

"As I remember, it was the fucking eggs that were burned. The fucking toast never got put in."

"I used to not mail your letters on purpose."

"Why are you saying these things? To castigate yourself, to somehow absolve yourself, or just to try to get a rise out of me? Even if it's true, I don't want to know it. That's all dead."

"I just always hated so the ways that people killed their time. I had this grand life all planned out, you see."

"I remember."

"Well, that's all dead too. Now I take what I can get, and I'm grateful to have it."

"Oh, don't overdo the 'chastened' bit, if that's what this is. Mr. Lowery doesn't sound like the scrapings to me. He doesn't look it, either. He looks like a very forceful person who knows what he's about. He sounds like somebody to conjure with, taking on the Mafia *and* the police. He sounds like a rather courageous man of the world. Just right for you. It certainly looks like he agrees with you."

213

"Does it?"

"You look terrific," I say—and am sorry I said it. So why then do I add, "You look marvelous."

For the first time since Claire came onto the porch, we fall silent again. We look unflinchingly at one another, as though we are strangers who dare, finally, to stare openly and unambiguously—the prelude to leaping precipitously into the most shameless and exciting copulation. I suppose there is no way we can avoid a little—if not a little more than a little—flirtation. Maybe I ought to say that. And then again, maybe I ought not. Maybe I ought just to look away.

"What were you sick with?" I ask.

"Sick with? It seemed like everything. I must have seen fifty doctors. All I did was sit in waiting rooms and have X-rays taken and blood taken and have cortisone injections and wait around drugstores to have prescriptions filled, and then bolt down the pills, hoping they'd save me on the spot. You should have seen my medicine chest. Instead of Countess Olga's lovely creams and lotions, vials and vials of hideous little pills—and none of them did a thing, except to ruin my stomach. My nose wouldn't stop running for over a year. I sneezed for hours on end, I couldn't breathe, my face puffed up, my eyes itched all the time, and then I began breaking out in horrible rashes. I'd pray when I went to sleep that they'd just go away the way they came, that they'd be gone for good in the morning. One allergist told me to move to Arizona, another told me it wouldn't help because it was all in my head, and another explained in great detail to me how I was allergic to myself, or something very like that, and so I went home and got into bed and pulled the covers over my face and daydreamed about having all the blood drawn out of me and replaced by somebody else's blood, blood I could get through the rest of my life with. I nearly went crazy. Some mornings I wanted to throw myself out the window."

"But you did get better."

"I began seeing Les," Helen says. "That's how it seems to have happened. The ailments all began to subside, one by one. I didn't know how he could bear me. I was hideous."

"Probably not so hideous as you thought. It sounds as though he fell in love with you."

"After I got well I got frightened. I thought that without him I'd start getting sick again. And start drinking again—because somehow he even got me to stop that. I said to him the night he first came to pick me up, looking so strong and cocky and butch, I said, 'Look, Mr. Lowery, I'm thirty-four years old, and I'm sick as a dog, and I don't like to be buggered.' And he said, 'I know how old you are, and everybody gets sick some time, and buggering doesn't interest me.' And so we went out, and he was so marvelously sure of himself, and he fell in love with me—and of course in love with rescuing me. But I didn't love him. And I wanted time and again to be finished with him. Only when it was over, when it should have been over, I got so frightened . . . So we were married."

I don't reply. I look away.

"I'm going to have a baby," she says.

"Congratulations. When?"

"Soon as I can. You see, I don't care any more about being happy. I've given that up. All I care about is not being tortured. I'll do anything. I'll have ten babies, I'll have twenty if he wants them. And he might. There is a man, David, who has no doubts about himself at all. He had a wife and two children even while he was in law school—he was already in the housing business in law school—and now he wants a second family, with me. And I'll do it. What else *can* she do, who was once the world's desire? Own a smart little antique shop? Be one of those fading beauties? Take a degree and go out and run something? Be one of those fading beauties?"

"If you can't be twenty years old and sailing past the junks at sunset . . . But we have had that discussion. It's no longer my business."

"What about your business? Will you marry Miss Ovington?"

"I might."

"What holds you back?"

I don't answer.

"She's young, she's pretty, she's intelligent, she's educated, and under that robe she seemed quite lovely. And as a bonus there's something childlike and innocent that I certainly never had. Something that knows how to be content, I would think. How do they get that way, do you know? How do they get so *good*? I wondered if she wouldn't be like that. Bright and pretty and good. Leslie is bright and pretty and good. Oh, David, how do you stand it?"

"Because I'm bright and pretty and good myself."

"No, my dear old comrade, not the way they are. They

come by it naturally, naïvely. Resist as you will, it's not quite the same, not even for a master repressive like yourself. You're not one of them, and you're not poor Arthur Schonbrunn, either."

I don't reply.

"Doesn't she drive you even a little crazy being so bright and pretty and good?" asks Helen. "With her seashells and her flower bed and her doggie, and her recipes tacked up over the sink?"

"Is this what you came here to tell me, Helen?"

"No. It isn't. Of course it isn't. I didn't come here to say *any* of these things. You're a bright fellow—you know very well why I came. To show you my husband. To show you how I've changed, for the better, of course; and . . . and other assorted lies. I thought I might even fool myself. David, I came here because I wanted to talk to a friend, strange as that may sound right now. I sometimes think of you as the only friend I've got left. I did when I was sick. Isn't that odd? I almost called you one night—but I knew I was none of your business now. You see, I'm pregnant. I want you to tell me something. Tell me what you think I should do. Somebody has to. I'm two months pregnant, and if I wait any longer, well, then I'll have to go ahead and have it. And I can't stand him any more. But then I can't stand anyone. Everything everyone says is somehow wrong and drives me crazy. I don't mean I argue with people. I wouldn't dare. I listen and I nod and I smile. You should see how I please people these days. I listen to Les, and I nod and I smile, and I think I'll die of boredom. There's nothing he does now that doesn't irritate me nearly to death. But I can't be sick alone like that ever again. I couldn't take it. I can take loneliness, and I can take physical misery too, but I can't take them together like that ever again. It was too horrid and too relentless, and I haven't courage any more. I seem to have used it all up; inside me I feel there's no courage left. I have to have this baby. I have to tell him I'm pregnant—and have it. Because if I don't, I don't know what will happen to me. I can't leave him. I'm too terrified to be sick again like that, itching to death, unable to breathe—and it doesn't help to be told it's all in one's head, because that doesn't make it go away. Only he does. Yes, *he* made it all go away! Oh, this is all so crazy. None of this had to be! Because if that wife of Jimmy's had been run down when he had it all arranged, that would have been it. I would have had what I wanted. And I wouldn't have thought twice about her, either. Like it or not, that's the truth about me. I wouldn't have had a moment's stinking guilt. I would have been happy. And she would have gotten what she deserved. But instead I was good—and she's made them *both* miserable. I refused to be terrible, and the result is this terrible unhappiness. Each night I toss in my bed with the nightmare of how much I don't love *anybody*."

At last, at long last, I see Lowery coming out of the woods and descending the hill toward the house. He has removed his shirt and is carrying it in his hand. He is a strong and handsome young man, he is a great success in the world, and his presence in her life has somehow restored her to health . . . Only it is Helen's bad luck that she cannot stand him. Still Jimmy—still those dreams of what might and should have been, if only moral repugnance had not intervened.

"Maybe I'll love the baby," she says.

"Maybe you will," I say. "That happens sometimes."

"Then again, I may despise my baby," says Helen, sternly rising to greet her husband. "I would imagine that happens sometimes too."

After they leave—just like the new couple from down the road, with smiles and good wishes all around—I get into my bathing suit and walk the mile along our road to the pond. I have no thoughts and no feelings, I am numb, like someone at the perimeter of a terrible accident or explosion, who gets a brief, startling glimpse of a pool of blood, and then goes on his way, unharmed, to continue with the ordinary activities of the day.

Some small children are playing with shovels and pails at the edge of the pond, overseen by Claire's dog and by a mother's helper, who looks up and says "Hi." The girl is reading, of all things, *Jane Eyre*. Claire's terry-cloth robe is on the rock where we always put our things, and then I locate Claire, sunning herself out on the raft.

When I pull myself up beside her I see that she has been crying.

"I'm sorry I acted like that," she says.

"Don't be, don't be. We were both thrown way off. I don't believe those things can ever work out very well."

She begins to cry again, as noiselessly as it is possible to cry. The first of her tears that I've seen.

"What is it, lovely, what?"

"I feel so lucky. I feel so privileged. I love you. You've become my whole life."

"I have?"

This makes her laugh. "It frightens you a little to hear

it. I guess it would. I didn't think it was true, till today. But I've never been happy like this before."

"Clarissa, why are you still so upset? There's no reason to be, is there?"

Turning her face into the raft, she mumbles something about her mother and father.

"I can't hear you, Claire."

"I wanted them to visit."

I'm surprised, but say, "Then invite them."

"I did."

"When was that?"

"It doesn't matter. It's just that I thought—well, I didn't think."

"You wrote them? Explain yourself, please. I'd like to know what's wrong."

"I don't want to go into it. It was foolish and dreamy. I lost my head a little."

"You telephoned them."

"Yes."

"When?"

"Before."

"You mean after you left the house? Before you came down here?"

"Down in town, yes."

"And?"

"I should never phone them without warning. I never do. It never works and it never will. But at night when we're having dinner, when we're so content and everything is so peaceful and lovely, I always start to think about them. I put on a record, and start cooking dinner, and there they are."

I hadn't known. She never speaks of what she does not

have, never lingers for so much as a moment upon loss, misfortune, or disappointment. You'd have to torture her to get her to complain. She is the most extraordinary ordinary person I have ever known.

"Oh," she says, pushing up to a sitting position, "oh, this day will be fine when it's over. Do you have any idea when that will be?"

"Claire, do you want to stay out here with me, or do you want to be alone, or do you want to swim, or do you want to come home and have some iced tea and a little rest?"

"They're gone?"

"Oh, they're gone."

"And you're all right?"

"I'm intact. An hour or so older, but intact."

"How was it?"

"Not all that pleasant. You didn't take to her, I know, but the woman is in a bad way . . . Look, we don't have to talk about this now. We don't have to talk about it ever. Do you want to go home?"

"Not just yet," says Claire. She dives off the edge of the raft, remains out of sight for a long count of ten, and then surfaces by the ladder. When she sits back down beside me, she says, "There's one thing we'd better talk about now. One more thing I had better say. I was pregnant. I wasn't going to tell you, but I will."

"Pregnant by whom? When?"

A wan smile. "In Europe, love. By you. I found out for sure when we got home. I had an abortion. Those meetings I went to—well, I went to the hospital for the day."

"And the 'infection'?"

"I didn't have an infection."

Helen is two months pregnant, and I am the only person who knows. Claire has been pregnant, by me, and I've known nothing. I sense something very sad, all right, at the bottom of this day's confidences and secrets, but what it is I am too weak right now to fathom. Indeed, worn down more than I had thought from all that has surrounded Helen's visit, I am ready to think it is something about me that makes for the sadness; about how I have always failed to be what people want or expect; how I have never quite pleased anyone, including myself; how, hard as I have tried, I have seemed never quite able to be one thing or the other, and probably never will be . . . "Why did you do this alone?" I ask her. "Why didn't you tell me?"

"Well, it was just at the moment you were letting yourself go, and I thought that had to happen by itself. You were surrendering to something, and it always had to be clear to both of us exactly what it was. Is *that* clear?"

"But you did want to have it."

"The abortion?"

"No, the child."

"I want to have a child, of course. I want to have one with you—I can't imagine having anyone else's. But not until you're ready to with me."

"And when did you do all this, Claire? How could I *not* know it?"

"Oh, I managed," she says. "David, the point is that I wouldn't even *want* you to want it until you know for certain that it's me and my ways and this life that you can be content with. I don't want to make anybody unhappy. I don't want to cause anyone pain. I never want to be anyone's prison. That is the worst fate I can imagine. Please, let me just say what I have to—you don't have to say anything about what you would have said or wouldn't have said had I told you what I was doing. I didn't want any of the responsibility to be yours; and it isn't; it can't be. If a mistake was made, then I made it. Right now I just want to say certain things to you, and I want you to hear them, and then we'll go home and I'll start supper."

"I'm listening to you."

"Sweetheart, I wasn't jealous of her; far from it. I'm pretty enough, and I'm young, and thank God, I'm not 'tough' or 'worldly,' if that's what that's called. Truly, I wasn't afraid of anything she could do. If I were that uncertain I wouldn't be living here. I did get confused a little when you wanted to shoo me out of the way, but I came back to the house only to get my camera. I was going to take some pictures of the two of them together. All in all, I thought it was as good a way to get through that visit as any. But when I saw you sitting alone with her, I suddenly thought, 'I can't make him happy, I won't be able to.' And I wondered suddenly if anyone could. And that stunned me so, I just had to go. I don't know if what I thought was true or not. Maybe you don't either. But maybe you do. It would be agony leaving you right now, but I'm prepared to do it, if it makes sense. And better now than three or four years down the line, when you're absolutely in every breath I draw. It's not what I want, David; it's not anything I am even remotely proposing. Saying these kinds of things you take a terrible risk of being misunderstood, and, please, please, don't misunderstand me. I'm proposing nothing. But if you do think you know the answer to my question, I'd like to be told sometime soon, because if you can't be truly content with me, then let me just go to the Vineyard. I know I could get through up there with Olivia until school begins. And after that I can manage on my own. But I don't want to give myself any further to something that isn't going to evolve someday into a family. I never had one that made the least bit of sense, and I want one that does. I have to have that. I'm not saying tomorrow, or even the day after tomorrow. But in time that's what I want. Otherwise, I'd just as soon tear the roots up now, before the job requires a hacksaw. I'd like us both to get away, if we can, without a bloody amputation."

Here, though the bright sun has baked her body dry, she shudders from head to foot. "I think that's everything I have the energy left to say. And you don't have to say a word. I wish you wouldn't, not just now. Otherwise, this will sound like an ultimatum, and it isn't. It's a clarification, that's all. I didn't even want to make it, I thought *time* would make it. But then it's time that just might do me in. But, please, it doesn't require reassuring sounds to be made in response. It's just that suddenly everything seemed as though it might be a terrible delusion. It was so frightening. Please, don't speak—unless there's something you know that I should know."

"No, there isn't."

"Then let's go home."

And last, my father's visit.

In the letter profusely thanking us for the Labor Day weekend invitation extended to him on the phone, my father asks if he may bring a friend along, another widower whom he has grown close to in recent months and whom he says he wants me in particular to meet. He must by now have discarded or used up the paper and envelopes bearing the name of the hotel, for the request is written on the back of stationery imprinted at the top with the words JEWISH FEDERATION OF NASSAU COUNTY. Imprinted beneath is a brief, pointed epistle to the Jews whose style is as easily recognizable to me as Hemingway's or Faulkner's.

Dear

   I am enclosing your pledge card from the Jewish Federation of Nassau County. I, as a Jew, am making a personal appeal. There is no need to recite our commitment to maintain a Jewish homeland. We need the financial aid of every Jew.
   Never again must we allow a holocaust! No Jew can be apathetic!
   I beg of you, please help. *Give before it hurts*.

> Sincerely,
> Abe Kepesh
> Garfield Garden Apartments
> Co-Chairman

On the reverse side is his letter to Claire and myself, written with a ball-point pen and in his oversized scrawl, though no less revealing than the printed message calling for Jewish solidarity (in those childlike hieroglyphics, all the more revealing) of the fanatically lavish loyalties that, now, in his old age, cause him to be afflicted throughout the waking day with the dull ache and shooting pain of wild sentiment ensnared.

   The morning we get his letter I telephone him at my

Uncle Larry's office to tell him that if he does not mind sharing our smallish guest room with his friend Mr. Barbatnik, he is of course welcome to bring him along.

"I hate like hell to leave him here alone on a holiday, Davey, that's the only thing. Otherwise I wouldn't bother you. See, I just didn't think it through," he explains, "when I rushed to say yes so quick like that. Only it's got to be no inconvenience for Claire, if he comes. I don't want to burden her, not with school starting up, not with all the work she must have to do to get ready."

"Oh, she's ready, don't worry about that," and I hand the phone over to Claire, who assures him that her school preparations were finished long ago and that it will be a pleasure to entertain the two of them for the weekend.

"He's a wonderful, wonderful man," my father quickly assures her, as though we actually have reason to suspect that a friend of his might turn out to be a rummy or a bum, "somebody who has been through things you wouldn't believe. He works with me when I go collecting for the UJA. And, I tell you, I need him. I need a hand grenade. Try to get money out of people. Try to get *feelings* out of people and see where you wind up. You tell them that what happened to the Jews must never happen again, and they look at you like they never heard of it. Like Hitler and pogroms are something I am making up in order to fleece them out of their municipal bonds. We got one guy in the building across the way, a brand-new widower three years older than me, who already made himself his bundle years ago in the bootleg business and God only knows what else, and you should get a load of him since his wife passed away—a new chippie on his arm every month. Dresses them up in expensive clothes, takes them in to see Broadway shows, wouldn't be caught dead driving them to the beauty parlor in anything but a Fleetwood Caddie, but just try to ask him for a hundred dollars for the UJA and he is practically in tears telling you how bad he has been hit on the market. It's a good thing I can control my temper. And between you and me, half the time I can't, and it is Mr. Barbatnik who has to call me off before I tell this s.o.b. just what I think of him. Oh, this one guy, he really gets my goat. Every time I leave him I have to go get a phenobarb from my sister-in-law. And I'm somebody who don't even believe in an aspirin."

"Mr. Kepesh," Claire says, "please feel free to bring Mr. Barbatnik with you."

But he will not say yes until he has extracted a promise that if they both come she will not think that she has to cook them three meals a day. "I want a guarantee that you are going to pretend that we're not even there."

"But what fun would that be? Suppose instead I take the easy way out and just pretend that you are."

"Hey, listen," he says to her, "you sound like a happy girl."

"I am. My cup runneth over."

Even though Claire is holding the phone to her ear across the kitchen table from me, I clearly hear what comes next. This results from the fact that my father approaches long-distance communication in much the way that he approaches so many of the riddles that elude his understanding—with the belief that the electrical waves transmitting his voice may not make it without his whole-hearted and unstinting support. Without *hard work*.

"God bless you," he calls out to her, "for what you are doing for my son!"

"Well—" beneath her tan, she has reddened—"well, he's doing some nice things for me."

"I wouldn't doubt that," my father says. "I'm delighted to hear it. But still and all he has practically gone out of his way to bring trouble into his life. Tell me, does he realize how good he has got it with you? He is thirty-four years old, a grown man already, he can't afford any longer to go around wet behind his ears. Claire, does he know enough by now to appreciate what he's got?"

She tries laughing the question off, but he insists on an answer, even if finally he must give it himself. "Losing your bearings no one needs—life is confusing enough. You don't stick a knife in your own gut. But that is just what he did to himself with marrying that glamour girl, all dressed up like Suzie Wong. Oh, about her and those outfits of hers the less said the better. And those French perfumes. Pardon my language, but she smelled like a God damn barber shop. And what was he up to living in that sublet apartment with red walls made out of cloth, and with whatever else went on there, that I will never be able to fathom. I don't even want to think about it. Claire dear, listen to me, you at last are somebody worthwhile. If only you can get him to settle into a real life."

"Oh, my," she says, not a little flustered by all the emotion that is flowing her way, "if it were any more settled around here . . ."

Before she can quite figure out, at the age of twenty-five, how to conclude that sentence, my father is roaring, "Wonderful, wonderful, that is the most wonderful news about him since he finished that fellowship to be a gypsy in Europe and came back on that boat in one piece!"

In the lot behind the general store in town, he steps

cautiously down from the high front step of the New York bus, but then, despite the scalding heat—despite his advanced age—*surges* forward, and not toward me, but on the wings of impulse, to the person who is no relation of his quite yet. There were those few evenings when she served him a meal in my new apartment, and then, when I gave my public lecture from *Man in a Shell* in the Scholar Series at the university, it was Claire who escorted him and my aunt and uncle into the library and sat beside him in the little auditorium there, identifying at his request which gentleman was the department chairman and which the dean. Nonetheless, now when he reaches out to embrace her, it is as though she is already pregnant with the first of his grandchildren, as though she is in fact *the* genetrix of all that is most estimable in that elite breed of creatures to which he is joined by blood and for which his admiration is overbrimming . . . if and when, that is, the membership does not go around shamelessly showing its fangs and its claws and leaving my father fit to be tied.

Seeing Claire swallowed up by this stranger, Dazzle begins leaping crazily around in the dust at his mistress's sandals—and, though my father has never had all that much trust, or found much to admire, in members of the animal kingdom who breed out of wedlock and defecate on the ground, I am surprised to see that Dazzle's display of unabashed dogginess in no way seems to deflect his attention from the girl he is holding in his arms.

At first I do have to wonder if what we are witnessing is not designed in part at least to put Mr. Barbatnik at ease about visiting a human couple who are not legally wed—if perhaps my father intends, by the very intensity with which he squeezes her body to his, to put his own not entirely unexpected misgivings on that score to rest. I cannot remember seeing him so forceful and so animated since before my mother's illness. In fact, he strikes me as a little nuts today. But that is still better than what I expected. Usually when I call each week there is, in just about every upbeat thing he says, a melancholy strain so transparent that I wonder how he finds the wherewithal to keep going on, as he will, about how all is well, wonderful, couldn't be better. The somber "Yeah, hello?" with which he answers the phone is quite enough to inform me of what underlies his "active" days—the mornings helping my uncle in his office where my uncle needs no help; the afternoons at the Jewish Center arguing politics with the "fascists" in the steam room, men whom he refers to as Von Epstein, and Von Haberman, and Von Lipschitz—the local Goering, Goebbels, and Streicher, apparently, who give him palpitations of the heart; and then those interminable evenings soliciting at his neighbors' doors for his various philanthropies and causes, reading again column by column through *Newsday*, the *Post*, and the *Times*, watching the CBS News for the second time in four hours, and finally, in bed and unable to sleep, spreading the letters from his cardboard file box over the blanket and reviewing his correspondence with his vanished, cherished guests. In some cases more cherished, it seems to me, now that they have vanished, than when they were around and there was too little barley in the soup, too much chlorine in the pool, and never enough waiters in the dining room.

His letter writing. With each passing month it is getting harder for him to keep track of who among the hundreds and hundreds of old-timers is retired and in Florida, and thus capable still of writing him back, and who is dead. And it isn't a matter of losing his faculties, either —it's losing all those friends, "non-stop," as he graphically describes the decimation that occurred in the ranks of his former clientele during just this last year. "I wrote five full pages of news to that dear and lovely prince of a man, Julius Lowenthal. I even put in a clipping that I've been saving up from the *Times* about how they ruined the river over in Paterson where he had his law practice. I figured it would be interesting to him down there—this pollution business was made to order for the kind of man he was. I tell you"—pointing a finger—"Julius Lowenthal was one of the most civic-minded people you could ever want to meet. The synagogue, orphans, sports, the handicapped, colored people—he gave of his time to everything. That man was the genuine article, the *best*. Well, you know what's coming. I stamp and seal the envelope and put it by my hat to take to mail in the morning, and not until I brush my teeth and get into bed and turn out the light does it dawn on me that my dear old friend is gone now since last fall. I have been thinking about him playing cards alongside a swimming pool in Miami—playing pinochle the way only he could play with that legal mind of his—and in actuality he is underground. What is even left of him by now?" That last thought is too much, even for him, especially for him, and he moves his hand angrily past his face, as though to shoo away, like a mosquito that is driving him crazy, this terrible, startling image of Julius Lowenthal decomposing. "And, unbelievable as it may sound to a young person," he says, recovering most of his equilibrium, "this is actually becoming a weekly occurrence, right down to licking the envelope and pasting on the stamp."

It will be hours before Claire and I are finally alone together, and she is able at last to unburden herself of the enigmatic decree issued by him into her ear while we four stood grouped in the fumy wake of the departed bus. The sun is softening us like so much macadam; poor confused Dazzle (barely grown accustomed to this rival) continues carrying on in the air around my father's feet; and Mr. Barbatnik—a short leprechaunish gentleman, with a large, long-eared Asian face, and astonishing scoop-like hands suspended from powerful forearms mapped with a body builder's veins—Mr. Barbatnik hangs back, as shy as a schoolgirl, his jacket folded neatly over his arm, waiting for this living, throbbing valentine, my father, to make the introductions. But my father has urgent business to settle first—like the messenger in a classical tragedy, immediately as he comes upon the stage he blurts out what he has traveled all this way to say. "Young woman," he whispers to Claire, for so it would seem he has been envisioning her, allegorically, as all that and only that, "young woman," commands my father out of the power vested in him by his daydreams— "don't let—don't let—please!"

These, she tells me at bedtime, were the only words that she could hear, pinned as she was against his massive chest; most likely, I say, because these are the only words he uttered. For him, at this point, they say it all.

And having thus ordained the future, if only for the moment, he is ready now to move on to the next event in the arrival ceremonies he must have been planning now for weeks. He reaches into the pocket of the nubby linen jacket slung across *his* arm—and apparently finds nothing. Suddenly he is slapping at the lining of the jacket as though performing resuscitation upon it. "Oh Christ," he moans, "it's lost. My God, it's on the bus!" Whereupon Mr. Barbatnik edges forward and, as discreetly as a best man to a half-dazed bridegroom, says in a soft voice, "Your pants, Abe." "Of course," my father snaps back, and reaching (still with a little desperation in the eyes) into the pocket of his houndstooth trousers— he is dressed, as they say, to the nines—extracts a small packet that he places in Claire's palm. And now he is beaming.

"I didn't tell you on the phone," he says to her, "so it would come as a total surprise. Every year you hold on to it I guarantee it will go up in value ten percent at least. Probably fifteen, and maybe more. It's better than money. And wait till you see the wonderful skill that goes into it. It's fantastic. Go ahead. Open it up."

So, while we all continue to cook away in the parking lot, my affable mate, who knows how to please, and loves pleasing, deftly unties the ribbon and removes the shiny yellow wrapping paper, not failing to remark upon its prettiness. "I picked that out too," my father tells her. "I thought that color would be up your alley—didn't I, Sol," he says, turning to his companion, "didn't I say I'll bet she's a girl who likes yellow?"

Claire takes from its velvet-lined case a small sterling-silver paperweight engraved with a bouquet of roses.

"David told me how hard you work in the garden you made, and the way you love all the flowers. Take it, please. You can use it on your desk at school. Wait till your pupils see it."

"It's beautiful," she says, and calming Dazzle with just a glance, kisses my father on the cheek.

"Look at the handiwork," he says. "You can even see the little thorns. Some person actually did that, by hand. An artist."

"It's lovely, it's a lovely gift," she says.

And only now does he turn and embrace me. "I got you something too," he says. "It's in my bag."

"You hope," I say.

"Wise guy," and *we* kiss.

At last he is ready to introduce his companion, dressed, I now realize, in the same spanking-new, color-coordinated outfit, except where my father is in shades of tan and brown, Mr. Barbatnik wears silver and blue.

"Thank God for this man," my father says as we drive slowly out of town behind a farmer's pickup truck bearing a bumper sticker informing the other motorists that ONLY LOVE BEATS MILK. The bumper sticker on our car, affixed by Claire in sympathy with the local ecologists, reads DIRT ROADS ARE DOWN TO EARTH.

Excited and garrulous as a small boy—much as *I* used to be when *he* was doing the driving around these roads —my father cannot stop talking now about Mr. Barbatnik: one in a million, the finest person he has ever known . . . Mr. Barbatnik, meanwhile, sits quietly beside him, looking into his lap, as humbled, I think, by Claire's buoyant, summery fullness as by the fact that my father is selling him to us much the way, in the good old days, he used to sell the life-lengthening benefits of a summer in our hotel.

"Mr. Barbatnik is the guy who I tell you about from the Center. If it wasn't for him I would absolutely be a voice in the wilderness there about that son of a bitch George Wallace. Claire, pardon me, please, but I hate that lousy cockroach with a passion. You shouldn't have to ever hear the kinds of things so-called decent people think in their private thoughts. It's a disgrace. Only Mr. Barbatnik and me, we make a team, and we give it to them, but good."

"Not," says Mr. Barbatnik philosophically, in heavily accented English, "that it makes much difference."

"And, tell me, what could make a difference with those ignorant bigots? At least let them hear what someone else thinks of them! Jewish people so full of hatred that they go out and vote for a George Wallace—it's beyond me. *Why*? People who have lived and seen a whole lifetime as a minority, and the suggestion that they make in all seriousness is that they ought to line up the colored in front of machine guns and let them have it. Take actual people and mow them down."

"This of course isn't everybody that says that," Mr. Barbatnik puts in. "This is just one particular person, of course."

"I tell them, look at Mr. Barbatnik—ask him if that isn't the same thing that Hitler did with the Jews. And you know what their answer is, grown men who have raised families and run successful businesses and live in retirement now in condominiums like supposed civilized people? They say, 'How can you compare niggers with Jews?'."

"What's eating this particular person, and the group that he is the leader of—"

"And who appointed him leader, by the way? Of anything? Himself! Go ahead, Sol, I'm sorry. I just wanted to

235

make clear to them what kind of a little dictator we're dealing with."

"What's eating them," Mr. Barbatnik says, "is that they owned homes, some of them, and businesses, and then came the colored, and when they tried to get out what they put in, they took a licking."

"Of course it's all economics when you get down to it. It always is. Wasn't it the same with the Germans? Wasn't it the same in Poland?" Here, abruptly, he breaks off his historical analysis to say to Claire and me, "Mr. Barbatnik only got here after the war." Dramatically, and yes, with pride, he adds, "He is a victim of the Nazis."

When we turn in the drive and I point out the house halfway up the hillside, Mr. Barbatnik says, "No wonder you look so happy, you two."

"They rent it," my father says. "I told him, he likes it so much, why don't he buy it? Make the guy an offer. Tell him you'll pay him cash. At least see if you get a nibble."

"Well," I say, "we're happy enough renting for now."

"Renting is throwing money down the drain. Find out from him, will you? What can it hurt? Cash on the barrelhead, see if he bites. I can help you out, Uncle Larry can help you out, as far as that goes, if it's a straight money deal that he's after. But definitely you ought to own a little piece of property at your stage of the game. And up here, you can't miss, that's for sure. You never could. In my time, Claire, you could buy a little place like this for under five thousand. Today that little house and—and how far does the property go? To the tree line? All right, say four, say five acres—"

Up the dirt drive and in through the kitchen door—and right past the blooming garden he has heard so much about—he continues with his realtor's spiel, so delighted is the man to be back home in Sullivan County, and with his only living loved one, who by all outward appearances seems finally to have been plucked from his furnace and plunked down before the hearth.

Inside the house, before we can even offer a cold drink, or show them to their room or to the toilet, my father begins to unpack his bag on the kitchen table. "*Your* present," he announces to me.

We wait. His shoes come out. His freshly laundered shirts. His shiny new shaving kit.

My present is an album bound in black leather containing thirty-two medallions the size of silver dollars, each in its own circular cavity and protected on both sides by a transparent acetate window. He calls them "Shakespeare Medals"— a scene from one of the plays is depicted on the face side, and on the other, in tiny script, a quotation from the play is inscribed. The medals are accompanied by instructions for placing them in the album. The first instruction begins, "Put on a pair of lint-free gloves . . ." My father hands me the gloves last of all. "Always wear the gloves when you handle the medals " he tells me. "They come with the set. Otherwise, they say that there can be harmful chemical effects to the medals from being touched by human skin."

"Oh, this is nice of you," I say. "Though I don't quite know why now, such an elaborate gift—"

"Why? Because it's time," he answers, with a laugh, and, too, with a wide gesture that encompasses all the kitchen appliances. "Look, Davey, what they engrave for you. Claire, look at the outside."

Centered within the arabesque design that is embossed

in silver and serves as a border to the album's funereal cover are three lines, which my father points out to us, word by word, with his index finger. We all read the words in silence—all except him.

FIRST EDITION STERLING SILVER PROOF SET MINTED FOR THE PERSONAL COLLECTION OF PROFESSOR DAVID KEPESH

I don't know what to say. I say, "This must have cost an awful lot. It's really something."

"Isn't it? But, no, the cost don't hurt, not the way they set it up. You just collect one medal a month, to begin with. You start off with *Romeo and Juliet*—wait'll I show Claire *Romeo and Juliet*—and you work your way up from there, till you've got them all. I've been saving for you all this time. The only one who knew was Mr. Barbatnik. Look, Claire, come here, you gotta look up close—"

It is a while before they can locate the medallion depicting *Romeo and Juliet*, for in its designated slot in the lower left-hand corner of the page labeled "Tragedies" it seems he has placed *Two Gentlemen from Verona*. "Where the hell is *Romeo and Juliet*?" he asks. The four of us are able to discover it finally under "Histories" in the slot marked *The Life and Death of King John*. "But then where did I put *The Life and Death of King John*?" he asks. "I thought I got 'em all in right, Sol," he says to Mr. Barbatnik, frowning. "I thought we checked." Mr. Barbatnik nods—they did. "Anyway," says my father, "the point is—what was the point? Oh, the *back*. Here, I want Claire to read what it says on the back, so everyone can hear. Read this, dear."

Claire reads aloud the inscription: " '. . . and a rose by any other name would smell as sweet.' *Romeo and Juliet*, Act Two, Scene Two."

"Isn't that something?" he says to her.

"Yes."

"And he can take it to school, too, you see. That's what's so useful. It's something not just for the home, but that he can have ten and twenty years from now to show his classes. And just like yours, it is sterling silver, and something that I guarantee will keep abreast of the inflation, and long after paper money is as good as worthless. Where will you put it?" This last asked of Claire, not me.

"For now," she says, "on the coffee table, so people can see. Come into the living room, everybody; we'll put it there."

"Wonderful," says my father. "Only remember, don't let your company take the medals out, unless they put on the gloves."

Lunch is served on the screened-in porch. The recipe for the cold beet soup Claire found in *Russian Cooking*, one of her dozen or so manuals in a Time-Life series on "Foods of the World" shelved neatly between the radio —whose dial seems set to play only Bach—and the wall hung with two of her sister's calm watercolors of the ocean and the dunes. The cucumber and yogurt salad, heavily flavored with crushed garlic and fresh mint from the herb garden just beyond the screen door, is out of the same set, the volume on the cuisine of the Middle East. The cold roast chicken seasoned with rosemary is a long-standing recipe of her own.

"My God," says my father, "what a spread!" "Excellent," says Mr. Barbatnik. "Gentlemen, thank you," says Claire, "but I'll bet you've had better." "Not even in Lvov, when my mother was cooking," says Mr. Barbatnik, "have I tasted such a wonderful borscht." Says Claire, smiling, "I suspect that's a little extravagant, but thank you, again." "Listen, my dear girl," says my father, "if I had you in the kitchen, I'd still be in my old line. And you'd get more than you get being a schoolteacher, believe me. A good chef, even in the old days, even in the middle of the Depression—"

But in the end Claire's biggest hit is not the exotic Eastern dishes which, in her Clairish way, she has tried today for the first time in the hope of making everybody —herself included—feel instantaneously at home together, but the hearty iced tea she brews with mint leaves and orange rinds according to her grandmother's recipe. My father cannot seem to get enough, cannot stop praising it to the skies, not after he has learned over the blueberries that Claire takes the bus to Schenectady every month to visit this ninety-year-old woman from whom she learned everything she knows about preparing a meal and growing a garden, and probably about raising a child too. Yes, it looks from the girl as though his renegade son has decided to go straight, and in a very big way.

After lunch I suggest to the two men that they might like to rest until the heat has abated somewhat and we can go for a little walk along the road. Absolutely not. What am I even talking about? As soon as we digest our food, my father says, we must drive over to the hotel. This surprises me, as it surprised me a little at lunch to hear him speak so easily about his "old line." Since moving to Long Island a year and a half ago, he has shown no interest whatsoever in seeing what two successive owners have made of his hotel, barely hanging on now as the Royal Ski and Summer Lodge. I had thought he would be just as happy staying away, but in fact he is boiling over again with enthusiasm, and after a visit to the toilet, is pacing the porch, waiting for Mr. Barbatnik to awaken from the little snooze he is enjoying in my wicker easy chair.

What if he should drop dead from all this fervor in his heart? And before I have married the devoted girl, bought the cozy house, raised the handsome children . . .

Then what am I waiting for? If later, why not now, so he too can be happy and count his life a success?

What am I waiting for?

Down the main drag and through every last store still there and open for business my father leads the three of us, he alone seemingly oblivious to the terrific heat. "I can remember when there were four butchers, three barbershops, a bowling alley, three produce markets, two bakeries, an A&P, three doctors, and three dentists. And now, look," he says—and without chagrin; rather with the proud sagacity of one who imagines he actually knew to get out when the getting was good—"no butchers, no barbers, no bowling alley, just one bakery, no A&P, and unless things have changed since I left, no dentists and only one doctor. Yes," he announces, avuncular now, taking the overview, sounding a little like his friend Walter Cronkite, "the old, opulent hotel era is over—but it was something! You should have seen this place in summertime! You know who used to vacation here? You name it! The Herring King! The Apple King!—" And to Mr. Barbatnik and to Claire (who does not let on that she already made this same sentimental journey some weeks ago at the side of his son, who had explained at the time just what a herring king *was*) he begins a rapid-fire anecdotal history of his life's major boulevard, foot by foot, year by year, from Roosevelt's inauguration right on up through L.B.J. Putting an arm around his sopping half-sleeve shirt, I say, "I bet if you set your mind to it you could go back before the Flood." He likes that—yes, he likes just about everything today. "Oh, could I! This is some treat! This is *really* Memory Lane!" "It's awfully hot, Dad," I warn him. "It's nearly ninety degrees. Maybe if we slow down—" "Slow *down?*" he cries, and showing off, pulls Claire along on his arm as he breaks into a crazy little trot down the street. Mr. Barbatnik smiles, and mopping his brow with his handkerchief, says to me, "He's been hoping a long time."

"Labor Day weekend!" my father announces brightly as I swing into the lot next to the service entrance of the "main building." Aside from the parking lot, which has been resurfaced, and the tumescent pink the buildings have all been painted, little else seems to have been changed as yet, except of course for the hotel's name. In charge now are a worried fellow only a little older than myself and his youngish, charmless second wife. I met them briefly on the afternoon in June when I came down with Claire to conduct my own nostalgic tour. But there is no nostalgia for the good old days in these two, no more than those clutching at the debris in a swollen stream are able to feel for the golden age of the birch-bark canoe. When my father, having sized up the situation, asks how come no full house for the holiday—a phenomenon utterly unknown to him, as he quickly makes only too clear—the wife goes more bulldoggish even than before, and the husband, a hefty boyish type with pale eyes and pocked skin and a dazed, friendly expression—a nice, well-meaning fellow whose creditors, however, are probably not that impressed by plans extending into the twenty-first century—explains that they have not as yet been able to fix an "image" in the public mind. "You see," he says uncertainly, "right now we're still modernizing the kitchen—"

The wife interrupts to set the record straight: young people are put off because they think it is a hotel for the older generation (for which, it would seem from her tone, my father is to blame), and the family crowd is frightened away because the fellow to whom my father sold out— and who couldn't pay his bills by August of his first and only summer as proprietor—was nothing but a "two-bit Hugh Hefner" who tried to build a clientele out of "riff-raff, and worse."

"Number one," says my father before I can grab an arm and steer him away, "the biggest mistake was to change the name, to take thirty years of good will and wipe it right off the map. Paint outside whatever color you want, though what was wrong with a nice clean white I don't understand—but if that's your taste, that's your taste. But the point is, does Niagara Falls change its name? Not if they want the tourist trade they don't." The wife has to laugh in his face, or so she says: "I have to laugh in your face." "You what? *Why?*" my outraged father replies. "Because you can't call a hotel the Hungarian Royale in this day and age and expect the line to form on the right, you know." "No, no," says the husband, trying to soften her words, and meanwhile working two Maalox tablets out of their silver wrapping, "the problem is, Janet, we are caught between life-styles, and that is what we have to iron out. I'm sure, as soon as we finish up with the kitchen—" "My friend, forget about the kitchen," says my father, turning noticeably away from the wife and toward someone with whom a human being can at least have a decent conversation; "do yourself a favor and change back the name. That is half of what you paid for. Why do you want to use in the name a word like 'ski' anyway? Stay open all winter if you think there's something in it—but why use a word that can only scare away the kind of people who make a place like this a going proposition?" The wife: "I have news for you. Nobody wants today to take a vacation in a place that sounds like a mausoleum." Period. "Oh," says my father, revving up his sarcasm, "oh, the past dies these days, does it?" And launches into a solemn, disjointed philosophical monologue about the integral relationship of past, present, and future, as though a man who has survived to sixty-six *must* know whereof he speaks, is *obliged* to be sagacious with those who follow after—especially when they seem to look upon him as the begetter of their woes.

I wait to intercede, or call an ambulance. From seeing his life's work mismanaged so by this deadbeat husband and his dour little wife, will my overwrought father burst into tears, or keel over, a corpse? The one—once again— seems no less possible to me than the other.

Why am I convinced that during the course of this weekend he is going to die, that by Monday I will be a parentless son?

He is still going strong—still going a little crazy—when we climb into the car to head home. "How did I know he was going to turn out to be a hippie?" "Who's that?" I

244

ask. "That guy who bought us out after we lost Mother. You think I would have sold to a hippie, out of my own free will? The man was a fifty-year-old man. So what if he had long hair? What am I, a hard-hat, that I hold something like that against him? And what the hell did she mean by 'riffraff' anyway? She didn't mean what I think she meant, did she? Or did she?" I say, "She only meant that they are going under fast and it hurts. Look, she is obviously a sour little pain in the ass, but failing is still failing." "Yeah, but why blame *me*? I gave these people the last of the golden geese, I gave them a good solid tradition and a loyal clientele that all they had to do was stick to what was *there*. That was *all*, Davey! 'Ski!' That's all my customers have to hear, and they run like hell. Ah, some people, they can start a hotel in the Sahara and make a go of it, and others can start in the best of circumstances and they lose everything." "That's true," I say. "Now I look back in wonder that I myself could ever accomplish so much. A nobody like me, from nowhere! I started out, Claire, I was a short-order cook. My hair was black then, like his, and thick too, if you can believe it—"

Beside him Mr. Barbatnik's sleeping head is twisted to one side, as though he has been garrotted. Claire, however—amiable, tolerant, generous, and willing Claire—continues to smile and to nod yes-yes-yes as she follows the story of our inn and how it flourished under the loving care of this industrious, gracious, shrewd, slave-driving, and dynamic nobody. Is there a man alive, I wonder, who has led a more exemplary life? Is there an ounce of anything that he has withheld in the perform-ance of his duties? Of what then does he believe himself

245

to be so culpable? My derelictions, my sins? Oh, if only he would cut the summation short, the jury would announce "Innocent as a babe!" without even retiring from the courtroom.

Only he can't. Into the early evening his plea streams forth unabated. First he follows Claire around the kitchen while she prepares the salad and the dessert. When she retires to shower and to change for dinner—and to rally her forces—he comes out to where I am preparing to cook the steak on the grill behind the house. "Hey, did I tell you who I got an invitation to his daughter's wedding? You won't guess in a million years. I had to go over to Hempstead to get her blender fixed for your aunt—you know, the jar there, the top—and who do you think owns the appliance store that services now for Waring? You'll never guess, if you even remember him." But I do. It is my conjurer. "Herbie Bratasky," I say. "That's right! Did I tell you already?" "No." "But that's who it was—and can you believe it, that skinny *paskudnyak* grew up into a person and he is doing terrific. He's got Waring, he's got G.E., and now, he tells me, he is getting himself in with some Japanese company, bigger even than Sony, to be the sole Long Island distributor. And the daughter is a little doll. He showed me her picture—and then out of the blue two days ago I get this beautiful invitation in the mail. I meant to bring it, damn it, but I guess I forgot because I was already packed." Already packed two days ago. "I'll send it," he says; "you'll get a real kick out of it. Look, I was thinking, it's just a thought, but how would you and Claire like to come with me—to the wedding? That would be some surprise for Herbie." "Well, let's think about it. What does Herbie look like these days? What is he now, in his forties?" "Oh, he's gotta be forty-five, forty-six, easy. But still a dynamo—and as sharp and good-looking as he was when he was a kid. He ain't got a pound on him, and still with all his hair—in fact, so much, I thought maybe it was a rug. Maybe it was, come to think of it. And still with that tan. What do you think of that? Must use a lamp. And, Davey, he's got a little boy, just like him, who plays *drums!* I told him about you, of course, and he says he already knew. He read about when you gave your speech at the school; he saw it in the *Newsday* calendar of what's happening around the area. He said he told all his customers. So how do you like that? Herbie Bratasky. How did you know?" "I took a guess." "Well, you were right. You're psychic, kiddo. Whew, that's some beautiful piece of meat. What are you paying up here by the pound? Years ago, a sirloin cut like that—" And I want to enfold him in my arms, bring his unstoppable mouth to my chest, and say, "It's okay, you're here for good, you never have to leave." But in fact we all must depart in something less than a hundred hours. And— until death do us part—the tremendous closeness and the tremendous distance between my father and myself will have to continue in the same perplexing proportions as have existed all our lives.

When Claire comes back down to the kitchen, he leaves me to watch the coals heat up, and goes into the house "to see how beautiful she looks." "Calm down . . ." I call after him, but I might as well be asking a kid to calm down the first time he walks into Yankee Stadium.

My Yankee puts him to work shucking the corn. But of course you can shuck corn and still talk. On the cork bulletin board she has hung over the sink, Claire has tacked up, along with recipes out of the *Times*, some photographs just sent her from Martha's Vineyard by Olivia. I hear them through the kitchen's screen door discussing Olivia's children.

Alone again, and with time yet before the steak goes on, I at last get around to opening the envelope forwarded to me from my box at the university, and carried around in my back pocket since we went into town hours ago to pick up the mail and our guests. I hadn't bothered to open it, since it wasn't the letter I have been expecting daily now, from the university press to which I submitted *Man in a Shell*, in its final revised version, upon our return from Europe. No, it is a letter from the Department of English at Texas Christian University, and it provides the first truly light moment of the day. Oh, Baumgarten, you are a droll and devilish fellow, all right.

Dear Professor Kepesh:

Mr. Ralph Baumgarten, a candidate for the position of Writer in Residence at Texas Christian University, has submitted your name as an individual who is familiar with his work. I am reluctant to impose on your busy schedule, but would be most grateful if you would send me, at your earliest convenience, a letter in which you set forth your views on his writing, his teaching, and on his moral character. You may be assured that your comments will be held in the very strictest confidence.

I am most grateful for your help.

Cordially yours,
John Fairbairn
Chairman

Dear Professor Fairbairn, Perhaps you would like my opinion of the wind as well, whose work I am also familiar with . . . I stick the letter back into my pocket and put on the steak. *Dear Professor Fairbairn, I cannot help but believe that your students' horizons will be enormously enlarged and their sense of life's possibilities vastly enriched* . . . And who next, I wonder. When I sit down at my place for dinner, will there be an extra plate at the table for Birgitta, or will she prefer to eat beside me, on her knees?

I hear from the kitchen that Claire and my father have got around finally to discussing her parents. "But *why*?" I hear him ask. From his tone I can tell that whatever the question, the answer is not unknown to him, but rather, wholly incompatible with his own passionate meliorism. Claire replies, "Because they probably never belonged together in the first place." "But two beautiful daughters; they themselves college-educated people; the two of them with excellent executive positions. I don't get it. And the drinking: *why*? Where does it get you? With all due respect, it seems to me stupid. I myself of course never had the advantages of an education. If I had—but I didn't, and that was that. But my mother, let me tell you, I just have to remember her to get a good feeling about the whole world. What a woman! Ma, I would say to her, what are you doing on the floor again? Larry and I will give you the money, you'll get somebody else in to wash the floors. But no—"

It is during dinner that, at last, in Chekhov's phrase, the angel of silence passes over him. But only to be followed quickly by the shade of melancholia. Is he teetering now at the brink of tears, having spoken and spoken and spoken and still not having *quite* said it? Is he at last about to break down and cry—or am I ascribing to him the mood claiming me? Why should I feel as though I have lost a bloody battle when clearly I have won?

We eat again on the screened-in porch, where, during the days previous, I have been making every effort, with pen and pad, to speak *my* it. Beeswax candles are burning invisibly down in the antique pewter holders; the bayberry candles, arrived by mail from the Vineyard, drip wax threads onto the table. Candles burn everywhere you look—Claire has a passion for them on the porch at night; they are probably her only extravagance. Earlier, when she went around from holder to holder with a book of matches, my father—already at the table with the napkin drawn through his belt—had begun to recite for her the names of the Catskill hotels that had tragically burned to the ground in the last twenty years. Whereupon she had assured him that she would be careful. Still, when a breeze moves lightly over the porch, and the flames all flicker, he looks around to check that nothing has caught fire.

Now we hear the first of the ripe apples dropping onto the grass in the orchard just beyond the house. We hear the hoot of "our" owl—so Claire identifies for our guests this creature we have never seen, and whose home is up in "our" woods. If we are all silent long enough, she tells the two old men—as though they are two children—the deer may come down from the woods to graze around the apple trees. Dazzle has been cautioned about barking and scaring them away. The dog pants a little at the sound of his name from her lips. He is eleven and has been hers since she was a fourteen-year-old high school girl, her dearest pal ever since the year Olivia went off to college, the closest thing to her, until me. Within a few seconds Dazzle is peacefully asleep, and once again there is only the spirited September finale by the tree toads and the crickets, most popular of all the soft summer songs ever heard.

I cannot take my eyes from her face tonight. Between the Old Master etchings of the two pouched and creased and candlelit old men, Claire's face seems, more than ever, so apple-smooth, apple-small, apple-shiny, apple-plain, apple-fresh . . . never more artless and untainted . . . never before *so* . . . Yes, and to what am I willfully blinding myself that in time must set us apart? Why continue to cast this spell over myself, wherein nothing is permitted to sift through except what pleases me? Is there not something a little dubious and dreamy about all this gentle, tender adoration? What will happen when the *rest* of Claire obtrudes? What happens if no "rest of her" is there! And what of the rest of me? How long will *that* be sold a bill of goods? How much longer before I've had a bellyful of wholesome innocence—how long before the lovely blandness of a life with Claire begins to cloy, to pall, and I am out there once again, mourning what I've lost and looking for my way!

And with doubts so long suppressed voiced at last—and in deafening unison—the emotions under whose somber portentousness I have been living out this day forge themselves into something as palpable and awful as a spike. *Only an interim*, I think, and as though I have in fact been stabbed and the strength is gushing out of me, I feel myself about to tumble from my chair. Only an interim. Never to know anything durable. Nothing except my unrelinquishable memories of the discontinuous and the provisional; nothing except this ever-lengthening saga of all that did not work . . .

To be sure, to be sure, Claire is still with me, directly across the table, saying something to my father and Mr. Barbatnik about the planets she will show them later, brilliant tonight among the distant constellations. With her hair pinned up, exposing the vulnerable vertebrae that support the stalk of her slender neck, and in her pale caftan, with its embroidered edging, sewn together early in the summer on the machine, and lending a tiny regal air to her overpowering simplicity, she looks to me more precious than ever, more than ever before like my true wife, my unborn offspring's mother . . . yet I am already bereft of my strength and my hope and my contentment. Though we will go ahead, as planned, and rent the house to use on weekends and school vacations, I am certain that in only a matter of time—that's all it seems to take, just time—what we have together will gradually disappear, and the man now holding in his hand a spoonful of her orange custard will give way to Herbie's pupil, Birgitta's accomplice, Helen's suitor, yes, to Baumgarten's sidekick and defender, to the would-be wayward son and all he hungers for. Or, if not that, the would-be *what*? When this too is gone in its turn, what then?

I can't, for the sake of us all, fall out of a chair at dinner. Yet once again I am overcome by a terrible physical weakness. I am afraid to reach for my wineglass for fear that I will not have sufficient strength to carry it the distance to my mouth.

"How about a record?" I say to Claire.

"That new Bach?"

A record of trio sonatas. We have been listening to it all

week. The week before, it had been a Mozart quartet; the week before that, the Elgar cello concerto. We just keep turning over one record again and again and again until finally we have had enough. It is all one hears coming and going through the house, music that almost seems by now to be the by-product of our comings and goings, compositions exuded by our sense of well-being. All we ever hear is the most exquisite music.

Seemingly with a good reason, I manage to leave the table before something frightening happens.

The phonograph and speakers in the living room are Claire's, carried up from the city in the back seat of the car. So are most of the records hers. So are the curtains sewed together for the windows, and the corduroy spread she made to cover the battered daybed, and the two china dogs by the fireplace, which once belonged to her grandmother and became hers on her twenty-fifth birthday. As a child on her way home from school she used to stop and have tea and toast with her grandmother, and practice on the piano there; then, armed at least with that, she could continue to the battlefield of her house. On her own she decided to have that abortion. So I would not be burdened by a duty? So I could choose her just for herself? But is the notion of duty so utterly horrendous? Why didn't she tell me she was pregnant? Is there not a point on life's way when one yields to duty, *welcomes* duty as once one yielded to pleasure, to passion, to adventure—a time when duty is the pleasure, rather than pleasure the duty . . .

The exquisite music begins. I return to the porch, not quite so pale as when I left. I sit back down at the table and sip my wine. Yes, I can raise and lower a glass. I can focus my thoughts on another subject. I had better.

253

"Mr. Barbatnik," I say, "my father told us you survived the concentration camps. How did you do it? Do you mind my asking?"

"Professor, please let me say first how much I appreciate your hospitality to a total stranger. This is the happiest day for me in a very long time. I thought maybe I even forgot how to be happy with people. I thank you all. I thank my new and dear friend, your wonderful father. It was a beautiful day, and, Miss Ovington—"

"Please call me Claire," she says.

"Claire, you are beyond your years and young and adorable as well. And—and all day I have wanted to give you my deep gratitude. For all the lovely things you think to do for people."

The two elders have been seated to either side of her, the lover directly across: with all the love he can muster, he looks upon the fullness of her saucy body and the smallness of her face above the little vase of asters he plucked for her on his morning walk; with all the love at his command, he watches this munificent female creature, now in the moment of her fullest bloom, offer a hand to their shy guest, who takes it, grasps and squeezes it, and without relinquishing it begins to speak for the first time with ease and self-assurance, at last at home (just as she had planned it, just as she has made it come to pass). And amid all this, the lover does, in fact, feel more deeply implicated in his own life than at any moment in memory— the true self at its truest, moored by every feeling to its own true home! And yet he continues to imagine that he is being drawn away by a force as incontrovertible as gravity, which is no lie either. As though he is a falling body, helpless as any little apple in the orchard which has broken free and is descending toward the alluring earth.

But instead of crying, either in his mother tongue or with some rudimentary animalish howl, "Don't leave me! Don't go! I'll miss you bitterly! This moment, and we four together—this is what should be!" he spoons out the last of his custard and attends to the survival story that he has asked to hear.

"There was a beginning," Mr. Barbatnik is saying, "there has to be an ending. I am going to live to see this monstrosity come to an end. This is what I told myself every single morning and night."

"But how was it they didn't send you to the ovens?"

How do you come to be here, with us? Why is Claire here? Why not Helen and our child? Why not my mother? And in ten years' time . . . who then? To build an intimate life anew, out of nothing, when I am forty-five? To start over again with everything at fifty? To be forever a beweeper of my outcast state? I can't! I won't!

"They couldn't kill everybody," says Mr. Barbatnik. "This I knew. Somebody has to be left, if only one person. And so I would tell myself, this one person will be me. I worked for them in the coal mines where they sent me. With the Poles. I was a young man then, and strong. I worked like it was my own coal mine inherited from my father. I told myself that this was what I wanted to do. I told myself that this work I was doing was for my child. I told myself different things every single day to make it just that I could last till that night. And that's how I lasted. Only when the Russians started coming so quick all of a sudden, the Germans took us and at three in the morning started us off on a march. Days and days and days, until I stopped keeping track. It went on and on, and people

255

dropping every place you looked, and sure, I told myself again that if one is left it is going to be me. But by then I knew somehow that even if I made it to the destination where we were going, when I got there they would shoot whoever of us was left. So this is how come I ran away after weeks and weeks of marching without a stop to wherever in God's name it was. I hid in the woods and at night I came out and the German farmers fed me. Yes, that's true," he says, as he stares down at his large hand, in the candlelight looking very nearly as wide as a spade and as heavy as a crowbar, and enfolding within it Claire's thin, fine fingers with their delicate bones and knuckles. "The individual German, he isn't so bad, you know. But put three Germans together in a room and you can kiss the good world goodbye."

"And then what happened?" I ask, but he continues looking down, as though to contemplate the riddle of this one hand in the other. "How were you saved, Mr. Barbatnik?"

"One night a German farm woman said to me that the Americans are here. I thought she must be lying. I figured, don't come back here to her, she's up to something no good. But the next day I saw a tank through the trees, rolling down the road, with a white star, and I ran out, screaming at the top of my lungs."

Claire says, "You must have looked so strange by then. How did they know who you were?"

"They knew. I wasn't the first one. We were all coming out of our holes. What was left of us. I lost a wife and two parents, my brother, two sisters, and a three-year-old daughter."

256

Claire groans, "*Oh,*" as though she has just been pierced by a needle. "Mr. Barbatnik, we are asking you too many questions, we shouldn't . . ."

He shakes his head. "Darling, you live, you ask questions. Maybe it's why we live. It seems that way."

"I tell him," says my father, "that he should make a book out of all he went through. I can think of some people I'd like to give it to read. If they could read it, maybe they would shake their heads that they can be the way they are, and this man can be so kind and good."

"And before the war started?" I ask him. "You were a young man then. What did you want to be?"

Probably because of the strength of his arms and the size of his hands I expect to hear him say a carpenter or a mason. In America he drove a taxi for over twenty years.

"A human being," he answers, "someone that could see and understand how we lived, and what was real, and not to flatter myself with lies. This was always my ambition from when I was a small child. In the beginning I was like everybody, a good cheder boy. But I personally, with my own hands, liberated myself from all that at sixteen years. My father could have killed me, but I absolutely did not want to be a fanatic. To believe in what doesn't exist, no, that wasn't for me. These are just the people who hate the Jews, these fanatics. And there are Jews who are fanatics too," he tells Claire, "and also walk around in a dream. But not me. Not for a second since I was sixteen years old and told my father what I refuse to pretend."

"If he wrote a book," says my father, "it should be called 'The Man Who Never Said Die.' "

"And here you married again?" I ask.

"Yes. She had been in a concentration camp also. Three years ago next month she passed away—like your own mother, from cancer. She wasn't even sick. One night after dinner she is washing the dishes. I go in to turn on the TV, and suddenly I hear a crash from the kitchen. 'Help me, I'm in trouble.' When I run into the kitchen she is on the floor. 'I couldn't hold on to the ditch,' she says. She says 'ditch' instead of 'dish.' The word alone gave me the willies. And her eyes. It was awful. I knew then and there that she was done for. Two days later they tell us that cancer is already in her brain. And it happened out of nowhere." Without a trace of animus—just to keep the record straight—he adds, "How else?"

"Too terrible," Claire says.

After my father has gone around to each candle to snuff out the flame—blowing even at those already expired, just to be sure—we step into the garden for Claire to show them the other planets visible from the earth tonight. Talking toward their upturned eyeglasses she explains about the Milky Way, answers questions about shooting stars, points out, as she does to her sixth-graders —as she did with me on our first night here—that mere speck of a star adjacent to the handle of the Little Dipper which the Greek soldiers had to discern to qualify for battle. Then she accompanies them back into the house; if they should awaken in the morning before we do, she wants them to know where there is coffee and juice. I remain in the garden with Dazzle. I don't know what to think. I don't want to know. I want only to climb by myself to the top of the hill. I remember our gondola rides in

Venice. "Are you sure we didn't die and go to heaven?"

"You'll have to ask the gondolier."

Through the living-room window I see the three of them standing around the coffee table. Claire has turned the record over and put it back on the turntable to play. My father is holding the album of Shakespeare medals in his hands. It appears that he is reading aloud from the backs of the medallions.

Some minutes later she joins me on the weathered wooden bench at the top of the hill. Side by side, without speaking, we look up again at the familiar stars. We do this nearly every night. Everything we have done this summer we have done nearly every night, afternoon, and morning. Every day calling out from the kitchen to the porch, from the bedroom to the bath, "Clarissa, come see, the sun is setting," "Claire, there's a hummingbird," "Sweetheart, what's the name of that star?"

For the first time all day she gives in to exhaustion. "Oh, my," she says, and lays her head on my shoulder. I can feel the air she breathes slowly filling, then slowly leaving her body.

After inventing a constellation of my own of the sky's brightest lights, I say to her, "It's a simple Chekhov story, isn't it?"

"Isn't what?"

"This. Today. The summer. Some nine or ten pages, that's all. Called 'The Life I Formerly Led.' Two old men come to the country to visit a healthy, handsome young couple, brimming over with contentment. The young man is in his middle thirties, having recovered finally from the mistakes of his twenties. The young woman is in her twenties, the survivor of a painful youth and adolescence. They have every reason to believe they have come through. It looks and feels to both of them as though they have been saved, and in large part by one another. They are in love. But after dinner by candlelight, one of the old men tells of his life, about the utter ruination of a world, and about the blows that keep on coming. And that's it. The story ends just like this: her pretty head on his shoulder; his hand stroking her hair; their owl hooting; their constellations all in order—their medallions all in order; their guests in their freshly made beds; and their summer cottage, so cozy and inviting, just down the hill from where they sit together wondering about what they have to fear. Music is playing in the house. The most lovely music there is. 'And both of them knew that the most complicated and difficult part was only just beginning.' That's the last line of 'Lady with a Lapdog.'"

"Are you really frightened of something?"

"I seem to be saying I am, don't I?"

"But of what?"

Her soft, clever, trusting, green eyes are on me now. All that conscientious, schoolroom attention of hers is focused upon me—and what I will answer. After a moment I tell her, "I don't know really. Yesterday at the drugstore I saw that they had portable oxygen units up on the shelf. The kid there showed me how they work, and I bought one. I put it in the bathroom closet. It's back of the beach towels. In case anything should happen to anyone tonight."

"Oh, but nothing is going to happen. Why should it?"

"No reason. Only when he was going on like that about

the past with that couple who own the hotel, I wished I had brought it along in the car."

"David, he isn't going to die just from getting heated up about the past. Oh, sweetheart," she says, kissing my hand and holding it to her cheek, "you're worn down, that's all. He gets so worked up, he *can* wear you to a frazzle—but he means so well. And he's obviously still in the best of health. He's fine. You're just exhausted. It's time for bed, that's all."

It's time for bed, that's all. Oh, innocent beloved, you fail to understand and I can't tell you. I can't say it, not tonight, but within a year my passion will be dead. Already it is dying and I am afraid that there is nothing I can do to save it. And nothing that you can do. Intimately bound—bound to you as to no one else!—and I will not be able to raise a hand to so much as touch you . . . unless first I remind myself that I must. Toward the flesh upon which I have been grafted and nurtured back toward something like mastery over my life, I will be without desire. Oh, it's stupid! Idiotic! Unfair! To be robbed like this of you! And of this life I love and have hardly gotten to know! And robbed by whom? It always comes down to myself!

And so it is I see myself back in Klinger's waiting room; and despite the presence there of all those *Newsweeks* and *New Yorkers,* I am no sympathetic, unspectacular sufferer out of a muted Chekhov tale of ordinary human affliction. No, more hideous by far, more like Gogol's berserk and mortified amputee, who rushes to the newspaper office to place a maniacal classified ad seeking the return of the nose that has decided to take leave of his face. Yes, the butt of a ridiculous, vicious, inexplicable joke! Here, you therapeutic con man, I'm back, and even worse than before! Did all you said, followed every instruction, unswervingly pursued the healthiest of regimens—even took it on myself to study the passions in my classroom, to submit to scrutiny those who have scrutinized the subject most pitilessly . . . and here is the result! I know and I know and I know, I imagine and I imagine and I imagine, and when the worst happens, I might as well know nothing! You might as well know nothing! And feed me not the consolations of the reality principle! Just find it for me before it's too late! The perfect young woman is waiting! That dream of a girl and the most livable of lives! And here I hand to the dapper, portly, clever physician the advertisement headed "LOST," describing what it looked like when last seen, its real and sentimental worth, and the reward that I will offer anyone giving information leading to its recovery: "My desire for Miss Claire Ovington—a Manhattan private-school teacher, five feet ten inches tall, one hundred and thirty-eight pounds, fair hair, silvery-green eyes, the kindest, most loving, and loyal nature—has mysteriously vanished . . ."

And the doctor's reply? That perhaps it was never in my possession to begin with? Or that, obviously, what has disappeared I must learn to live without . . .

All night long, bad dreams sweep through me like water through a fish's gills. Near dawn I awaken to discover that the house is not in ashes nor have I been abandoned in my bed as an incurable. My willing Clarissa is with me still! I raise her nightgown up along the length of her unconscious body, and with my lips begin to press and tug her nipples until the pale, velvety, childlike areolae erupt in tiny granules and her moan begins. But even while I suck in a desperate frenzy at the choicest morsel of her flesh, even as I pit all my accumulated happiness, and all my hope, against my fear of transformations yet to come, I wait to hear the most dreadful sound imaginable emerge from the room where Mr. Barbatnik and my father lie alone and insensate, each in his freshly made bed.

www.vintage-books.co.uk

TU

ACCOUNT

TURF ACCOUNT

Steve Smith Eccles
with Alan Lee

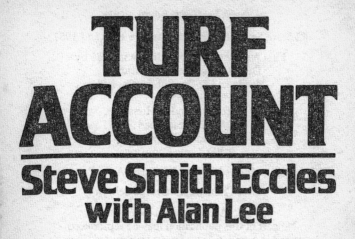

Queen Anne Press
Futura

A Queen Anne Press/Futura BOOK

© Steve Smith Eccles and Alan Lee 1986 and 1987

First published in Great Britain in 1986 by
Queen Anne Press, a division of
Macdonald & Co (Publishers) Ltd
3rd Floor
Greater London House
Hampstead Road
London NW1 7QX
A BPCC plc Company

This edition published in 1987 by Queen Anne Press/Futura

Cover Photograph: George Selwyn

ISBN 0 7088 3619 4

Reproduced, printed and bound in Great Britain by
Hazell Watson & Viney Limited,
Member of the BPCC Group,
Aylesbury, Bucks

To Di, Sandra, George and Penny
who have to live with me!

Brushing through the birchwood switches
Cramming at the open ditches
Taking what the fate provides them
Danger calling death beside them
'Tis a game beyond gainsaying
Made by God for brave men playing.

WILL H. OGILVIE

INTRODUCTION

Time was, if you believe the old-stagers of the racing game, when every jump jockey was a little like Steve Smith Eccles. Frankly, I don't believe a word of it. There is something special about the pocket battleship from coal-mining country in Derbyshire: it is called flair. He shows it on and off the racetrack, and it sustains him through the varied scrapes and crises in which his extravagant lifestyle lands him.

Often infuriating, sometimes outrageous but never, ever boring, Steve is certainly a throwback to another age, and it is one of the great regrets of his life that, all too often, his own gregarious nature seems foreign to most of his contemporaries in the riding game.

'Ecc', as he is affectionately known within the weighing-rooms of England, shares some — but not all — of the traits of another great sporting extrovert, Ian Botham. He is a fighter, a survivor and an incurable adventurer, sometimes blind to the consequences but never short of motivation. Life, he believes, is for living hard and full, and if nobody else wants to join him, he will go ahead and do it all alone.

He drinks, sometimes too much. He drives, sometimes too fast. He is a nocturnal creature who can forget his cares and worries, his bumps and bruises, in the throes of a party. And because he has always managed to divorce the working side of life from play, because he has never allowed his social life to detract from his tough, competitive riding, he has reached the top of the tree and he can afford to spoil himself.

Suddenly, when John Francome retired in 1985, the punters

9

promoted Smith Eccles to favourite to be the next champion jockey. Steve took a deep breath and tried to ignore the implications. He had seen it all before, long ago, when he was a mere twenty-one-year-old and nowhere near as proficient. The reality had not matched the expectation then, and he did not intend to allow his feet to leave the ground this time.

For all his extravagances, he has become essentially a pragmatist. He grew up in an area where virtually everyone went down the pit. He was one of the fortunate few to stay above ground, and he has never allowed himself to forget his good fortune. There has always been an anxiety to prove himself in his chosen lifestyle, blended with an acceptance that, whatever tomorrow may bring, it can hardly be as grim as life might have become if he had trodden the traditional coal-mining path.

No one can say he has failed, despite the fact that, in the 1985-86 season, he still did not become champion. As in each of the preceding half-dozen years, he rode more than his share of big-race winners and finished in the top few. He was also involved in controversy, gossip and front-page headlines. Injured several times, his face was disfigured more than once. He had rows inside and outside racing, had desperate disappointments and days of high elation. All this he has faithfully chronicled in the following pages with a diligence and discipline that some would not suspect of him. Steve bared his thoughts in words, I put them on paper. We both hope the end result is worthy of the character at the centre of this story.

Alan Lee

JULY

SUNDAY 28 JULY

It's been an odd sort of summer. The new season is six days away and I feel as if I need a holiday more than anything. I'm knackered. Since the first day of June, eight short weeks ago, when last season's jumping programme ended, I have been on the go virtually non-stop. I have ridden in America, Australia, New Zealand, Belgium, Jersey and Ireland, and the occasional spells I have had at home seem to have consisted of a hectic round of parties. That's what comes of living in Newmarket, headquarters of flat racing, during their busy months.

Mind you, I'm not complaining. The close-season might have been exhausting, but it has undoubtedly been a success. I've ridden a few winners, gained a lot of experience, done myself some good in all kinds of ways. More than that, I've also had a good time, which is an important factor in my life. Perhaps I belong to a different age, an age when sportsmen counted the laughs first and the pounds later; certainly, I find myself increasingly alone among modern jockeys in the way I live my life. But I adhere to the simple, clichéd philosophy that you are only young once. I don't intend to allow my active years to slip past unused.

There is a lot to look forward to this season. On paper, indeed, my chances of success look better than they have ever done and I notice that the bookmakers are quoting me as low as 5-2 to be champion jockey. The odds, frankly, are ludicrous — it would be more realistic to give 5-2 against me getting through the season in one piece!

In National Hunt racing, you are constantly being reminded that you are only as safe as your last ride. Everyone has falls. They are an

11

unavoidable and inevitable hazard of the occupation. There is luck involved — the best jumpers can get brought down, or make one mistake and fall — and although good jockeys can to some extent see the pitfalls before they occur and so make their own luck, no one is immune from danger. All you can do, once you have attained the happy level of being able to pick and choose rides, is to pace yourself, turning down spare rides on notoriously bad jumpers just for the sake of another £46 fee. Better to refuse the cash and be fit for a winner tomorrow.

All too often, something will go wrong just when you kid yourself you are on top of the job. Racing is that kind of cruel leveller — it will build you up to a certain pitch and then knock you flat again with a single blow.

Success naturally spawns pressure. Even the expectation of success adds an extra strain. I will begin this season painfully aware that the racing public are expecting me to do well, indeed that many of them are expecting me to be champion. Hard as I will try to ignore it, that knowledge could affect my riding. It only needs a few things to go wrong, a little confidence to drain away ... everyone is human.

The one certainty about the coming season is this. I don't know where it will happen and I don't know when, but more than once in the coming months I will experience genuine fear. There is no escaping it. Every jockey has his fear factor, every jockey will be frightened during a race several times in the course of a jumping season. The good ones can cope, conquer it and carry on as if it never happened. The bad cases never do. One jockey can always see fear in another. We know the tell-tale signs. Thankfully, it is seldom obvious to anyone outside the job, and nine out of ten jockeys will give up and get out as soon as they see the red light and realise their 'bottle' has gone. The few who try to battle on are a pathetic sight to see.

It is for these reasons, among others, that I cannot begin this diary with any brash predictions. I am not even thinking about winning the championship. With the retirement of my old mate John Francome, who was incomparable during his last few years of riding, the title race is likely to be more open than at any time since I started riding. A good start is important; weather will play its part; injuries could be decisive. Skill, of course, is a not insignificant factor, allied to the ammunition — in horse terms — to show it. Weighing all these things up, I reckon there are six perfectly good candidates for the crown: Jonjo O'Neill, Chris Grant and Neale Doughty in the north, Peter Scudamore, Hywel Davies and myself in the south. And I am perfectly prepared for someone outside this half-dozen to surprise us all.

One advantage of my working summer is that I will begin the season fully fit. There will be no holiday pounds to sweat off — I haven't had a holiday — and no race-rustiness to oil because I have hardly stopped race-riding.

It will not take me long to get back into the routine of the season, I'm sure of that. Although I feel tired now, a few meetings, hopefully a winner or two, and I will be back on auto-pilot. There are memories to keep me going, too. The summer has certainly filled in a few more pieces of life's rich tapestry and I have plenty of tales to tell in the weighing-room, arising from the world tour I undertook with the British jockeys team during June. Tales like the one about the young jockey who struck lucky with an Australian girl and was getting down to important matters in his hotel bed when a radio station announcer phoned, demanding an instant live interview about his winner at the big meeting that day. He managed to prove it is possible to do two things at once . . . !

So many things happened to me on that trip it is hard to know which to relate first. I recall being thrown in a Baltimore swimming-pool fully-clothed on my 30th birthday, the day after we had beaten the Americans; I remember being boldly chatted up on a plane across the States — by a male steward; I remember the L.A. women, the foul New Zealand weather, the stunning Australian hospitality. I shall never forget riding out in the darkness before dawn near Melbourne and I will certainly always cherish the memory of riding two big winners on the Saturday afternoon TV card at Moonee Valley. Most of all, it strikes me, I got used to being away from home. There were, of course, times during the three-week tour when every one of us got fed up, and one memorable occasion at Auckland airport when I threatened to get on the next plane back to London, but I did get used to the lifestyle, the confinements and the freedoms of hotel life, and the cameraderie which is naturally created in a travelling party of seven.

We all felt that we were riding for Britain, for Queen and Country, rather than simply for ourselves, and it was striking just what a difference this made. We celebrated each other's winners as if they were our own; we strained every muscle to pick up points for third or fourth place which just might swing a match; winning, as a team on faraway foreign soil, meant a lot. Team riding did have its amusing moments, of course. During the hurdle race at Moonee Valley, I was rounding the home turn on the favourite. Peter Scudamore was on my outer, beaten but battling for a place, and he suddenly yelled: 'One up your inner, Steve'. I moved across to close the gap and heard an unmistakeably Welsh scream. I had just cost my own team-mate Hywel Davies any chance of winning. Fortunately, I went on to win, but Hywel did not allow 'Scu' to forget . . . .

Being lucky with my weight, I could always tuck into a hearty bacon, eggs and brown sauce breakfast while Hywel and Peter set off for the sauna each morning. And, being naturally gregarious, I enjoyed the social life of being abroad, and usually outstayed my team-mates on our evenings out. I enjoyed all the good points of foreign racing, especially in America and Australia, but in New Zealand we saw things which made us all appreciate British standards. In a place called Tauranga we had to ride a hurdle race over obstacles which were literally five-bar gates staked into the ground. For the chases they simply added brush on top to create a homespun fence. Frankly, it was dangerous, and no English race-course would have contemplated such death-traps. We all came through unscathed, however, and I have since ridden in Jersey, Belgium and Ireland — all in the space of one hectic long weekend in mid-July.

Now I am ready and eager for the business of the home season. Today, I spoke to all the trainers who are likely to engage me on a regular basis, and I have to admit things look good. John Jenkins, always sure to run plenty of horses on the firm ground at the beginning of the season, ought to give me a good start as I will be sharing the work on his string with Simon Sherwood, last season's champion amateur; Nicky Henderson will not run many early on, but he has some impressive animals for when the season is seriously underway and I will ride 30 of the best; Jeff King, who provided me with a dozen winners last term, has more horses of a higher quality this time; my Newmarket neighbour Gavin Pritchard-Gordon will have his usual few nice jumpers; there will be Duke of Milan and Dark Hansel, two lovely horses, to ride for Nick Gaselee, and Kathies Lad — who won at both Cheltenham and Aintree in the spring — for Alan Jarvis ... yes, things look good. But despite my confident front, I never count my chickens. This time next week the season will be a day old and everything could look different after one fall.

MONDAY 29 JULY

You can never accurately predict the bad fall but you can take precautions to avoid it. Bill Clay, a nice guy who trains in Uttoxeter, phoned up today to offer me a ride on Saturday. It is a novice chaser having his first attempt over fences — on the first day of the season. I hate turning down rides but I had to refuse. What an idiot I would look if, with all the good horses I can look forward to riding this season, I broke my leg on that. Bill is not too happy, but there are times as a freelance when you just have to risk upsetting people.

AUGUST

SATURDAY 3 AUGUST

The season began with a race against time and traffic. Stayed last night with John Francome at Lambourn after flying back from Ireland, where I had a ride on Thursday. Set off in plenty of time for the drive down to Newton Abbot, I thought, even allowing for the inevitable Saturday morning West Country holiday traffic. But the M5 was worse than I've ever known it — bumper to bumper all the way. I watched the clock ticking on, imagined my fancied ride in the first being snapped up by somebody else, and decided it was time for action. My Porsche can travel a bit, given a clear run, so I opted for the hard shoulder and, with a wary eye in the mirror for flashing blue lights, cruised along at 95 mph.

It was some sort of journey, that. But I got to the course in time, won the first event on Kyoto and the third on The Owls. I could hardly have asked for a better start.

SUNDAY 4 AUGUST

Jonjo has broken his collarbone. I read it in the papers this morning and felt so sorry for the poor guy. He had a wretched time with injuries last season but, with Francome out of the way, he was favourite with many bookmakers to be champion this time. It didn't take long for fate to catch up with him again — his second ride at the Market Rasen evening meeting, on a moderate horse in a very moderate selling hurdle, and there he was back in hospital — out for maybe three weeks. It could have been me; we tread a very fine line between success and disaster in this game.

16

MONDAY 5 AUGUST

Just one ride, which did not oblige. But I have had a good weekend staying, as usual, at the Palace Hotel in Torquay. It must be six years now since I began to camp here for the early-season Devon meetings and I always look forward to coming back. The facilities are vast and include tennis courts inside and outside, on which Francome and I have challenged all-comers every autumn. If it doesn't seem quite the same so far this year it must be because John is not here with me. We share a similar sense of humour and outlook on life; I miss him a lot. I also have a feeling that he is pining, too. When I stayed with him last week it was not the normal bouncy 'Franc'. It struck me then that he might be miserable because he would be missing out on Devon this year . . . but then again, maybe he was just worried about his imminent new life in training. I caught him reading a book called 'How to train racehorses', which should amuse the boys!

The hospitality the Palace staff always show to me was illustrated again tonight. I got back to the hotel, after having some dinner, around 11.30 p.m. and noticed that the water pump on my car was leaking. The hotel manager immediately summoned one of his garage staff and the fault was fixed on the spot while the manager bought me a drink in the bar — very civilised.

Mind you, life has had its literally painful moments at the Palace. About five years ago, I went to the traditional start-of-season ball always held down here after the opening day at Newton Abbot. A footloose bachelor, I took a fancy to two different girls at the ball; one had to be given the elbow and she did not take it well. The following day I had a message to say she was waiting for me in the lobby of the hotel and when I strolled down to see her it was obvious that time had not healed. She had brought along a friend and, with a face like thunder, she gave me little time for explanations. I could tell she was about to hit me. I threw up an arm to catch the intended blow and was just telling her to be sensible when I got stars before my eyes as what felt like a paving slab hit me on the back of my head. Concentrating on one potential assailant, I had unwisely ignored her mate, who had slipped round behind me and swung her handbag with regrettable accuracy. I can only assume that, with malice aforethought, she had slipped something blunt and heavy inside it as it gave me a fierce headache, not to mention an entirely undeserved reputation with the giggling reception staff of the Palace . . . .

TUESDAY 6 AUGUST

I agreed to drive to Finmere, a 390-mile, six-hour round-trip from Torquay, for a Jockeys' Show Jumping event today. Under normal circumstances I would not have gone but this year the proceeds are all going to the appeal fund set up for Bob Woley, an ex-jockey. I knew it was a good cause, and this morning 'Franc' and I went to see Bob in the spinal injuries unit of Stoke Mandeville Hospital, and the visit had quite an effect on me.

I remembered Bob as a big bull of a man, a character much liked and enjoyed by all his fellow jockeys. Now, after a fall which has paralysed him and taken away the great love of his life, he is a shadow of his old self. For a change, sitting there in his company, I was entirely lost for words, welcoming the chatter of 'Franc', who had seen Bob in that state before. It could happen to any of us riding today, and if I ever ended up in that position I don't think I would want to go on living. I drove on to Finmere in a mood of near depression; but I was glad I had decided to go.

WEDNESDAY 7 AUGUST

I always say that the most hazardous part of my job is not riding horses over obstacles but having to contend with some of the other lunatics who are somehow let loose on our jumping courses. The situation is often at its worst in the West Country, where a number of Devonshire farmers, not to mention their sons and daughters, ride the family horses and any others they are allowed to sit on. Some ride like cowboys, apparently imagining they are acting in a particularly violent western and that the other jockeys in their race are all Indians. There are a couple of girls in particular who ride down here and should undoubtedly be locked up as dangers to civilisation. Today on the Devon course on Haldon Hill the weather was consistent with our worst summer in years — hosing down with rain — and the recipe for accidents only needed the addition of the cowboys. Rain on firm ground creates a surface like an ice-rink and guiding a horse round bends

18

in such conditions is tricky enough without the crazy, untutored riding of some of this lot. They took no notice at all of the conditions, however, and I was very grateful indeed to come through the day not only in one piece but also with a third winner chalked up.

Although all three winners have been for John Jenkins, I am having to bite my tongue over the situation, as neither Simon Sherwood nor I ever quite know which horses we are supposed to ride. It is frustrating, of course, but most jockeys would give a lot to have a share of the Jenkins stable's early action, so it is best to say nothing.

Simon also rode another winner today and he is emerging as one of the old school. Apart from being a very tidy rider, he is a nice fellow who is far from reluctant to have a night out on the town. I had begun to wonder if I was the last of the breed!

THURSDAY 8 AUGUST

Most jockeys will tell you they very seldom hear the noise of the crowd when they are riding a race, and I am usually no different. But there is an exception to every rule. I rode a horse called Sailing By, running for the second day in succession and attempting a hat-trick of wins in the first four racing days of the season. He failed spectacularly. At Devon's very first hurdle, the horse made such a bad mistake that his nose hit the ground and I slid forward out of the saddle until I was no more than a foot from the ground, clinging onto the horse's neck with my head under his. I was convinced I had gone past the point of no return and I could clearly hear the jeers of the crowd as the horse — heavily backed to favourite — galloped past the stands with his jockey in this desperate and undignified position. Using all the strength and balance I could muster, I somehow struggled slowly onto the horse's back and as I slipped into the plate, the jeers turned to cheers and a thunderous round of clapping broke out as many substantial wagers were, at least temporarily, rescued. All this had hardly helped Sailing By's prospects, though, and combined with it being his third race in a week, I was far from disappointed to finish fourth after such a hairy adventure.

When it is cold and raining, as it was today, Haldon is one of

19

racing's most uninviting places and I was just warming myself in the bar with the day's first whisky after racing when I happened to overhear a conversation. It was plainly a mother talking to her daughter; equally plainly, they did not know who I was, as mother was in the middle of giving daughter her views on Simon Sherwood, which went something like this: 'He's a very nice boy, dear, but what a pity he spends so much time with that Steve Smith Eccles ... he'll ruin him, you know.' I briefly considered introducing myself, but I'm not one to cause unnecessary embarrassment!

FRIDAY 9 AUGUST
Checked out of the Palace this morning after a six-night stay. It cost me around £200 but I consider it money well spent. I feel fresh and relaxed and I have enjoyed the first week of the season without the strain imposed by constant driving. With four meetings in this part of the world, I would have thought it logical to stay down but I am obviously in the minority. I compare my approach with that of Richard Rowe, Josh Gifford's stable jockey. Richard lives in Findon, West Sussex, a four-and-a-half-hour drive from either of the Devon courses, and he has ridden at each of the four meetings this week, yet commuted every day. On petrol costs alone he can hardly have saved any money, and with four nine-hour round trips I very much doubt if he has actually enjoyed the opening week of a long season. On Saturday, he got so badly caught in the traffic that he missed his first two rides, but even then he didn't reconsider and stay down for the other meetings. I know it takes all sorts, but I really can't understand it.

SATURDAY 10 AUGUST
Last season it took me two months to ride my first four winners. This time I have reached that figure already after winning on Celtic Story in the novice chase at Worcester tonight.

We have evening meetings at each end of the jumping season and I think it is fair to say that they are more popular with the public than the jockeys. They attract big crowds because more people can come along after work (or, in the case of a Saturday, after a day in the garden, at the shops or under the wife's thumb) but as far as the jockey is concerned it means a late finish, probably no dinner, and perhaps a long drive home in the dark.

My own drive home this evening was eventful. I was moving at a decent speed through Alcester, the first town out of Worcester, when I saw a gorgeous blonde hitching a lift on the pavement. I screeched to a halt 20 yards or so further on and watched in the mirror as this attractive creature tripped along the road and hopped in next to me. Only then, at close quarters, did I realise I had made a grave mistake. The blonde turned out to be a fellow in drag. It gave me the shock of my life but I proceeded to give 'him' the shock of his, driving him on to Stratford at an alarming speed before gratefully depositing him and continuing on my way with a silent vow to be more careful of future hitch-hikers.

SUNDAY 11 AUGUST

There is no real day of rest once the season gets properly under-way. During August and September, when the meetings are scattered, we all have a few days off now and again, but once the time comes, during October, for racing every day, it is a seven-day-a-week existence, Sundays being the day on which most jockeys plan their week ahead. Even today, I spent two-and-a-half hours on the phone to my trainers, only to discover that none of them — with the exception of John Jenkins — has anything close to being ready to run. John, of course, has had another tremendous start with nine winners in eight days, and no other trainer even tries to compete with his striking rate at this end of the season.

Sunday lunch is a luxury, a time when I greatly appreciate having very few weight problems, and after indulging myself with the joint and the roast potatoes I set to work in the garden — and not at all unwillingly. Gardening may be a chore to many, but to me it is a release. I love trees and plants and take great pride in tending my acre, even though I do pay a regular gardener, a World War II bomber pilot named Joe Pryor, to look after it. For me, it is a rare chance to switch off from racing.

WEDNESDAY 14 AUGUST

The glamour of this life is not even skin-deep. Having set off early this morning, heading for Fontwell, I was caught in the rush-hour chaos around the Dartford Tunnel. We were stationary for half-an-hour and time was beginning to run short, so for the second time this season I took to the hard shoulder. This time I was not so lucky — a police car appeared, followed by the notebook, and all my protestations about being a jockey late for work had no effect at all. I didn't have the nerve to adopt the tactics of one controversial colleague of mine who, when stopped on the motorway for driving at 105 mph and told he would probably lose his licence for it, glibly replied that it made no difference at all to him as he was a leukaemia sufferer with only a few months to live. The poor, duped policeman took pity and put his notebook away.

After all the fuss, I raced into the Fontwell weighing-room half-an-hour before my race wondering if the hassles of my lifestyle were all worthwhile. Then I went out and won on The Somac and, instantly, I knew they were.

THURSDAY 15 AUGUST

Rode two losers, back at Newton Abbot, including Celtic Story, which fell five out in the novice chase. He wouldn't have won anyway, but I spent some time thinking back through the incident and apportioning blame. It is important always to assess why you have had a fall, particularly if you are likely to be riding the horse again. I am very self-critical about my riding but I believe it is the only way to improve. No one ever stops learning in this game and if you have made a mistake, such as giving a horse a kick into the fence when you should have been taking a pull, then try to correct it the next time.

FRIDAY 16 AUGUST

John Jenkins and Philip Mitchell both train at Epsom and it would be fair to say that they don't see eye to eye. They are about the same age, both have tasted success and both are strong-willed ... all of which helps to explain the remarkable scenes in the foyer of the Plumpton weighing-room today, when I am convinced they would have come to blows if I had not stepped in. The argument arose because both had a runner in the three-year-old hurdle and both believed they had booked Simon Sherwood to ride. Simon, having been advised yesterday morning that John would not be running his horse Asticot, had agreed to ride Billion Boy for Philip. Some time between 9.30 and 10.00 a.m. yesterday, however, John obviously changed his mind and Asticot appeared among the declarations, S. Sherwood's name next door. Poor Simon, who was just the pawn in this affair, found himself with two rides and neither trainer was prepared to release him.

Philip was the first of the pair to arrive at Plumpton and duly made out his declaration sheet for Billion Boy with Simon down to ride. When John arrived, he ripped up Philip's sheet and wrote out his own, naming Simon. I observed all this, and with interest, because I thought one of them would ask me to deputise on their horse, so it came as something of a blow when they seemed willing to ignore S. Smith Eccles and fight over S. Sherwood.

John lost his temper first, only yards away from the stewards' room and close to disaster. I moved in to an argument which had nothing at all to do with me and told him to calm down, because if he started a fight he would lose his licence (and, although I refrained from saying so, this meant I would lose rides!). Fortunately, he saw sense, backed down and told me to ride Asticot, which unfortunately got beaten ... by Billion Boy. Philip diplomatically said later that he and John were friends again, but I am not so sure.

Another eventful day at least provided a winner, Kyoto hacking round to win the handicap chase under 12 stone 8 pounds. He is the best two to two-and-a-half-mile chaser around at this time of year, and we are trying to get him invited to America for the Colonial Cup — another trip to look forward to.

SATURDAY 17 AUGUST

With no rides at the two meetings, Bangor and Market Rasen, I took the chance of a rare Saturday off — well, nearly off. I was still up and out of the house by 7.00 a.m. to school some horses for Gavin Pritchard-Gordon, but the rest of the day was my own.

SUNDAY 18 AUGUST

I made the most of my free day and enjoyed myself rather too much, judging by my head this morning. Last night's dinner party was lively and lengthy and I am paying the price. I often spend some time on Sundays reflecting on the week gone by, and I have little to complain about today, the hangover apart. I've ridden two more winners this week and survived my first fall of the season, always an important landmark to pass. Simon and I have each ridden six winners now, which is the sort of start to boost confidence. I find it very noticeable in the weighing-room that there are still plenty of tense faces; a lot of jockeys fancy their chances of being champion this season, and they are all champing at the bit, trying to get those first few winners under the belt.

MONDAY 19 AUGUST

My bags are packed for another week away. Today racing was at Worcester, where I rode two losers before going on down to Lambourn. In the morning I shall be doing some schooling for Nicky Henderson, and I'm looking forward to seeing how his good horses are coming along.

TUESDAY 20 AUGUST

Comparing Nicky's horses with John Jenkins' right now is like comparing a broodmare with a greyhound. John has a team specifically prepared for this time of year but Nick is content to wait, maybe impatiently, for the good ground. I did, however, school an experienced and successful American import called Running Comment, who will be out soon. I have high hopes of him, having been in the States with the British team last year when 'Franc' won a chase on him very comfortably.

WEDNESDAY 21 AUGUST

Drove down to Devon fearing I might fall asleep on my way to the start. My bedroom at the Francomes' house is directly above the piano room, in which John has a habit of playing at very odd times of day and night. It was 5.00 a.m. when he started tinkling today, just when I needed another few hours kip.

I managed to stay awake for my one ride, which was just as

well as things turned out. It was pouring with rain — again — and my horse Aboushabun seemed to take offence. He was in front coming to the water jump near the stands when suddenly he ducked out. There was nothing whatever I could do as he veered off, crashing through the rail, snapping the plastic as if it were a matchstick. The bottom of my boot hit the rail, taking the heel off, and if I had been riding three inches longer, I have no doubt that it would have taken my foot off instead. I didn't give it much thought at the time, but this evening, lying in my bath at The Palace, a shiver crept up my spine when I reflected on what might have been.

THURSDAY 22 AUGUST

Hywel Davies rode two winners today, breaking his duck for the season, and the broad smile on his face was one of undisguised relief. Hywel, the Welshman who won the Grand National in April, is another of whom the public have high expectations this term and, always an intense man, he had worn a permanently worried frown as that elusive winner refused to arrive for almost three weeks. It is a mental barrier as much as anything, and I am sure he will ride in more relaxed fashion from now on.

FRIDAY 23 AUGUST

The *Sporting Life* is on strike, a calamity for everyone involved in racing. Jockeys, especially, survive and organise their lives by knowing the four-day declarations for imminent meetings, and the *Life* is the only national paper which publishes them. It is not so bad at this time of year, when there is seldom more than one meeting each day anyway, but when there are two, three or even four possible venues to ride at on any one day, rides can take some sorting out. Seldom have I been so anxious for swift arbitration in any industrial dispute.

SATURDAY 24 AUGUST

For any freelance, the unwritten law is 'never turn down work'. But there are times when common-sense prevails. Today I had the choice of a six-hour round trip to Hereford for one ride on a no-hoper, or a leisurely Saturday off, catching up on some sleep. No prizes for guessing my decision.

MONDAY 26 AUGUST

Pressure on a jockey is automatically increased when he knows that his horse's connections have had a punt. If you get beaten on one that is really fancied you know there will be no pats on the back when you return to unsaddle. Sometimes, however, the reaction is not at all what you expect. Take today. I rode a four-year-old called Taraius for John Jenkins. He had run in last season's Triumph Hurdle, and so should have outclassed everything in a Newton Abbot novice hurdle: the owners backed him to 4-6 and, knowing that, I threw everything in to try and get the horse's head in front. I failed, finished second — and, to my surprise, came back to be told by the trainer that I had been too hard on the horse!

THURSDAY 29 AUGUST

Had a haircut today, which was quite an achievement. It is such menial things, which other people take for granted, that I find so hard to fit in during the season. I have to book three days in advance with my hairdresser, and invariably I end up cancelling the appointment when an unexpected ride turns up.

My three days in Devon were not a great success; indeed, they were an irritation. I lost a couple of expected rides to Jonjo O'Neill, whom John Jenkins summoned from deepest Cumbria. They both got beaten — for which Jonjo was certainly not to blame — but John is well aware that I am unhappy at the situation. So far, I am biting my tongue.

FRIDAY 30 AUGUST

Gavin has a nice three-year-old called Boom Patrol. I schooled him for the first time today, just gently popping him over some hay-bales in Gavin's indoor school, and I was impressed. You will hear a lot more of the animal.

Schooling young horses is very satisfying to me. I did my apprenticeship with a fine trainer, Tom Jones, who taught me the proper method of schooling, step-by-step, and when I am called upon by any of my trainers I like to make sure things are done the right way. A horse's first school over obstacles is the most important. You need a decent lead horse who behaves impeccably, and you do not want the young horse to be frightened by what he is doing. If he is, and he carries that fear onto the racecourse when he first runs in a hurdle race, he could be ruined for a very long time. I have known trainers whose idea of schooling is to rush a novice across a couple of full-size hurdles, probably clattering through them both, and then send him to the races, where they cannot understand it when their charge runs as if he is scared and bewildered.

SATURDAY 31 AUGUST

That six-hour round-trip to Hereford confronted me again, but this time I had a feeling it would be worthwhile. Nicky Henderson's first runner of the term was the American horse, Running Comment, and although he was no more than half-fit, he trotted up. On firm ground at either end of the season, he will be a real force.

If Nicky was smiling, his Lambourn neighbour and mentor Fred Winter was not. Fred also had his first runners: both started favourite but one jumped awfully, losing all chance, and the other ran out. It's a great leveller, this game.

SEPTEMBER

SUNDAY 1 SEPTEMBER

At various stages of the season, and usually on a Sunday, I make a habit of sitting quietly in my own snug — a retreat from the world — and taking stock of what has passed. Today I looked back on August and concluded that it was a very satisfactory first month of the season. I am riding well, I am full of confidence and I have so far clocked up seven winners. That puts me second in the table behind John Jenkins' other jockey Simon Sherwood, but the gap is small. No one has broken away from the pack as John Francome did last season. There is still all to play for.

MONDAY 2 SEPTEMBER

Back to international business today. The British team of three — Peter Scudamore, Hywel Davies and myself — are taking on Ireland and France in a three-leg challenge match sponsored by the Irish-based pen manufacturers A.T. Cross. This was the opening leg in Galway, and in many ways it was typically Irish. There were a lot of non-runners, some chaotic moments in the presentation ceremonies and a good deal of the customary Irish 'it'll be all right on the night' outlook.

For us, it *was* all right, Britain taking a decent lead into the next leg, which is in France in three weeks time. We had arrived at Shannon airport by private plane, and three cars had been sent from Galway to ferry us to the racecourse. Jonjo O'Neill, (riding for Ireland on this occasion) Hywel and I were billetted with a man named Paul who had a fast car he insisted on driving at about 20mph. I kept telling him to take off the handbrake but it made no difference, so we decided between us that there would be a change of driver on the return trip. I took the wheel, initially to Paul's obvious apprehension and later to his utter alarm. He sat in the back seat with his eyes closed, frequently crossing himself, and I have never seen such relief on a man's face as I saw on Paul's when we arrived at Shannon in about half the time it had taken us on the outward journey.

There was more fun to come. Back at Birmingham airport after a suitable amount of celebrating on board, there was a longish walk along concourses and down escalators to the customs desk. Finding an unused wheelchair was a temptation impossible for me to resist, and our manager David Nicholson did not take much persuading to sit in it, while I pushed him at considerable speed, scattering all in our path. Now, David — commonly known as 'The Duke' — has his critics for his superficial domineering manner. He frightens people, but under it all he is soft and, having ridden for him often, I know he is game for a laugh. On this occasion, however, he got rather more than he bargained for. The escalator loomed up quicker than I had expected and the pilot of our wheelchair, yours truly, opted to bail out, while D. Nicholson, still seated with his head hunched inside his coat, toppled onto the moving steps and, somehow, stayed intact to make one of the more unusual entrances this particular customs team can ever have seen.

TUESDAY 3 SEPTEMBER
When you are down in this game, life tends to kick you in the teeth. The current case of Mark Perrett proves my point. A year ago, Mark was riding a lot of winners in good style and people were speaking of him in glowing terms as a star of the future. Then he fell out with Stan Mellor, the trainer who retained him, and suddenly he was effectively 'out on the street'. Hugh O'Neill, a middle-of-the-road Surrey trainer, offered him his rides, and no sooner had he got going than Mark broke his leg. I heard the news today when Hugh phoned up to book me for one of his horses. I accepted with no particular pleasure.

THURSDAY 5 SEPTEMBER
The season is not yet six weeks old and Jonjo O'Neill has just

suffered his second bad injury. This time it is a broken wrist — and he did not even do it on a racecourse, but in schooling. I am beginning to think Jonjo must have brittle bones, because every time he has a heavy fall he seems to break something. I do not, however, go along with the view that he wants to pack up riding or that he should. He has certainly not lost his nerve, which is the all-important thing; like most of us who have been around a few years he refrains from the unnecessary risks we might have taken as kids, but he still rides as hard as ever. He also still sees it all the same way I do — as being paid pretty well for doing something enjoyable. The day he stops is the day his problems begin to mount up. I hope he is not out for long.

SATURDAY 7 SEPTEMBER

Anthony Webber is an enigma. Even he would not claim to be the most stylish or rhythmical jockey around, but however much one might criticise him, the fact remains that horses do run for him. Today at Stratford he rode the winner of the novice chase, a horse of his father's called Ayle Hero. It was impossible to fault the ride he gave his horse until after jumping the last. Then, instead of coming across towards the inside rail to keep a course towards the post, he seemed to lose his sense of direction, carrying straight on towards the water-jump. I was chasing him in second place and could see this happening, so I stoked up my horse, knowing that Anthony would have to take a smart left turn to avoid the water and might be thought to have impeded me if I could get close enough. He saw the danger just in time and veered left, but I wasn't quite within striking distance and I had to be content with second place and a spot of ribbing at Anthony's expense.

WEDNESDAY 11 SEPTEMBER

First racing since Saturday. Rode in a novice chase at Fontwell, a hilly track where the downhill fences take prisoners at every meeting. Caution and commonsense is demanded, especially in the game of Russian Roulette, which is very often the closest thing to a novice chase. Yet today there were jockeys urging bad horses down that hill at a crazy, neckbreaking speed. I shouted to one such lunatic to take it steady, but he took no notice. I passed him at the next fence — he was lying on the deck — and completed the race, grateful to be in one piece.

I have some sympathy with these jockeys though. In almost every case they are struggling riders who have to grab every opportunity and ride each horse they get on as if their life depends on it. But in giving everything, they take commitment to a dangerous degree at which they are risking serious injury to themselves and also putting the health of other riders at risk.

THURSDAY 12 SEPTEMBER
I am lying alone in bed at the Palace, Torquay. I feel I want to be sick, but I can't. Every bone in my body aches and I am honestly not sure which day of the week it is anymore — and all because I took a spare ride in a fillies' hurdle race at Newton Abbot.

It wasn't as if it looked a risky ride. The horse, Joscilla, was trained by Les Kennard and went off a warm favourite. But we got no further than the sixth hurdle before the horse ploughed straight into the obstacle and fired me into the firm autumn ground. I don't remember much more. The doctor probably should have signed me off for the compulsory seven-day period stipulated for concussion. Somehow I escaped. But God knows how many brain cells I killed with that fall. I must sleep . . . .

FRIDAY 13 SEPTEMBER
A suitable date for the way I feel. Getting out of bed was a monumental effort, and I felt as if I had been run over by a steamroller until an hour's soaking in a hot bath got rid of a certain amount of the stiffness.

The last thing I felt like doing was riding, but somehow I got through my one booked ride. Unfortunately it was the first race on the card, which gave me far too much time in the bar. Whisky can be an effective painkiller, I kept telling myself, but things did get out of hand, and for some reason I ended the evening in the bar of the Grand Atlantic Hotel, Weston-super-Mare!

SATURDAY 14 SEPTEMBER
This promised to be a good day, but it didn't turn out that way. It

was the day on which John Francome was to have his first runner over jumps since taking up training — and I had the ride. The horse was Crimson Knight, and I use the word 'was' advisedly, because tonight Crimson Knight is dead and instead of celebrating an immediate success for one of my closest friends I am sharing in a nightmare.

I was on a high for 'Franc's' race, having just won the novice chase. I had taken the mickey out of John for bringing in his colours in a plastic shopping bag instead of the smart leather bags most trainers use, and I was enjoying the new experience of having him give me riding instructions in the paddock.

The horse was fancied, and with good reason. Turning for home, I challenged for the lead with Crimson Knight cruising. The moment he hit the front he found another gear, and he was running away from the pack as we approached the third-last hurdle. He met it on a long stride but instead of taking off, he stepped into the hurdle and we came down. What could I have done? Even as I lay on the grass I asked the question. But there was no good answer. When you have hit the front and you're flying, instinct insists you go for the long one if it's there. But this did not help the way I felt. John had ridden his first and his 1000th winners at Worcester and I had had the chance to give him his first training success there.

It made things much worse when word reached me later in the afternoon that the horse had dropped dead in his box, some time after the race. John had already left the course; someone would have to tell him on the phone. Knowing his phlegmatic approach, I guessed he would take it in his stride, but even if he did not feel upset, I did. Tonight I felt so low I didn't want to talk, drink or eat.

MONDAY 16 SEPTEMBER
Up at six o'clock to ride out for Alan Jarvis, who trains at Royston, only a short drive from Newmarket. He had told me yesterday that the ground was too firm for him to school any horses, but I decided to go anyway. Putting myself around like this, turning up to school or ride work at each of my trainers in turn, is a way of securing rides once their horses do run.

Alan Jarvis offered me a £10,000 retainer a few years ago and got as far as paying me the first instalment. It was big money then — probably the biggest sum ever offered to a jump jockey — but for various reasons we drifted apart before the middle of the season. Despite the inevitable gossip, there was no bad feeling between us; indeed, I like the guy a lot, and I look forward to riding his very good two-mile chaser Kathies Lad again this season.

TUESDAY 17 SEPTEMBER
Ever since that fall at Newton Abbot I've been suffering from bad headaches. The three days off at the start of this week would normally have been a frustration, just as the season has begun to get going, but the way I feel right now, they are very welcome.

WEDNESDAY 18 SEPTEMBER
I phoned Jonjo and Mark Perrett to try and cheer them up. Jonjo is his usual bouncy self and will be back in the saddle before too long, I expect. But Mark was depressed and in a lot of pain. He also said I was the first jockey to phone him in the two weeks since his fall. I'm afraid that does not say much for my profession.

THURSDAY 19 SEPTEMBER
My day began at 5.15 a.m. when I set off to school in Lambourn. Then it was on to open a shop for a friend in Street, Somerset, before riding at nearby Wincanton. Yet another fall — my third in the last five rides — which will do nothing for my head. Bought fish and chips on the way home. There is quite an art, I have discovered, to eating them while driving at 90 mph.

FRIDAY 20 SEPTEMBER
Huntingdon is my favourite course, partly because it is my most local track but also because it holds so many good memories. I had my first ride there, and my first 'chase winner. I've been leading jockey there for the past six or seven years, and I know the track so well that I have won races there that I had no right to. Having said all that, I logged a bad memory onto the Huntingdon file today when I turned up to ride Tamertown Lad for John

Jenkins and found that I had been 'jocked off'. John backed off when I had a go at him, saying that it was not his fault, and that the decision had been taken by the owners. But I remained upset, not just by the fact that Graham Bradley rode the horse and won, but that nobody had told me I was not required until I reached the course. As it was Huntingdon, I had only a short, sulky trip home, but what if it had been Wincanton? Would I still have received the same treatment?

SATURDAY 21 SEPTEMBER

A long weekend away, on team duties, began today. After racing at Warwick where I drew a blank, I joined up with the British and Irish teams to fly by private plane to Rennes in France for tomorrow's second leg of the A.T. Cross International. Then on Monday and Tuesday, in the unlikely settings of Plumpton and Sedgefield, I am in the South team for a match against the North. I have my doubts whether this event will work.

It turned out to be a long day. The Irish were late into Birmingham, so our plane was late arriving at Rennes. Then we had a long drive to Laval, and a hotel near the racecourse. We did not arrive until past midnight and I went straight to bed.

SUNDAY 22 SEPTEMBER

Last year we raced against the French in Paris. This is a bit of a contrast. Laval is a sleepy old market-town, as I discovered when I took a stroll before breakfast this morning. Considering that, the crowd at the races was enormous — almost 20,000 apparently — and it is easy to see why they brought the match here.

The French idea of a steeplechase is very different from ours. In England, the fences are uniform, with slight variations such as the open ditch and the water; in France, you race over all shapes and sizes, including stone walls and steep banks. That in itself would have made things tricky, but the course also followed a complicated route and when Tony Mullins, the engagingly voluble one in the Irish team, announced that he would make the pace, I feared trouble. Sure enough, Tony was still ahead when he went the wrong way in mid-race and found himself disqualified. It might make a big difference — Frank Berry won the race for

Ireland, but we picked up plenty of place points and still have a healthy lead going into the last leg at Chepstow. The French, I'm afraid, are tailed off.

Another long day ended with a flight to Gatwick and a car transfer down to Brighton, where we will be spending the next two nights. Summoning some energy reserves I quizzed the hotel receptionist about the best night-clubs to patronise. 'It's Sunday,' she replied sullenly. 'They are all closed.' They would be, wouldn't they.

MONDAY 23 SEPTEMBER

My prediction about the North v South match proving a failure very nearly came true in the most unfortunate way. There were two match races at Plumpton today, and 15 minutes before the first of them was due 'off', the northern jockeys had still not arrived. I can't remember ever seeing so many worried faces on a racecourse before, nor so much relief when Graham Bradley, Phil Tuck, Chris Grant and Colin Hawkins sprinted breathlessly into the weighing-room even as the stewards were meeting to decide what action to take. I don't think many if any spectators in the surprisingly big crowd had any inkling of the panic, which was just as well.

'Brad' has always been a cool customer. He told me the saga of the boys missing a train connection in London and getting a cab all the way to the course, not daring to stop and ring up for fear of losing vital minutes. Then he went out and rode a well-judged race to win the first event. Sam Morshead won the next for us and our place points give us a ten-point advantage.

Tonight, I decided, Brighton would know I was in town. After a good fish meal attended by the eight jockeys in the match, Colin Hawkins and I set off in search of a night-spot. We were not discouraged by the obvious number of gays on the seafront, nor even by first impressions of the Brighton Belle Club. It was only after a drink and a look around that we realised we were conspicuous. Of all the men in the club, we were the only whites!

TUESDAY 24 SEPTEMBER

Sedgefield is a strange place. The course is in the middle of nowhere and, from the riding viewpoint, there is a lot wrong with it. But somehow it is always well-patronised and today's event helped draw their biggest crowd in years. So I was wrong. The match worked; people came to watch, appeared to enjoy what they saw and everyone wants to do it again next year. That is fine by me. I love riding in team events — especially when we win, as happened today — and the great thing about this competition is that, on two difficult tracks, there were no problems in any of the four races because all eight of the competing jockeys were experienced and skilful. It makes so much difference.

WEDNESDAY 25 SEPTEMBER

Jamie Bouchard, a jockey mate of mine from a few years back, turned up at Devon today, soon after I had won the novice chase on Aboushabun. He has been in America for some time, and it is strange how seeing a face from the past can immediately conjure up the vivid image of a half-forgotten experience. In this case, Jamie Bouchard reminds me of the day I broke my neck.

Oddly enough, it was at Devon and Exeter that it happened. The Grand National was just eight days away and I recall having some attractive booked rides at Newbury the day after the Devon meeting. I had gone down to ride one for Ian Wardle in the handicap hurdle, and long before the business end of the race, I realised I had no chance. Approaching the last flight, I noticed that there was a gap in the hurdle, where one of the leaders had flattened it. I did the natural thing, steering my beaten horse through the gap rather than trying to jump it but, freakishly, he tripped on the fallen piece of brush and catapulted me out of the plate. The first thing to hit the ground was my head and the first thing I felt was a shock-wave shooting up my arm. This I thought, was nothing trivial.

A jockey's self-defence mechanisms demand that he should pretend he is not badly hurt, no matter how severe the fall or agonising the pain, and in the doctor's room I persuaded everyone who asked that I had done no more than twist my shoulder. In my heart I knew it was more serious — but I wanted to take those rides at Newbury the next day. I asked Jamie to phone up a physio in Hungerford the jockeys always use, and he managed to make me an appointment for later that evening. Jamie then put me in his car and we set off, after I had swallowed a couple of painkilling pills.

The pain hit me, half-an-hour up the motorway. The tablets had no further effect. I was in agony, and I told Jamie, with some reluctance, that there was no point in stopping at Hungerford, I just had to get home. Like the good friend he was, he drove me all the way to Newmarket, where I slept through an uncomfortable night before seeing a specialist the next morning.

He took x-rays and sent me back to bed, and it was late afternoon when he phoned and asked how I felt. 'Not good,' I replied. 'In fact, bloody awful.' 'I'm not at all surprised,' he said. 'You've broken your neck.' I didn't believe him at first. I had always thought that if you broke your neck, that was it — paralysis, wheelchair, end of career — but he explained that my spinal cord had remained intact with one vertebrae fractured and two others displaced. The ambulance, he added, was on its way.

The sequel to the story is quite uncanny. Exactly 12 months later I was riding in the same handicap hurdle on the same Devon card. Coming to the last, again with no chance, I saw there was a gap in that very same hurdle. If it is true that your whole life can flash before you, mine did in that moment. Quite what the trainer of my horse thought, let alone the spectators, I prefer not to know, but I yanked the horse's head back as hard as I could and pulled him up. Nothing in the world could have persuaded me to try and cross that hurdle, much less negotiate that gap.

THURSDAY 26 SEPTEMBER

One of my perennial problems is that I tend to dislocate my right knee if I fall heavily on it. It causes agony while it is out but I can put it back myself, leaving only a stiffness for the next day or so. It happened today at Uttoxeter. I had already ridden one winner, and looked as if I might ride another on the horse which fell. When I gave up my final ride, that won too!

On the way home I stopped off to see my parents. They have always lived in the Derbyshire village of Pinxton. It is a mining community and my Dad, Stan, was down the pit from the age of 14, until he retired quite recently. It had always been traditional in our village that the sons followed the fathers into the mine, but I don't think Dad would have let me, even if I had wanted to. Fortunately, the thought never crossed my mind.

FRIDAY 27 SEPTEMBER

The years might be catching up with me. I was suffering today, riding in the heat, and I wonder if I can go on burning the candle at both ends. It is not, however, affecting my riding, and I scored my third novice chase winner in successive days on Celtic Story. I've always said that novice chases sort out the men from the boys!

SATURDAY 28 SEPTEMBER

On Thursday I came across a young claiming rider named Ricky Balfour. I'd neither heard of him nor seen him ride before, and I left Uttoxeter not caring whether I ever did again after a reckless piece of riding in the novice chase which could have caused chaos. Today, just my luck, I was up against him in another chase, and he followed his Uttoxeter tactics of setting off at a lunatic pace and trying to make all, never giving his horse a chance to recover from mistakes but winding him up and slinging him into the next fence. I kept my wits about me behind him, which was just as well, as he careered through the wing of a fence half-way round, and nearly took two more with him. He also rode in the novice chase, and I watched him knocking spots off a no-hoper at the back of the field. It was a sad sight. I understand that the lad does not get many rides and wants to make an impression, but he is going the wrong way about it.

OCTOBER

TUESDAY 1 OCTOBER

I've been feeling lousy lately and can't decide why. It's nothing specific, I'm just not bouncing and bubbling as I should be. So today I had an appointment in London with Dr Michael Allen, the Jockey Club's chief medical officer. He gave me a thorough check and, late this evening, telephoned me at home to tell me that my chest x-rays were clear. This was a big relief. When you are feeling rough it is, I suppose, natural to fear the worst and although the doctor has not immediately been able to tell me what *is* wrong, he has been able to reassure me about what is not wrong.

WEDNESDAY 2 OCTOBER

By this time of year I'm usually sparking, eager to go anywhere for a potential winner. But my state of mind was summed up today when I had to drag my reluctant self to Ludlow for one ride. It is a three-hour-plus drive to Ludlow and by the time I got there I was wishing I hadn't bothered. But I got down to concentrating on the race in hand, and decided that my horse, Balmatt, had only a notorious runner-up called Karnatak to beat. I chose to track Karnatak until the last possible moment and then, trusting his reputation as a reluctant finisher, try to beat him for toe after the last. It worked to perfection and I passed him ten yards from the line to win. The best-laid and most sensible plans often come to nothing in the hurly-burly of a race but it is a nice feeling when one does work. The drive home seemed a lot sweeter and quicker. '

THURSDAY 3 OCTOBER

John Jenkins had booked me for one ride at Fontwell on a horse called First Temptation. He warned me it was a small horse and he wasn't wrong ... I've seen bigger rabbits. But the man knows how to train them — he won by half-a-length and another long drive was justified.

Got home late and a glance at the results told me that 'Sharky' Sherwood has ridden another winner. Every time I get one, he replies, and he is still a few up on me.

FRIDAY 4 OCTOBER

I've seen everything now. The first event at Hereford today was a hurdle race with only three runners. The favourite ran out when clear, his market rival took it up, but then fell to leave the outsider to come home alone. But Robin Dickin, the jockey of the faller, remounted with what turned out to be a broken collarbone. He finished all right, though what further damage he might have done I can't imagine. For this piece of extraordinary bravado his percentage of the place money works out at a princely £4.50!

Newmarket to Hereford is 166 miles, and I did a spot of wally-watching. I noticed that around 90 per cent of the idiots who accelerate while you are overtaking them, or cut you up on roundabouts, have beards. If you come across one sporting a beard *and* glasses, you are in big trouble.

SATURDAY 5 OCTOBER

A landmark in every jumping season is the first televised meeting. For me, this always means reminding myself to curb my bad language down at the start. Whenever I watch TV videos the boom mike always seems to pick out my voice uttering some expletive as the starter calls us into line. My mother does not approve!

It was Chepstow who hosted the cameras today and an additional attraction was the finale of the A.T. Cross International. We came into this last leg with a decent lead and I looked like putting the result beyond doubt when, in the first of the remaining two races, I sent my mount Yacare into a clear lead on the run-in. But with the race won, he stuck his head in the air and tried to pull himself up. Rhythmic Pastimes, ridden by Ireland's Tommy Carmody, got up to beat me in a desperately close photograph. It was a horrible feeling, the race and the points slipping away like that — only made worse by the fact that the winner is normally my ride. Carmody also won the international chase, but we scrambled enough points to hang on and win the match.

MONDAY 7 OCTOBER
There are only four jump jockeys based in Newmarket — Simon McNeil, Jeff Barlow, Johnny McLaughlin and myself — and whenever we travel together, usually to a midweek midland meeting, a late night is guaranteed. It was Southwell today; all four of us were on parade and a pub-crawl back down the A1 meant I managed to get home at 3.00 a.m. Perhaps it's no wonder Jeff's wife threatens to divorce him every time I phone up to go racing with him!

WEDNESDAY 9 OCTOBER
I didn't have a ride at Cheltenham and I wasn't sorry — still not feeling right, and I slept all afternoon.

FRIDAY 11 OCTOBER
The schooling grounds at Lambourn are the scene of many a lost temper before breakfast and today, as I got down to schooling some of Nicky Henderson's young horses, I am afraid we added to the record of the place with a sizeable barney.

I have been brought up to believe that you should only school novices with an experienced lead horse. Nicky has different ideas, and we had no lead horse at all this morning. In my view it was the blind leading the blind, and the horses did not learn much. I said so, and Nicky said his piece in reply. He is the boss; he has to train the horses and answer to the owners. But I am not sorry I made the point, even if the atmosphere was frosty afterwards.

SATURDAY 12 OCTOBER
An unwelcoming day. The weather is still unseasonably warm, the ground unkindly firm, and all I had to cheer me was two moderate rides at Uttoxeter. The novice chase was full of amateurs and

41

conditional jockeys, and I felt quite the father figure down at the start. I loudly told everyone that I would lead them on Celtic Story, and when one lad came upsides me at the third fence I snarled and growled at him and he dutifully dropped back, never to be seen again. I got beaten by half-a-length but had no trouble in running.

SUNDAY 13 OCTOBER

Every jockey loses a ride now and then, but some hurt more than others. Gavin told me this morning that the owners of Work Mate were upset over the way I rode the horse at Southwell last Monday, and are insisting I don't ride him again. Fair enough, the horse was favourite and trailed in near the back, prompting an inevitable stewards' enquiry. But my explanation that the torrential rain had altered the going, and that Work Mate could not act on the soft, was accepted because it was the absolute truth. The owners appear to be suggesting something more devious, which particularly annoys me as I have devoted a lot of time and patience to their horse. Work Mate was never a natural jumper but I put in a lot of hours schooling him and, last season, he repaid the effort by winning two hurdles and a chase. And this is the thanks I get.

Oddly enough the same thing has happened to Peter Scudamore. He has been 'jocked off' Ace of Spies, a very useful horse on whom he has won two hurdle races. 'Scu' taught that horse everything about jumping, but after one disappointing race the owner has got rid of him. This can be a cruel job sometimes. I don't know about 'Scu', but I don't intend to bite my tongue when next I meet the owners of Work Mate.

TUESDAY 15 OCTOBER

Morning schooling sessions are a pleasure to me on days when I am not in a tearing rush to get to the races. I had no rides at Newton Abbot today so I popped a few of Di's horses over the obstacles. I'll be doing this a lot more for her when I finally pack up riding and I really enjoy seeing the horses improve as they learn.

The rain has arrived at last and it's pissing down. I built a big log-fire this afternoon and put my feet up.

WEDNESDAY 16 OCTOBER

I had never ridden for John Ffitch-Heyes before, but I knew of the man and I could even spell his name. It seems I was not quite so familiar to him, however. He phoned me last night to ride a couple for him at Plumpton today but I was bewildered when I answered the call and he asked for 'Stan'. 'Who?' I replied. 'Stan Smith Eccles' he repeated — and I could tell he wasn't joking. Still, I've only been riding 15 years. I can't expect people to know my name yet, can I!?

My other ride was for Philip Mitchell, a headstrong horse called Eurolink Boy I had happened to draw in the North v South match last month. As I finished third on him I kept the ride — but today was different. Today was his first time over fences, and I'm not likely to forget it. He stuck his head in the air going to the first, and I quickly realised that there was no way I could stop him. He dived through the fence, somehow keeping his balance and his rider at the other side, and then steamed down that sharp Plumpton hill as if we were in a five-furlong sprint. He met the downhill fences well, more by luck than judgement I would say, but by now I freely admit I was *frightened*. There is a railway station at the bottom of the Plumpton hill, well-used by the punters who flock down to this pleasant little Sussex course from 'the smoke'. I had serious doubts whether we would negotiate the turn before the station and had a momentary vision of leaping the rails onto platform two.

Alarming though he is, however, he is not that bad a horse. He turned the bend all right and then I had him under control. Up past the stands I kept a tight hold on him, and as we turned down the hill for the last time I was ten lengths second. Loose horses were darting in and out, making life even more hazardous, but I let my animal go again and he responded, joining the leader after the second last and going away to win. I think I can say I earned my percentage of this one!

THURSDAY 17 OCTOBER

Sometimes, being popular has its drawbacks. My phone has been red-hot today with two trainers blowing their top at me on the subject of one three-year-old hurdle at Market Rasen tomorrow.

Patrick Haslam, who trains in Newmarket, had asked me to ride Armorad for him. I had been up to school the horse, I knew he was fancied and I took the booking early in the week after putting in a precautionary call to John Jenkins to see if he was likely to run any of his in the race. The answer was initially negative, but then John phoned this morning to say he wanted me to ride one for him after all. In a situation like this a jockey cannot win. I phoned Patrick to try and get off Armorad and he was furious. I phoned John again to tell him I wasn't available and *he* was furious. I eventually opted to ride Armorad on the freelance basis of first come, first served. But it was not a happy decision.

FRIDAY 18 OCTOBER

Armorad got beaten. It had to happen after the rows of yesterday, and the only relief was that the Jenkins horse did not win either.

I drowned my sorrows on the way home with two of the Newmarket Musketeers, Messrs Barlow and McLaughlin. The 90-minute journey took us eight hours!

SATURDAY 19 OCTOBER

The day began with that warm glow of anticipation a jockey gets when he has a full book of decent rides on a major card. It ended with a feeling of utter deflation.

It was Kempton, the first London meeting of the season and the best-class programme seen anywhere to date. I rode Running Comment, Rhythmic Pastimes, Duke of Milan, Hot Match and Billion Boy — all previous winners and all with some sort of chance. It was a mouthwatering prospect and I set off early to avoid the crowds and ensure I had time for a game of pool in the plush new Kempton weighing-room complex which now makes it such a popular venue among the jockeys. On the drive down the M11 and across the north of London I weighed up my prospects for the afternoon and concluded it was the sort of day on which I ought to have one winner, might well have two, and could conceivably have even more.

I had none. It was gloriously sunny weather, there was a large crowd and the atmosphere was perfect. But I got beaten on everything, including three favourites. Two seconds and a third was the sum total of my efforts and I drove home in a mood diametrically opposed to the sunny enthusiasm of my outward journey just a few hours earlier.

SUNDAY 20 OCTOBER

I am too fed up for even the usual Sunday routine of ringing round my regular trainers. Yesterday was a big disappointment and, although there were excuses for the defeat of each of the five I rode, it was still a bitter pill to swallow after waking up to a day of such promise.

I cheered myself up this evening with my regular Sunday programme: 6.00 p.m. switch on Channel Four for the American football; 7.30 p.m. drive to the Willie Thorne Snooker Centre in Newmarket. If I hadn't been a jockey I think I would like to have played American football, and I never miss my Sunday night diet of quarterbacks and first-downs. As for snooker, well, I'm improving and I enjoy it.

MONDAY 21 OCTOBER

No jump racing in Britain today. None of us objects to the occasional free day but I am baffled by the logic of the race-planners at the Jockey Club. Take last week, for instance — again, Monday was a complete blank, yet on Wednesday there were meetings at Plumpton, Towcester and Wetherby. Surely it would have made more sense to run one of the three on the Monday?

I drove to London tonight for a British team reception hosted by Austin Reed of Regent Street. They have kitted out the jockeys' team in a uniform of blazer, slacks and tie, and it is striking just what an impression we create when travelling abroad through the fact that we *look* like a team.

TUESDAY 22 OCTOBER

Oh dear, more bad news. Gavin phoned this morning and said somewhat ominously that he'd like to see me. I drove down to his yard and he broke the news that another one of his owners has complained about my riding. This time the horse concerned is

Hot Match, who finished last of four at Kempton on Saturday. The owner was not pleased with the way I rode him and wants someone else. I believe the horse is badly handicapped at present, and at Kempton he was giving lumps of weight to the other three, coming up against a horse called Peter Anthony who is a real flier on fast ground. Not surprisingly, Hot Match couldn't go the pace and was well beaten. I did not think his defeat had anything to do with my riding. Fortunately, Gavin agrees. He has told the owner concerned that I am his jockey and he will continue to put me up on his horse. So now the ball is back in the owner's court. I appreciate Gavin sticking by me, but this is certainly turning into a few days I will be keen to forget.

WEDNESDAY 23 OCTOBER

The arrangement with John Jenkins is not working out quite as I had hoped. In fact it is increasingly clear that Simon Sherwood is getting most of the Jenkins' rides, which is why he is some way ahead of me at the top of the jockeys' table. He rode another winner for John at Cheltenham today and is riding with a great deal of style and confidence. I'm pleased for him, if disappointed for myself, but as regards the championship I must say I currently fear Hywel Davies the most. He is in third place, but his main retainer Tim Forster has hardly run any of his stars yet, and it will be a formidable stable once they get going.

THURSDAY 24 OCTOBER

This was a day off with a difference — no rides, no food and virtually nothing to drink. With two meetings on it's very frustrating to be sat at home, but the ground is still hard and spare rides are like gold-dust. Tomorrow, however, it is Newbury — the first jumping of the term on one of my favourite courses — and I ride Dhofar for Gavin in a handicap hurdle. He is well weighted with only 10-2, and Gavin has warned me he does not expect any overweight. So this morning, after a cup of tea and a slice of toast, I took two de-appetiser pills and resigned myself to eating nothing more before the race.

I take these tablets because I hate saunas and I have no willpower to control my eating voluntarily. They certainly work, in that I rapidly lose all urge to eat, but their side-effects are not pleasant. They make me feel tense and nervous and I find it hard to sleep when I've taken them — I lie awake with my brain racing. I only hope it's worth it. Putting up overweight creates a poor impression and is rightly considered unprofessional if your horse is at all fancied. But the effort and sacrifices demanded to lose the necessary pounds can seem painfully futile if the end result is a mention in the *Sporting Life* reading 'tailed off', 'never dangerous' or — perhaps the most frustrating of all — 'caught on line'.

FRIDAY 25 OCTOBER

Dhofar was far from tailed off and, although at the final flight there seemed a danger he might be caught on the line, he sprinted away again to make the wasting worthwhile and give yours truly something extra to celebrate: my 500th winner. I had done my homework about this race, and a snap poll of the other jockeys in the weighing-room confirmed my fears that no one wanted to make the running and give my horse the strong gallop he needs over two miles. So, in the parade ring, I told Gavin we had no choice but to make the running ourselves — and we did exactly that, knocking three seconds off the Newbury two-mile record in the process. Another plan which worked!

Dhofar was my second win of the day, but the horse which broke a worrying barren run stretching back three weeks and a day was Kings Bridge. Off-course punters, I hear, were surprised to see that I rode this horse. I have news for them all — so was I. The horse is owned by Freddie Starr and trained by John Jenkins. I had phoned John last night to ask him if he ran Rhythmic Pastimes on Saturday. He said he didn't and mentioned nothing about any other possible rides, so I rang off. Imagine my surprise when the phone rang at seven o'clock this morning and John asked me to ride Kings Bridge in the first at Newbury today!

Kings Bridge, I discovered, had useful form in Ireland, but he was out of the handicap here and I had to put up a couple of pounds overweight. Even the de-appetiser pills did not enable me to ride at 10 stone. My first sight of the horse was far from encouraging — he is an ugly animal who looks as if he might recently have been released from pit duties. But as is his habit,

John had produced him fit and well, the horse jumped admirably and came through after the last to win, giving John his 40th winner of the season and bringing me a great deal of relief after an especially rough fortnight.

Completing 500 winners leaves me with one overwhelming emotion — total admiration for Stan Mellor and John Francome, the only men to have ridden twice that number. Right now, I cannot see myself lasting that long!

SATURDAY 26 OCTOBER
A Saturday meeting at my local course, Huntingdon, would normally guarantee me a healthy list of rides. Today, with no respite from the drought and the firm ground, I had only one — but it was an important one. Gavin had talked the owners of Hot Match round to his way of thinking and I was on board again. Once more, I thought the horse had too much weight with 11 stone 10 pounds, and once again he was outpaced. But second place was an improvement and everyone seemed much happier this time.

SUNDAY 27 OCTOBER
My phone calls brought the response from trainers I have come to expect: 'If it rains, we'll run some horses. If not, we will just go on waiting.' I would do and say exactly the same in their shoes, but I must say this Indian summer is dragging its feet and I'm about fed up with it.

I habitually complete all my phoning before lunch on a Sunday and tend to get very tetchy with anyone who bothers me afterwards. I regard Sunday afternoon and evening as my sacred free time and if I do pick up the phone — because I never take it off the hook — I am pretty short-tempered, making it very clear to callers that they should modify their telephoning times in future. People in racing — and I mean trainers as well as jockeys — are on duty most hours of the day, seven days a week, and I feel I am entitled to cut myself off from the job just for a short time each week.

MONDAY 28 OCTOBER
Fakenham is one of the charming eccentricities of the English

jumping scene. Set just a few miles from the north Norfolk coast, the tip of a triangle with Kings Lynn and Norwich, it is part of a sleepy and ancient town and has attractions one would never associate with, shall we say, Ascot or Newbury. The only approach road, for instance, is riddled with stones, boulders and ruts to test any tyre or exhaust system. The grandstand, over 100 years old, looks quaint enough but it houses the weighing-room and I can relate from bitter experience that, on a December afternoon, there are many better places to be; the few, high windows steam up, the pipes and the walls attract condensation and the room becomes damp, uncomfortable and uncivilised.

Having said that, I am all for preserving the Fakenhams of the jumping world. You meet real people here, real jumping enthusiasts. Plenty of them speak with Norfolk accents I find it impossible to understand, but they love the game and this course is always well patronised. For some reason it also draws hordes of the green-wellies brigade, the Hoorah Henries and their Penelope and Samantha girlfriends. The ladies do the scenery no harm.

It was packed today. They don't race here often, and the locals like to make the most of their chances. So do a few trainers. Rex Carter, based just down the road in Swaffham, turned out three winners, while Philip Mitchell, who trains in Epsom but treats Fakenham like a favoured local course, had two. I didn't have any, but I still enjoyed the day, and in the wooden shack which passes for a bar, I stood with a whisky after the last race half listening to the strains of a Norfolk earbasher whose views I could neither understand nor enthuse over. It wouldn't happen at Ascot, I thought — but that doesn't necessarily make Ascot any the better.

TUESDAY 29 OCTOBER

I am trying to improve my golf. There is not much chance of playing the game regularly in this job, but on recent days off I've taken to spending the afternoons at the Newmarket course, investigating its ample rough. I play off 24 and rely on connecting lustily with the occasional drive, but if I had more free time to spend on the course, I think I could get quite attached to the game.

WEDNESDAY 30 OCTOBER

The drought must surely end soon. The Ascot meeting was televised today but there were only 25 runners on the entire card and I didn't ride one of them. Instead I sat at home in front of the TV, critically appraising the styles of my fellow jockeys, and secretly wishing I was out there with them.

THURSDAY 31 OCTOBER

A bad month ended on an appropriate note. I drove all the way to Wincanton for one ride on a horse with no logical chance, only to be told when I got there, a shade car-weary, that he was a non-runner. I drove on to spend the night in Torquay before tomorrow's Devon meeting and had plenty of time to reflect on the misfortunes of October. The score adds up to 28 rides, only five winners, a few rows with trainers and owners, and a general frustration that the season has still not properly got underway. Things can now only improve.

NOVEMBER

FRIDAY 1 NOVEMBER

Losing any race on an objection figures among the greatest irritations in a jockey's life. Whatever the justice of the verdict, the rider will invariably feel aggrieved as he has done his bit in getting his horse first past the post. All the effort is suddenly for nothing, and the deflation most acute, when the stewards reverse the placings. It is not often, however, that a horse is demoted after winning his race by as much as seven lengths, as happened to my mount Kings Bridge at Devon today.

This was the horse on which I had won a competitive 'chase at Newbury after being booked to ride, by John Jenkins, only on the morning of the race. This time things were a little different. The race had been mapped out for the horse and I was always going to ride him. We were also expected to win and the owner, Freddie Starr, was bubbling with wit and confidence before the off.

The race panned out into a two-horse finish. Over the final three fences I raced neck and neck with Brendan Powell, riding a prolific winner called My Bonnie Prince. I knew instinctively that all was not well with Kings Bridge as he began to go severely left-handed, and when I resorted to the whip after the last he ran away from it, veering across My Bonnie Prince. The interference was obvious, though accidental, and although by now I was convinced that Kings Bridge was lame, I roused him to run on again and we went away to win by that wide margin of seven lengths.

As soon as we passed the post I pulled the horse up and jumped off — the usual routine followed by a jockey who is aware he has a lame horse under him. I was expecting a steward's enquiry and had no immediate qualms when Brendan told me his owners wanted him to object. Having won by so far I thought I had a very reasonable chance of keeping the race. The stewards, however, viewed the video of the offending incident and decided otherwise. It was sickening for me, probably worse still for Freddie who likes nice trophies on his mantlepiece and had rather taken a fancy to this one. My day was not improved by my one other ride, also for John Jenkins, in the seller. I think I could have finished faster than my horse if I had got off and run.

SATURDAY 2 NOVEMBER

What a difference a day makes. Yesterday I had two disappointments, today two winners — and one of them came through the rare privilege of a walkover. With the going still very firm at Sandown, Rhythmic Pastimes was the only horse to stand his ground for a £3,000 novice chase and the only effort demanded of me was to don the correct colours, weigh out, mount, and canter down to the first fence and back. Not a difficult way to earn my riding fee, plus the ten per cent of the prize money. It was only the second walkover of my entire career.

I had to work rather harder on my other winner but as it was Duke of Milan I enjoyed every second. I couldn't settle him in as I had hoped to, because an amateur rider named Tom Grantham, riding Tom's Little Al, was on my withers all the way, but the 'Duke' jumped immaculately as ever and came right away to win comfortably, breaking the track record by all of three seconds.

Sandown has always been among my favourite tracks. I tend to do well here, which is a big factor, but I also consider it a fair and challenging course which happens to have just about the best facilities you could hope to find on an English racetrack.

If I thought I'd had a good day, however, Peter Scudamore had a far better one. He rode four winners on the other big card at Chepstow, all for his guv'nor David Nicholson. I was pleased for them both. 'The Duke's' stable had a disastrous time last season, suffering from some sort of virus, and I am quite sure 'Scu' was tapped up by other trainers, and perhaps even tempted to move. He loyally stayed on, however, and it seems he is now beginning to see some reward.

TUESDAY 5 NOVEMBER

No jockey likes to be unseated during a race. The difference between a horse falling and simply ejecting his rider, giving him no chance of staying in the plate, can be extremely slim, and we all accept that the occasional dreaded 'U' is inevitable in a chase. To be unseated over hurdles, however, is undignified and degrading. The first emotion of a jockey when this happens is usually embarrassment, though when I suffered the fate at Fontwell today I must say I first felt relief that I was unscathed as my mount had roguishly attempted to duck into the wing of the third last hurdle, which could have had very painful consequences for both of us. But after that, and on the long way back to the weighing-room, yes, I felt embarrassed.

I celebrated Guy Fawkes' night at Oliver Sherwood's Lambourn home. All the trainers in the village seemed to be around Oliver's bonfire and as the beverage on offer was a particularly potent mulled wine I have not for some while seen such a drunken gathering.

Racing folk tend towards the manic side of humour when off-duty and socialising. Tonight was no exception and the star turn during a variety show of misbehaviour was performed by trainer Nicky Vigors who drove a car straight through the blazing fire and leapt out on the other side howling with laughter. Amused but appalled, I remarked that he must be crazy, but he retorted: 'Not as crazy as you think ... it's not my car!'

WEDNESDAY 6 NOVEMBER

Fortified by the mulled wine, I won on both my rides at Newbury. I got a novice hurdler up on the line to win by a hard-fought neck but derived far more pleasure from victory on Rhythmic Pastimes in the novice chase. He had not jumped well early in his chasing debut and I had been easy on him, trying to teach him something and do little more than get him round safely. With that achieved, and a Sandown walkover in the bag, he took on Fulke Walwyn's highly-rated Arctic Stream today over two-and-a-half miles. A wide grin crossed my face when he met the first fence wrong but fiddled it expertly. He had learned a lot, and from then on he hardly put a foot wrong. He went round this testing track like an experienced handicapper and won on the bridle, beating Arctic Stream by 12 lengths, which might have been doubled if I had changed up a gear. It is a great feeling when a horse of obvious ability can be helped to make the difficult transition from hurdles to fences and then shows the benefit with a performance like this, and I drove home in high good humour.

THURSDAY 7 NOVEMBER

It is a golden rule of mine never to go racing when I don't have any rides. I don't believe it looks good, a jockey hanging around like an out-of-work actor at an opening night, and anyway I get very bored watching a meeting in which I have no involvement. But today I broke that rule and drove to Kempton for a business meeting. The business was conducted quickly enough and then I wished I was somewhere else. Restless and out of place, I left the course as quickly as was polite.

FRIDAY 8 NOVEMBER

Cheltenham's Mackeson meeting is regarded by most people in jumping as the launch of First Division National Hunt racing. The crowds roll up by tradition, the prize money is high and the Mackeson itself is, of course, an institution. Today was the first day of the meeting and here I was, a top jockey, sitting at home without a single ride. Frustration is one word for it . . . .

SATURDAY 9 NOVEMBER

My dejection at having no ride in the Mackeson was lifted by winning on Kumbi in a valuable long-distance chase later in the afternoon. I reckon Kumbi must be the biggest and strongest horse in training — he ploughed straight through the tricky downhill fence which accounts for so many, yet never even broke stride, and stayed on really well up the taxing final hill to give 'Ginger' McCain, a trainer I like enormously, his first Cheltenham winner in a long while. He and the horse's owner are already talking about taking Kumbi to Aintree for his third crack at the Grand National but, from my own point of view, I am far from convinced he is the sort of conveyance any right-minded jockey would wish to be on when jumping those awesome fences. On park courses he can get away with his blunders, and an able pilot can stay on board. At Liverpool Kumbi may not fall, but he has already twice displayed a penchant for getting rid of his rider. I can hardly blame 'Ginger' for being keen, though. He trains in homely premises at Southport, Aintree being his local course, and it would be a dream come true for him if he could produce another National winner to follow in the legendary footsteps of his greatest horse Red Rum, who is still in his number one box now.

The afternoon belonged to Richard Linley, who won the Mackeson for the third time in four years, on Fred Winter's Half Free. But the evening was scheduled to belong to Fred's ex-jockey, one J. Francome, due to receive his seventh and last champion jockey's award at the annual ball staged in the banqueting rooms at Cheltenham. Unfortunately, John had made something of a cock-up. His memory for dates not being his greatest quality, he had some time ago accepted an invitation to host a celebrity sports forum in Birmingham tonight. Programmes had been printed, the Francome name had been freely touted as an inducement to potential ticket-buyers, and the organisers were understandably miffed when they phoned John a few days ago to make final arrangements and were informed that not only had he forgotten all about it but that he was also due at the ball. The Francome phone was apparently busy for some minutes after this revelation and the upshot was that his speech — which some of us have come to look forward to as much as the meal and the ball itself — was delivered, with a delicious disregard for convention, just before the soup course, whereupon the ever-controversial 'Franc' made his apologies and jumped into his Porsche (sadly a newer model than mine) to hotfoot it to Brum!

Typical John, he didn't leave us without a laugh. Sporting his usual deadpan face as he drawled his jokes, he told one about three trainers — Fred Winter, Mercy Rimell and David Nicholson — having an audience with God at which each was to be granted one wish. Fred asked if he could win the Gold Cup again before he died and, sure enough, God allowed him his ambition and even told him the year it would happen. Mrs Rimell's wish was to train another Champion Hurdler before she died. God granted this and revealed the relevant year. Then David who, remarkably, has never trained a winner at the Festival meeting, was called to make his request. He asked, not surprisingly, when he would be allowed to train a Cheltenham winner. 'Good gracious no,' replied God. '*I'll* be dead before that happens!'

SUNDAY 10 NOVEMBER

I had stayed overnight with Pete Scudamore and the drive back to Newmarket with a pounding head and all the hangover trimmings was a long and painful experience. On arrival, I abandoned plans to phone trainers — some of whom, I guessed, might be feeling just as rough — and went straight to bed.

MONDAY 11 NOVEMBER

Plumpton was the only southern meeting today and I had no booked rides. Catching up with the planning I should have done yesterday, I phoned John Jenkins at ten o'clock to ask him what I might ride for him during the rest of the week. He told me he would not be running much until the weekend but then, to my astonishment, he said: 'What are you doing today?' When I told him I had a day off, he said: 'Right, get yourself down to Plumpton and you can ride one for me in the last.'

I had noticed in the *Life* that he was due to run a novice hurdler which had no declared jockey, but had glibly assumed he must have booked someone else. With John, however, this should never be assumed. Amazed though I was to pick up a ride in such a casual manner, I packed my bags for the week and set off for Sussex. The horse ran promisingly and finished third so I did not consider it a wasted journey, and I drove back only as far as Lambourn, to spend the night with 'Franc'.

TUESDAY 12 NOVEMBER

Despite being dragged bodily from my bed to ride out for John and earn my usual generous breakfast, I was in good form this morning. One of the horses I have most been looking forward to partnering is Kathies Lad and he was to make his seasonal debut at Devon, in quite a valuable chase. He won, too, despite being only half-fit and not being given too hard a race. With luck, the two of us can add further to last season's successes at Cheltenham and Aintree.

I spent the evening with Simon Sherwood, thus exploding the myth that rival sportsmen never socialise. Simon and I are actually good buddies, and will hopefully remain so whatever may befall us in the contest for this season's jockeys' title. Anyone who imagines us at daggers drawn would have been startled to observe us together in The Swan Inn at Shefford, near Lambourn, where the Sherwood brothers were celebrating today's win by one of their hurdlers, Atrabates, with the horse's owners. There appeared to be dozens of them, and it transpires they are all members of the Atrabates Cricket Club. They certainly know how to celebrate.

WEDNESDAY 13 NOVEMBER

Some day soon the rains will come. Then, I guess, it will teem down for a fortnight and we will all moan about it. Right now, however, everyone in racing is praying for some rain to ease one of the longest autumn droughts I can remember. Underfoot conditions are now so bad that today there were two walkovers on the Wolverhampton card — something I have never known before.

I was at Newbury for a single ride on Nick Henderson's Smart Reply. We quietly fancied him, but to no avail. He ran deplorably and I retired to The Five Bells, a welcoming pub between Newbury and Lambourn run by a charming and hospitable lady called Dottie Channing-Williams. It is among the favourite haunts of all racing people in this area, and deservedly so.

THURSDAY 14 NOVEMBER

Every experienced jockey knows that trying to sneak up the inside rail on a bend is a dangerous manoeuvre at the best of times, and can often be construed as asking for trouble. It is a common sight to see the 'door closed' by the man in front when he senses someone attempting this and, unbeknown to the crowd up in the stands, there is frequently a good deal of shouting and swearing between the jockeys involved. On some courses it is more hazardous than others. Wincanton, for instance, has a final bend on which there is often trouble, and today Peter Scudamore and Graham McCourt had such a tussle, as Graham cheekily tried to slip up 'Scu's' inner that they conveniently left the race for me to win on a horse called Comedy Lane. Their argument, loud and angry on the course, resumed in the weighing-room where I feared for one moment that these two normally mild characters would come to blows. I kept out of the way and went out to ride another winner on Duke of Milan. To complete a highly satisfactory day, it is now raining hard.

FRIDAY 15 NOVEMBER

In 99 cases out of 100, a jockey involved in a photo-finish knows his fate. To the crowd it might seem well-nigh impossible to separate the horses, but a jockey has a sixth sense which tells him whether he is in front, or just behind, as the winning-post flashes past. I usually manage to look across at the post without interrupting my riding, and today, in a televised chase at Ascot, I was unhappily convinced that Richard Rowe on Paddyboro had touched me off in a desperately tight finish. I was riding Destiny Bay, a decent horse of Nicky Henderson's having his first run of the season; and I was so sure I had been beaten that I returned to the runners-up position in the winners' enclosure and was virtually back in the weighing-room when the announcement gave me the race and a mix of surprise and delight.

A winner on TV always gives a jockey a boost, and today I had two, which makes six winners in the last six racing days. Things are at last starting to happen after a sticky patch, but as usual, whenever you get up, something happens to knock you down.

I had been asked to go to Newcastle tomorrow. It is a hell of a journey, one I normally wouldn't relish at all, but as it was the David Steele-John Jenkins team who had booked me to ride their very good hurdler Wing and a Prayer, I had agreed. The race was a valuable one — the Fighting Fifth Hurdle — and I was also swayed by the hint that I was back in favour with Mr Steele who, despite the fact that I have ridden him a lot of winners, seemed to be reluctant to have me on his string of horses this season. So, although I had little chance of picking up any further rides in what is virtually foreign territory to a southern jockey, I was looking forward to going. Imagine my surprise, then, when I arrived at Ascot at midday, asked my valet John Buckingham to lay out my tack after racing so that I could take it to Newcastle, only to have him tell me that I wouldn't be going. Wing and a Prayer had been pulled out of the race at the overnight stage and no one had thought to tell me. Having turned down a number of rides at Ascot, I have now had to scramble to get back on them. I've only been successful with one, Gavin's Boom Patrol, so my Saturday plans have to some extent been wrecked.

SATURDAY 16 NOVEMBER

We have to try to cut ourselves off from emotion in this job. It is a mistake to become too attached to any particular horse. We all have our favourites, our heroes and our villains, but the game is so fickle, balanced on that knife-edge between success and disaster, that feelings should never run any deeper than that.

Sadly, however, attachments, emotions and heartbreak cannot always be avoided, and I reckon every jockey in England felt sorry for Dermot Browne today. Dermot, 'Murphy' as he is known, has always been synonymous with the very good hurdler Brownes Gazette; he has always ridden the horse, and until recently he also owned him. He might have won the Champion Hurdle last March, but poor Dermot was left at the start when the horse spun and jigged sideways when the tapes rose; I, more than anyone, remain thankful for that incident if sympathetic for Dermot's embarrassment. Brownes Gazette was again being aimed for the Champion. Today's Fighting Fifth at Newcastle, in which I had been intended to ride, was the first step along the way. For Brownes Gazette it was also the last step.

I was watching the race on TV in the palatial weighing-room's set under the main stand at Ascot. Along with many other jockeys, I winced and cursed as Brownes Gazette crashed through the rails, for no obvious reason, midway through the race. All too soon, though, it was very evident the horse had suffered a massive heart attack and was dead. I watched poor Dermot, himself unscathed, kneeling by his beloved horse, and thanked God it wasn't me.

My own day, by contrast, was never likely to make headlines

of the right or wrong kind, and when Boom Patrol ran far too freely and faded with utter inevitability up the final hill, I drove home with no great sense of hardship. I was simply glad that tonight my name is not Dermot Browne.

SUNDAY 17 NOVEMBER

The first celebration of the day came with the bleary morning awareness that it was still pouring with rain. Soon, perhaps, some of the best horses available to me, kept so far under protective wraps, will be brought out.

The next good thing was Sunday lunch. A luxury many jockeys, fighting off the excess pounds and forced to resist every temptation, can never contemplate, it is one I seldom like to miss. Today I look Di to the White Hart at Risby, near Bury St Edmunds, a place I can recommend to all. Nancy, who runs the restaurant, recites her menu as if it was the Ten Commandments and I seldom have any trouble polishing off a couple of generous helpings.

MONDAY 18 NOVEMBER

Jump racing is at its worst on Mondays at Leicester. A personal opinion, certainly, but one shared by many in the sport. For one thing, the quality of the programmes is low on Mondays, and for another, Leicester is just about the most dismal, uninspiring course in the country. There is no glamour and laughter here, and I don't know a jockey who enjoys coming. It is, nevertheless, part of the job, and although I woke this morning with a sense of gloom as I reviewed the day ahead and discovered only a single ride in the Leicester seller, the compensations were that the course is only a short drive from home, and that even riding one loser guarantees me a profit of around £25 on the day. It is important to keep such matters in perspective.

I didn't win on the horse but I was back home by three. The ground has certainly eased after the weekend rain but now, as if the fates are conspiring against racing, snow is forecast.

TUESDAY 19 NOVEMBER

With flat racing finished for the year, there are two or three jump meetings almost every day, and it is now that the freelance's job tends to become complicated. The phone calls, both in and out, increase, along with the tricky demands of diplomacy. In my position I can hardly avoid treading on a few toes, disappointing a few people and upsetting a few more; but in all the ducking and diving I must do to sort out my rides, the first priority has always got to be which horses and which meetings are likely to supply me with winners.

It was snowing as I glanced out of the window during my morning session of phoning and book-keeping, but it doesn't look likely to last. It certainly didn't deter me from driving down to London for one of my favourites among the annual racing dos, the Stable Lads Boxing night. Held at the Hilton, it comprises a dinner followed by the boxing and is always great entertainment. As I manage to have my card marked on all the Newmarket lads, there is also a few quid to be made, punting on the fights.

THURSDAY 21 NOVEMBER

Quite a day. My waking hours totalled 20, of which something over eight were spent behind the wheel of my car. It began at 5.00 a.m. with a drive to Lambourn through the murk and mist of an ugly morning. I covered the 134 miles from Newmarket in one hour 50 minutes, schooled six horses for Nicky Henderson, grabbed a swift bite to eat and then climbed back in the car for the long slog north to Haydock Park. I had four rides booked, of which I gave three a decent chance. It was the only no-hoper, Bob Champion's dogged plodder Prince Bai, who provided me with the day's most painful relic, giving me a crashing fall at the final fence, and then adding insult to injury by treading on my nose.

John Jenkins' fancied hurdler Romana ran a bad race; his other runner Shangoseer was not good enough to finish closer than fifth and Kumbi made too many mistakes. Another promising day gone west. I was deflated from lack of a winner and exhausted from the efforts of the day. But there was still one engagement I had no intention of missing. It was the night of the retirement party for John Burke, who has been a close friend and drinking partner for years. I couldn't see him go out of the ranks without being present, so it was back into the car, destination Worcester.

As usual, I forgot my disappointment once I was in sociable company and the time flew. It was 1.00 a.m. by the time I reached my bed for the night in Lambourn, and I felt less tired than I had done eight hours earlier.

FRIDAY 22 NOVEMBER

It goes without saying that Cheltenham gave me my biggest thrills last season, or perhaps of any season. To win the Champion Hurdle on See You Then and the Triumph Hurdle on First Bout in the space of three days gave my career a fantastic lift at an apt time; some said it dragged me from the shadows of J. Francome. I have both horses to ride again this season and, although it could present me with an agonising choice if they both make it to Cheltenham on Champion Hurdle day, I like to think there will be some good days to enjoy on each of them before that. They are two very different horses: See You Then has class and speed, First Bout is a stayer, a streetfighter. But they could both be very good indeed, and today the preparation work began when I schooled First Bout over a few hurdles on the Lambourn gallops. He may have his first run in another three weeks but has some condition to shed before then.

I went on to ride three at Newbury — no luck. My nose is bloody sore and I dread having another fall.

SATURDAY 23 NOVEMBER

If I thought I was in pain last night, it was nothing compared with tonight. I am bruised, battered and, if not quite bowed then admittedly well below par. It is all the fault of a horse called Indamelody who conclusively proved the point that no matter how well a horse may jump during exercise at home it is dangerous to be confident until he shows it on a racecourse.

It was Hennessy day at Newbury, one of the biggest jumping days of the calendar, and experience had insisted that I set out early and got inside the course fully 90 minutes before the first. I was right, too. The crowds grew to such a pitch that some jockeys and trainers were still absent when we were called to go out for the opening novice hurdle. Josh Gifford and his number one rider Richard Rowe were among the missing men, and it later transpired that they had abandoned their car in the five-mile queue which stretched back from the course onto the M4, and run the remaining distance to the track. All in vain — the first race was run without them.

For some reason I have never quite been able to fathom, the Sloane Ranger population of London appears to descend on Newbury in their entirety every Hennessy day. In their identical Sloane uniforms and with their identical plummy Sloane accents they seem a world apart from most of the regular racegoers and we never see them from one November to the next. But they turn up, they swell the crowd and some of them — the girls, that is — are not at all bad looking, so who am I to complain?

The performance which won the Hennessy deserved a large audience. It was stunning. Galway Blaze was so far superior to this competitive field of chasers that his jockey, Mark Dwyer, was looking around for non-existent dangers as they jumped the cross-fence, five from home. He absolutely trotted up and although he was undoubtedly well-handicapped it gave yet another illustration of just how fine a trainer is Jimmy Fitzgerald. He may train in Malton, an awfully long drive from Newmarket, but I wouldn't mind the chance to get on some of his horses.

My personal calamity followed the big race. It was potentially an exciting novice chase with Indamelody, a good, staying hurdler, The Breener, one of last season's leading novices, and Some Machine, David Nicholson's expensive purchase from Ireland, all jumping fences for the first time. But it became something of a damp squib. Some Machine was tailed off from early on, and my horse never settled at all. He rushed at his fences, attacking them as if they were as small as the hurdles he is used to jumping, and although we survived one bad mistake in front of the stands, he easily got rid of me with another monumental error at the ditch on the far side of the course. At home, he had impressed me with his jumping: it is a different matter in a race.

The fall alone would have been bad enough, but the horse behind ran all over me. I tried to get up but my leg gave way and I sagged back onto the turf. The ambulance men who quickly surrounded me were convinced I had broken my leg and took some elaborate and perhaps over-zealous precautions. I had my

legs strapped together and was lifted onto a stretcher for the
ambulance ride across the track. The ambulance reversed right
up to the door of the medical room, at the back of the weighing-
room block, and screens were erected as I was wheeled out. It
crossed my mind that some of the gawping sightseers who always
gather at such moments might have thought I was dead, when
actually the main thing on my mind was convincing the doctor
that there was nothing seriously wrong with me at all. I had
already investigated the damage in the ambulance and confirmed
that the top of my foot was badly swollen. I had also taken a kick
on the shin, which was more painful than anything. But I was
satisfied that nothing was broken and I managed to brazen it out
well enough for the doctor to allow me home rather than recom-
mending a hospital stay. I did have to go for some x-rays, thankfully negative, and when Di got me home I used the ultrasonic
lamp we have to treat her horse's injuries in order to disperse the
swelling.

SUNDAY 24 NOVEMBER
You find out who your friends are when you have had a bad fall
and I was quite touched by the number of phone calls I had today,
asking after my progress and wishing me well. The press were on,
of course, but a good number of jockeys and other friends called
too, and I felt improved enough to astonish them all with the
news that I might even ride tomorrow.

MONDAY 25 NOVEMBER
I did not exactly feel up to an early-morning run, but the bruising
had begun to go even if much of the aching pain was till there. I
found I could just about fit my boot over the injury so I decided to
risk it and ride Oversway for Di at Folkestone. I turned down
another couple of rides, not wanting to take too many chances,
but I was pleased with the way things went. We finished second,
running on well, and although I was sore afterwards I'd done it no
further damage. I am certainly fit enough to partner my old chum
Kathies Lad in a big chase on my local Huntingdon track tomorrow.

TUESDAY 26 NOVEMBER

Kathies Lad came to the last fence a stride or two behind The Mighty Mac. I was sure we would win. Monica Dickinson's horse is a brilliant jumper and an exciting front-runner, but we had closed steadily on him during the final half-mile and now I had plenty in reserve and felt poised to pounce for the first prize. We met the fence on a long stride, which seemed perfect as Kathies Lad had been jumping really well but now, most unusually, he put down on me — put in an extra short stride — and inevitably got no more than half-way the height of the fence, catapulting me from the saddle and into the ground with a resounding thud. It was exactly what I did not need after the traumas of the past week. Losing out on a good winner was one pain; a third bad fall in a week was another. I managed to get to my feet and hobble to the ambulance this time. Once more, the doctor cleared me to ride tomorrow, but this time I know I have more than bruises to contend with. My head is aching already.

WEDNESDAY 27 NOVEMBER

I was awake at one o'clock this morning, searching for painkillers as the headaches raged. I am probably concussed. The pills allowed me to sleep but I still felt dreadful when daylight came. I should not have ridden at Plumpton, a long and fraught drive from Newmarket ... but there was the chance of a winner, maybe two, and I am still trailing in the title race. I persuaded myself to go and have regretted the decision ever since.

Of my three rides, two were second and the other fourth. All three might have won, and the last of them, Nicky's I'm Somebody, cruised into a long lead between the last two hurdles and looked uncatchable. The punters who had backed him down to favourite were probably counting their money, and I guess their sums had come to something pretty healthy judging by the angry reception I got as I returned to unsaddle after being caught in the last few strides. They thought I had been caught napping, sitting on my lead instead of riding the horse out. I think they are wrong and that they are talking through their pockets, but I cannot be sure any more. I know I feel rough and that I am now in the middle of a very bad patch, full of falls and defeats.

I am feeling low, my head still thumps and the drive home was desperate. It gave me time, too much time, to think about the past few days and I came to the conclusion that Simon Sherwood will be champion jockey this season. Trainers are jumping on the bandwagon that inevitably surrounds a new and successful name, while some of the trainers I had been counting on are not supporting me as I'd hoped. Simon is riding with tremendous zest and confidence, while right now my own confidence is draining away.

THURSDAY 28 NOVEMBER

At eight this morning I was on the road to London for the Jockey Club appeal, demanded by Freddie Starr after his horse Kings Bridge had been demoted at Devon four weeks ago. I thought we had little chance, but as jockey I had to go. On all known journey times I had left plenty of leeway for the trip to Portman Square and my part of the hearing before scooting back for three rides at Warwick in the afternoon. But a mixture of snow, accidents and traffic jams meant that at 10.20 a.m., ten minutes before the appeal was due to begin, I was stationary, still five miles from the Jockey Club. I took an instant decision, phoned my solicitor at the hearing and told him my plight, then did a U-turn and headed for Warwick.

Immediately, I wondered what on earth I was doing — not only risking the wrath of Mr Starr, but doing so for the dubious privilege of riding Green Bramble and Indamelody, horses who had given me some memorable tumbles. But, if they have sometimes seemed dangerous conveyances, they also both have ability and Green Bramble finally got me off the 29-winner mark which had anchored me for a fortnight, winning gamely with a big weight, while Indamelody got round safely this time.

Drove home with yet another headache and went to bed still not knowing the result of the appeal.

FRIDAY 29 NOVEMBER

I switched on the TV this morning to check whether the Leicester meeting at which I was due to ride had survived a heavy frost, and got a nasty shock. Richard Linley and his wife Beverley were involved in a car crash on icy roads after yesterday's Wincanton meeting. Richard is critically injured and Beverley is dead. And I thought I had problems.

It made me feel sad and sick. I have always maintained that a jump jockey is in as much danger driving in wintry conditions every day as he is out on the track, but that knowledge can never prepare you for death and injury when it happens to friends. It certainly made me reflect that there is more to life than riding horses, and I was not sorry when Leicester was abandoned.

SATURDAY 30 NOVEMBER
Richard remains critical after two major operations. I hear the atmosphere at Sandown yesterday was sombre, and there was still a degree of disbelief among the jockeys there today.

Out of that sorrow, however, emerged a day I shall remember for a long time. I rode one of the most rewarding winners of my career to give J. Francome his first success as a trainer at last. What's more, it was on a horse which went off at 25-1; it was in a big three-year-old hurdle, and it was on TV. So, for John, some good may have come out of that depressing day at Worcester in September. Di was standing with 'Franc' on the huge Sandown terraces and she told me later that he had got surprisingly emotional as the horse, That's Your Lot, skated in by six lengths. He certainly received an incredible ovation in the winner's enclosure.

I went on to finish a close second on Dhofar in the big handicap hurdle, then win the long-distance chase on the remarkable Kumbi, who would be a bloody good horse if ever he learned to jump! My efforts on this one left me ridiculously weak, and I got off my ride in the last and got Di to drive me home. I'm clearly not right. I shouldn't be exhausted like this, even after three testing rides, and I've decided to have a few days off and not ride again until Wednesday.

DECEMBER

MONDAY 2 DECEMBER

Reading is a hobby of mine, a relaxation; nothing too heavy, nothing demanding great intellect or powers of concentration, much more a means of switching off from cares and worries, of escaping from the real world. Wilbur Smith's thrillers, set in South Africa, give me the sort of release I seek from a book. I was just getting stuck into one of his best, my feet up in front of a generous log fire, when John Jenkins phoned. What he had to say persuaded me to revise my immediate plans.

John has asked me to ride Foyle Fisherman for him at Fontwell tomorrow. Nothing remarkable about that until you know that this is one of the horses owned by David Steele, with whom I had understood I was still not exactly flavour of the month. Simon had been riding all his horses recently ... perhaps he has done something to upset him? Anyway, the request was coupled with an offer to ride another of Mr Steele's horses at Cheltenham on Friday. This one, called Ivy League, came over from Ireland with a reputation as high as his price tag. He is reputed to have cost around £120,000, which makes him one of the most expensive National Hunt horses in training. Rides like that one are not to be sniffed at — and if I'm to ride him, I really have to go to Fontwell tomorrow. I can hardly say no.

TUESDAY 3 DECEMBER

Fontwell is a long way for one ride, but it seems a much shorter drive back after a winner. It was a near thing, but I pulled the race out of the bag on Foyle Fisherman, beating Fandango Light a neck after a real battle up the run-in. The horses raced close together and the jockey of the beaten animal objected, but I was rightly confident the result would stand. Mr Steele was beaming brightly, John Jenkins was happy and I was glad I came back a day early.

It has, in fact, been a long day. I started out around 7.00 a.m., schooling Kathies Lad at Alan Jarvis's place. The plan had been to run the horse in the big 'chase at Cheltenham on Saturday, which would have given me a tricky problem as I have also been asked to ride Duke of Milan in the race. My first really delicate decision of the season has now been made for me, however, as 'Kathies' is clearly not quite right after that heavy fall at Huntingdon last week ... which makes two of us!

WEDNESDAY 4 DECEMBER

John Francome had some unkind words for the stewards during his career and in one memorably hilarious after-dinner speech he referred to them as 'cabbage patch kids'. Now that he has retired, maybe they are missing his regular visits and want someone to replace him. Me, for instance? Today at Worcester I was called before them twice. They fined me £25 for undoing my chin strap as I walked back after the first race, overruling my plea that the strap was tight and aggravating one of my many recent head-aches. Then, later in the afternoon they accepted my explanation for dropping my hands on a desperately tired horse and being touched off for second place — though I had the distinct impression they came within a whisker of 'doing' me for this one, too. The stewards are a necessity on every racecourse and I'm sure most of them do a fine job; but they remain an occupational hazard for every jockey!

It was, all in all, not the happiest of days. My weekend plans are now in chaos as my retaining trainer Nicky Henderson has altered his plans and decided against sending First Bout — last season's Triumph Hurdle winner — to Cheltenham for his seasonal debut. Instead, he is sending me to Lingfield to ride Green Bramble. This means I must pass up four decent outside rides at Cheltenham and involves some reluctant and unpleasant phone calls.

THURSDAY 5 DECEMBER

I went to Uttoxeter for a single ride. Anywhere else and I might have turned it down, but I always combine trips to Uttoxeter with a visit to my parents, who live virtually on the route. We are a close-knit family; my mother, whose philosophy to life is that if you are not eating, you're not very well, loves the chance to feed me up and ruin my weight, and my Dad usually enjoys coming racing with me. Not today, though: he was a good judge.

From the time I left Newmarket this morning to the time I got back tonight, the rain never relented. It was torrential, quite the most spectacular I have seen in ages, and it made for a thoroughly unpleasant day. The racing itself was bad enough — jockeys can wear supposedly waterproof breeches but no garment can protect against that kind of rain. Walking around at the start was miserable for horses and jockeys alike. But the driving was much worse.

I passed three separate accidents on my way to Derbyshire, and the return trip, in equally fierce rain but also in darkness, left my eyes like lumps of lead. I was more exhausted from driving than if I had ridden five or six horses at a meeting, and I could not help thinking of poor Richard Linley. It was this part of our job which was responsible for the death of his wife and for his own serious injuries — the man in the street, even the racing follower who sees jump jockeys at work every week, can never appreciate that often the most exacting part of our business is having to drive long distances each day in the worst weather an English winter can produce.

FRIDAY 6 DECEMBER

David Steele must have thought owning racehorses was an easy route to fame and fortune while Wing and a Prayer and Beat the Retreat were winning race after race last season. He is now beginning to see the other side of the game I have a feeling he is becoming quickly disillusioned. He rang me last night and mentioned quite casually in conversation that Wing and a Prayer was dead — in fact that he died only a couple of days after his last run at Newbury. I was stunned, not so much by the death of the horse but by the fact that John Jenkins had not mentioned it to me either on the phone or at the races. That I found very hard to understand.

Mr Steele had another setback today. So too did I. Ivy League should have won his race at Cheltenham if he was even to begin to justify his lofty reputation and his enormous purchase price, but after running well for a long way he faded to finish eighth. With any other horse you would probably not have been disappointed. With this one, Mr Steele was very plainly dismayed and although I urged him to give the horse another chance, he is already talking about selling him — inevitably at a big loss. Sometimes, I find owners impossible to fathom.

SATURDAY 7 DECEMBER

Luck comes and goes in fickle fashion in this job. You fly for a few weeks, then you spend days on end wondering where on earth the next winner is coming from. You don't have a single fall for an age, then you have five or six in a week.

Simon Sherwood is currently a vivid example of my point. He is still top of the championship but he has not ridden a winner for a fortnight, and today's events at Lingfield just about summed up his current fortunes. First, he somehow forgot to weigh in after finishing third in the three-year-old hurdle. He must, I suppose, have had things on his mind. It was just a careless oversight, but the stewards fined him and disqualified the horse. Then, in the last race of the day, he was aboard the odds-on favourite — a novice hurdler of his brother's called Idleighs Run. He must have thought that this was the race to end his lean run, but instead it made things many times worse. Twice, down at the start, poor Simon was unseated by this very unruly animal. On the second occasion, with the race now certain to start without him, Simon hurled his cap to the ground in a fury while 21 other jockeys hooted with laughter. He later saw the funny side himself, but it took him a time to force a smile.

Ben de Haan is another good rider for whom precious little is going right. Ben now rides the majority of Fred Winter's good horses, the very same horses which made John Francome champion so many times. But now that Ben has landed the job, the stable has hit a bad patch and the winners have dried up. I was pleased to see him put on two fo Sheikh Ali Abu Khamsin's best horses — Half Free and Gaye Brief — at Cheltenham today but it was somehow inevitable both would be beaten.

My day was a mixed one. I had been upset to miss some rides at Cheltenham, and was feeling decidedly sick when, after finishing second on a Nicky Henderson horse behind Franc's That's Your Lot — which I won on a week ago — I heard that one of my lost rides, Copse and Robbers, had won the three-year-old race at headquarters. But things did get better. Di's horse Oversway ran a blinder, just being touched off into second place, and I finished up winning both divisions of the novice hurdle. One of the winners was a horse called Juven Light, trained by Reg Akehurst, and unless this was a freak performance, he could be very high class.

I went home to my first decent dinner in days, the wasting dilemma over again for a while. But, as so often after a few days of strict dieting, I was full up after the starter and simply could not cope with the main course.

SUNDAY 8 DECEMBER

I enjoy schooling, and pride myself on doing it well, but unless the circumstances leave no option I object to trainers asking me to school on a Sunday morning. Eric Eldin left several messages last night asking me to school his one jumper this morning and I'm afraid I ignored them all. What is wrong with the six working days of the week?

MONDAY 9 DECEMBER

Went to a West End theatre this evening for the first time in my life. Growing up in Derbyshire mining country, and then living in Newmarket and being permanently busy, it is something I had just never got around to doing. Tonight, after a lengthy Sports Writer's Lunch in Kensington, Di and I went to see The Sloane Ranger Revue with the Francomes. I hardly knew what to expect and somewhat to my surprise I greatly enjoyed it. In fact I enjoyed the whole day. It all made a change from the usual week-day diet of driving to a racecourse and galloping round.

TUESDAY 10 DECEMBER

Schooled First Bout again at Nicky's place — very pleased. Last week he had been a bit sketchy at the hurdles, the rust of the summer and autumn months showing through, but today he was much more his old self. He goes to Ascot on Saturday but will probably need the race to bring him on to full fitness.

I drove on from Lambourn down to Plumpton in fog. In fact the fog was so bad at the course that I feared they might abandon the meeting. I only had one ride, Foyle Fisherman again in the second race on the card, so as soon as the first-race jockeys had filed out of the weighing-room I galloped through and weighed out. That little trick ensured I would be paid my riding fee even if they abandoned after one race. I don't think David Steele would have been too pleased if that had happened but in the event the meeting went on, visibility improved, and Foyle Fisherman cheered him up by winning easily.

WEDNESDAY 11 DECEMBER

When I started my career with Tom Jones, there were plenty of jumping trainers in and around Newmarket. They all tended to run their horses at Huntingdon whenever possible, and as I was the locally-based rider I usually had a full book of rides there. For some years now I have been top jockey on the course but with Newmarket now housing so few jump trainers my supply of mounts from the area has dwindled quite alarmingly. I only had two rides there today, neither of which finished in the frame. It remains my favourite track and I know my way round it better than anyone else riding, but I would welcome a few more opportunities to prove it.

THURSDAY 12 DECEMBER

We had quite a house-party last night, the guests including John Francome, Simon Sherwood and Di's brother Tim Thomson-Jones. So out on the gallops this morning Mrs Di Haine, small-time permit trainer, had a celebrated team of riding-out jockeys. Tim, however, was not at his best. The after-effects of the dinner party were all too plain when he schooled a horse called Tar Flame over hurdles. He clattered clumsily through two flights before Tim pulled him up and demanded to know if we had had the damned horse's eyes tested. When I got on him myself I could see his point. Although I managed to pop him over a couple of fences he was jumping very stiffly. When a horse can't or won't bend his back there is usually something wrong in that area, and we will have to get him checked.

Simon left us to drive down to Somerset and visit Richard Linley in hospital. There just hasn't been time for me to get down there yet, but I have sent Richard a crate of half-bottles of champagne. He may not consider he has much worth celebrating right now, but anything which cheers him up a little must be worth trying.

FRIDAY 13 DECEMBER

And I'm glad I am not superstitious about such things! Racing was at Warwick today, and I positioned myself by the door of the weighing-room as the lads went out to ride in the novice chase. As they filed past I shouted: 'It's Friday the 13th boys — just hang in there!'

It was not the luckiest of days for some. Tim was kicked in the face, fracturing a cheekbone, and Kevin Mooney was stood down for seven days with concussion. Me? I just got beaten on two favourites.

SATURDAY 14 DECEMBER

In our hearts I honestly think both Nicky Henderson and I were convinced that First Bout would be beaten today. He is not fully wound up, he had not raced since March, and was in a pretty hot contest at Ascot. Both of us would have been pleased if he had finished in the first three. But perhaps he is even better than either of us think, because he slaughtered his opposition and won virtually as he pleased. I knew from some way out that I could pick off the others and, jumping superbly, he strode away up the straight to win very impressively.

The bookmaker reaction was predictable but premature. They now make him joint-favourite for next March's Champion Hurdle with See You Then, our other star and current holder of the hurdling crown. I think they are wrong. First Bout is a very nice horse and, personally, I can't wait to ride him over fences when the time comes. But in terms of a Champion Hurdle, I don't think he is in the same class as See You Then. If I had to make my decision now which one to ride in the big race, it would not take me long to make up my mind.

Today's other big meeting was at Doncaster and, between races at Ascot, I watched events up there on the weighing-room television. Hywel Davies had a shocking fall in the two-mile chase, and I recalled that it was at Doncaster last season that he might have been lucky to come out alive from an even more horrific tumble. I wondered what he thought when he went back to the course. It is certainly true that most jockeys have bogy courses, where nothing ever goes right for them and where, eventually, they dread having to ride.

MONDAY 16 DECEMBER

Richard Linley is, naturally enough, still a daily topic of conversation among the jockeys. The bulletins we are receiving now are more encouraging. His condition seems to be improving steadily. But any mention of his plight inevitably creates a sombre mood so it was good to be able to laugh today over something which happened to him. Beverley's parents are apparently keen winemakers, and they took a bottle into Richard when they visited him a few days ago. At 2.00 a.m. that night there was a dramatic explosion next to Richard's bed which set nurses running in all directions, panicking because they thought a bomb had gone off. It turned out that the home-made wine had popped its cork rather extravagantly. The bottle had smashed, the cork had made a hole in the hospital ceiling, and Richard was discovered in fits of laughter.

This was related to me at Leicester where I rode one winner (Indamelody getting his jumping together) and felt certain I had ridden two. It was a desperately close thing between my horse Paulatim and Cross Master but, looking across on the line as I always do, I judged that I had won by a head. Cross Master's jockey plainly thought so, too, as he steered his horse straight into the runners-up position in the unsaddling enclosure. I duly swung into the winner's spot, exchanged a few cheerful words with

Nicky, and had returned to weigh-in when the announcement came that I had been beaten by a head. I could hardly believe the evidence of the photograph.

It was a mad evening — predictably mad, as I had been driven to the races by Jeff Barlow. It is only a 75-mile run from Leicester to Newmarket and we were both finished riding by three o'clock, but it was after 11.00 p.m. when I staggered into my house, led astray again and dallying dangerously in our favourite watering-hole, The Haycock on the A1.

TUESDAY 17 DECEMBER

Foyle Fisherman was sent to Folkestone today aiming for his third victory on consecutive Tuesdays. He failed gallantly, finishing third in a race which would have done justice to a far grander meeting than this one, but despite the fact that penalties had increased his load to 12-2 and he was conceding pounds to the two horses which beat him, David Steele was inconsolable. He now wants to sell this one as well as Ivy League. I think he is wrong, as both horses are sure to win more races, but the owner pays the bills and what he says is law.

From Folkestone I followed the fast motorway route back to Lambourn, taking the M20, M26, M25 and M4, thankful as I drove that I am having my career in an age when long journeys can be undertaken without much recourse to slow country roads or even slower, unreliable trains.

At Nicky Henderson's Windsor House yard we had an early-evening conference, also involving head lad 'Corky' Brown. We talked through the horses one by one, mapping out plans and hopes for each of them. It was a productive discussion. Nicky has a high-class team of horses here this season and he is sensibly being patient with the big guns. We still, for instance, don't accurately know when See You Then will reappear on the race-course, but there will be no hurry with him. The Champion, in March, is really the only race which matters.

WEDNESDAY 18 DECEMBER

No jockey is perfect. Even John Francome was not infallible — he made the occasional blunder; but what made him the best was that his cock-ups were far less frequent than anyone else's. There are times when you make a mistake so bad and so obvious that the best policy is to admit it and apologise. That happened to me today. I had gone to Worcester for one ride — Jeff King's Veleso in a three-mile handicap chase. I won three times on the horse last season, and although he was not expected to add to that score today he might well have run decently. But he didn't get the chance. I fell off him at the first fence. He didn't make much of a mistake, just put in an extra short stride: but I fell off. As there were plenty of runners, and I was upsides in front when we met the fence, I took the inevitable kicking as the rest of the field galloped over me. I was not badly hurt, but the ambulance picked me up anyway, and on the way back across the course I agonised over what I should say to Jeff. Having been a brilliant jockey himself, Jeff tends to judge everyone else by his own standards and so is a notoriously hard taskmaster. I knew that if I trumped up an excuse he would crucify me, so I didn't even try. As he walked to meet me I just said: 'Sorry Jeff, I fell off.' I waited for the explosion but, instead, he burst out laughing. Honesty really is often the best policy.

THURSDAY 19 DECEMBER

My life has just flashed before me. I feel so shaken I cannot think straight. I have come within an inch of killing someone. I have also done untold damage to my car, let alone my nerves. I was almost home when it happened. The annual Bollinger dinner took place in London last night and I stayed down, heading back up the M10 this morning as I had no rides booked anywhere. I had left the motorway and was travelling at moderate speed along a country road when, up ahead of me, an accident unfolded. It was a strange experience. I knew it was going to happen and I was powerless to do anything about it. A car was backing out of a drive. A motorbike was approaching at high speed. As if in slow motion, I saw the inevitable collision, winced at a noise like a gunshot and watched in horror as the rider of the motorbike cartwheeled high into the air and flew towards me. He hit the road with a sickening thud and slid into my path. I was not moving that fast but it still required rapid reactions to swing the car off the road — the only place I could go to avoid him. I skidded across the verge and came to rest in a hedge. When I extricated myself the bike-rider was already getting some attention. He was in a bad way but he was alive. He was also lying right next to my tyre-mark. When I got home I was literally shaking, both at what had happened and what might have happened. And after all the bad conditions I have driven in recently, this occurred in bright daylight on a dry, mild morning.

FRIDAY 20 DECEMBER
Loyalty rates high in my book, so when the Lambourn trainer David Murray-Smith rang up today to offer me the ride on Rhyme'n'Reason, second favourite for tomorrow's Welsh Grand National, I had to turn it down. I have already taken the ride on Ginger McCain's enigmatic Kumbi, and although form dictates that he has far less chance than Rhyme'n'Reason I shall not desert him or let down Ginger. I can't pretend I didn't feel a few pangs of regret at refusing, however, and I was not in the best of moods as I drove up into Norfolk for this afternoon's meeting at Fakenham.

The day was bitterly cold and miserably damp, which made Fakenham the last place on earth a jockey would want to be. Condensation dripped on my head from the weighing-room ceiling as I sipped a cup of tea and surveyed the surroundings. There was one wash-basin, one urinal and one shower between 30-odd jockeys. There was no hot water at all. This was the downbeat end of the racing scale, one that those who only frequent Ascot and Cheltenham will never know.

It did, however, have its compensation in the shape of a winner. Gavin's Boom Patrol came here today and I regarded him as a bonking certainty. He was backed down to even-money and he did the job, but made hard work of it, only winning by half a length. I'm afraid he is not the horse we thought he was. At least it meant Gavin's lads had something to celebrate, and some cash in their pockets, at their Christmas party tonight. I went along through a sense of duty. I don't enjoy large gatherings of stable-lads because they not only have very good memories but generally jaundiced memories too. They will mercilessly remind you of each and every occasion you got beaten on a horse they had backed, but they seem to forget the winners!

SATURDAY 21 DECEMBER

The last day of racing before the brief Christmas recess was a mixed and surprising one. I got a lift down to Chepstow with Bob Champion (though I get so screwed up inside, sitting in a passenger seat, I am much better off driving myself) and as we discussed the meeting ahead I thought that I was likely to win the juvenile hurdle on Ana Waslawi but that I was unlikely to win on either of my other booked rides. I was completely wrong.

Ana Waslawi, who cost £20,000-plus, had run very well to be second behind That's Your Lot a fortnight ago and although he often misbehaves at home we had high hopes that he would develop into something pretty useful. But today I am afraid his temperament let him down disastrously, and as the field turned into the back straight I was already in trouble. The horse was digging in his toes and trying to pull up, plainly determined to take no serious part in the race. I got him round, but he trailed in at the back of the field and I could only suggest to Nicky and the owners that they rapidly have him gelded before trying again. If that fails he could turn out to be a quick and very expensive flop.

It was a very different story on Nicky's Pikes Peak in the two-and-a-half-mile novice hurdle. He won in the style of a very good horse, and I will look forward to riding him again. And then there was Kumbi, running the race of his life to finish third in the Welsh National. Rhyme'n'Reason, eventually ridden by Frank Berry, was a long way behind me, so on this occasion loyalty paid off.

Mark Perrett's desperate bad luck goes on. Only just recovered from a broken leg, and still short of rides since his split with Stan Mellor, he got on a good horse of Jenny Pitman's called Smiths Man in the National — and broke his leg again. He didn't even fall, simply felt the leg snap. Not surprisingly he came back in agony and I should think his season is over. Only a year ago people were talking of him as a future star, a potential champion ... it can be a very cruel game, this.

Before leaving the course I handed out my first Christmas gift, a bottle of scotch to the valets. John Buckingham, famous for winning the Grand National on the 100-1 shot Foinavon, is my personal valet, but all of them do a tremendous job under sometimes very trying conditions. Their day starts hours before the first jockey arrives at a course and ends considerably after the last one has left. They seldom see a race run, they have to put up with a lot of moaning — not to mention a lot of mud — but they manage to stay quite amazingly cheerful.

MONDAY AND TUESDAY 23 AND 24 DECEMBER

The days when most people buy their final presents: the days when I buy all of mine.

I've told all my trainers that I will not ride at lighter than 10 stone 7 pounds over the next week, which gives me some leeway to indulge my appetite. My parents are due to come and stay with Di and I, but it hardly seems like Christmas yet. It has been a busy time recently and even now, late on Christmas Eve, I am still arranging my holiday rides.

WEDNESDAY 25 DECEMBER

Unlike machines, racehorses cannot be switched off when the workforce is on holiday. So at 7.30 a.m. on this Christmas morning I was out on the Newmarket gallops, giving Di's chaser Oversway a piece of work. He is due to run at Newbury next Monday, and even Christmas Day cannot disrupt a horse's race preparation. From breakfast-time onwards, however, I did not give horses, trainers or racecourses another thought. I ate and drank too much. I enjoyed it, too.

THURSDAY 26 DECEMBER

Kempton Park on Boxing Day is one of the big jump-race meetings of the season. It is also one of the most hectic, and crowds clog up the M3 and all other approach roads to Sunbury hours before the scheduled start. Like the Sloane Rangers at Newbury on Hennessy day, there is a peculiar breed of spectator attracted to this meeting. The racing is so good that thousands of regular racefans are always present, but the once-a-year brigade are there in their droves, curing their hangovers and their excesses in the open air or dragging along unwilling children to avoid another day of mending broken toys. Kempton does not have limitless viewing facilities, and on Boxing Days there are always hundreds perched in positions from which they can see no more than the flash of colours as the horses gallop past. Some experience it once and never come again. Others are hooked by the atmosphere of Bank Holiday escapism, of Christmas cigars and new coats, and come back each year. All I can add is that anyone who left Kempton with a smile today was lucky. Rain was falling steadily when I got up this morning and it set the tone for one of the most miserable Boxing Days I can recall. I left Newmarket very early to beat the crowds, and got to Kempton in time to enjoy a game of pool. But once the racing began any glamour apparently attached to this prestigious day was stripped away. All that was left was a freezing wind, driving rain and flying mud. Goggles were useless after a few hundred yards; there was nothing for it but to pull them down and take the mud full in the face. The thought of a blazing log fire, a lunchtime drink and a decent Boxing Day meal flashed mischievously across my mind and I wondered what on earth I was doing in this job. The feeling always passes, usually hastened by a winner, but today even that tonic was missing.

First Bout ran a stinking race. After his impressive win at Ascot it was too bad to be true. I was struggling a mile out, and although he plugged on to finish fourth he felt anything but a champion. This Christmas Hurdle has become a bogy race for Nicky Henderson; last year See You Then ran equally badly in the race. But he went on to triumph at Cheltenham. So why should Nicky worry about the omens now?

Wayward Lad won the King George again, at long odds. The pundits had written him off as a light of other days, and considered that the race was between Combs Ditch and Burrough Hill Lad. But for some reason Wayward Lad often sparkles at Kempton. Graham Bradley gave him a lovely ride and I was delighted for him — he is one of the best northern jockeys, if not the best.

FRIDAY 27 DECEMBER

Back to Kempton with a heavy heart for the second day of the holiday meeting, perennially as different from the first as lemonade is from champagne. After the heady excitement and the huge crowds of Boxing Day, normality reluctantly returns. There is an ordinary crowd for an ordinary card, but at least the sun shone.

I had only two rides, both for Nicky Henderson, and neither of them won. I'm having another quiet spell now, but I was sharply reminded of how rapidly fortunes can change when Richard Dunwoody rode four consecutive winners, after almost three weeks without a winner at all.

I cheered myself up in the time-honoured way, by eating. Another of Kempton's popular features among the jockeys is the tearoom, where a lady called Josie fusses around us like a mother hen and provides some super sandwiches. In fact, if it wasn't for the racing, I might have enjoyed the last two days much more!

SATURDAY 28 DECEMBER

The ground was white with frost when I peered out of the bedroom window this morning. My first thought was that there would be no racing today, and my second thought was that that would suit me fine. True, it was Newbury I would be missing, a good meeting on a favourite course, but when your luck is out and your energy low even those like myself, lucky enough to enjoy their job, begin to run short of enthusiasm. The radio confirmed my impression. There would be no racing anywhere in the country. I settled contentedly for a weekend at home and dug out a Jack Higgins thriller to see me through to the start of 'Grandstand'.

MONDAY 30 DECEMBER

As we are still frozen solid and Newbury is off again, I booked an appointment to have my hair cut this afternoon. But I never got there. Just after breakfast Alan Jarvis phoned to ask if I was free to go and work some of his horses on the beach at Yarmouth. I agreed to go along and I'm glad I did. Galloping along at the water's edge with the wind blowing in fresh off the sea gave me a feeling that was both solitary and exhilirating. It was another side of racing, an unexpected side. I didn't get my haircut but I had a good day.

TUESDAY 31 DECEMBER

This is the half-way point in the season, and a bleak one at that. There was no racing in England for the third day running, and I'm no longer happy about it. I've had my break, now I am eager to get back riding, chasing the winners, striving to be champion. I'm in there fighting, still in second place behind Simon Sherwood and very much within striking distance. I have got through so far without serious injury. There have been plenty of falls, plenty of highs and lows. But the really big days of the season are still to come. The reckoning is still in front of us all.

JANUARY

WEDNESDAY 1 JANUARY

Bank Holidays mean nothing to jockeys. Nothing, that is, except a confusion of meetings from which to choose, and the regular suspicion that you are in a national minority in not having a hangover when the day begins. I was sensible last night — a few drinks with some friends and to bed not long after the New Year struck — and my compensations this morning were a clear head and a clear road for the drive to Cheltenham, where the major holiday meeting was staged. It was not, however, a good road. After a cold night ice lay in lethal patches on the surface, and I passed four separate accidents on the short stretch of motorway between Newmarket and Huntingdon. Although I was at the wheel of Di's mother's Mercedes, my car being in dock after the pre-Christmas prang, I kept to a steady speed. One idiot flashed past, doing something over 100 mph. I glanced across and confirmed that, in the usual style of motoring maniacs, he had a beard!

The two best novice hurdlers seen out this season won at Cheltenham. Ten Plus, trained by Fulke Walwyn, was the first to go in and I won the other division on Nicky's Pikes Peak. It will be some race, if and when these two meet back at Cheltenham in March, but an awful lot can happen before then.

THURSDAY 2 JANUARY

Racing's betting underworld has been alive with fanciful rumours that all is not well with See You Then. Based presumably on the fact that he has not appeared in public since winning his crown last March, the gossip has it that he will not be ready to defend his title, and some of the bookies have taken sufficient notice to extend his odds. I can tell you, however, that if jockeys were allowed to bet I would plunge heavily on him now. Nothing, to my mind, will get near him on the big day.

I say this despite suffering an unnerving indignity when I schooled the horse today for the first time this season. No sooner had my backside touched the saddle than I was unceremoniously bucked off. As I flew gracelessly through the air I caught a fleeting glimpse of Nicky Henderson's face. It was a portrait of shock and alarm and I could well imagine what was flashing through his mind. Day one of the champion's proper preparation, and here he was about to set off around the Berkshire countryside, capable of causing untold damage, chiefly to himself. To Nicky's eternal relief, not to mention mine, I had managed to cling onto the reins and made certain that the damage was confined to a couple of bruises on my own body and pride. See You Then, having had his fun, was far more amenable to being mounted second time around, and proceeded to jump like a stag. We could not be more pleased with the way he has come on. Physically he has developed very well and, while there will still be no rush to get him onto a racecourse, I cannot see a hurdler to beat him right now.

First Bout certainly shouldn't beat him. He ran again at Cheltenham today in a two-and-a-half-mile race. Ran well, too, finishing third behind two older horses in Corporal Clinger and Galas Image. Kempton can now at least be dismissed as a freakishly bad day — but I still have no doubts which of our two horses I want to be on in March.

A surprise and welcome face at Cheltenham today was Sam Morshead. All of us in the weighing-room have been concerned about Sam as he has been absent since a fall on the flat at Warwick all of five weeks ago. His concussion was so serious that he apparently could not walk downstairs without feeling dizzy. He is still not fully recovered now and, although it was good to see him back amongst us I wonder if he will see this as a sign that his career might not have long to go.

FRIDAY 3 JANUARY

Fred Winter phoned up to offer me a ride at Sandown tomorrow. This is only because he runs two horses in the race and one of his retained riders, Jimmy Duggan, is being sent to the other meeting at Warwick, but it still gave me a kick. When Fred asks you to ride for him you can't be too bad a pilot.

SATURDAY 4 JANUARY
Fred Winter phoned again. Warwick is off, Duggan is available so yours truly is not needed after all. Still, the thought was there. Sandown, all things considered, was a bit of a disaster as Indamelody, who seemed to have taken to jumping fences after his temperamental start, put me over his head again. Horse and rider unhurt — but it's back to the drawing-board with this one.

Pete Scudamore won yet another big race, this time the Anthony Mildmay-Peter Cazalet Chase, on Run And Skip. He is riding like a demon, and was absolutely brilliant today.

MONDAY 6 JANUARY
After winning my regular Sunday night snooker match 6-0 I went out this morning and invested in my own cue. I just might start to take this game seriously — the way things are going I could end up making more money from snooker than from racing. The weather has closed in again. Nottingham was frosted off today, and there is not much hope for tomorrow.

WEDNESDAY 8 JANUARY
As it's a few degrees warmer down south I got up this morning full of hope that I would be heading for Plumpton to ride a decent novice of Jeff King's. Switched on the radio and what do I hear? Plumpton is waterlogged! That's the trouble with this time of year — the weather operates in extremes, and if racing is not off for one thing it will be off for another. It plays hell with us poor jockeys trying to plan our lives.

THURSDAY 9 JANUARY
Back to work. Wincanton is often a good bet for a resumption after a spell of abandonments; it's a popular track, both with the working fraternity of trainers and jockeys and with the paying public. There is a hard core of West Country farmers who come to every meeting, and I happen to know that the course attracts fans from consider-

able distances. It's not that it is very accessible, either. Quite the opposite in fact. You approach the course down some winding, hedge-bordered country lanes which begin to look as if they lead nowhere; it is not near a single large town and is, in fact, one of the least convenient of all the southern tracks to reach.

For all that, it was good to see the lads for the first time since Saturday, and good to be earning again. Most people tend to forget that a jockey's income abruptly dries up when the weather halts racing. Only those with seasonal retainers have anything to fall back on. I had only the one ride but I expected him to win. It was Ogden York, a novice hurdler which Di used to train. He's now with John Francome, and he had twice run well without winning, so we had every right to fancy him today. But he was a big disappointment, disliking the soft ground and dropping into the also-rans very quickly. 'Franc', however, is not one of those trainers who will mope and moan about such setbacks. Five minutes after the race he was in the weighing-room for a cup of tea, laughing and joking with us just the same as he used to be when riding. I must say I admire this phlegmatic side of his nature, even if it has tended to offend the more serious-minded people in our sport. John's attitude to life is that there is always a tomorrow, so why worry. It's an outlook which should ensure he lives a long time.

FRIDAY 10 JANUARY

Schooling half-a-dozen horses in pouring rain soon after dawn is not always my idea of a good time, but it served its purpose today. All six of them jumped well and I was able to sweat off an excess pound or two. I've been as fat as a pig since Christmas, and the shortage of recent racing has not helped one bit. I managed to do 10 stone 3 pounds on Green Bramble today at Ascot, but the horse is still not right. He ran left-handed at every fence, losing about three lengths each time, and in the circumstances he did well to finish fourth in a race marred by Brown Chamberlin breaking down. He has always been a bad-legged horse, but plenty of people had begun to fancy him quietly for the Gold Cup. Simon Sherwood had been paid a big retainer to ride him for the rest of the season. This was only the second time he had sat on him, and it will also be the last. Barring a miracle, Brown Chamberlin will never run again.

SATURDAY 11 JANUARY

My quiet time goes on, but 'Scu' can do no wrong. He rode a double at Ascot today, and has now overtaken me and gone into second place in the table. His greatest quality is his strength in a finish, and that was evident on both today's winners, Tickete Boo and Very Promising. I can say with absolute certainty that a weaker, less experienced jockey would have been beaten on them both and I was staggered to hear that there had been some phone calls to the course from TV viewers complaining the 'Scu' had overused his whip. That may have been a valid criticism of his riding in his early days, but not any more. If those armchair critics had been a shade more observant they would have seen that although 'Scu' uses his stick very vigorously he is for much of the time either waving it past the horse's head or slapping him harmlessly down the shoulder.

As for me, I seem to be following my annual pattern. Don't ask me why, but I always suffer a famine of winners during January. I might just as well pack up for two or three weeks and grab that much-needed holiday.

MONDAY 13 JANUARY

If Sunday racing ever does come to Britain, and I have very mixed feelings about the prospect, it might have one welcome side-benefit. Mondays could then be scrapped as a racing day — you would not hear a single moan from the jockeys' room. The cards on a Monday are invariably uninspiring, and the venues are no better. I usually end up going to one of the dreary midland courses to race in front of a few hundred diehards. Leicester runs it close but for me, Wolverhampton is the most soulless course of the lot; with my confidence short and my luck poor, I drove there today in hardly the sunniest of spirits. It gave me my first winner since 1 January!

It was a typical Wolverhampton day — cold, grey and with the threat of rain. It was a typical Wolverhampton card, too, and although I had three reasonable rides I have reached the stage where I didn't expect any of them to win. When Bright Arrow, one of Nicky's young hurdlers, stopped suddenly in the straight from a promising position I thought it was an omen for another blank day, but my old pal J. Francome came to the rescue, and I rode his useful flat horse Asswan to win the other division of the novice hurdle.

Breaking fast out of the 'gate' is crucial to obtaining your position in a race. I stare across at the starter through my distinctive dark goggles, waiting for the moment he brings down his hand to lift the tape. Alan Johnson

On tour with some of my closest jockey mates (LEFT TO RIGHT) *Peter Scudamore, Hywel Davies, John Francome and Jonjo O'Neill. 'Franc' and Jonjo are both now training.* Caroline Norris

A jockey's valet does very much more than just put out the right silks. John Buckingham even lets me share his ice cream on a hot autumn racing day. Alan Johnson

TOP   *A memorable and emotional winner for me, giving John Francome his first training success with Thats Your Lot at Sandown.*   Alan Johnson

ABOVE   *Nothing went wrong with this leap – Rhythmic Pastimes winning an October hurdle race at Ascot. Later on, his confidence went to pieces.*   Alan Johnson

TOP *Early morning on the Lambourn gallops, My guv'nor Nicky Henderson directs operations.* Fiona Vigors

ABOVE *Away from it all on the French ski-slopes . . . but when will they open that bar?* Courtesy of Steve Smith Eccles

It always seems a long walk back to the weighing room after being beaten on a fancied horse. Alan Johnson

The season's greatest day. Nick and I look tense as See You Then walks out to defend his championship hurdler title

. . . striding up that long Cheltenham hill to the line

. . . the moment of truth as we tackle 'Scu' and Gaye Brief at the last

. . . and now it's all smiles as the champion returns. Caroline Norris

Every jockey I know reads the Life *like a bible – when they wake up in the morning, often at the races, and then again before bed.* Alan Johnson

*Kathies Lad (*RIGHT*) is still the best two-mile handicap chaser in training, and he gave me my one winner at a highly eventful Aintree meeting.* Alan Johnson

WEDNESDAY 15 JANAURY

Are retainers worthwhile? I found myself asking that question again today as my commitment to Nicky caused more headaches for the weekend ahead. Already, I have had to turn down a couple of potential winners to ride inferior horses for the Henderson yard. It's not Nicky's fault; he offered me the retainer, I took it, and naturally I'm pleased enough to have the link when his top horses run. But there is no doubt at all that a retainer complicates life. It means that I am not a genuine freelance any more, and I am not convinced that I like the restriction. This is something to consider for next season, I think.

I got a shock when I stepped on the scales at Windsor today. I was 10 stone 5 pounds stripped, which meant I could not possibly ride at less than 10 stone 8 pounds. I have never been so heavy and I can't quite understand it. It cost me a ride today, as Jeff King was understandably adamant that he would not put up five pounds overweight on a handicap chaser, and although the horse concerned trailed in last under Simon Sherwood, I am going to have to do something about the problem before it takes root.

Windsor is one of England's two figure of eight tracks, Fontwell being the other, and they certainly take some riding. If you get a horse on the inside rail for one bend, he will be on the outside for the next bend, so a good deal of dodging about is called for; small wonder that some horses don't act very happily on this track.

'Scu' rode another winner. I didn't, and drove home with only a supper-less night to look forward to.

THURSDAY 16 JANUARY

No breakfast, no lunch, and yet again no winners. It was desperate ground at Lingfield (it's always bottomless mud there even if the ground is good elsewhere), but the day did have its redeeming features. I am still fit and healthy, which is saying something, the rate jockeys are getting hurt at present. And I finished up spending a sociable evening in London with my pal and rival, S. Sherwood. At times of adversity, enjoy yourself — that's my motto.

FRIDAY 17 JANUARY

The racing hacks were out in force at Kempton this evening. Nicky had arranged for See You Then to have a racecourse gallop with two of his other horses, and it seems that to many people this was the big event of the day. A lot of the crowd stayed on and they cannot have been disappointed at what they saw. The rumour-mongers who had been renaming the horse See You When must have slunk away silently as he cruised past the two stablemates, jumping brilliantly. He blew hard afterwards, as you would expect, but I told anyone who asked that I consider him a ten-pound better horse than he was last season, and I am more convinced than ever that he will win at Cheltenham.

I am also becoming increasingly convinced that 'Scu' will be champion jockey. Maybe it's a maudlin view from the depths of my bad patch, but I honestly think he will take some catching, the way he is riding right now. When you are in a purple patch like this, you ride with enormous confidence, and Peter won a race today that summed it up perfectly. Solar Cloud, the four-year-old he was riding, veered all over the course, yet 'Scu' kept him going to win by a neck. If he had been out of form and low on confidence, he would have been beaten.

SATURDAY 18 JANUARY

The big races were at Doncaster and Kempton, but I went to the bread-and-butter meeting at Warwick, with no complaints, though. I rode a welcome winner, Paulatim, winning the novice chase in comfortable style. Nicky's main object in sending me here, I think, was to ride an ex-Irish hurdler called Charlie's Cottage. They have expected a lot of this horse and Nicky had plainly not lost faith despite several disappointments. But today, tried over a new, longer trip, he not only never looked like winning, he also made a very unhealthy noise. There may well be something substantially wrong with him. He is certainly not the horse they thought he was when they bought him.

MONDAY 20 JANAURY

Di knows now not to bother cooking me any dinner when I go racing with the Newmarket Musketeers. It was the usual routine today. Short drive to Leicester, one ride on a no-hoper, finished work by 3.00 p.m., home by 11.00 p.m. ....

TUESDAY 21 JANUARY

I knew as soon as I took the ride that I had made a mistake. It was only the fact that it was John Burke who phoned me which lowered my guard. Burkey is such a good old mate that I'd love to help him out in his new career as an assistant trainer. He offered me two rides at Nottingham today, one in a novice hurdle, the other in the novice chase. Neither had any chance, but I took them anyway.

On the way up the A1 this morning I had second thoughts. There was a maximum field for the novice chase. I had nothing to prove; it was too risky. I asked John when I got there to find someone else, and immediately felt relieved. It was funny how things turned out. It was not the novice chase but the hurdle which caused the carnage ... I was out the back, just concentrating on getting round safely and teaching the horse a little. One fell in front of me, bringing down two more. Suddenly, there was nowhere to go, and as I crossed the hurdle I knew we were galloping all over one of the prostrate jockeys. I had no clear idea who it was but I heard the crunch as we hit him, felt the shock waves shoot up my horse's legs and knew instantly that I had done the bloke some serious damage. As soon as I had weighed in after the race I headed for the ambulance room, and there he was. It turned out to be a young claimer called David Chinn and he looked as if he had been trampled on by a herd of hungry elephants. His silks were ripped to shreds and the doctor was busily engaged in literally stitching his ear back on. Meanwhile, a couple of other jockeys were also being treated and Anthony Webber was being dispatched to hospital. It was a depressing mess, even though there was nothing at all I could have done about it.

WEDNESDAY 22 JANUARY

The Musketeers led me astray again last night, The Haycock Inn taking our custom until a late hour. Unusually for me I had a thick head this morning, and didn't exactly relish the long drive to dismal Wolverhampton. It was raining and blowing a gale, but it was still worth going. Smart Reply, the American-bred horse of Nicky's which had disappointed over hurdles, took to fences much more readily and won by 30 lengths. That was my 44th winner of the season, and although I have had a long lean run, I am actually closing the gap on Simon — now only five behind.

It occurred to me on the unpleasant drive home that this time last year I was lying on a beach in Barbados.

THURSDAY 23 JANUARY

The best thing about today's racing was that I didn't have far to come home! It was at Huntingdon, but even my favourite course failed to cheer me or change my current luck. I not only drew a blank, which is becoming a familiar January tale, but I also inwardly accepted that I am really not riding with my usual zest and confidence. It is a worrying admission, but an honestly-held view. I am finding it very hard to rouse myself for the run-of-the-mill race days which, after all, dominate the jockey's calendar. Apart from longing for a holiday, I am also anxious for the major occasions to hurry along, those days when I need no motivating to test myself and my mounts against the best.

I could have fancied each of my three rides today, but a second on Nicky Henderson's four-year-old, Attiki, was the closest I came to scoring. Di's Oversway just failed to stay three miles, and John Francome's Ogden York ran as if he is in the same state as me — a bit run-down and in need of a rest!

FRIDAY 24 JANUARY

Doncaster is one of those crossover northern courses, like Haydock Park, and to a lesser extent Wetherby, at which southern jockeys will appear now and again to ride in major races. These three tracks would be the north's equivalent of Sandown, Ascot and Kempton, where we often see the leading northern riders down for big events. Today's card on the Town Moor course at Doncaster was not all that special apart from a valuable novice hurdle, called the Rossington Main, which is annually competitive, and this year had drawn a better field than ever. There were about a dozen previous winners lining up, including the horse I had driven up there to ride, Asswan. I knew there were a number of fancied runners, and I honestly had no idea how well my horse would fare against them but as it turned out he beat them all ... then lost the race to an unconsidered 50-to-1 shot.

As usual at Doncaster the ground was good and fast, which greatly appealed to my horse — and, as usual, the wind whipped mercilessly across the moor, cutting through the silks and chilling all of us jockeys to the bone. I was pleased, though, to be riding only in the big hurdle event. I have long held a dread of the Doncaster fences, which I believe to be the worst in the country. They are so formidably big and bushy that they deter horses, even some usually good jumpers, and there always appear to be too many falls here for comfort.

I had driven Jeff Barlow to the meeting. He had ridden two hurdlers at Huntingdon yesterday, both of which had fallen, and when he fell again in the opening hurdle race today I have a feeling his confidence for his ride in the later novice chase was at a pretty low ebb. I wished him well, silently glad that I was staying in the weighing-room, and I was as relieved as he was to see him return safely after an uneventful ride round.

SATURDAY 25 JANUARY

My situation in Newmarket has plenty of advantages, but I have to say that on mornings like this one it is not the most convenient place to live. Frost had bitten into the ground nationwide over-night, and inspections were called at all four planned meetings. Three of them — Ayr, Doncaster and Folkestone, were rapidly abandoned, but at Cheltenham, the feature card of the day and the place where I had five booked rides, a decision was delayed several times. I could understand the course management's anxiety to keep the meeting on; in other circumstances, I would openly have applauded their efforts. But as I hovered restlessly at home between the telephone and the radio I admit to wishing they had called it off at eight o'clock and had done with it.

Eventually I set off, grimly daring them to call it off when I was half-way through the long, westward journey. But they didn't, and although when I got to Prestbury Park I discovered that my five rides had been whittled down to three — one withdrawn due to the ground and another reclaimed by a re-routed Peter Scudamore — it was still a good card on which I had two genuine winning chances.

I might easily have won on them both. Prime Oats, one of Nicky's best four-year-olds and having only his second run over hurdles, ran very well indeed in the Triumph Hurdle Trial and in my view would have won but for being hampered by the eventual third just before jumping the last. Even after that he was only narrowly beaten by Tangognat, who is currently favourite for the Triumph in March. I'm not afraid of him.

At this time of year the Triumph is still a lottery. I would never have an ante-post bet in it even if I was allowed to — much of the early form is unreliable and first-year jumpers tend to run in and out of form before settling down as they gain experience. Prime Oats has not even won a race yet and if he should go to Cheltenham still a maiden he has a chance of being ballotted out of an always over-subscribed event. But if he takes his place in the line-up, then on what I know and have seen of the juveniles this season, I shall look forward to a very good ride on him.

By contrast, I don't know if I shall ever sit on Misty Spirit again, but I was certainly grateful to pick up the ride on him today. He is trained in the north by a man named Don Lee, and I confess I had never heard of him until he phoned to book me. I thought at first the horse would have no chance as the opposition included the long-range Gold Cup favourite Dawn Run, over from Ireland to gain experience of the Cheltenham fences. But when I took a closer look at the race I realised I was not entirely without hope. My horse had a decent, consistent record in northern handicaps, whereas Dawn Run, for all her brilliant ability, is still not the steadiest of jumpers; I had severe reservations about her prospects of putting in a clear round at Cheltenham.

Well, Dawn Run completed the course all right, but well before the end she had unshipped her jockey, Tony Mullins. A delightful Irishman, and the son of the horse's trainer, Tony would still not be everyone's idea of a tidy steeplechase jockey, and he was unseated from both his rides in 'chases today. He was well in front on Dawn Run when horse and rider parted company, leaving the big race of the day in the hands of Misty Spirit and yours truly. I accepted the chance eagerly, but reflected later that neither the horse nor I will receive due credit for the victory. I will be amazed if we get more than a passing mention as all newspaper accounts of the race dwell on the misfortune of the great mare. Still, I've got another winner and a nice payout in my pocket; the Mullins family have to go back home to Ireland and return to the drawing-board. Who am I to moan?

Finished a good day with a Chinese meal in Baldock. A place called the Golden Rickshaw sounds authentic enough and the food is excellent, as I can testify after the latest of several visits. What I can't work out is that the manager — who is a racing nut and always finds me a table even when they are full — goes by the name of 'Wally'. Nothing very Chinese about Wally, is there?

SUNDAY 26 JANUARY

My major dilemma of an otherwise slovenly day was whether to devote my evening to the Superbowl on TV or go for my regular game of snooker. I finally opted for the American football, it being the highspot of a season I had followed so closely, but the match was so one-sided I was soon wishing I had played snooker.

The weather has altered dramatically. After what has been a pretty mild winter so far it looks as if we are in for a cold snap and the frost was so thick this morning that I can't see there being any racing at Leicester tomorrow.

MONDAY 27 AND TUESDAY 28 JANUARY

All racing has been frozen off. I am not one who chafes at having a couple of days off — I'm happy enough to laze around in front of a log fire with a good book. But the frustrating part of it is organising rides for meetings which have precious little chance of going ahead. You have to go through the motions every day, phoning up your regular trainers and confirming their plans, and if more than one or two days in succession are abandoned you know that you are in for problems, with rides you had managed to space out through the week being concertinered to a point where you have to start upsetting trainers again.

WEDNESDAY 29 JANUARY

What began as a good day and might have turned into an excellent one actually became a near-disaster for the simple reason that I broke my number one golden rule and took a ride on a novice chaser from outside my usual string of trainers. I had been lulled into it because the trainer was Roddy Armytage, highly respected and particularly successful with his young 'chasers. The horse concerned, Two Eagles, is not without ability, and was in fact going reasonably well. It wasn't his fault that he was brought down, nor was it mine, but it could easily have put me out for weeks. The first thing to hit the ground was my nose, which currently feels as if it is twice the size of the rest of my face. Then a following horse kicked me on the wrist. This was potentially much worse. For an awful few moments I believed that it was broken, such was the pain. In fact I have been lucky to escape with bruising, as much to pride as body.

Because of all this I had to give up my final ride. It didn't concern me at first. Although Young Nicholas is a very nice horse he was having his first run of the season, carrying 11 stone 11 pounds in soft ground, and Nicky Henderson assured me he had no chance. Peter Scudamore stepped in for the ride and, damn me, went and won on him. This Windsor meeting had begun so well, too. I won the handicap chase on a horse called Socks Downe, giving Jeff King his first winner of a frustrating season. But when I might have gone on to ride a double and further close the gap at the top of the championship table, I instead ended up battered and sore, not to mention having given a winner to one of my closest rivals!

My one consolation tonight is that things could be very much worse. I was only offered the ride on Two Eagles because Mr Armytage's regular jockey, Anthony Webber, is injured yet again. After the latest of a sequence of recent falls, poor 'Ant' was reported to have blood coming from his ears and nose. I fear that this game will finish him before long. Like Sam Morshead, of whom there is still no sign of a return, he is probably suffering accumulated concussion, which can get so bad that you feel dizzy for days even if you fall on your backside.

THURSDAY 30 JANUARY
It was with some relief that I woke to hear the announcement that both today's meetings had been abandoned. Often this radio bulletin — sometimes the sight of the purple printed message on the teletext service — leads to a bout of purple language from S. Smith Eccles, but this morning I was so sore — I would have struggled to ride anyway. See You Then is due to run on Saturday and I can't afford to be below par for that, so this afternoon I went into Newmarket for some ultrasound treatment on my wrist, which has stiffened up badly.

FRIDAY 31 JANUARY
Thank God. I shall be very pleased to see the back of January — never my favourite month anyway, and this year, it seems right now, the bringer of more bad tidings and bad breaks even than usual.

Nicky Henderson has twice rung up to ask if I am OK for tomorrow and although I am happy enough that the injury is nothing serious, I knew he would expect me to prove it to him at Sandown today. He is a trainer who, quite properly, will not allow his jockey to ride a top-class horse if he is anything less than 100 per cent, so my relief can well be imagined when I came through the public examination with flying colours — riding Nicky a novice chase winner on Paulatim. He did the job well but I almost made a botch of it in the closing stages. As we approached the final fence my horse was hanging into the eventual runner-up, who was alongside on my left. I knew I had to pull my whip through into my left hand and satisfy the stewards that I was doing everything to keep the horse straight, but I found the manouevre trickier than planned. The problem is that I am entirely right-handed, and although I can hold the whip in my left, and wave it about down the horse's flank, it is no more than a gesture. Somehow, I did enough to persuade Paulatim to respond and check her course, and the race was won without recourse to the stewards' room. But afterwards in the weighing-room as I joked about it with the other lads I was surprised to hear how many of them owned up to being similarly inadequate with the stick in their 'wrong hand' in a driving finish. It is

something every one of us practises, but not all of us can be ambi-
dexterous!

All the top three jockeys in the table rode a winner this afternoon — Simon, after a very lean patch, celebrating his 50th of the
season — so at the end of January and the start of the serious
business of the campaign's major events, we are bunched up with
all to play for: Sherwood 50, Scudamore 49, Smith Eccles 47.
Luck and injuries will play a big part, I am sure ... but it is
proving to be every bit as open a race as I predicted when the
season began.

FEBRUARY

SATURDAY 1 FEBRUARY

The reputations of two equine champions were laid on the line today; both survived the public examination in very impressive style. We were at Sandown, a big day's racing on one of our biggest and plushest tracks. There is something special about this place, tucked into a green corner of stockbroker territory in plummy Esher. It is not only a highly challenging course, it also has facilities which are the envy of virtually every racetrack in the country. It has a buzzing, big-time atmosphere and, like many other jockeys who have experienced the thrill of a decent winner or two here, it figures largely among my favourite courses.

Today, though, could have been special for me on any course in England because it was the day on which I was reunited with See You Then, my chance ride and unforgettable winner in the 1985 Champion Hurdle at Cheltenham. The naked nerves of trainer Nicky Henderson, a more emotional man than me and today quite visibly tortured by anxiety as we awaited the race, were testimony to the importance of the occasion as the horse made its first competitive appearance in ten and a half months.

It was a significant day too for my pal Peter Scudamore, now with his first Gold Cup in his sights as well as his first outright jockeys' championship. The switch of jockeys on the brilliant black giant, Burrough Hill Lad, had caused considerable media controversy. Many people thought owner Stan Riley had been cruelly hasty in ditching Phil Tuck, who had after all ridden the horse to the Gold Cup two years earlier, after a couple of disappointing setbacks. But 'Scu' could not afford to waste any sympathy. He had to take a clinically professional view of a heaven-sent opportunity and simply hope that the big horse came back to his best and got to Cheltenham sound.

'The Lad' took the stage first, contesting the valuable Gainsborough Chase off top weight of 12 stone. 'Scu's' mental state may easily have been confused, because among his opponents was Run and Skip, the tiny but tenacious horse from John Spearing's Warwickshire yard, who had begun the season as a middle-of-the-road handicapper yet developed — chiefly under 'Scu's' inspired riding — into a Gold Cup candidate in his own right. It can't have been easy for Pete to desert this great servant after some marvellous wins, notably in the Welsh Grand National and in the Mildmay Chase on this Sandown course. But I felt he was doing the right thing, and the race bore me out.

I had expected to be viewing the race on TV in the weighing-room but instead I was out there on the course, having picked up the ride on the Irish-trained Rainbow Warrior when Jonjo had a bad fall in the previous event. The poor guy has suffered quite enough recently, and I feared this was another serious setback when I saw him being loaded onto a stretcher with his leg in a splint. There was relief all round when it turned out to be a case of bruising alone. At least it provided me with a decent ride and, as it turned out, a share of the prize money. I led the field into the straight for the last time, Run and Skip having lost all chance with a bad mistake at the first of the notorious 'railway fences' in the back straight. But I could sense 'Scu' simply biding his time on the 'Lad' and, sure enough, he took it up at the perfect moment and went away to win by ten lengths.

See You Then's victory in the following race, the Oteley Hurdle, was every bit as smooth. Giving away stacks of weight to decent hurdlers such as Asir, Tom Sharp and Sabin du Loir was one of his problems; the other, potentially more serious, was that he was palpably not fully fit. He still carried plenty of condition, which was always the plan with Cheltenham still six weeks away, so I was delighted when a slow pace was set which played into my horse's hands. I came to take it up after the last and only had to push him out to win tidily by two-and-a-half lengths. I appreciated the relieved looks on the faces of the Henderson camp, back in the winner's enclosure!

It was, all in all, a brilliant day's racing. Although not personally involved, I relished a titanic novice chase battle between Berlin and Desert Orchid, enjoyed my close rival Simon's win on Ballinacurra Lad, and even bore the disappointment of defeat on my four-year-old hotpot, Arnhall, with no more than a pang of regret and a conviction that he will be better on good ground.

I left Sandown marvelling once again at the great quality of racing it perenially provides and saying a silent thank you to their young and efficient clerk of the course, Mark Kershaw. It is fashionable for jockeys to knock clerks and, in truth, some of them are so poor they ask for it. But in a job where people only tend to notice you when things go wrong, Mark is a great example of how things should be done. He achieved wonders today to keep racing on after a sharp frost, and he was later, as ever, courteous and helpful to trainers, jockeys and pressmen alike. I only wish there were more up to his standard.

SUNDAY 2 FEBRUARY
I made a major breakthrough in my snooker career — a break of 20! It may not sound much if you are accustomed to watching the likes of Davis and Thorburn but it meant potting six consecutive balls and to me that was the equivalent of climbing a particularly steep mountain.

MONDAY 3 FEBRUARY
That fall from Two Eagles at Windsor last week re-educated me over the merits and demerits of accepting chance rides. I could have gone to Wolverhampton today and earned 50 quid, but it was a novice chase and, set off by renewed throbbing from my wrist, the alarm bells rang in my brain. I refused the ride and stayed at home, a little poorer but very much safer, and ultimately more content.

TUESDAY 4 FEBRUARY
Luck is so important in this game, and you cannot be champion jockey without at least your fair share of it. Today, my luck was non-existent, whereas Peter Scudamore's fortunes are currently

flying so high that he can do no wrong. I had three booked rides at today's Warwick meeting, two of them holding a reasonable chance of winning. All three, believe it or not, were ballotted out under the Jockey Club rule which comes into play when too many horses declare for any race. One ballotted out would have been unfortunate, three was almost unbearable.

'Scu' meanwhile, had gone to yesterday's Wolverhampton meeting to ride two absolute no-hopers. Both were duly beaten out of sight. But when Graham Bradley didn't show due to an attack of food poisoning, Pete took the ride on Stearsby for Jenny Pitman and won on him. Then, with Graham McCourt absent through flu, he picked up another chance ride on King Ba Ba — and won on that one, too. You can say, of course, that he deserved the breaks because he had bothered to go there and I had stayed at home, but then that is Pete all through. I freely admit he is more thoroughly dedicated to chasing winners than I am, which in all probability means that he will be champion jockey this season, and I won't. That double yesterday has taken him to the front of the field for the first time, and both Simon and I know we have a battle on hand to knock him off the perch now. Our cause may not be helped much by the weather. This morning's newspapers gloomily predicted with what seemed total confidence a major freeze-up on the way here from Siberia. That could easily put paid to racing for a week or so.

WEDNESDAY 5 FEBRUARY

I am writing this entry a day late for a very good reason. It is now Thursday the 6th, and I have just got home from yesterday's Ascot meeting. I think this needs some detailed explanation . . . .

9.00 a.m.

Still not sure whether I am riding at Ascot or Ludlow. The weather has begun to bite and there is an inspection at Ascot in half-an-hour. If racing goes ahead, I will be there to ride River Ceiriog for Nicky. The dilemma is that Smart Reply runs at Ludlow and will probably win, but to get there in time I will have to leave home by 9.30 a.m. I am hovering by the phone, my bag packed and ready to go.

9.30 a.m.
Still waiting. But the phone has rung twice — some good news and some bad. The bad came from Nicky, who tells me that Young Nicholas, my intended ride in the Schweppes Hurdle at Newbury on Saturday, will not now run. The good news came in a surprise call from John Spearing, offering me the ride on Run and Skip in the Gold Cup. With 'Scu' committed to Burrough Hill Lad and Sam Morshead, who rode the horse previously, still out injured, John had a headache. I was very happy to solve it for him. I also hear that Tony Mullins has been 'jocked off' Dawn Run and Jonjo will ride her at Cheltenham. I'm sorry for Tony but not surprised. I think it is the right decision — in the Gold Cup you need everything going for you; mistakes there cannot be forgiven.

9.45 a.m.
Ascot plan to inspect again at 11.00 a.m. which effectively makes my decision for me. It's a shade irritating because I am sure River Ceiriog won't win and I think Smart Reply will. But as both horses are trained by N. Henderson, I have to go where he tells me.

10.30 a.m.
Left home for Ascot. It may yet be abandoned, so I plan to stop off at Alan Jarvis's home at Royston and ring the course ... I am beginning to think I will have to buy a car phone.

12.30 p.m.
Arrive at Ascot. They have had four inspections but racing is on. It was obviously touch and go, and they have put back the first race by half-an-hour, but you have to applaud them for the effort which has clearly gone into keeping the meeting on, even if I am doing it through clenched teeth after this morning of indecision.

2.15 p.m.
River Ceiriog did not win. But he did run a blinder to take third place behind two good animals. He might be better than I thought. I have also just heard that Smart Reply was beaten at

103

Ludlow, so I missed nothing by having to come here. Now I need a drink.

8.00 p.m.
I have had a drink; in fact, I've had several. Peter Shilton, the England goalkeeper and an old friend, had invited me up to the Metropole Casino box at the races. As I had no further rides after the first race, I got up there early in the afternoon, which is always dangerous. One generous scotch led to another and by the time racing was over, Peter and I had acquired the taste for the stuff and so we went on to a pub in Ascot with another England footballer, Tony Woodcock. With the news that all tomorrow's racing is already off, we have now come to another decision. I am leaving my car here, good sense prevailing, and we are off up to the West End for a night out at that exclusive and expensive haunt of the famous, Tramp.

4.00 a.m.
Thursday — back at Ascot. Emerged from a thoroughly good night with the lads and found, to my great surprise, that the Siberian weather had struck while I was 'underground'. It was snowing hard and, by the time my taxi-driver had navigated back to the racecourse where I could collect my car, it was lying thick on the ground. The journey home could be interesting.

7.00 a.m.
I have reached Royston and I have had enough. The snow is bad and becoming worse by the hour. It's been very slow going, and I am whacked. Pull into a layby, flick back the reclining seat, and settle down for a welcome nap....

9.00 a.m.
This is serious: I've just woken up to find the snow half-way up the car. I forced open the door and surveyed the dire truth — I am stuck.

1.00 p.m.
Home at last! Unshaven, dishevelled and exhausted, I tottered

across a field, through thick snow, to knock up a farmer and persuade him that my plight merited the use of his tractor. He relented and brought the tractor round onto the road to tow my car out of the drift. Once I was back in the centre of the road I was OK again, and managed to stay awake long enough to cover the few miles remaining of the longest journey I have ever undertaken from Ascot to Newmarket.

Today's meeting at Huntingdon was abandoned, which was really just as well — I don't think I would have been in a state to do myself justice even if I had got to the course on time! The entire country, I hear, is now blanketted in snow — and I'm off to bed.

SATURDAY 8 FEBRUARY

Racing has ground to a halt. The freeze-up is every bit as bad as the forecasters promised and I, for one, have come to the conclusion that it will be at least another week before we have a chance of resuming. So, on impulse, I am going to grab that holiday I have been hankering after for so long. I considered a return to Barbados, which would certainly be pleasantly warm, but finally rejected the idea in favour of a skiing trip to France. I've never been before, which is one very good reason for trying it in my book, and I have to say I am also attracted by the tales of hectic apres-ski which filter back through friends of mine who are regular winter sports fans. So today I have been on the telephone trying to round up a suitable team for the expedition. One unexpected refusal came from J. Francome. In years gone by he would have not needed a second bidding — he would have been with us like a shot. I don't know whether he is finding the pressures of training getting on top of him or whether he is just getting old!

SUNDAY 9 FEBRUARY

The weather continues to be desperate and, on the basis that there is no time like the present, we are booked to fly out of Gatwick this afternoon for a week on the piste. My skiing squad is a bare three — Paul Barton, Oliver Sherwood and myself. To my great chagrin, I discovered that Oliver's brother Simon has already gone on a separate skiing holiday without telling me. I shall be having words with him when I see him.

I have no regrets at all about leaving England in February. It is a cheerless, tedious month in which there is little pleasure to be had from racing even when it survives the weather. Even the cancellation of yesterday's big meeting at Newbury caused me to shed no tears, although I do have a certain sympathy with Schweppes, whose sponsorship of the big handicap hurdle at Newbury looks a dubious investment — it has now been lost to the weather four times in the past six years. The three holiday-makers drove down to Gatwick for an afternoon flight to Italy, followed by a long but picturesque coach ride into the mountains and on to the French border. It was late when we arrived at the hotel and I admit to just a slight pang of doubt about the week to come. What if I break my leg, with Cheltenham a month away? I put it quickly out of my mind and turned my attentions to the matter in hand. Racing, I vowed, would remain firmly at the back of my thoughts for this rare week of escapism.

SUNDAY 16 FEBRUARY

We landed at Gatwick hale and healthy. The week passed rapidly and, at times, riotously. I never thought there could be anything to compare with the thrill of riding good horses over fences but I now admit that skiing at speed rivals it. It was pure exhilaration, hard work now and again but great fun throughout; and thankfully, none of us sustained anything more lasting than the odd bruise. Even my tortured, temperamental knee stood up to the unaccustomed strain very well until our final afternoon, when a few jolting pains reminded me of my infirmity. The skiing crowd is certainly a change from the racing fraternity I mix with every day of the ten-month season and, interestingly, the three of us hardly talked shop at all. I think each one of us was grateful for the chance of a mid-winter break in which the season's stresses and strains, highs and lows, could temporarily be pigeon-holed.

Immersed in the day-to-day routine of the long racing campaign, it is all too easy to cut adrift from the reality of the outside world. To a certain extent, racing folk live a cocooned existence, mixing chiefly with their own kind and spending virtually all their waking hours doing something connected with their job. It is a peculiar lifestyle. I have no great desire to change it, as I still consider myself fortunate to be well paid for doing something I love. But it has to be said that racing can become almost incestuous in its atmosphere and the occasional week, entirely divorced from thoughts of runners and riders, horses and handicaps, restores a healthy balance to a dangerously one-track mind.

It occurs to me, driving home tonight, that it ought to be possible to make this an annual winter break — God knows, the British February is usually dire enough to allow at least a week's escape with barely a missed meeting; already I have enlisted the support of Paul and Oliver for a repeat performance in 1987, and we have opted for Austria for our next venture.

TUESDAY 18 FEBRUARY
Having craved all season for a holiday, and finally got one, I now need a rest to get over it. I'm just about recovered now, two days after arriving home!

The weather has still not broken, nor is there any immediate prospect of it doing so. Nightly TV forecasts from the mournful Michael Fish or the manic Ian McGaskill follow a tediously similar pattern; the isobars seem unchanged from day to day and no-one can predict when any remotely warmer air might be able to force a path into the country.

Everyone in racing faces certain problems during a prolonged break such as this. Some face considerably more than others. I am among the more fortunate, in that I make enough money while the weather is fair to survive an enforced holiday of a few weeks; I even welcome it at first, although I am prepared to admit it will not be long before the novelty of free time wears thin. But in jump racing only a dozen or so of the jockeys are in this category; the vast majority, the middle-of-the-road boys who scratch around for their daily riding fee and the scores of young hopefuls trying to make their way in the game, can get into quite serious hardship if a freeze lasts much beyond a week or two. A few have outside jobs which sustain them and others are attached to stables — but even for them, the prospect of riding out two lots every morning with the temperature ten degrees below freezing is an unenviable way of making a few quid.

The trainers have a different kind of headache. Although the lack of racing can hit their pocket as it means there is no prize money going into the pot, they are at least still receiving their weekly training fees from the frustrated owners who cannot run their horses. But it is the trainer's responsibility to keep those horses as fit as possible during bad weather, and when the freeze bites as deeply as it has done now, that can be an awesome task. For some, set in the bleakest and worst-hit parts of the country and lacking the plush indoor or all-weather facilities owned by their luckier neighbours, it is pretty near impossible and there will inevitably be some plump and unfit horses appearing when racing eventually does resume. With that in mind, I was relieved and delighted to hear that my retaining trainer, Nicky Henderson, has discovered an arduous but effective method of ensuring his string is kept on the go, come what may.

Nicky has an all-weather paddock in his Lambourn yard, but the term 'all-weather' is in this case inapplicable. Even such surfaces as that cannot cope with constant temperatures well below zero and Nicky soon discovered that the paddock froze solid each night and was quite unusable at exercise time in the morning. There was only one way to overcome that and I must say I would have found it distinctly unappealing. But my guv'nor is an extremely dedicated trainer so, every two hours, through the night and every night, a tractor and harrow is driven around the paddock to keep it loose and functional. Various members of the Henderson staff take their shifts, but I happen to know Nicky is shouldering a good deal of this bleak and unpleasant task himself. It obviously works, too, as he informed me today that the group of horses he is particularly anxious to keep fit have not missed a day's exercise since the weather took its icy grip on the country. See You Then is reported to be in good shape, although we are all obviously hoping to get another race into him before the Champion Hurdle.

SUNDAY 23 FEBRUARY

Boredom has set in. There is not the slightest change in the weather, the long-range forecast is equally grim and S. Smith Eccles is becoming more irritable by the day. Those around me, and especially Di, are, I am afraid, beginning to feel the sharp edge of my tongue as the tedious days drag on. I have virtually given up reading the *Sporting Life* now, as the four-day declarations which are still appearing daily for the forthcoming scheduled meetings mean nothing when they have precisely no chance of ever being run. I speak to Nicky regularly, but there seems little point in phoning even the other trainers who habitually give me rides. They have enough to think about in these circumstances without having a frustrated jockey moaning down the telephone.

If things were different I could enjoy the scene outside. Snailwell, the tiny hamlet where we moved into an old cottage a little over a year ago, is a charming sight for anyone interested in photographing typically English winter scenes. I can just picture it on the front of a postcard. The village is protected from further building and so its character is much as it has always been; the Snailwell Stud surrounds it, and the facilities for inhabitants extend to one pub, but no shops. Out in my garden there is a well from where the villagers once drew their daily supplies of water. A good job they don't still have to do so — they would need a pick-axe to break up the ice each day!

Even the ducks and chickens I keep are looking miserable, no doubt feeling the chilly pinch through their feathers. I am keeping them well fed but, unfortunately, I am also eating rather too heavily myself. Boredom is the reason, of course — with so little else to occupy me, I am picking at food in a way I would never do when I am busy racing. Although I am riding out for Di on the odd occasion, it is not enough to keep the flab at bay and I fear I am now about five pounds heavier than I should be; something will have to be done.

THURSDAY 27 FEBRUARY

Three weeks have now elapsed since the last racing in Britain and I would wager there is not a jockey or trainer in the country who is not champing at the bit for a resumption. The most appalling thought of all is that the Cheltenham Festival is now less than a fortnight away, and it is going to need a fairly rapid and complete thaw to allow that meeting — the biggest of the season for all of us involved — to escape the unthinkable fate of joining the list of abandonments. And that thaw still looks a long way off as I gaze out of the window in my snug, normally just a hideaway room on Sundays or when I want an hour alone in the evening but, just recently, almost a permanent residence.

It is small consolation, but right now there is at least nothing to stand in the way of social engagements and, yesterday, for the first time in years, I was able to accept an invitation to the William Hill Golden Spurs luncheon in London. Season after season, I have had to decline through a clash with riding commitments, but as the Worcester meeting had inevitably been called off days ago, I joined a strikingly large contingent of jumping people, all relieving the tedium besetting us all. From there, I went on to the opening of a new restaurant in St James's called Silks which, as you may gather, has a racing theme. A pleasant day, but another which did nothing for the ever-increasing amount of overweight I am carrying.

FRIDAY 28 FEBRUARY

My month's work consisted of just four rides and one winner — on that long-ago opening day of February at Sandown. Today's abandonments have brought the total number of meetings lost this season up to 104, closing fast on the record of 136 which was established in the 1967-68 winter. It is enough to turn any man to drink — but unfortunately I can't even take that option. I am now in strict training. On the possibly absurd assumption that the weather will relent in time for Cheltenham I am determined to get back into decent physical shape and get some idle muscles working again.

I have started a diet, which chiefly revolves around exercising some self-discipline and keeping off the biscuits and chocolate I had taken to chomping between the more serious meals. Bread and potatoes are also strictly rationed from now on. I have decided to start running regularly and so, this morning, well wrapped up against another raw day, I set off jogging around the Suffolk lanes. As my boredom threshold is lower than most, however, I quickly get fed up with the tedious plod of a run and so I took a football with me to kick around on the fields and footpaths as a distraction. Tonight, I am continuing my exercise kick — by playing a game of snooker. . . .

MARCH

SATURDAY 1 MARCH

Panic is descending on the ranks of National Hunt trainers. Cheltenham is now just ten days away and we woke up this morning to the sight of a fresh and intense blizzard. It is the fourth consecutive Saturday without racing and although Messrs Fish and McGaskill are now hinting vaguely that the middle of next week could see a temporary end to this wretched spell, even that would give the ground scant time to thaw completely, and the poor trainers no time at all to get any racecourse work into their Cheltenham horses.

SUNDAY 2 MARCH

Spent the morning checking and confirming my Cheltenham races, keeping my fingers firmly crossed for the weather. I currently have ten engaged rides over the three days, which means there are only four races, open to professionals, in which I am still free. The Smith Eccles squad looks very promising, too.

I have expanded my training programme to include riding out two lots each morning for Di. I still feel podgy, but my dedication did not extend to going without Sunday lunch. I downed it ravenously with the silent promise that it would be my final treat before the Festival.

This evening was spent in mourning. After all these months of snooker practice, I have suddenly lost my partner. Tommy Keddie, one of my oldest and dearest pals, is leaving town and going to drive trucks for his sister's haulage firm in Carlisle. Tommy and I go back to my early days in Newmarket when we both came here as raw-boned wide-eyed teenagers from working-class backgrounds. That was 14 years back, yet still I have a vivid memory of turning up at my first 'digs' and finding myself allotted to a room smaller than my current kitchen — and I had to share that room with five other lads. Three sets of bunk beds were squeezed into the box-room and us half-dozen innocents, all thrust into stable-work without really knowing what to expect or where it would take us, had to make do and get along with each other.

Coming straight from a comfortable home and a close-knit family, it came as a major shock to me and after three nights in 'digs' I almost packed my bags and caught the bus home. I often wonder what would have happened to me if I had given up at that point. Would I have ended up following my father and my other ancestors, going daily down a Derbyshire coalmine? Somehow I can't imagine it. I have been down the pit just once, when, later in my apprenticeship, I had a weekend at home and my father took me down to show me what I was missing. I don't mind admitting it frightened me — and we ventured nowhere near the deepest interior, the part where Dad said he would often spend hours on his stomach, hacking at the coalface in incredibly claustrophobic conditions. No, I don't think I was made to be a miner ... but then Tommy Keddie, after all these years in Newmarket, has gone back to *his* roots. It makes me realise how lucky I am. But I'm still short of a snooker partner!

MONDAY 3 MARCH

Another sharp frost this morning, but unless I am engaging in entirely wishful thinking, I swear it is now appreciably milder than it has been for weeks. Shall I chance another run before my sparse supper?

TUESDAY 4 MARCH

This morning I felt like the kid waking up on Christmas Day to find that Santa really has left a sackful of presents at the foot of the bed. My usual wary peer through the curtains produced a sight which at first I refused to accept. But after blinking sharply, rubbing my eyes and staring once more, I had to believe it — it was pouring with rain! What's more, it has rained for most of the day, taking at least some of the frost out of the long-suffering ground.

I celebrated by getting back into a racing mood. After riding out, I went to take part in a video being made by Ladbrokes, chatting about my Cheltenham rides and their chances. Now that TV is allowed in betting shops, I can just imagine the scene next Tuesday lunchtime; the punters glued to this video, drinking in the confident thoughts of jockeys like me. What they may not realise is that jockeys as a breed are some of the worst tipsters in the game!

WEDNESDAY 5 MARCH

Racing in Britain resumes after an absence of exactly one month — the trouble is, the surviving meeting happens to be at Catterick, way up the A1 in the north of Yorkshire and foreign soil to us southern jockeys. So I endured yet another day off, but at least the thaw does seem to have begun in earnest. There is still a good bit of frost hanging around, most particularly in the south, and we may not resume racing down here until the weekend. But the long-range forecast is encouraging for Cheltenham which, after all this time twiddling our thumbs, is all that really matters.

After riding out this morning I popped into Gavin Pritchard-Gordon's Newmarket home for a bite of breakfast. The chat got around to the subject of trying to keep fit during the bad weather and when I told Gav of my excess poundage he beckoned me downstairs and showed me what looked like a half-built canoe! A rowing machine, he told me, is the ideal way to stay fit. I tried it out for five minutes and saw exactly what he meant. As I creaked to my feet every muscle in my body ached and it came home to me just how much of an effect enforced idleness can have. Impetuous as ever, I decided on the spot that I would go out and buy one of these machines, which certainly appear (by the area of aches) to get muscles in the stomach, back and legs working in unison. I can set it up in a spare room and install a tape player so that the music saves me from giving up too soon through boredom.

THURSDAY 6 MARCH

Another slight frost this morning retarded the thawing process a shade and put paid to today's two scheduled meetings, but it was still a day of big racing news, dominated by the story that, for the second year running, Burrough Hill Lad is a late withdrawal from the Gold Cup. He had been promoted to favourite after his win at Sandown and, among those supposedly in the know, was widely expected to repeat his 1984 win. But, just as he did last year, the big horse has suffered an untimely training setback — on this occasion, apparently the result of working on the beach at Burnham. Beach work is favoured only by a proportion of trainers during a freeze-up; there are those who regard it as a high-risk surface on which horses are all too likely to break down. This incident is bound to refuel the debate.

My first feeling on hearing the news was one of self-preservation. This may sound odd, but let me explain. The story of Burrough Hill Lad was actually related to me over the telephone, by David Nicholson. Although nothing was said directly, I suspected that David was phoning to sound me out over the prospect of Peter Scudamore — now without his Gold Cup ride — reclaiming the engagement for Run and Skip. It wasn't long later that the phone began to ring in earnest, with pressmen wanting to know if I was still riding the Spearing candidate. At six this evening I finally received the call I had been expecting. It was 'Scu'. I told him that I had accepted the ride on an understanding with John Spearing that I would keep it, whatever may befall Burrough Hill Lad. 'Scu' told me he already knew this, having spoken to Mr Spearing himself.

The trainer's solution had apparently been to inform 'Scu' that he must sort it out with me. Now, Pete is a good mate of mine and I didn't blame him for trying to get the ride back but I also had no intention of backing down. 'What would you do in my position?' I asked him, and he immediately knew he was chasing a lost cause.

A couple of hours later, after several more newspaper calls, I was cheered up when Jeff McCarthy, one of Run and Skip's owners, rang up himself. He rapidly banished my sense of foreboding over what he was about to say by insisting: 'As far as we are concerned, you will ride the horse. Take no notice of the speculation to the contrary.' I give him and his colleagues full marks for loyalty. 'Scu' has won some big races for them, and I knew more than a few owners who would have been utterly unscrupulous in these circumstances, but these guys know the terms on which I was booked and they are standing by them. For my part, I have to go to Stratford racecourse on Sunday morning to ride Run and Skip a piece of work and then watch some videos of his recent races. That is a small price to pay for the privilege of a Gold Cup ride on a horse now down to 10-1 third favourite. Tonight, for the first time, it occurred to me that I have a genuine chance of becoming the first jockey to ride the Gold Cup and Champion Hurdle double at the Festival meeting.

FRIDAY MARCH 7

My first ride in a month — and I had to go to the relative wilds of Market Rasen for it! With Sandown frozen off, I was keen to get my eye back in with a spin on something, so I took the ride on a little hurdler for Newmarket trainer Gerry Blum at the Lincolnshire track. I don't go there very often, although it is not a difficult journey, and after riding out for Di this morning I was glad I had taken the decision. I schooled one horse for her and then had a real blow. I was exhausted! I've been running, I've worked at my diet and now I've even got a rowing machine — but nothing keeps a jockey fit like race-riding, and I knew then that there would be some very tired riders going round at Market Rasen.

The course was in an awful state — like a ploughed field — and one of the bends was positively dangerous. But I still came away with a sense of having achieved something. My horse didn't win — finished third, in fact — but like a cricketer reporting back after the winter break, I have had my first innings and I feel more confident for it.

SATURDAY 8 MARCH

This game can mock you all too often. Us professional jockeys, kicking our heels for a month and now anxious to make an impression again, were all upstaged today by one Mr Gerald Oxley, gentleman amateur rider. Gerald was partnering the Queen Mother's Special Cargo in the Horse and Hound's Grand Military Gold Cup, salvaged from yesterday's abandoned card and run as the first race today. Now, this race is restricted to amateurs who have served in a branch of the armed forces and it often provides some memorably unorthodox styles, but there was nothing wrong with Mr Oxley's performance. At the last fence on the far side, three from home, his leathers broke, and he was obliged to see out the business end of the race with his legs swinging down the horse's neck. Undeterred, he somehow conjured a late burst from Special Cargo to get up on the line and win. It was an effort of which any top professional would have been proud.

I managed nothing remotely as memorable. The decisive factor, when racing resumes after such a lengthy break, is how much work your trainers have managed to get into their horses, and the three I rode today all 'blew up'. Two were for Jeff King, who is based on the Marlborough Downs and has obviously had problems keeping his string going. The one thing which did greatly please me, however, was my weight — I managed to do 10 stone 3 pounds quite comfortably.

I stayed the night with the Francomes and did nothing very extravagent. In fact, we played Trivial Pursuits. I did not win....

SUNDAY 9 MARCH

An early start, on the road to John Spearing's yard just west of Stratford. Run and Skip has never struck me as a very handsome animal to look at and today the impression was amplified. He does not even give a great feel when first you sit on him, but his recent record bears no criticism. In each race he has run, his bravery and wholehearted enthusiasm for the game has shone through, and if there will inevitably be more gifted horses in Thursday's Gold Cup field, I can't believe there will be any who outdo my fellow for sheer effort.

After riding a piece of work on him I was shown video recordings of his major races this season. Although I had ridden in most of the races, one is always far more concerned with one's current mount than any other horse and this was certainly an instructive session. The horse, I know, likes to be up with the pace all the way, and it will be fascinating to take part in a duel for the lead with Dawn Run!

Back home by lunchtime, I made some calls to trainers simply to reconfirm my Cheltenham rides. I was pleased with the result and now, after weeks of inactivity and a growing belief that the big meeting would not take place, the adrenalin is beginning to flow for what is always the biggest week of my year.

MONDAY 10 MARCH

There was a time when I didn't believe in caution. Not any more. Today, I declined all offers to go to the meeting at rustic old Southwell and occupied the time at home with a couple of lengthy sessions on my newly-acquired rowing machine.

Southwell on a Monday is rarely an appetising prospect, inevitably combining bad horses with a dodgy track, and with Cheltenham now 24 hours away, I considered it would have been madness to risk an injury which could put me out of the festival. Mind you, as I say, I have not always been so prim and sensible. Ten years ago, when I was a silly young boy, I took a spare ride in a chase at this very Southwell meeting and, of course, the thing fell. I cracked my collarbone but somehow managed to ride my Cheltenham horses, heavily strapped and dosed up with painkilling drugs. On the Wednesday, I rode Sweet Joe in the Sun Alliance Chase and by the time the race began my latest injection had worn off and I was gritting my teeth against the pain. Sweet Joe won, the first big winner of my career, but in the midst of the celebrations I silently accepted that a painful lesson had been learned. Nowadays, I avoid riding the day before Cheltenham unless one of my regular trainers has a hurdler he fancies — and then, although it is hard to refuse to ride, I go in some trepidation. Cheltenham means that much to me.

I have also come to believe that the great Festival races are best watched from a seat in the weighing-room, while sipping a cup of tea, if you do not have a decent ride offered. The days are gone when I could get any kick out of riding a no-hoper among class horses at this meeting, so I am not at all dismayed to have just the two rides tomorrow, both of which are for Nick Henderson. The first is River Ceiriog, a nice sort of novice but still a maiden and most unlikely to cut much ice in the opening event of the meeting, the Waterford Crystal Supreme Novices Hurdle. His most recent race, at Ascot last month, was his best yet, but I shall be more than happy if he runs well and finishes in the first six or seven. But then, of course, there is See You Then . . . .

I have no doubts whatever that he is the best hurdler in training and that, given the necessary luck in running, he will win the 'Champion' for the second year running. But I have to admit to being horrified when I turned on Channel Four's Teletext service at lunchtime and discovered that he is one of 24 horses declared for the race, making it the biggest Champion Hurdle field since 1964. Included in the number are a few who have no right to be taking part — mediocre horses, even a novice or two among them, whose participation in the most prestigious hurdle race of the year can only be designed to give their owners something to swank about to their chums. I believe the conditions of the race should be better framed to prevent such anomalies in the future, but as for tomorrow, my biggest worry in the race will simply be in trying to keep out of their way and steer See You Then a clear path. If I can negotiate that problem, I shall be a very disappointed man if he gets beaten.

TUESDAY 11 MARCH

Nobody in the county of Gloucestershire is more amazed or delighted tonight than yours truly. See You Then is once more the champion hurdler, which is an enormous relief, and River Ceiriog is the champion two-mile novice, which is little short of a miracle. It has been a fantastic day, quite one of the best of my career, and it has also been a very long day.

Nick had asked me to school Prime Oats, our Triumph Hurdle fancy, in Lambourn this morning before driving on to the course. I made the mistake of electing to set off in the early hours rather than driving down at my leisure last night, and so it was that, shortly after five this morning, I was poking my Mercedes tentatively through thick fog at the start of the long cross-country drive. My frustrations turned to temper as the murk persisted for much of the journey, but somehow I pulled into the drive at Windsor House in time to go out with Nick's first lot, a little chastened but otherwise none the worse for the experience.

I popped Prime Oats over some hurdles on the schooling grounds, a worthwhile exercise as he turned out to be a bit rusty, and then I worked Green Bramble, who felt in very good order for his bid to win the Ritz Club three-mile chase on Thursday — he might well have won last year at the Festival but for falling at the second last when in front, and although he has been out of sorts for much of this season, there seemed to be very little wrong with him this morning.

On the way back from the downs I saw Fred Winter, who wished me luck for the Champion Hurdle and asked if I was suffering from butterflies. I was able to tell him with complete honesty that I felt quite calm about the whole thing. Nerves, I know, affect different people in very different ways, but apart from feeling a bit shaky before my first-ever ride in the Grand National, they have rarely affected me at all. Even though I was acutely aware of the importance of the day, and although the adrenalin was pumping that shade more strongly than usual, I had none of the doubts, the fright and the apprehension which afflicts a really nervous person. Now Nick is a different story — naturally restless and a born worrier, I was in no doubt about his state this morning and I did not attempt to discuss much with him other than the races immediately ahead.

Arriving at Prestbury Park on the opening day of the Festival is always a moment of supreme anticipation. The three days' biggest jump racing on the calendar lies ahead, days in which the hopes and dreams which have been nurtured for months beforehand will either come to fruition or be dashed into deflating disappointment. Very often, of course, the expectation far outweighs the reality — so Tuesday morning is a time to savour.

Today, the crowds seemed bigger than ever, the tented village had certainly sprouted another river of tarpaulin since last year but the atmosphere was just the same as ever — exciting, intoxicating, with just a hint of Irish madness attached. I had arrived early to be sure of avoiding the worst of the traffic and I sipped tea in the weighing-room after changing into the colours of Mr Bobby McAlpine, owner of River Ceiriog, for the first event of the meeting.

If I state that the race amazed me I am not doing it justice: it was quite unbelievable. With the usual maximum field of novices, I intended to give my horse some daylight and keep him up with the pace, a plan I carried out entirely to my satisfaction. At the top of the hill I hit the front, increasingly delighted with the way he had run, yet fully expecting him to weaken rapidly after the second last.

Frankly, I could not have been more than slightly disappointed if he had done so, after running well for so far. But River Ceiriog was not going to fold up.

Turning into the straight we were still in front, and as we approached the last I risked a look over my shoulder, still in my heart believing that one of the well-backed hotpots would be cruising upsides to take it off me. But that one glance was enough to tell me that nothing was travelling more sweetly than me. I returned my gaze straight ahead, my heart momentarily in my mouth at that familiar but ever formidable sight of the famous hill looming ahead. But plainly it troubled me more than the horse; River Ceiriog just lengthened his stride, flew the last and stormed up the run-in to win unchallenged.

What happened back in the unsaddling enclosure is something of a blur. I remember there being relative silence as we walked in, which can only be because nobody in the vicinity had availed themselves of the 40-1 which now suddenly seemed absurdly generous. I also remember the stunned look on the guv'nor's face, and the fact that he was virtually speechless — as indeed we all were. I don't remember much else! In looking forward to Cheltenham I had set my sights on winning the Champion Hurdle and regarding any other winner as a tremendous bonus. The last thing I had planned for was to receive the bonus before the big race!

Very soon, my thoughts had turned once more to See You Then. I donned the green and white check silks and strolled out once more to the parade ring, where the terraces were now packed to bursting point with eager punters. My first sight of the horse was, I can now confess, a little alarming. He had had just the one run this season, shortly before the freeze-up, and to me he still looked on the tubby side of fit. I consoled myself with the thought that Nick had kept him constantly on the go, and would hardly be likely to have left him short of work, and kept my worries to myself.

The race itself, however, gave me no worries at all. I managed to keep See You Then clear of the pack, cruised up behind Gaye Brief going to the last and let him sprint away up the hill with that devastating turn of foot which marks him as a true champion.

There was never a moment when I was anything but convinced we would win, and it all went absolutely as we had planned. It was the perfect way to ride my 50th winner of the season and, not having any further rides to worry about, I was able to sample a little celebration champagne.

The most remarkable fact to emerge from my two races is that River Ceiriog covered the two miles in a time two seconds faster than See You Then, an astonishing performance for a horse who came here today as a maiden. Days like this don't happen very often and, when they do, I never want them to end. I was sensible tonight, just enjoying a couple of drinks and then a bite to eat before going back to the cottage Di and I have rented for the week in Condicote, near David Nicholson's yard and Peter Scudamore's home. I thought of them both as I pulled in — here am I with two winners on the opening day of the meeting, while 'the Duke' has never trained a single Festival winner and 'Scu' has never ridden one. I hope their luck changes.

WEDNESDAY 12 MARCH

What could possibly follow the events of the opening day? I am realistic, if nothing else, and I was not looking for any more miracles. When I woke this morning and surveyed the day's card I reached the conclusion that I had four good, worthwhile rides but that I would be hard-pushed to ride another winner. And so it proved. My reservations were as follows: Pikes Peak, who ran in the two-and-a-half mile Sun Alliance Novices Hurdle, is a potentially high-class horse, but would prefer the ground softer; Kathies Lad, in the Queen Mother Champion Chase was taking on the very best two-mile chasers from Britain and Ireland, and looked likely to be just outclassed; Highland Gold, trained by 'Ginger' McCain, was one of 32 handicap hurdlers declared for the marathon Coral Final which is annually the most difficult race of the meeting in which to find the winner; and Classified, now ten and one of Nick's most faithful servants, was going for the Mildmay of Flete Chase not completely wound up. The National is his objective and the stable had a more fancied runner in the Mildmay, the Tsarevich, which duly won for the second successive year to give Nick his third winner in two days.

Although my assessment turned out to be correct, however, I was far from disappointed with any of my horses. Pikes Peak galloped on bravely to be second and Kathies Lad — despite not looking properly fit in the paddock — ran a blinder behind Buck House and Very Promising. I hope Alan Jarvis takes him back to Liverpool, where I think he can win again.

One of the great gambles of the meeting came off today when Motivator won the Coral final for Newmarket trainer Mick Ryan and his flamboyant main owner, financier Terry Ramsden. Never a man to hide his light under a bushel, Mr Ramsden had been boasting about this horse for some time; today, not being short of readies, he put his money where his mouth is and collected the interest. The Irish, by contrast, have been suffering terribly. When Omerta won the amateur riders' chase, the fifth event on today's card, it was their first success of the meeting, and I imagine it probably came too late to save quite a number of empty wallets among the hordes who invade across the Irish Sea. For me, the Irish people make Cheltenham week what it is, and while I am very much against them running off with too many of our prizes I was actually quite pleased when they had a winner . . . especially as it was only an amateur's race!

Cheltenham being where it is, in the centre of England, most jockeys travel home each night. I am one of the few to stay in the area, but I am more and more convinced it is a good move, especially to have a cottage away from the frenzy which overtakes Cheltenham's town hotels each night of this crazy week. I went back to Condicote tonight feeling relaxed and well, and if I don't win the Gold Cup tomorrow it will not be through any fault in my preparation.

THURSDAY 13 MARCH

By 11.30, almost three hours before first-race time, a queue of cars snaked away from the course and back towards Winchcombe, to the east, and Gloucester and the M5, to the west. It was a sight to warm the heart of anyone involved in jump racing, but I must say I was glad I hadn't taken a chance on arriving an hour later.

The atmosphere was absolutely electric, as it always is on

Gold Cup day. If the first two days attracted record crowds, I can only imagine today's was an all-time high for the final day — almost twice the number that were here either on Tuesday or Wednesday.

On the short drive in from Condicote I mulled over my rides and decided that all four could be fancied. But, without wishing to be negative, I just could not imagine Run and Skip winning the Gold Cup. The way I saw it was this: Dawn Run had the speed and the class, but her jumping was suspect. If she jumped round, she would win; if not, I expected last season's winner Forgive 'n' Forget to triumph again, as I had heard some very good reports of him earlier in the week. That did not mean I would not be in there trying my best, but deep down I thought a place was the best I could hope for.

Paradoxically, I felt my best chance of another winner was with the least experienced of my four rides. Prime Oats had got into the Triumph Hurdle field despite still being a maiden and I gave him a really decent chance of upsetting the form horses. That, however, was one which did not work out to plan. I finished in the pack, Prime Oats showing us that he was still a shade more backward than we had hoped, and the race was won by a rank outsider in Solar Cloud — trained by David Nicholson and ridden by Peter Scudamore.

If I could not win the race myself, I considered this the ideal result, I know a little of the torment, not to mention the teasing, that these two guys have been through, as the years have totted up and their Festival winner tally has remained rooted at nil. 'Scu', in particular, had ridden a phenomenal amount of runners-up, and he must have feared he was in for another one here. Having virtually pinched the race by kicking on down the hill, Solar Cloud was rapidly coming back to the chasing field on the long, exhausting run-in, and it took all Pete's renowned finishing strength to get him home, accompanied by a totally understandable clenched fist from an exultant jockey. The enclosure was an emotional place after this overdue victory for the local stable and, back in the weighing-room, a beaming 'Scu' was showered with some very sincere congratulations.

We professionals had some time to catch our breath while the

Foxhunters Chase was run, and then we were out for the Gold Cup, which was a race I doubt I shall ever forget. If there has ever been a better or more spectacular Gold Cup I would love to see it — this one was simply a privilege to have taken part in. That Dawn Run won — becoming the first horse ever to complete the double of Champion Hurdle and Gold Cup — is part of history, while the race itself is, I am sure, engraved on the memory of at least four jockeys — Jonjo O'Neill, who rode the winner, Graham Bradley (Wayward Lad), Mark Dwyer (Forgive 'n' Forget) and myself.

My plan had been to take Dawn Run on at the head of affairs and try to force her into mistakes. This made for a strong gallop and some pretty thrilling racing from the off, and it seemed to me that the plan had worked when I caught sight of Jonjo apparently struggling with the mare as we hit the top of the hill for the final time. The trouble is, neither J.J. O'Neill nor Dawn Run ever know when they are beaten.

My horse was still in front three from home. At the second last he hit the top of the fence, halting his rhythm, but it was then that I experienced the marvellous courage of Run and Skip. He may have begun the season as a mere handicapper, but he was showing the world now that he was perfectly entitled to his place in this Gold Cup field. He plugged on bravely, and if the three-horse drama a few yards in front of him deservedly took the glory, I could have asked no more from my horse.

Those who have seen one of the countless TV repeats of the race will know that Dawn Run came back when the race looked lost, touching off Wayward Lad on the line. What followed will go down in Festival history as the most extraordinary scene ever witnessed in the winners' enclosure. There had been a form of pandemonium two years earlier, when Dawn Run won the Champion Hurdle, but that was vicarage tea-party stuff compared to this wild cavorting invasion by hundreds and hundreds of exuberant Irishmen. Jonjo was lifted high on their shoulders, then Tony Mullins, the deposed jockey yet still very much part of the Dawn Run team, received the treatment. I have never seen a racing crowd respond like that to any winner and I doubt if I shall see its like again.

There just had to be an anti-climax, of course, and it came in a manner which I suppose I could have predicted with the enigmatic Green Bramble falling at the last in the Ritz Club Chase and giving me a bruising which cost me my final ride of the meeting. He had run a good race but he was out of contention when he came down — the race was won by the Scudamore-Nicholson team, now making up for lost time.

If the day closed on a painful and disappointing note, this has still been a marvellously memorable Festival. Anyone who rides two winners at Cheltenham has to be very satisfied, especially when they include the Champion Hurdle, and I have been lucky to have some great losing rides, too. Tonight, I think, I might break out of my self-imposed chains and let my hair down. . . .

FRIDAY 14 MARCH

I began the day with a hangover, an unsurprising relic of a night when quite a few refugees from Cheltenham cut loose. I drank some farewell toasts to my pals from Ireland, and generally had a good time. After looking a good thing to win the Ritz Club award as top jockey at the meeting for the second successive season I had lost out — to 'Scu' — because he had ridden more seconds than I had (we kid him that he's a seconds specialist at Cheltenham, but that may have to change now). But that was only a minor setback to a week which gave me ample cause to celebrate.

Today brought the inevitable anti-climax. It happens every year and it is never any easier to handle. All through the winter, the racing talk is of Cheltenham. It arrives with a thumping of drums and pumping adrenalin, it holds everyone involved on an emotional high, then all too quickly it is over and the realisation that there is a full year to wait for the next Festival — and an awful lot of mediocre racing to get through — bursts the bubble in which we have all existed. Very often, I have come down to earth at Wolverhampton, riding a moderate novice on a murky Friday afternoon with a dull-faced crowd of no more than a few hundred looking on. Today, at least the scenery was better at Lingfield Park, the rural Surrey course they advertise with good reason as 'Lovely Lingfield'. I had a quiet day — a third-place being my nearest bid for a winner — and opted to stay down for tomorrow's meeting on the same track rather than dragging myself back to Newmarket.

One sad piece of news punctuated an otherwise forgettable day. Anthony Webber has been forced to retire, on doctor's orders, after taking one too many bangs on the head. It is obviously the right thing to do, but I always have sympathy for a jockey of Anthony's visible enthusiasm when his retirement is dictated rather than planned. He was never the most stylish rider of my generation but he was bloody effective, and a good number of trainers will miss him.

SATURDAY 15 MARCH

Peter Scudamore rode four winners at Chepstow today, convincing me that he will be champion jockey if he stays fit until the end of the season. I know this may sound like another slice of defeatism — it was not all that long ago that I was resigning myself to Simon Sherwood taking the title — but if nothing else, I am a hard realist about my own shortcomings and I totally accept that 'Scu' is prepared to work harder at this game than I am.

It would not always have been this way. Time was when I would go anywhere for a ride, be it the dodgiest novice chaser in the book or the best hurdler in the country. I took no account of risks and paid no heed to the luxuries of life. But I have been going round a good few years now and I have seen a lot more of life, both inside and outside racing. It is no longer attractive to me to earn £50 to ride a horse which has an even-money chance of decanting me at the first fence, with all the painful ramifications that may have. When I take a ride from outside my retaining stable, I want to get on that horse thinking it has at least some chance of winning — and then I will give it everything.

'Scu' is a few years younger than me. He is also hungrier for success. Winning the championship, as a specific entity, must mean more to him than it does to me because it seems he is prepared to be on the phone for hours at a time every evening in an attempt to book a ride in every race at the meeting he goes to. He will many times ring up trainers he doesn't know and others he has never taken a ride for, in the constant quest for winners. I am not saying he is wrong — I would not admit I am wrong. But we are very different people, and the difference in our make-up is likely to make him champion jockey. The current state of play is that Pete has ridden 62 winners, Simon 53 and I am on 51 after an easy success on Juven Light at Lingfield today.

SUNDAY 16 MARCH

The thing I most needed after the past week was a quiet, slovenly day in an armchair ... and that is exactly what I had today. With no snooker partner and the passing of the American football season, both my usual Sunday pursuits are off the menu so I became a goggle-eyed telly addict for the afternoon and evening, simply trying to recharge somewhat over-used batteries.

MONDAY 17 MARCH

My guv'nor Nicky flew to Ireland today with an urgent mission. The Italian owners of See You Then have been on to him with a request that their horse should pass up his engagement at the Aintree National meeting and instead try for a rich hurdle race in Italy. You can't blame them for wanting to show off their champion in their homeland, but Nicky is anxious to run the horse at Liverpool. As a compromise, he has agreed to try and buy these fellows another horse to run in Italy. Watch this space for developments.

I set off on the previously arduous journey from Newmarket to Plumpton and was mildly amazed to get there in one-and-a-half hours. The M25, now open almost all the way round London, is beginning to pamper us racing gypsies. Before they built it, this journey was a three-hour nightmare, and I hate to think how long it used to take before there were any motorways at all. It was a worthwhile trip, too — Foyle Fisherman won again, restoring a contact with John Jenkins I seemed to have lost over recent weeks.

TUESDAY 18 MARCH

In two days' time flat racing begins again up at Doncaster. The only difference this makes to my way of life for the next couple of months is that jumping receives substantially less of the racing publicity than has been the case up to now. Otherwise, life goes on as before. But here in Newmarket, headquarters of the summer game, I can feel the atmosphere building up to a crescendo.

The town sleeps during the winter, while I am chasing busily around the country. Now it is as if an electric charge has been passed through the place — everyone is buzzing and bubbling, and when I ride out on the Heath at dawn there is the animated sight of up to 2,000 horses queuing to use the gallops, trainers and their staff bustling about with furrowed brows, and touts with their high-powered glasses and notebooks clocking the action. I have very little time to follow the flat myself, except on the odd occasion when jumpers I have ridden turn out in distance events, but when living in Newmarket it is impossible — and undesirable! — to avoid being drawn into the social scene.

The post-Cheltenham jumping today could also aptly have been described as flat, my one ride at Nottingham resulting in the worst of all results, unseated from the favourite in a novice hurdle. It was made worse by the fact that the horse, Gavin's Bell Founder, was absolutely running away and would undoubtedly have won if I had remained on board. The only consolation was that I picked myself up unscathed. Only my pride was hurt on a day when Simon Sherwood injured his neck, a hospital case which will cost him a week's rides, and there were nasty-looking falls for Peter 'Scu' and Graham Bradley. So perhaps I should be counting my blessings.

WEDNESDAY 19 MARCH

Many jockeys are superstitious. As a general rule, I am not, but I am considering the point very carefully tonight. Yesterday morning I bought a new pair of shoes — red sneakers to wear with jeans at the meetings where it is not necessary to dress up. I wore them to Nottingham yesterday, when I was unseated, and I wore them again to Worcester today, where I was obliged to pull up on every one of my four rides. So since I mistakenly purchased these sneakers, I have failed to complete in any one of five races.

THURSDAY 20 MARCH

Reading this morning's *Sporting Life* I was astonished to see the name of P. Scudamore chalked up against a particularly dodgy jumper in the novice chase at Towcester. I wondered what on earth Pete was thinking of, taking a ride like that at this delicate stage of the season, midway between Cheltenham and Liverpool and with the jockeys' title still at stake. So, when I got to the course, I sought him out and told him so. In fact I gave him a bit of a bollocking for being stupid and, to his credit, he took the point and did get out of the ride.

Sure enough, the horse buried the deputy pilot Allen Webb at one of the uphill fences, leaving him motionless for several minutes. That could have been the end of 'Scu's' season and the end of his bid for the championship. He came up later and thanked me, but he really shouldn't accept rides like that in the first place. No one thinks any the better of you for it. I know, as I have previously said, that the reason he will probably be champion ahead of me is that he is prepared to chase rides rather more than I do, but there must come a time when you touch the brake and hold back for the sake of expediency and good health.

FRIDAY 21 MARCH

There was decent racing at Newbury, but no luck for me, although there was hope for the future from two runners-up. Whitsunday, a chaser having his first run under rules after three point-to-point wins by no less than 25 lengths, shaped very impressively before being run out of it from the last, and I was very unlucky on another horse of Nicky's, the novice hurdler Arnhall. We knew that he hates being in front, and it was my plan to hold him up behind the leaders until the last possible moment, as he has plenty of finishing speed. This was thwarted by complete accident. At the second last flight I was nicely tucked in behind the pacemaker, ridden by Phil Tuck, when he fell and broke a leg. This left me a very reluctant leader, and I had no alternative but to go for home. Just as I had feared, Arnhall folded up after the last and was beaten one-and-a-half lengths into second place.

In both races I had been beaten by horses trained by Captain Tim Forster and ridden by Hywel Davies. It was a welcome change of luck for them both. The poor Captain had lost no fewer than three of his better horses this week, all killed in various ways, and must have been in the depths of despair, while Hywel, who takes the job every bit as seriously as his pal 'Scu', had been very short of winners and getting extremely low about it. Amazingly, they went on to register a four-timer, which must be one of the greatest swings of the fortune pendulum this season has seen. I'm pleased for them both.

SATURDAY 22 MARCH

I stayed at the Francomes last night, and heard another of John's ambitious schemes for his life. Training is not turning out quite as well as he had hoped yet, and he tells me he is tempted to take a year off and spend it travelling around the world. He wants me to go with him. Now, there are times when I get depressed about my lot and there is nothing I would rather do than pull up stumps on the jockey's life and set off to explore the world, but it only takes a few minutes to convince me it is a fantasy I could never live out. Being a Gemini, I am a Jekyll and Hyde character and it is only in one of my guises that these ideas even enter my head; fortunately, I always return to my more familiar role in time to realise that I have too many responsibilities, too many commitments both to myself and to those close to me, to ever carry through something so outrageous. Basically, I come from a very solid family background and I have pretty settled, domesticated views of life. John, however is the type who might just carry out the threat. I only hope he realises that to do that would probably ruin his training career for good. It is hard enough to set up a training establishment once and get the trust of sufficient owners. To do it twice is asking too much.

Besides, I won a big race today, so all is right with my world! Pikes Peak duly justified favouritism in the Philip Cornes Hurdle final at Newbury and is proving to be one of the stars of the season, unlike John Jenkins' Ivy League, who flopped yet again and is now looking a very expensive piece of dogmeat.

SUNDAY 23 MARCH

Tom Jones taught me most of what I know about horses and racing when I worked for him as an apprentice. I respected him enormously and still do, so the relationship continues very much in the style of master and servant, trainer and apprentice, despite the fact that I now live with his daughter. There are occasions, however, when the barriers are broken down — usually when we get drunk together after a family get-together. We had just such a party today, lunch blending into supper and Sunday becoming Monday almost before I knew it, and it is amazing how a decanter of port can stimulate good debate!

MONDAY 24 MARCH

A car service, haircut and paperwork were all I had in the diary today. But I wasn't sorry not to be riding. The spring winds outside whipped up to such a temper that they knocked down my chicken shed and a fence, and left one of my plum trees leaning drunkenly. It would not have been much fun riding a novice chaser around Wolverhampton in this.

TUESDAY 25 MARCH

Sandown ran a very strange card today, which included two races for amateur riders and one for conditional jockeys, leaving three open to the professionals. With the fields small, I didn't get a single ride, which at least left me clear to repair the storm damage in my garden, even if it wasn't very welcome in most ways.

Pete Scudamore is still going very well and has now extended his lead to ten in the jockeys' table. More than two months of the season still remain, but in my heart I have accepted that I am most unlikely to finish as champion. I had a very good chance when the season began — indeed, I may never have a better one — but winners are hard to come by at this end of the campaign and, as I have said, I am not prepared to risk my neck riding anything outlandish. If 'Scu' was injured tomorrow, and ruled out of the remainder of the season, I would have to sit down and give serious thought to trying to catch him, but if he stays fit I shall still be content with what I have achieved this year.

WEDNESDAY 26 MARCH

The Italian Job has resolved itself. Nicky bought a horse called Duplicator, a top Irish four-year-old trained by Mick O'Toole, and that will be sent over for the race in Italy over Easter. I, by coincidence, will be heading the opposite way to Ireland, having been offered the ride on Run and Skip in the Irish Grand National at Fairyhouse.

THURSDAY 27 MARCH
Racing was at Ludlow and Southwell, and my only offered ride was a novice hurdler for Nick in a race at the Shropshire track. Now, Newmarket to Ludlow is a pig of a journey at the best of times, and today I felt very disinclined to attempt it for the sake of one little horse without a hope in hell of winning. Fortunately, the owner saw things the same way — he didn't want to go either, so Nicky took the horse out and everyone was happy.

I filled in the time organising my trip to Ireland and assuaging my slight pangs of guilt over not staying at home to scratch around for half-a-dozen rides at one of the Bank Holiday meetings here. Maybe I should be doing that. Call it complacency if you like, but I know I would probably have taken the opposite decision if I still felt I had any chance in the championship. So, bearing in mind my predilection for the social habits of the Irish, I will fly out to Dublin on Saturday night and make a decent weekend of it, with the lure of a tilt at the big race to top it off on Monday.

FRIDAY 28 MARCH
When I listed 'bird-watching' among my hobbies in the *Turf Guide* (the bible of racing folk) I did not have my tongue in cheek — I really did mean the feathered variety. Plenty of people are willing to believe that the only birds I study are two-legged, but in fact I have made myself pretty knowledgeable on ornithology and I love visiting bird sanctuaries to look at unfamiliar species. Today I drove to the Norfolk coast with just that in mind. I have a lot to think about at the moment, and when I have things to contemplate and decisions to take I very often head for the beach and a solitary stroll. With the sea breeze blowing the cobwebs out of my brain I could think clearly, and an afternoon visit to the sanctuary completed an enjoyably worthwhile day, far from the crowds I often crave but sometimes loathe.

SATURDAY 29 MARCH

Races cut up badly over the Easter holiday, and this year is no exception. It annually gives owners and trainers their best chance of winning a little event with a poor animal, and it always draws big crowds into the courses, so it should not be knocked, but there was some very modest fare at Towcester today. I did manage to ride a winner on Nicky's novice chaser Edenspring, however, before hurrying on to catch the 8.00 p.m. flight out of Heathrow with a friend named Mick Curtain. We booked into Jury's Hotel in Dublin and had a relatively early night; it is likely to be the only one during our stay.

SUNDAY 30 MARCH

A trip to Ireland really is like going home for me. I have a lot of affinity with their way of life here, and I just love their sense of humour. Today we met up with some of the Irish jockeys, notably Tommy McGivern, and needless to say it was a day of riotous sociability.

MONDAY 31 MARCH

Run and Skip had been allotted top weight of 12 stone in the National. He was also just 'over the top' after so many brave efforts in tough company this season, and it was bottomless mud at Fairyhouse this afternoon after 24 hours of solid heavy rain. A combination of these three factors made certain that the Irish National did not join my list of big races won.

Conditions were dire by English standards — the Irish relish the boggy ground rather more than we do — and although my horse ran his heart out yet again, the writing was on the wall a long way from home. I was still in fourth place as we jumped the third last, but with no chance of winning. I was wondering whether to pull up or not when a panting and snorting alongside announced the arrival of my good Yorkshire pal Graham Bradley, riding Righthand Man for Mrs Dickinson. His horse was in the same state as mine — thoroughly knackered — and in his broadest, most breathless tones he muttered: 'Eee, ah wish ah could pull up'. Seeing the chance of ending the agony in a bit of fun, I replied: 'Just follow me', and turned sharply left-handed, steering him off the course. The expression on Brad's face was a picture — horror and shock with just a degree of relief — but we were soon laughing about it on the muddy, wet walk back to the weighing-room. Significantly, the first three places in the race were all occupied by horses carrying less than ten stone. It was not a day for class weight-carrying animals; the moderate sloggers won out.

In the bar I bumped into 'Ginger' McCain, who I expect to be seeing rather a lot this week, as I shall be staying very close to his Southport stables for the National meeting. This initiated a farewell session on the whisky, which progressed to a local pub which boasted, among its decorations, a stuffed pheasant. Or rather, it used to. That stuffed pheasant, now mysteriously headless, somehow ended the night inside my pocket. It will be something to surprise the boys with later in the week....

Back in London, I checked the day's results and found I had not missed a single winner by opting for Ireland. But Simon Sherwood rode four winners at Newton Abbot. Perhaps I will struggle for second place in the table, now.

APRIL

THURSDAY 3 APRIL

I don't always look forward to Liverpool, but this year has been different. With an enviable National ride in Classified, and three likely winners in River Ceiriog, See You Then and Kathies Lad, I would not willingly have swapped places with any other jockey as we drove north up the M6 this morning. By tonight, I was not so sure. What a difference a day can make!

Di usually comes up with me for this three-day meeting and, this year, we had decided to stay in Southport, at the busy but remote Royal Clifton, rather than risking the Irish contingent, who set up base at Liverpool's Holiday Inn. In my younger days, I would have been with them, but there are important horses to be ridden this year — and, anyway, I reasoned, an awful lot of racing people stay in Southport and it is certain to be just as much fun.

The first thing to go awry was not long in coming. Just as at Cheltenham, the opening event of Liverpool's three-day meeting is a valuable two-mile novice hurdle. River Ceiriog had trounced most of this opposition three weeks before, and I saw no good reason why he should not do so again, despite having to give weight away all round. I had carefully scrutinised the form of every horse in the race and, although there were dangers, I set off to the start as confident as any jockey has the right to be.

Three hurdles from home I was cruising. I had held the horse up longer than at Cheltenham, trusting in his finishing kick, and as I went past half the field on the bridle I felt my confidence had been entirely justified. Two out, I was disputing the lead and I thought it only a matter of time before I saw off all challengers. But as we approached the last the alarm bells began to ring in my head. One horse, his jockey clad in the distinctive blue-and-white hoops of Terry Ramsden, was still with me and showing no sign of throwing in the towel. I went for everything. River Ceiriog hit the final flight, but I am not sure it made the slightest difference to the outcome. All the way up the run-in I was coming off second-best and, at the line, the margin was three-quarters of a length.

I have to say I had given I Bin Zaidoon no chance, which I suppose is always dangerous with a horse of Mr Ramsden's. The man himself was waiting to welcome his winner, surrounded by what seemed like a dozen minders. He is certainly a colourful character, probably good for the game, and on most other occasions I would have enjoyed the scene, but not today. I had been so sure that River Ceiriog would win, and this came as a savage setback. With hindsight, it doesn't seem so bad. Things seldom do. He was, after all, giving the winner pounds, which means that strictly on the book he was still the best horse in the race. I don't think the tight Aintree circuit suited him and nor, looking back, do I think I rode him to his best advantage. He is a relentless galloper, suited by being up at the head of affairs, and maybe he was held up too long.

But the fact remains I was bitterly disappointed, a feeling which was not assuaged when Indamelody, another horse I had fancied — if more quietly — ran well enough but could finish only third in the stayers' handicap hurdle. The meeting seemed to be crumbling beneath my feet. And so, not having any further rides, and having met up with some of the Irish jockeys I had been with in Dublin only a few days ago, I decided to have a few drinks and try to put the dejection out of sight and out of mind....

FRIDAY 4 APRIL

Thursday ran inconveniently into Friday, and I have an awful feeling I have made a fool of myself in the most spectacular fashion. In brief, since my last ride on Thursday, I have got drunk, had a fearful row with Di, been hijacked in my own car and then stupidly confessed the lot on television. The first three circumstances are temporarily painful but no more; the last may have altogether more serious ramifications.

To explain myself I need to go back to early yesterday evening. I drove back to Southport with Di to check into the hotel, still feeling sorry for myself. The Irish boys, most of whom were over for a busman's holiday, had bought me a scotch or two and cheered me up with their wit, but I was still sober and still depressed. So I took it out on Di. It was unfair, of course, but it happened. I told her I was going out for the evening in Liverpool and, to put it mildly, we had a ruck. It was made fairly plain that I had better find somewhere else to sleep and, the lady not being short of character, I knew she meant it.

I left the hotel, now angry as well as depressed. But when I got into my car I couldn't face the long drive back into the city, so instead I just drove around the corner to a place where I knew there would be a welcome — Ginger and Beryl McCain's house. I find the McCains great company, and I was soon beginning to forget my problems, helped by liberal quantities of scotch and some excellent food. I left them at a respectable hour, certainly before midnight, and faced up to my dilemma again. It didn't even occur to me to try and find another hotel room — I knew the two major hotels in Southport were full and I was in no state to go farther afield, so I decided to spend the night in the back of my car. It was no big deal — I have used it before as a last resort, and being a Mercedes it is not uncomfortable. The problem was, I was by now quite drunk, and as I stumbled back into the car I must have left the keys either in the doorlock or in the ignition — I honestly can't remember which. Oblivious to this, I covered myself up with a couple of overcoats against what was a distinctly chilly night, and then settled down to sleep.

The next thing I was aware of was a strange sensation of movement. It can only have been an hour or two later, and I was in that indefinable limbo somewhere between sleep and wakefulness. I tried to concentrate my befuddled brain, and there really was no doubt. Then it hit me — where I was, what I was doing there and the dramatic realisation that, if I wasn't driving the car, someone else had to be. I burst out from under my covering of coats, sat up sharply in the back seat and said something abrupt and absurd: 'What the hell do you think you're doing?'

The driver, I now saw, was a teenage bloke, a joyrider no

doubt, and the effect on him of my sudden words and actions was, I imagine, not unlike that on someone convinced he has seen a ghost. He gave a terrified squeak, slammed on the brakes, swerved the car rapidly and awkwardly onto the hard shoulder and, without pausing for polite conversation, opened the door and legged it. He was halfway across a field which bordered the road before I had fully realised what he was doing, and then there seemed no point in chasing him. I surveyed the scene and counted my problems. Thanks to an obliging traffic sign I was able to ascertain that I was on the M57, approximately 20 miles from Southport, so that was one potential teaser solved. But I still had to get myself back to the hotel, and I was well aware I would not have passed a breathaliser. Still, there was no option; I could hardly just sit there, on the hard shoulder of the motorway, waiting for an inevitable police patrol car to come along. So I got back into the driver's seat and, feeling slightly shaky for the experience and no doubt a little hazy for the alcohol, I navigated back to Southport surprisingly accurately, re-parked in the hotel car park, locked all the doors and dozed off again — this time in the driver's seat and with the engine left on to heat the car.

When at last I woke again in daylight and reconstructed the events, it seemed scarcely believable. I was stone-cold sober now, and ready to admit that it might also have been frightening. But, after all, it had turned out all right, hadn't it — and it was a great yarn to tell the lads in the weighing-room. So I set off for the races, if not exactly with a song in my heart then certainly feeling much bouncier than I had been yesterday evening.

To be honest, I was bursting to tell someone the story, and as the first person I saw was my valet Johnny Buckingham, he was regaled with the entire saga. Knowing me as well as he does, he didn't disbelieve it, either — indeed, he was so struck by it that he, naturally enough, relayed it to a few other willing listeners. By this time I had also retold the story once or twice, and before I knew what was happening everyone on the course seemed to have heard it in some form or other and I was being asked to go on television for a chat with their usual interviewer Jonathan Powell. I saw nothing wrong with the idea and answered Jonathan's questions faithfully, glossing over the row with Di, but otherwise being brutally honest right down to confessing that the reason I had not chased my kidnapper was that I was thoroughly drunk.

Tonight, just a few hours on, I realise this admission was stupid, quite probably one of the silliest things I have ever said, and I am fully expecting trouble over it. Not from the police — I have not reported the matter and there is nothing they could now do about it — but perhaps from Nicky and his owners, if they should take the view that it was careless at best and irresponsible at worst first to get drunk and then blunder into a situation as potentially dangerous as that, during one of the season's most important meetings. Nicky thought the whole thing very amusing when he first heard of it but, like me, he has now had time to appraise the question not of what did happen but what might have happened. What if there had been two blokes instead of just one? What if the joyrider had been armed, maybe with a knife? And what if he had crashed the car? All these possible consequences have now occurred to me, and I must say the affair does not seem quite so funny any more.

The conspiracy of circumstances which led me into the trap could, I suppose, all have been avoided, though it really stemmed from the bitter disappointment which beset me following River Ceiriog's defeat. Oddly enough, that horse is owned by Mr Bobby McAlpine, who also owns Baby Sigh, the only horse I had to ride today. He had absolutely no chance in one of the best four-year-old races of the season, but I put him in the race and did my best on him. He finished tailed off, just as I imagined he would.

There was no way I was going to involve myself in another drinking session tonight, and as I have not yet patched up my differences with Di, I checked into another, smaller hotel in Southport, where the Francomes are staying. I was in thoughtful mood and determined to keep a low profile, so after an early dinner I retired to bed at 10.30 p.m., anxious to catch up on some sleep in the knowledge that my riding tomorrow might be scrutinised that bit more critically than usual.

SATURDAY 5 APRIL

My usual papers, the *Daily Express* and *Sporting Life*, were waiting for me on the table when I went in to breakfast. Normally, I would have picked up the *Life* first — especially on National morning — but my eye was drawn irresistibly to the front page of the *Express*, and it gave me quite a turn. Splash headline, dramatic words and a picture, too — my kidnap saga, leading the front page. I suppose I should have seen it coming, but it had honestly never occurred to me that the papers would give the story such treatment.

I glanced sheepishly around the room and noticed a good deal of whispering and nudging going on. That told me all I needed to know. The story was obviously in their papers, too. I didn't much enjoy my breakfast. It's all very well being a celebrity, but I could predict all too clearly the frosty reaction such notoriety might bring from one or two owners I ride for, and I couldn't really blame them.

As ever on National day I left very early to beat the traffic queues outside the course. I was prepared for the ribbing in the weighing-room, which was all good-natured, but I was taken aback by my reception when I went out for my ride on Kathies Lad in the day's first race. There was a fantastic crowd at Aintree, probably the biggest I have ever seen there, and I don't suppose there were many in the mass who had not read about my adventures in their morning papers. As I walked Kathies Lad out of the parade ring, the jibes were many and audible.

'Do you need a chauffeur, Steve?'

'Had your car pinched lately, Smith Eccles?' ... And other, less polite enquiries. It was, I admit, a little unnerving. I had already detected that a proportion of people didn't believe the story at all, while others were convinced that there was rather more to it than I had made out. The fact that there wasn't didn't help me. I knew I had already said far too much about the business and that now I had to ride at my very best and strongest to avoid any possibility of the muttering becoming plain indignation. I have never let my social life affect my riding, but I knew that plea was going to sound pathetic if I failed to do myself justice now.

Well, I am proud of the ride I turned in on Kathies Lad. In the season's richest two-miles handicap chase, he won for the second successive year and, it transpired, did so despite considerable pain from a plate which twisted into his hoof during the race. It must have been that which made him jump violently left at the last, but although many spectators expected a stewards' enquiry, I always felt I was clear of the chasing horses and had hampered nobody. Brave horse that he is, Kathies then sprinted away on the run-in to win by two-and-a-half lengths and I came back feeling considerably relieved.

That, I thought, was the hard bit done. I expected See You Then to win the Sandeman Aintree Hurdle, and I expected that I would be required to do little more than steer. But, not for the first time this week, I was wrong. He had never attempted two miles five furlongs before, but he had won a slow-run race at Doncaster over only a furlong less, so, before the event, we were not unduly concerned about his ability to get the trip. He had previously trounced every horse in the field, so we were justified in thinking he should win and the betting market, which had him at 9-4 on, supported our conviction.

The horse did not help his chances by pulling hard early on. I had a battle to settle him, but once he stopped fighting me he was travelling smoothly. Turning out of the back straight, Aonoch made his move under Jimmy Duggan. I had expected that and I went with him, tracking him into the straight, always going well. See You Then got close to the second last, losing momentum, but now it was clear that I had a struggle on hand. The ground was sticky after morning rain and I wondered, aghast, if my horse could produce his devastating finishing speed.

Coming to the last I had to press the button, ask the horse questions he had never needed to answer at Cheltenham. For a time, it seemed he would respond like a true champion. I got the rail and drove him up the inside of Aonoch, who was staying on gallantly. I was within a neck of him 100 yards from the line, but even as I got there, I had the horrible sensation of running out of petrol. See You Then simply had no more to give, and was beaten by a length. We had taken him to Liverpool for easy pickings and come unstuck. I don't think he liked either the track or the trip. He is a top-class two-miler and I suspect he will be kept to that from now on.

Nicky did not condemn me at all, but I still felt low. In the minutes which followed I rode the race time and again in my head, and I know there is nothing more I could have done to win. It was, however, another nasty pill to swallow, and at a most unfortunate time.

I had to get myself motivated again for the National. I sat sipping tea in my corner of the weighing-room, while all around me the excited chatter which traditionally precedes the greatest spectacle of the jumping season ebbed and flowed. The youngsters, those for whom it was all new, were the most animated, but some old heads, too, were bubbling. It seemed to me, as I sat a little detached from the hubbub, that everyone was asking everyone else how they would run and nobody was listening to the obviously optimistic answers. And then came the ritual in which National jockeys always get all their colleagues to sign the racecard over the name of their ride. It is a harmless souvenir, but I was in no mood to join in, and after signing several I was a bit short when the teaboys came round asking me for my autograph.

The reason why the National meant nothing special to me is that, in my previous six attempts, I had only managed to complete the course once. I had twice finished up fishing in Bechers Brook and I had never looked like winning the race, so history did not exactly fill me with confidence or enthusiasm. Having said that, I considered Classified to be one of the best National rides I had ever had. He is not a big, robust horse but he is an athlete, a natural, safe jumper, best at two or two-and-a-half miles on park courses but not short on stamina, as he showed when completing in fifth place last year. This season he had been trained specifically with the National in mind, and he was spot-on for the occasion. I cheered myself up with the thought that he might even improve my dismal Aintree record.

In many diverse ways, the National is unique. One striking thing about it is the noise which assails the jockeys' ears as the tapes go up and the field surges away from the packed stands. In any normal race you are oblivious to the crowd, but here the roar is deafening. There is another audible cheer from the crowd out at Bechers, for those who get that far. This year, as usual, there were plenty who failed. I had jumped off towards the outer, ignoring the usual scrum for the rail, because the first six fences are in a straight line and there is plenty of opportunity to track over to the inner once your horse is settled. I broke fast and first out of the gate, always doubly important in this enormous field of 40, and as we went to the first I noticed Graham McCourt, on Tim Forster's Port Askaig, ranging upsides.

I called across: 'This is it then, here we go'.

He shouted back: 'I'll just be glad to get over this first fence'.

The first always catches out a few horses. It is the steepness of the drop which is the surprise element, and although Classified — suitably steadied a few yards before take-off — met it perfectly, I still landed with a jolt. Even as I did so I heard the tell-tale tinkling of irons from my right which always signifies a faller. Poor Graham had hit the deck and Richard Rowe, on the third favourite Door Latch, had come to grief with him. Back in the weighing-room much later a laconic Rowe was heard to report that it was such a pity because he had been going so well at the time!

The third fence is the first big ditch. It sorts out the men from the boys, and Classified was foot-perfect. Once over that, I had a feeling of rising confidence. Barring accidents, I knew I was in for a decent ride, and I actually began to enjoy myself.

Essex, the Czech entry, was weaving all over the course, and I was fully occupied avoiding him for a while, but by Bechers I was in the clear again. Jumping this extraordinary brook is like going into space, but Classified was brave and accurate. We landed running and I decided that the time was right to tack over to the inside. By the time we crossed the Melling Road, only West Tip and Richard Dunwoody were on my inner and I was perfectly satisfied with my position.

Over the awesome Chair and past the stands again, lying about sixth, a loose horse began to worry me. He was jumping the fences, edging right at each one, so I made sure I stayed on his inside. Sure enough, at the 17th he went quite violently right, bringing down one runner and badly interfering with another. That, then, was another danger met and matched.

At the 22nd — Bechers for the second time — I took the lead. I didn't really want to be there, but Classified had jumped to the front and was plainly enjoying it all, so there was absolutely no point in restraining him. By now, too, I had changed my thinking about the Grand National — thanks to Classified. I defy anyone to find a thrill comparable with jumping these Aintree fences on a thoroughly good horse. I can't describe it, and I can only imagine it must be like being high on drugs, only without the side effects.

I knew, however, that there was only a certain amount of fuel left in Classified's tank, and when Chris Grant on Young Driver ranged alongside at the third last, I felt pretty sure we were not going to win. I was also well aware that West Tip was creeping ever closer up the rail.

'Rambo' Grant — if you saw his spindly body you would appreciate the nickname — is a great character of the northern courses, but all the same I tried a bit of psychology, calling across to him to go steady as we still had a long way to go. It didn't work — his response was to wave his whip and kick for home, leaving me trailing.

I badly wanted to complete, but while there was still a chance I had to ask Classified for one final effort. To his eternal credit, he responsed, albeit at one tired pace. It is in these final yards that the National can be a cruel race. A horse may have relished the jumping but now, when he has nothing left to give, his jockey is still obliged to demand more. In any other race I would have pulled him up but we plugged on, while up ahead West Tip remorselessly gunned down Young Driver on the run-in through a coolly inspired piece of riding. Richard was fantastic, and as I saw him go past the winning post from 20 lengths further back I was delighted for him. I was also delighted for myself. Third place in the National may not earn much of the glamour, but it earns the owner a good payout, and it gave me an experience I shall never forget. Nicky was ecstatic, too ... and nobody, surely, could say my riding had in any way suffered through my well-publicised social activities.

If the weighing-room is noisy before the National, it is nothing to the uproar immediately afterwards, as all the boys talk each other through the race fence by fence, reliving every slice of the action. By now, I even felt up to joining in, although I was shattered by the effort I had expended. It is always an anti-climax to have to go out and ride in the last race on the card, the only other one open to professionals, and this year it was worse than ever. Most of the crowd had gone and an ordinary novice hurdle seemed somehow irrelevant. My horse, Bell Founder, ran a stinker and, all things considered, I think I may try to avoid taking a ride in the race next year.

I was too tired to drive back to Newmarket, so I went back to my small Southport hotel and wound down with another evening at Ginger McCains. It has been an emotional, memorable day in many ways but at the end of it I fear the Aintree chapter is not yet closed.

SUNDAY 6 APRIL

I phoned my parents, and was not surprised to hear that they were upset by the publicity I had received. The local Derbyshire press had also been in touch with them over the story, which struck me as unnecessary and possibly malicious, and my mother was ready with a few stern words of advice for me. I didn't have to do any explaining, she had already worked out the truth of the story, and as usual her advice was sound.

I drove home and, not without difficulty, patched things up with Di. It is silly to think that all this stemmed from an over-reaction to one defeat, but that is the case. I know now I was foolishly stubborn, and that the mess I got myself into on Thursday night was self-induced. It was also unprofessional, and I am not proud of that. We all make mistakes, but just at the moment I seem to be making more than my share.

WEDNESDAY 9 APRIL

Ascot: one of the last major meetings of the season. There are still plenty of whispers around about my Liverpool escapade, but I try hard not to discuss it now — I want to put it behind me. I thought I would ride a winner today on Juven Light, but he ran unaccountably badly, as did my other mount, Joy Ride. Poor Jeff King is having a wretched time, and there was no spark at all in the horse. It can happen to any trainer, and it is not always possible to pinpoint a reason. I just hope things come right for Kingy, because I like him a lot.

There is talk today of Peter Scudamore being offered the job as stable jockey to Fred Winter next season. It might be difficult for him, after spending so long under the wing of David Nicholson, but I think he would be silly to turn it down.

THURSDAY 10 APRIL

I had arranged to go to Southwell to ride two of Nicky's hurdlers, so I took a spare ride offered. Then Nicky took his two horses out, and I was obliged to make the journey for one no-hoper. At this late stage of the season, such is life. I have now slipped to fourth place in the table, behind Hywel Davies, so I need to get my finger out.

FRIDAY 11 APRIL

As the Saturday meeting is again at Ascot I had arranged to stay the night with Nicky Henderson in Lambourn. I knew what I was letting myself in for and I went prepared for an inquest into the happenings of a week ago. Fortified by riding a winner for Jeff King at Towcester, I arrived at Windsor House at the cocktail hour, accompanied by Di, and Nick and I went into conclave to talk things through.

I made no attempt to offer excuses or cover anything up. There was tension in the air and I knew Nick had taken some flak from certain owners, so for his sake as well as mine I simply made a clean breast of it, told him I had done wrong and that I would not do anything so unprofessional again. It was a frank talk, and very worthwhile for both of us. I still want to ride for Nick next season and I am pretty sure he wants me around, so clearing the air today was essential.

SATURDAY 12 APRIL

I thought I had had a stroke of luck this morning when Fred Winter approached me on the Lambourn gallops and asked me to ride his novice chaser Gold Bearer at Ascot this afternoon. It turned out, however, to be a case of being in the right place at the wrong time, because Gold Bearer dumped me on the deck at the third fence. In fact, Fred's first three runners of the meeting, all fancied, ended on the floor, so it was as well that Lambourn pride was retrieved by Nick's very promising chaser Whitsunday, who jumped splendidly and made all the running to give me my 57th winner and give Nick a dilemma. The ground is sure to dry up soon, discouraging him from running his better horses, but as this was the horse's first win under rules, he will be anxious to win another with him before he has to turn to handicapping next season. I'm glad it's not my problem.

Nick had a valuable double, as Pikes Peak graduated to handicap company and slaughtered the opposition. But this was a ride I was frustrated in missing. Nick decided to put the stable claimer Michael Bowlby on him to take off seven pounds and, as he won, the move was justified. It's not a precedent which delights me, however.

'Scu' has decided to join Fred Winter next season, and announced it to the press before racing. David Nicholson was then interviewed on TV and gave me the distinct impression that it was not the best news he has had this week. I hope they remain friends, but I don't think 'Scu' could have taken any other course. Fred may have had a quiet season by his own standards, but it is still one of the best jobs in racing.

MONDAY 14 APRIL

With no racing today, and rides booked at Devon tomorrow, the temptation was too great — I drove down to Torquay this afternoon with 'Sharky' Sherwood and booked into the Palace Hotel. It was the first time I had stayed there for months but the welcome was as overwhelming as ever, from the manager Paul Uphill — who found rooms for us both despite the fact that they were officially full up — down to Jeff the barman, Vic in the restaurant and David the head porter. I think if I could use the Palace as my HQ for the entire racing season I would not hesitate to do so.

TUESDAY 15 APRIL

In torrential rain there is no worse racecourse to be stranded on than Haldon in Devon. Set on the side of a hill, open to all the elements, it attracts the very worst of bad weather and then revels in it. It is a long, galloping course, and when you are at the farthest point from the stands on a grim, wet and windy day like today you might just as well be on horseback in the middle of Dartmoor. It was so wet, indeed, that racing was put back half-an-hour, and conditions were barely tolerable when we did start. I thought it was going to be one of those days when Kathies Lad, widely regarded as a good thing for the feature event, showed very little interest and was beaten after jumping three fences. I fear he is over the top and has simply had enough for the season. But my day was redeemed when Bluelimit won the handicap hurdle. It was a chance ride for me, the horse being trained by David Elsworth, and I know the owners had a nice touch on him.

A final thought today for the unsung heroes of muddy meetings, the valets. Racegoers never see them, these tireless backroom workers, but you can take it from me that they earn their money at all times, never more so than when the weather is as it was today and their job becomes a thankless slog. John Buckingham, who looks after me, has already been mentioned, but there are a dozen or more like him up and down the country. Those on duty at Devon today would have still been in the weighing-room three hours after the last race, probably covered in mud. It's not a job I can ever see myself doing, but I'm very thankful they are around.

WEDNESDAY 16 APRIL

Jonjo's falls really are becoming inconvenient. At Cheltenham today we were going round together in the three-mile handicap hurdle, both on horses with little chance. I was telling him a particularly funny joke and was just about to deliver the punch-line when he came down! He got a pretty severe kicking, but he couldn't wait to get back into the weighing-room and hear the end of the joke.

THURSDAY 17 APRIL

If ever I have a daydream about going into films when I give up riding, I shall remember today and dismiss the idea immediately. John Francome and I had been asked to make a video advertising a Timeshare company with whom we have linked up. It was hardly a taxing part for us — we had just the one line to introduce ourselves, and we had to say it together. But every time we began, we would catch sight of each other's anxiously concentrating expressions and burst out laughing. We did get through it eventually ... on take 51.

FRIDAY 18 APRIL

I have won a big race; I have been spoiled to pieces and I feel as if, just for once, I have sampled the jet-set world in which the leading flat jockeys exist. I have to say I could get a taste for it!

It was Scottish Champion Hurdle day at Ayr, and Nicky had entered River Ceiriog for what will undoubtedly be his final race of the season. Now, the drive up to Scotland would not have been an appealing prospect but, thankfully, we were spared the ordeal and instead, travelled in considerable style. Nick's wife Diana drove us from Lambourn to Wolverhampton where we boarded Bobby McAlpine's private executive plane, stopping off at Chester to pick up the owner himself, and then flying on to land near the Ayr course.

I had always maintained that River Ceiriog was the best two-mile novice in the country, even after his defeat at Liverpool and, although he was today taking on the second, third and fourth horses home in the Champion at Cheltenham, he was getting weight from them all and I gave him a decent chance. We decided that he should make his own running if necessary, as he is a much better horse with a strong gallop, and the plan worked to perfection. Nothing else so much as got in a blow at him, and he was a very convincing winner, fully redeeming himself for the Aintree disappointment.

That put me in a high good humour, maintained by the natural wit of my northern jockey pals — especially Colin 'Jack' Hawkins, a night bird when he gets the chance, and today sporting a fierce black eye from some mysterious fracas on the streets of Ayr last evening.

A perfect day ended in another painless plane journey. We were back in Lambourn almost before we knew it, and in plenty of time for a celebratory glass.

SATURDAY 19 APRIL

Schooled Indamelody over fences again. He is potentially a very useful chaser but he has no confidence to go for the long ones; if he is to get round safely he just has to get in close to the obstacles and pop over, which is frustrating for a jockey and rather self-defeating within a race. It is engrained in every decent jockey to look for the stride approaching each fence and, if it is right, to commit the horse to the long take-off. With a horse of Indamelody's disposition, that isn't possible, but it is very hard to change the basically good habits built up over the years. The horse is scheduled to go to Nottingham for a novice chase next Tuesday, which should be interesting.

I had thought this was going to be a very ordinary day at the office, with just a couple of rides at Stratford, but it turned out quite well, as I got Welsh Oak up to win the handicap hurdle for David Gandolfo.

SUNDAY 20 APRIL

There is little to report, except for a big lunch, long afternoon kip, and a lazy evening. I am badly missing my snooker partner Tommy, and so far I have not found a suitable substitute.

MONDAY 21 APRIL

The Newmarket cavaliers are breaking up fast. Simon McNeil came with me to Southwell today and, after a miserable journey in driving rain, he confided that he is moving to Lambourn at the end of the season. Soon, I might be the only jump jockey left in town.

TUESDAY 22 APRIL

Pete Shilton rang. He offered me a ticket for tomorrow night's England v Scotland game, which was good of him — but I think the main purpose of his call was to quiz me on Indamelody's chances. I told him that if I could get him round, he would definitely win, and I hope he took my advice. The horse jumped better than before, making just the one mistake, and although he looked beaten from the third last, the combination of his staying ability and my stick up his backside carried him to the front on the run-in. That puts Nicky about £35,000 ahead of his nearest rival in the winnings league, so it looks as if he will be champion trainer for the first time.

What a contrast is provided by John Jenkins, who has hit troubled times after his usual flying start to the season. I rode two for him today and they both ran like dead horses. It puzzles me that John knows they are wrong, yet keeps running them in the belief that all will come right. It's not his fault if there is a virus in his yard, but I don't think he is doing sick horses any favours by keeping them hard at work.

WEDNESDAY 23 APRIL

I don't know what has happened to our climate. This entire season, the weather has veered from one extreme to the other, always either too wet or too dry. Right now, it is unseasonably boggy, and although Worcester's meeting today surprisingly survived a morning inspection, my trainers have taken their horses out. I have plenty of potential rides left, but they are all waiting for the usual spring-time fast ground.

THURSDAY 24 APRIL

My worst fall of the season has written me off for a week ... but I consider myself fortunate to have got away so lightly. When I hit the deck, I was horribly convinced I had broken my neck again. The cause of my distress was Rhythmic Pastimes, a horse I have won on several times and one of two rides for John Jenkins which took me down to Taunton today. A few months back, Rhythmic was potentially a decent dual-purpose horse who had won his hurdle races regularly and was adapting capably to fences. I well remember him trouncing some useful opposition in a two-and-a-half mile chase at Newbury. But his jumping went to pieces soon after that, and his confidence has obviously vanished. John put him back over hurdles today, sensibly thinking that it might restore his nerve, but the remedy seems to have been applied too late. He was backing off as we went towards the first flight, then suddenly he launched himself at the hurdle, landing in its roots and taking a crashing fall, while firing me head-first into the ground.

I felt my head disappear into my shoulders and thought: 'Not again'. The ambulancemen rapidly put me in a collar and stretchered me back to the weighing-room where, although a break was ruled out, the doctor diagnosed bruising of the neck, back and legs plus concussion, and signed me off for the statutory seven days.

FRIDAY 25 APRIL

Concussion is in many ways worse than breaking a bone. Today I feel sick, dizzy and disorientated, and I know it is a feeling which will not go away for several days. It is the first time in four or five years that I have had a week's compulsory leave, and I have no clear idea what to do with it. I don't think I'll be missing much racing, although I had taken the ride on Arctic Beau for John Thorne in tomorrow's Whitbread Gold Cup at Sandown. He only has 10 stone, and if the ground dries up he has a great chance. The one consolation is that I can now eat again!

SATURDAY 26 APRIL

I watched the Whitbread on TV, and silently applauded the great ride 'Sharky' gave Plundering to win the race for Fred Winter. Arctic Beau ran a blinder to be third in ground far softer than he likes. No one will be more worried about this result than Nicky Henderson, whose old boss Fred is now just a few thousand behind him in the winnings table. It could make an interesting finale to the season. My neck and shoulders are still stiff and sore. For much of the day I have either been soaking in hot baths or applying the ultrasound machine; it has helped a bit, but I have got a blinding headache.

SUNDAY 27 APRIL

Di has taken a few days off to be with me, and we set off today on a four-day mini-holiday, kicking off with a stop at my parents' Derbyshire home. It's funny that my family appear from all quarters when they get wind that I am going to be around, and today the place with packed with aunts, uncles and cousins. But this sort of reunion happens all too seldom, and I really enjoyed it.

MONDAY 28 APRIL

Princess Anne has had her critics in the past but I won't hear a bad word said against her. I think she is a great sport — especially after tonight. We had travelled north to Beverley for a dinner-dance run in aid of Riding for the Disabled and the Injured Jockeys Fund. We had a great night on a table dominated by jockeys, and I somehow managed to manoeuvre myself into having the last waltz with the Princess. She was appreciably taller than me in her high heels, and I mumbled something to the effect. With that, she kicked off her shoes and danced barefoot!

TUESDAY 29 APRIL

A great day in the Lake District, and a riotous evening with some good friends, had a sad postscript. We had arranged to stay with Jonjo O'Neill and his wife Sheila at their lovely Cumbrian home, and tonight we went out to a marvellous restaurant on Lake Ullswater, along with Ron Barry — a recently retired character of the weighing-room — and his wife. Midway through the meal I said to Jonjo that it was great he was coming out with the British team to Australia in June. He replied that he wasn't. At first I wondered whether he had business commitments, or perhaps that Sheila was unhappy about it, but then Jonjo stunned me by saying he was going to hang up his boots. Apparently, there were complications following his latest bang on the head. Three days later he was feeling very sick and had to be admitted to hospital. Lying there in bed, dreading yet more surgery, he just arrived at the conclusion that he had reached the end of the road. A month ago, he told me of his plan to go on riding for two or three more years because he still enjoyed it. He always thought it would be terribly difficult to take the decision to stop, but now he related that, when he realised enough was enough, it was all very easy.

We will miss him like hell in the weighing-room, because I don't know of a more popular or genuine guy. To lose both 'Franc' and Jonjo in a year is a bitter blow, but at least, like John, he will be staying in the game through training.

WEDNESDAY 30 APRIL

This is the end of the most enjoyable, relaxing few days I have had in a long time. Di and I drove back home after a good lunch on Lake Windermere, and with my headaches now cleared up, and most of the stiffness gone from my neck, I am looking forward to riding again — though I must say I wouldn't at all mind another seven days off some time soon!

MAY

THURSDAY 1 MAY

The show is back on the road ... and what a bloody show it is! Despite a vague attempt at evasion, I had to undertake the three-hour cross-country drive to Hereford for a single ride in their first race, then head south for two more at Wincanton's evening meeting. None of them obliged — and I fear life is going to continue in this vein for the remaining month of the season, because, all too often, I will be chalked down to ride moderate horses at two meetings in a day.

Events would have been far more tolerable, however, had I not bumped into Matt McCourt, the Oxfordshire trainer, in the car park at Wincanton. He told me that Graham, his son, had broken his wrist, and asked me to step in for the ride on Oyster Pond. I should have known better, but I reasoned that this was a reliable old handi-capper he was asking me to ride, and he might even win; needless to say, he didn't. At the second-last ditch he stumbled on landing, and I ended up on the deck, bringing down two following horses as I fell. I got a very unpleasant kick on the side, and although the doctor did not sign me off, my hip-bone currently looks as if it has got a football attached. All in all, I think I prefer being on 'holiday' in the Lakes!

FRIDAY 2 MAY

I am too old for these double-shift days. Today it was Plumpton followed by Taunton — one ride at each and an endless drive in between. My hip had loosened up last night, aided by a whisky or two and a few dances at Stringfellows, the London nightspot, but I still had a huge and colourful bruise to show off in the weighing-room before going out to win on Gavin's Boom Patrol. I had been concerned that a longish break, and a couple of outings on the flat, might have turned him against hurdling; but, oddly, he has never jumped better, and I could not have won by less than 20 lengths if I had tried. I fancied completing a long-range double with my one ride at Taunton, but got beaten into second. Exhaustion had by then set in, and rather than flog back to Newmarket through the night, I booked in at Torquay. Graham Bradley stayed down, too, and it was a thoroughly good decision.

SATURDAY 3 MAY

The rains have ended and the ground is drying fast all round the country. Last time I was at Taunton, little more than a week ago, they needed a tractor to tow vehicles out of the mud in the car-park, but last night it was rock-hard. The ground was firm at Worcester tonight, too, and I think the runners will quickly diminish from now on in.

At the end of a week which has taken me to virtually every corner of England — I hate to think what my mileage has been — there was another frustration in store when I got beaten a short-head on Welsh Oak tonight. Just to sum up the way luck runs in cycles, 'Scu', for whom nothing can go wrong right now, finished second in the novice chase, and then got the race on an objection to move even farther clear at the top of the championship.

Yet again, I failed to get home. This time, it was my old pal Johnny Burke who kept me out — and eventually put me up for the night. I always enjoy 'Burkey's' company, and it is good news that he is to start training next season. Many try and fail, but Johnny will not lack for knowledge or effort.

SUNDAY 4 MAY

My Bank Holiday plans were all made in advance. I was to go to the mixed meeting at Haydock to ride two horses for Nick Henderson and one for Mick Naughton. It is the last really valuable meeting of the season, also the last televised jumping, and I was looking forward to it. But soon after ten this morning Nick phoned to tell me he had taken his two horses out and he wanted me to go and ride one at Fontwell instead, which won't seem quite the same. I then had to spend an hour on the phone trying to scrape one or two more rides together to make the journey viable. I ended up with a tally of three, but I can't see any of them winning.

After that, it was to lunch on the lawn at James Toller's house. James is one of the young and friendly Newmarket flat trainers, but he had invited a whole bevy of 'hooray henries' who, I'm afraid, took a considerable amount of stick from me. The Pimms flowed very freely. It was also very well mixed, and by mid-afternoon I was all for taking on the world at snooker. I settled for a couple of bloodstock agents I know, thinking they would be easy meat for a few quid but, what with my lack of recent practice and the Pimms (and the scotch which followed) I soon discovered I could hardly see a ball, let alone pot one. I lost.

MONDAY 5 MAY

There is a moral here somewhere, if only I can find it. Mike Furlong and I were both called before the stewards at Fontwell for the 'crime' of failing to do up our chinstraps as we mounted our horses. We were each asked if we had anything to say. I said no, but he launched into an elaborate and prolonged account of why his mind had been elsewhere. The net result? I was fined £50, and so was he!

I had plenty of time to mull over the implications of this. I spent most of the evening drumming my fingers on the steering wheel as the Bank Holiday traffic crawled ponderously away from the Sussex coast. I was not even nourished by a winner; Nick's Master Bob, carrying 12 stone, was caught on the line and beaten a short-head, just when I thought my journey had been worthwhile after all.

TUESDAY 6 MAY

Ana Wasslaawi had not been seen out since pulling himself up at Chepstow just before Christmas. He has been gelded since and, although he still acts the monkey at home, Nick ran him at Kempton tonight in the hope that he might reform and deign to show the limitless ability he possesses. It was a vain hope. The horse at first refused to take any interest, then, after I had somehow forced him over two flights of hurdles, he switched on and raced impressively to the third last. I was lying second now, thinking I might win, but as soon as I made the initial twitch towards asking him the question, he dug his toes in again and I had to pull him up before the second last.

He will doubtless now be called one of racing's great rogues, but I am not so sure. I remember a horse called Oscar Wilde, once trained by Fred Winter. He too had plenty of talent but often looked markedly reluctant to show it. He was sold on to John Jenkins' yard and, one day, they found him dead in his box. When the vet opened him up he discovered the poor animal had only one kidney — and that was shrivelled to the size of a walnut. While the pundits had been labelling him a thief and the punters had been much less polite, Oscar Wilde must have been in terrible pain every time he ran a race. I just wonder whether something similarly serious is amiss with Ana Wasslaawi, because I have never believed horses are clever enough to behave as he is doing.

WEDNESDAY 7 MAY
No racing. I tried three times to cut the lawns, but each time I wheeled out the mower and prepared to start, down came the rain. I'm sure this is the complaint of many more serious gardeners than me in this oddly unco-operative spring. It didn't break my heart — I simply gave up and read a book instead.

THURSDAY 8 MAY
It may sound like wishing life away, but I think I am in the majority among the jockeys I know in longing for the end of the month, the end of the season. Ten months of racing six days a week, with all the driving it entails, is perhaps a more demanding season than any other sport requests of its principals. Almost every year, May becomes a drag for me, a month in which incentives are few and time is for killing.

FRIDAY 9 MAY
Indamelody has cropped up regularly in the pages of this diary, not because he is one of my favourite horses but because he is certainly one of the most challenging and interesting rides in Nicky Henderson's yard. A very capable handicapper over hurdles, he has not exactly taken eagerly to fences, yet he un-deniably has ability. Last month at Nottingham I got him safely round — with him, the most important obstacle overcome — and then made up ground rapidly on the run-in to win a novice chase.

This, I felt, had done the horse's confidence immeasurable good, but when he next ran, burdened with a heavy weight, Nick decided to take a few pounds off his back by giving the ride to our claimer, Mike Bowlby. Now Mike is a very decent little rider, but I would maintain that Indamelody is not a boy's ride, and it is not pique at having lost the ride which prompts me to report I was not at all surprised when the combination ended up on the floor. I was, however, dismayed, wondering whether the tender work we had done on the horse's confidence would now be laid to waste. Today at Stratford I was to find out.

For the first time, Indamelody was declared for a handicap chase, running against horses far more experienced than him over fences. Despite that, the punters made him favourite on the strength of his two novice wins and, it must be said, his almost irrelevant hurdles form. I was not so confident. Stratford is a tight little circuit where horses can often rush at the fences so, in the circumstances, I was delighted when my horse finished a close-up third, having jumped well until he got a bit low over the last two. We may yet get another race out of him before the season is over.

SATURDAY 10 MAY

My choice of how to spend the day was straightforward enough: accept the six-hour round trip for two rides at Hereford, neither of which had any real chance; or stay at home with my feet up watching the cup final on TV. I did not find it very difficult to plump for the latter, but I confess to having a few pangs of guilt as the day progressed. Was I doing the right thing? Was it natural to feel lethargic at this end of the long season, or was I verging on the unprofessional? I put such thoughts out of my mind, enjoyed a splendid cup final, and saw with some relief that neither horse was placed.

SUNDAY 11 MAY

The morning papers gave me depressing food for thought. An amateur jockey named Michael Blackmore was killed by a fall at Market Rasen's evening meeting last night. I have never met him, indeed I don't think I had ever heard of him until now, but the news is still stunning. There is no escaping the conclusion that it could happen to any of us tomorrow. There but for the grace of God. . . .

Two better pieces of news on the social front — my old snooker partner Tommy Keddie is coming back to town after a brief and abortive move to Carlisle, so Sunday evenings will soon revert to their previous pleasurable pattern at the Willie Thorne Snooker Centre; and, much to my surprise, an invitation to Robert Sangster's 50th birthday party has flopped onto my door-mat. It is in two weeks' time on the Isle of Man and I have a sus-picion it could be quite a thrash.

MONDAY 12 MAY
I spent the entire day in my armchair reading a Jack Higgins novel called *Solo*. This time, there were no pangs of guilt what-soever.

TUESDAY 13 MAY
Bad news from home: one of my aunts has died, the second family death in a couple of months. As we are a close family, and as there is some sorting out to be done, with no racing to concern me today I drove up to Derbyshire to lend a hand.

THURSDAY 15 MAY
Jeff King and I have been friends for years. When he was riding I openly admired his ability. To me, he was among the top two or three jockeys around. I also appreciated his sense of humour and the uninhibited way in which he lived his life, never being afraid to say what he thought and always being around to buy a drink in the bar at the end of a long day. There are now too few around like 'Kingy' and I have to say I may even have modelled myself on him a little. But, with all that said, he can also be the most infuri-ating bloke I know, especially when he takes the berating of beaten jockeys to extremes. Tonight was just such an example.

I had wanted to do both meetings today, taking in a ride for Jeff at Ludlow before coming on to Uttoxeter for the evening card. In the end I had to settle for riding one of Nicky's novice chasers at the Uttoxeter course, which at least meant I could pick up my parents and give them an evening's racing to help take their mind off their recent troubles.

I was on my way back to the weighing-room after being well beaten on Nick's horse when someone hailed me. It was Jeff, asking if I was all right to ride a horse called Kings Jug for him in the handicap chase. I agreed, and if I lacked a little enthusiasm, I certainly listened when he told me he thought the horse had every chance of winning. The race, however, never went to plan at all, and although Kings Jug made up a stack of ground in the straight and finished fastest of all, I knew that Jeff was not going to be ecstatic.

I was right. He was, in fact, in a fury, and I was the one on the end of his temper. Maybe he was right, maybe I had not ridden the greatest of races; but I had never even sat on the horse before and I had discovered he had a mind of his own. He was not an easy ride, and I felt I did not deserve quite such a bollocking. When it continued in the weighing-room a few minutes later I began to get very angry myself and we might easily have come to blows.

Every trainer is entitled to tell a jockey exactly what he thinks of the ride he has given his horse. Many never accept that entitlement, keeping their thoughts to themselves, while most others get the criticism out of the way and then forget it. This time I believe Jeff went too far, and even if he had right on his side I don't feel I should be spoken to quite like that. I wonder if I will ride for him again?

FRIDAY 16 MAY

The compensations of night racing in May occasionally come in the shape of a good social evening to follow. Tonight, for instance, I rode two bad novice hurdlers for Nicky and then, in company with Dermot Browne, set off to examine what Stratford had to offer. We found two good pubs and then, with a journey to Bangor facing us tomorrow, put up for the night at the Moat House Hotel, set on the banks of the Avon.

SATURDAY 17 MAY

Dermot had taken a bad fall last night, suffering a few kicks after hitting the deck. He felt better after a drink or two but a night's sleep in a strange bed had stiffened him up again and, half-way to

Bangor, he was plainly in agony and in no state to even consider riding today. So he had to come just for the trip — which was virtually what I did, too. Torrential rain ruined the chances of my two rides, so I set off for the cross-country dash back to the evening meeting at Warwick in a dismal mood, made worse when I got there to find one of my two mounts had been taken out. I was left with Bluelimit, top weight in the handicap hurdle, and after two or three hard recent races he just couldn't cope with the ground and the extra poundage on his back. He did not, however, go down without incident.

Three from home I was still going well as a gap opened up on the inner. It was only a narrow gap, but it was a good position, and race-riding tactics dictated that I should try to get there. As I made my move, with the hurdle looming, I could sense someone else had the same idea, but I had to keep going. I got there first and the other fellow, with nowhere to go, crashed out through the wing of the hurdle. It turned out to be Kevin Mooney and, thankfully, there was not much damage. No blame was attached. He understood, as would any good jockey, that this was a classic 'him or me' situation in which someone has to lose out.

The jockeys' title race has taken an interesting turn. It had looked to be in Peter Scudamore's pocket, but after a lean week or two for him it is not so clear. 'Sharky' Sherwood has been banging in the winners relentlessly and after winning the first at Warwick tonight he was only six behind. I could well imagine 'Scu' jumping up and down in frustration as he had visions of another championship vanishing at the last but, having taken on the daunting drive to Newcastle to ride one for his good mate Nigel Twiston-Davies, the gods smiled on him. Not only did that one win, but he picked up a spare ride on that grand old chaser Silent Valley — and got that one home, too. So, at eight winners ahead and with only a fortnight left, I reckon P. Scudamore is the new champion.

TUESDAY 20 MAY

The things I do for a game of tennis! Newton Abbot's final two-day meeting began today, and none of my regular employers were running anything, but by scrubbing around on the phone I

managed to pick up a ride for Jimmy Frost, an old friend, basically to ensure I could get down to the Palace Hotel for the last
time this season. I was expecting no more than the £50 riding fee
as recompense for the journey so it was to my great surprise when
Stars and Stripes — who began the race with a series of duck-eggs
next to his name in the form guide — responded to an energetic
finish on my part and won the handicap hurdle.

WEDNESDAY 21 MAY

My two rides at today's evening meeting were previously
unknown to me and, frankly, I shall shed no tears if I never see
either of them again. They certainly made it an eventful night.

The first of them was for Cheltenham trainer Owen O'Neill.
The girl leading the horse around the parade ring warned me that
he was 'a bit keen' but this did not exactly set alarm bells ringing
in my head. It is the type of comment a jockey very often hears
from proud, committed stable staff. This one, however, happened
to have understated the case.

The routine at Newton Abbot is that, before cantering down
to the two-mile start, jockeys take their mounts past the stands to
show them the last hurdle. My horse was a shade impatient. We
were, remember, approaching the hurdle from the 'wrong' side —
in other words, it was leaning towards us, but this animal wanted
to jump the thing and nothing I could do would deter him. He had
taken off. So, hanging on and hoping, we ploughed through the
hurdle, the horse miraculously kept his feet and I belatedly
managed to get a stranglehold on him and get him down to the
start. He jumped well enough in the race, too, but could finish
only fourth. Maybe he prefers his hurdles back to front!

After that little episode I was all for a quiet ride round in the
last race of the night, when I was chalked up for another of
Jimmy Frost's horses. I had not expected, however, to earn my
riding fee quite so easily. This one, called Getaway though
heaven knows why, was a lazy sort and Jimmy told me to wear a
pair of spurs to wake him up. They made absolutely no difference. When the tapes went up, he plodded three strides and then
mulishly refused to go another yard. Variety, they say, is the spice
of life. After tonight, I am not so sure.

FRIDAY 23 MAY

The sun shone at last, so the golf clubs came out of hiding. Today's racing for me was an evening card at Towcester, so I had plenty of time for a round on the Newmarket course ... which was just as well, the way I play.

I have just one ride tonight — Indamelody. He was back over hurdles again but he has had his fair share of work this season and I feared he might just have gone over the top. The way he ran, dying under me from the third last, I was right.

SATURDAY 24 MAY

In any rating of the 1986 social calendar, I guess Robert Sangster's 50th birthday party will be upstaged only by the Royal Wedding. It lived up to expectations in every way and was, quite simply, the most memorable shindig I have ever been privileged to attend.

This was, of course, a racing day and I had to back out of a couple of rides at Warwick, one of them for my guv'nor Nick — but, as he was heading for the Isle of Man too, I think he felt he couldn't complain. So, at 6.00 p.m., a crowd of us boarded a specially chartered Boeing 737 at Gatwick and the party was underway. I must say I could easily have foregone the next bit, as landing a thing of that size on the tiny Manx airstrip would be hair-raising at the best of times, let alone in driving rain. But we survived, and after a rapid change of clothes at the Golf Links Hotel to which Di and I had been billetted, it was on to the palatial Sangster residence, where an enormous marquee had been erected in the grounds.

The guest list extended to something over 500 and, by the look of the place, there had been very few regrets. The cream of the racing world was present, and if I was surprised to find myself the only National Hunt jockey there, I did not let this detract from the enjoyment. Paul Anka's cabaret, Charlie Benson's uproarious speech and a constant flow of pink champagne all stand out as memories, and as night became morning the celebrations continued unabated. It was around 6.00 a.m., and the birds were singing, when we finally pulled up stumps and staggered back to bed. Quite a night!

SUNDAY 25 MAY

Part two of the Sangster celebrations was as impressive as part one. Food and yet more drinks (champagne naturally) were provided at our hotel from 12.30 p.m., so I was out of bed just in time to partake, and then the party moved on to Castletown race course for the Isle of Man's big Derby meeting. I had been asked to ride in the hurdles race, but decided I would enjoy the social side of the weekend instead. When I saw how tight the track was, I felt I had made the correct decision. Robert's horse won the Manx Derby so more champagne arrived. Really, considering I have only met him socially a few times, I feel quite honoured to be part of the enclave at this gathering.

It ended for the night at the Palace Casino and, as I have to ride tomorrow, I exerted some self-discipline and went to bed at midnight. Just before I retired, Nicky started to give me my riding instructions for tomorrow. It was a good job Di was beside me, because they would quickly have faded into a sleepy oblivion otherwise.

MONDAY 26 MAY

I proved today that, whatever others may think, my social life never affects my riding — and then I proved the maxim that you never can tell what is around the next corner.

I felt a degree or two short of death when I dragged myself and Di out of bed at 6.00 a.m. for the early flight back to Gatwick but, in the true spirit of 'the old Ecc', I kept kicking. Di dropped out of the day as soon as we got home, taking to her bed again, but I went on to Huntingdon and proceeded to ride two winners for Nick. If I say so myself, I rode them both like a demon and no one was more aware than me of their significance. Nick and Fred Winter, to whom he was once assistant trainer, have for the past month been fighting quite a scrap over the trainers' championship. Fred, never one to be beaten lightly, sent out nine horses today at five meetings, and Nick badly needed some winners to stay in front. Well, only one of Fred's troops came home victorious, so my double, and a win for Master Bob at Fontwell, makes virtually certain that I am now retained jockey at jumping's champion stable.

I was feeling pretty bucked by all this as I went out for my last ride of the day. John Jenkins' State Diplomacy went off as favourite for the handicap hurdle, so I thought I had every chance of riding my first treble of the season. I should have known better. We got no further than the second flight. Something fell in front of us, we were brought down, and another horse crashed on top of us ... or so I'm told. To be honest I remember very little about it, because for the first time in my career I was unconscious.

They tell me I was still motionless as the remaining runners passed me on the next circuit. They also tell me I came round in time to tell the ambulance staff what they could do with their stretcher. The upshot, naturally, was a seven-day rest period for my second bout of concussion inside a month. So that's it: end of story, end of season. The highs and the lows of this funny old game, all captured in a single afternoon.

TUESDAY 27 MAY

I had planned to finish the season this weekend with a trip to Sweden, where I have been offered good rides in their Grand National and Champion Hurdle. That must now go by the board. Quite apart from the concussion, an x-ray in Cambridge today confirmed that I have also cracked a rib. My main worry now is whether I will be fit enough to fly to Australia with the British team next week. I spent much of the afternoon in hot baths trying to soothe away the worst of the aches.

WEDNESDAY 28 MAY

I did nothing today because I was not up to doing anything. My head is still woozy, my brain working slowly as if scrambled. And I don't recommend cracked ribs, either. It is not just the energetic pursuits which have to be scrubbed from the agenda — I can't even sneeze or laugh.

THURSDAY 29 MAY

My ribs are feeling easier, my head is slowly clearing and I'm on my way to London for the annual social gathering of 300 jump jockeys at the Sportsman Club awards dinner. It is a great gesture by Max Kingsley and his directors to give these awards every year, though I wonder if they realise what havoc they are turning loose on the West End when the ceremony is over?

I had another cheque to pick up for finishing third in the championship with 63 winners. I had a good year. Yes, of course I fancied being champion, but in all honesty there was hardly a stage of the season when I considered myself favourite. First Simon, who had a fantastic first season as a professional, built up a good lead and then 'Scu' came with a rattle. A place in the top three was always the best I could hope for, but I did have the satisfaction of winning some big races along the way. Also, despite my current state, I finished up in one piece. I had two rounds of concussion, a cracked rib, a damaged ankle and various bruises, but when I think of Sam Morshead, Mark Perrett and Anthony Webber, I think myself very lucky.

As my season ends I feel like the hero in *Papillon*, the Frenchman who keeps escaping from prison and, in the closing shots, gets away from Devil's Island, from where no one has ever escaped before. He has made a coconut raft and he is floating out to sea, lying on his belly. Suddenly, he looks up at the sky, shakes his fist and bellows defiantly: 'I'm still here, you bastard'.

STATISTICS

HOW THE JOCKEYS FINISHED 1985/86 SEASON

	1st	2nd	3rd	Unplaced	Total
P. Scudamore	91	61	52	335	539
S. Sherwood	79	50	53	181	363
S. Smith Eccles	63	47	32	184	326
H. Davies	58	45	30	264	397
R. Dunwoody	55	51	61	337	504
R. Rowe	48	48	42	240	378
R. Lamb	46	34	31	163	274
C. Grant	42	49	37	194	322
J.J. O'Neill	38	35	27	162	262
G. McCourt	38	43	28	217	326

BIG RACE WINNERS 1985/86 SEASON

MACKESON GOLD CUP HANDICAP CHASE 2¹/₂m
(Cheltenham, Nov 9)
1. Half Free 9-11-10   R. Linley 9-2
2. Newlife Connection 6-10-2 S. Sherwood 5-1
3. Another City 6-10-1   P. Tuck 12-1
Distances: head, 8L. Winner trained by F. Winter. 10 ran

HENNESSY COGNAC GOLD CUP HANDICAP CHASE 3m 2f 82yds
(Newbury, Nov 23)
1. Galway Blaze 9-10-0   M. Dwyer 11-2
2. Run And Skip 7-10-9   S. Morshead 7-1
3. Door Latch 7-10-8   R. Rowe 9-1
Distances: 12L, 5L. Winner trained by J. FitzGerald. 15 ran.

STILL FORK TRUCKS GOLD CUP HANDICAP CHASE 2½m
(Cheltenham, Dec 7)
1. Combs Ditch 9-11-9   C. Brown 13-2
2. Final Argument 9-10-11   P. Tuck 9-4 fav
3. Western Sunset 9-11-5   R. Dunwoody 9-2
Distances: 7L, 5L. Winner trained by D. Elsworth. 7 ran.

CORAL WELSH GRAND NATIONAL HANDICAP CHASE 3¾m
(Chepstow, Dec 21)
1. Run And Skip 7-10-8   P. Scudamore 13-1
2. Golden Ty 7-9-11   Mr. A. Orkney 100-1
3. Kumbi 10-10-3   S. Smith Eccles 18-1
Distances: 6L, 2L. Winner trained by J. Spearing. 18 ran.

KING GEORGE VI CHASE 3m
(Kempton, Dec 26)
1. Wayward Lad 10-11-10   G. Bradley 12-1
2. Combs Ditch 9-11-10   C. Brown 3-1
3. Earls Brig 10-11-10   T.G. Dun 7-1
Distances: neck, 12L. Winner trained by Mrs. M. Dickinson. 5 ran.

ANTHONY MILDMAY, PETER CAZALET MEMORIAL HANDICAP CHASE 3m 5f 18yds
(Sandown, Jan 4)
1. Run And Skip 8-11-1   P. Scudamore 7-2
2. Contradeal 9-10-0   S. Shilston 5-2 fav
3. Buckbe 7-10-0   C. Brown 10-1
Distances: ½L, 2L. Winner trained by J. Spearing. 8 ran.

EMBASSY PREMIER CHASE FINAL 2½m
(Ascot, Jan 11)
1. Very Promising 8-11-10   P. Scudamore 5-4 fav
2. Mr Moonraker 9-11-10   B. Powell 9-1
3. I Haventalight 7-11-10   S. Sherwood 10-1
Distances: short head, 10L. Winner trained by D. Nicholson. 8 ran.

OTELEY HURDLE 2m
(Sandown, Feb 1)
1. See You Then 6-11-12   S. Smith Eccles 3-1
2. Sabin Du Loir 7-10-7   G. Bradley 7-2
3. Tom Sharp 6-11-0   P. Tuck 4-1
Distances: 2½L, ½L. Winner trained by N. Henderson. 9 ran.

WILLIAM HILL IMPERIAL CUP HANDICAP HURDLE 2m
(Sandown, Mar 8)
1. Insular 6-9-10   E. Murphy 14-1
2. Hypnosis 7-10-2   C. Brown 11-1

3. Peter Martin 5-10-2   K. Mooney 14-1
Distances: ³/₄L, neck. Winner trained by I. Balding. 19 ran.

WATERFORD CRYSTAL SUPREME NOVICES HURDLE 2m
(Cheltenham, Mar 11)
1. River Ceiriog 5-11-8   S. Smith Eccles 40-1
2. Deep Idol 6-11-8   N. Madden 4-1 fav
3. The Clown 5-11-8   R. Stronge 100-1
Distances: 15L, 1¹/₂L. Winner trained by N. Henderson. 29 ran.

ARKLE CHALLENGE TROPHY CHASE 2m
(Cheltenham, Mar 11)
1. Oregon Trail 6-11-8   R. Beggan 14-1
2. Charcoal Wally 7-11-8   B. Powell 11-1
3. Desert Orchid 7-11-8   C. Brown 11-2
Distances: ³/₄L, 8L. Winner trained by S. Christian. 14 ran.

WATERFORD CRYSTAL CHAMPION HURDLE 2m
(Cheltenham, Mar 11)
1. See You Then 6-12-0   S. Smith Eccles 5-6 fav
2. Gaye Brief 9-12-0   P. Scudamore 14-1
3. Nohalmdun 5-12-0   J.J. O'Neill 20-1
Distances: 7L, 1¹/₂L. Winner trained by N. Henderson. 23 ran.

QUEEN MOTHER CHAMPION CHASE 2m
(Cheltenham, Mar 12)
1. Buck House 8-12-0   T. Carmody 5-2
2. Very Promising 8-12-0   P. Scudamore 11-2
3. Kathies Lad 9-12-0   S. Smith Eccles 11-1
Distances: 3L, 8L. Winner trained by M. Morris. 11 ran.

DAILY EXPRESS TRIUMPH HURLDE (4-y-o) 2m
(Cheltenham, Mar 13)
1. Solar Cloud 11-0   P. Scudamore 40-1
2. Brunico 11-0   D. Browne 16-1
3. Son Of Ivor 11-0   T. Carmody 16-1
Distances: ³/₄L, short head. Winner trained by D. Nicholson. 28 ran.

TOTE CHELTENHAM GOLD CUP CHASE 3¹/₄m
(Cheltenham, Mar 13)
1. Dawn Run 8-11-9   J.J. O'Neill 15-8 fav
2. Wayward Lad 11-12-0   G. Bradley 8-1
3. Forgive 'N' Forget 9-12-0   M. Dwyer 7-2
Distances: 1L, 2¹/₂L. Winner trained by P. Mullins. 11 ran.

JAMESON IRISH GRAND NATIONAL HANDICAP CHASE 3¹/₂m
(Fairyhouse, Mar 31)
1. Insure 8-9-11   M. Flynn 16-1

2. Omerta 6-9-9   Mr. L. Wyer 4-1
3. Bold Agent 10-9-7   J.P. Byrne 16-1
Distances: 10L, 8L. Winner trained by P. Hughes. 15 ran.

CAPTAIN MORGAN AINTREE LIMITED HANDICAP CHASE 2m
(Liverpool, Apr 5)
1. Kathies Lad 9-10-13   S. Smith Eccles 11-8 fav
2. Lefrak City 9-10-7   H. Davies 7-2
3. Badsworth Boy 11-11-10   R. Earnshaw 4-1
Distances: 2½L, ½L. Winner trained by A.P. Jarvis. 6 ran.

SANDEMAN AINTREE HURDLE 2m 5f 110yds
(Liverpool, Apr 5)
1. Aonoch 7-11-9   J. Duggan 16-1
2. See You Then 6-11-11   S. Smith Eccles 4-9 fav
3. Sheer Gold 6-11-1   G. Bradley 6-1
Distances: 1L, 15L. Winner trained by Mrs. S. Oliver. 9 ran.

SEAGRAM GRAND NATIONAL HANDICAP CHASE 4½m.
(Liverpool, Apr 5)
1. West Tip 9-10-11   R. Dunwoody 15-2
2. Young Driver 9-10-0   C. Grant 66-1
3. Classified 10-10-3   S. Smith Eccles 22-1
Distances: 2L, 20L. Winner trained by M. Oliver. 40 ran.

WHITBREAD GOLD CUP HANDICAP CHASE 3m 5f 18yds
(Sandown, Apr 26)
1. Plundering 9-10-6   S. Sherwood 14-1
2. Buckbe 7-10-7   B. Powell 15-2
3. Arctic Beau 8-10-0   R. Dunwoody 9-1
Distances: ½L, 15L. Winner trained by F. Winter. 16 ran.

SWINTON INSURANCE BROKERS TROPHY HANDICAP HURDLE 2m
(Haydock, May 5)
1. Prideaux Boy 8-11-2   M. Bowlby 15-2
2. Gala's Image 6-10-7   H. Davies 9-1
3. Janus 8-10-3   M. Hammond 25-1
Distance: 2½L, 6L. Winner trained by C. Roach. 20 ran.

INDEX

173